THE WAKE

of

FORGIVENESS

Bruce Machart

Mariner Books
Houghton Mifflin Harcourt
BOSTON   NEW YORK

First Mariner Books edition 2011

Copyright © 2010 by Bruce Machart

ALL RIGHTS RESERVED

For information about permission to reproduce selections from this book,
write to Permissions, Houghton Mifflin Harcourt Publishing Company,
215 Park Avenue South, New York, New York 10003.

www.hmhbooks.com

Library of Congress Cataloging-in-Publication Data
Machart, Bruce.
The wake of forgiveness / Bruce Machart.
p. cm.
ISBN 978-0-15-101443-9
ISBN 978-0-547-52194-7 (pbk.)
1. Czechs — Texas — Fiction. 2. Spaniards — Texas — Fiction.
3. Horse breeders — Fiction. 4. Landowners — Fiction. 5. Vendetta — Fiction.
6. Lavaca County (Tex.) — Fiction. I. Title.
PS3613.A272525W35 2010
813'.6 — dc22   2009047459

Book design by Brian Moore

Printed in the United States of America

DOC 10 9 8 7 6 5 4 3 2 1

For my mother . . .

and for Marya — this and any that may follow

AUTHOR'S NOTE

Some years ago, I acquired a map of Lavaca County, Texas, that was printed in 1896, and I noted that a large parcel of land had been owned at that time by one Mr. Patrick Dalton. Because Dalton is a name that goes back many generations in my family — as my godfather's name, as my own middle name, as my son's name — this seemed, since I had just begun to imagine the fictional town of this novel, a kind of serendipity. Two years later, once the novel's landscape had become all but indelible in my imagination, I discovered that there exists, way up in the northeast corner of the state and some 350 miles from the events of this story, an actual Dalton, Texas, an old timber settlement with a current population of fewer than one hundred residents. Hence the need for clarification: Though Lavaca County and many of the towns and landmarks depicted in this work are quite real, as are some historical figures who appear as minor characters, all are used fictitiously. Likewise, Jackson Gregory's novel *Judith of Blue Lake Ranch* was in fact serialized in the *Shiner Gazette* during December of 1924, but I have fictionalized it here, altering to varying degrees both its characters and storyline. The Dalton, Texas, of this novel is entirely a product of my imagination.

It is good for a man that he bear the yoke in his youth. He sitteth alone and keepeth silence, because he hath borne it upon him. He putteth his mouth in the dust; if so be there may be hope.

—LAMENTATIONS 3:27–29

The harvest is past, the summer is ended, and we are not saved.

—JEREMIAH 8:20

A Winter Harvest

FEBRUARY 1895

THE BLOOD HAD COME hard from her, so much of it that, when Vaclav Skala awoke in wet bed linens to find her curled up against him on her side, moaning and glazed with sweat, rosary beads twisted around her clenched fingers, he smiled at the thought that she'd finally broken her water. He pulled back the quilt, a wedding gift sent six years before from his mother in the old country, and kissed Klara on the forehead before climbing from bed to light the lamp. He struck a match, and there it was, streaked down his legs and matted in the coarse hair on his thighs—dark and half-dried smears of his wife's blood.

And it kept coming. He saddled his horse and rode shivering under a cloudless midnight sky to the Janek farm to fetch Edna, the midwife. By the time they made it back, Klara's eyes were open but glazed in such a way that they knew she wasn't seeing through them anymore. Her pale lips moved without giving voice to her final prayer, which entreated the child to come or her own spirit to stay, either one.

When the baby arrived, their fourth boy, blood slicked and clot flecked, he appeared to have been as much ripped from flesh as born of it. Klara was lost, and Edna tended to what had been saved, pinching the little thing's toe to get the breathing started, cleaning him with a rag dipped in warm milk and water, wrapping him in a blanket.

Vaclav Skala stood at the foot of the bed, grinding his back teeth slowly against a stringy mash of tobacco he'd chewed flavorless half an hour before. He watched Edna, a slight young woman with narrow hips and long hair as black as her eyes. She bunched pillows beneath the dead woman's shoulder blades and behind her head before resting the baby on his mother's stomach. Taking one of Klara's breasts between her thumb and finger, she puckered the nipple so the baby could get hold of it. The little thing threw his hands up about his face and worked his legs beneath the blanket, and Edna held him unremittingly to the breast until he hollowed his cheeks and found it with his mouth. "It's no hind milk in her yet," she said, "but he might get some of the yellow mother's milk. We'll be needing a wet nurse. It's several up county who might do it."

Vaclav stepped back into the doorway and looked down the dark hallway toward the room where his other three boys were sleeping. "We'll be needing a hell of a lot more than that," he said. "Let him get what's left of her if he can. He's done taken the rest."

Just before dawn, after Edna had washed the body and wrapped it in clean bedding, Vaclav carried it out and up into the loft of the barn so the boys wouldn't find her when they woke. Then he dragged the drenched mattress from the house and out through the young pear grove to the hard-caked plot of earth where he planned one day to build his stable. There, beneath the wash kettle, he kindled a fire with last year's fallen mesquite branches. The mattress was soaked through and heavier than Klara's body had been, and Vaclav found himself cursing its weight even while he recalled how Klara had stitched the ticking and stuffed it with goose feathers before their wedding night; how, when he lay pressed for the first time between her tender skin and the soft warmth of the bed she'd made for him, he'd startled his bride, so loud was his laugh.

Now, as the horizon gave way to the pink glow of another south Texas dawn and the mockingbirds came to life in the pear grove, Vaclav worked his knife along the mattress seam, undoing his wife's work, as he would find himself doing for years. With several inches

4

of the stitching cut away, he reached in and pulled out the feathers, one bloody handful after another, and fed them to the fire, which spat and sizzled before blazing into yellow flames and thick white billows of smoke.

In the near pasture, the cattle stood lowing against the fence, and had Vaclav been paying attention the way he usually did, he would have puzzled at their behavior, wondering what it was that kept them clustered against the fenceline instead of in the center of the parcel near the three square bales of hay he'd set out for them the day before. Instead, he stood staring into the fire, adding the steady fuel of feathers, looking into the flames so he wouldn't have cause to look at his hands, which were chapped and creased deeply with calluses and stained with the blood of the only woman he'd ever been fond of.

The townsfolk would assume, from this day forward, that Klara's death had turned a gentle man bitter and hard, but the truth, Vaclav knew, was that her absence only rendered him, again, the man he'd been before he'd met her, one only her proximity had ever softened. He'd known land in his life that, before a few seasons of regular rainfall, had been hard enough to crack a plow point, and he knew that if, by stubbornness or circumstance, that earth became yours to farm, you'd do well to live with the constant understanding that, in time, absent the work of swollen clouds and providence, your boots would fall loudly, giving rise to dust, when you walked your fields.

With the sun breaking clear of the horizon and the ticking gutted of its down, Vaclav whittled his knife against a brick of lye soap and added a handful of shavings to the boiling kettle water. He squinted against the sharp fumes of Klara's strong soap, and when he got the bloodstained ticking into the kettle, the water roiled and frothed red like so much sick stew.

Softly, a cool wind came up from the north and swirled the smoke around the kettle and out into the newly lit morning. Across the pasture, hidden in the far hedgerow near the creekside stand of trees, three half-starved coyotes raised their twitching snouts to catch a breeze laced of a sudden with the hot, iron-rich scent of blood. Their mouths flooded with anticipation as they hunkered their bellies low and inched forward, shifting their feet beneath them and waiting, their reticence born more of caution than patience. In the pasture, the cows went to lowing again, pressing themselves together against the fencewires.

With a twisted mesquite branch, Vaclav moved the ticking around in the boiling liquid and then threw that wood, too, on the fire. When he turned toward the house and weaved his way through the grove, he found the back door swung open, his three young boys standing just inside wearing nightclothes and wet cheeks. The oldest, Stanislav, was only five, but he held on to his brothers' shoulders the way a father would. The wind gusted enough to ripple Vaclav's shirt, and when it calmed he heard the baby crying inside. Standing in the bare yard, he took his plug of tobacco from his shirt pocket and tore off a portion with his teeth. Edna appeared behind the boys and turned them away from the door. "Their breakfast's gone cold on the table," she said. "They're asking after her."

He nodded and spit tobacco juice into the hard earth near the porch, and then, without washing his hands or taking off his boots, he stepped into the house where, for all but one wailing newborn, as in the pasture and the hedgerows, even hunger had been plowed under by fear.

Turning the Earth

MARCH 1910

His two good horses he saves for racing, for the straight make-shift furlongs of the moonlit creekbed, for the chance to take more land from his godforsaken neighbor, Patrick Dalton, whose Scots-Irish surname remains on the town map and postmark but no longer on the largest deed in the county. Nowadays, that deed is in Vaclav Skala's name, for just shy of six hundred acres, nearly a third of it taken, over the past four years, by wit and force and fast horses from Dalton himself.

As likely to spit tobacco juice on a woman's shoes as to tip his hat at her, Vaclav has, since his wife's death fifteen years ago, only one source of weakness: his pair of towering roan quarter horses. For them, there are well-oiled leather bridles and carrots pulled straight from the mineral-rich earth. For them, hand-forged shoes and alfalfa and sweet feed and as many good mares to mount as he can find without insulting their bloodlines.

The horses, they're beautiful, though no longer the most beautiful in Lavaca County, and they don't work the fields. They race, they rest, they eat, they mate, and they race. They don't pull a plow. That work Vaclav leaves to his four sons, and when Guillermo Villaseñor drives his two Spanish-bred stallions and three olive-skinned daughters up the farm-to-market road from town, and when the carriage clears a thick stand of mesquite trees with arthritic branches and thorns long enough to skewer a foot in a way only careless barefoot boys and Jesus might fully appreciate, and the girls get their first glimpses of their future husbands, what they see, instead of blond-haired and handsome Czech farm boys, like they've been told by their father to expect, are weathered young men straining against the weight of the earth turning in their wake, their necks cocked sharply to one side or the other, their faces sunburned despite their hats and peeling and snaked with raised veins near the temples, their boots sliding atop the earth they're sweating to unearth. The four of them work harnessed two abreast in front of their father, who's walking in their work, one foot in each furrow, spitting stained juice between his front teeth and periodically cracking a whip to keep the boys focused and the rows straight.

The boys are moving toward the carriage—which is coming toward them, coming to change everything—but at first they don't see it, don't see the horses or the puffs of dust coming up from their hooves, don't see these fine animals, longer of leg than any the boys have known before and higher of step, their withers soaked through and shining black with sweat despite the cool morning breeze, their carriage one of wealth and women and a future the boys could not have dreamed up if they'd been left, any short night of their lives, to their beds long enough to dream much anything at all.

Here in these parts, in the black-soil heart of Lavaca County, where the Czech farmers have run off all but the last of the red-haired and ruddy settlers who came before them; where, if a man has two bits' worth of good seed and a strong back and a certain degree of stubbornness—that and a good wife who lives long enough and with enough of God's favor to grant him sons—he might harvest two hundred acres of cotton without calling on even his neighbors for help; here, where men make their own worth, they don't have much use for outsiders, and until this week there's been neither a man nor woman in the county who's often laid either an eye or a thought on a Mexican.

In the last three days, Villaseñor and his two armed escorts have been busy throwing their weight—and nearly their weight in gold—around town. On Monday, in town at the First Federal Bank and Trust, where Lad Dvorak sat at his desk working through the inventory list of the Butler farm foreclosure, Guillermo came tracking mud through the doors with his men. His hair was black and oiled back and tinged with gray in such a way that he looked to have spent the duration of his life walking into the same wet and gypsum-laden wind. His spectacles he wore down low on his nose, and he spoke with an accent that sounded to the tellers more refined somehow than their own.

One of his men stood at the door with his rifle while the other brought in the saddlebags, some eight of them in all, and then they held the door open and refused to do their business until the rest of the customers were cleared out and the doors bolted. Guillermo's daughters were taking lunch at the inn, forbidden, as usual, to accompany their father on occasions where money changed hands, of which there had been hundreds over the years, and perhaps, had they been in the bank, Lad might have been rendered as slack jawed and inarticulate by their lovely Spanish features as he was presently by the weight of their father's saddlebags.

Lad lifted the first of them to his desk, saying, "Most of it's silver, I'm betting."

"A man should know better than to make his bets blind," Villa-señor said. "I wouldn't have my good horses shod with silver."

Lad laughed and worked his fingers through the patchwork of bristled hair on his chin while Villaseñor's men stood with their rifles held casually and crosswise beneath their bellies, their thumbs hooked behind their belts. Lad figured them for nearly forty, but they wore the mustaches of boys, combed straight and too thin to hide the skin of their upper lips. Their shirts were laundered, creases pressed in the sleeves, but their boots were caked with mud and, by the smell of it, dung. They were two of the shortest men Lad had ever seen, and he snorted and jerked his head at them and said, "If it's something worth protecting in these bags, mister, I'd expect your boys here to be a shake bigger than a pair of well-fed housewives."

The men didn't flinch, and Lad knew then that they didn't speak English. Villaseñor acted, too, like he hadn't heard. He took his spectacles off, pulled a folded handkerchief from the vest pocket of his suit coat, and when he replaced the spectacles, he squinted and a tight smile creased the corners of his mouth while he spoke to his men in Spanish. They laughed, turned their backs, and went toward the door. The two tellers backed away from their windows, eyes wary. One of Villaseñor's men unlatched the door and went outside. The other propped his gun against the far wall, pulled a cigar from his shirt pocket, and waved the chewed end beneath his nose before putting it in his mouth. He unbuckled his belt and dropped a hand down into the front of his britches to make some adjustments, and when he got himself situated to his liking he pulled the belt tight under the slump of his belly and buckled up. He had an audience in the two tellers, and he gave them a wink and went back to sucking on his cigar.

When his partner came back in the door, he carried a smallish box that looked, for all its varnish and shine, like a coffin built for a rich man's tomcat. He turned the bolt on the door and put the box beside the first saddlebag on Lad's desk.

"And what of this?" Lad said.

"That's *my* wager," the old man said. "I'm betting that after we weigh these coins and you hand me a voucher, you and your boys are going to need what's in this box."

"Is that so," Lad said, winking at his tellers. "And what would that be?"

"Shoeblack. My men's boots need some attention."

Now they all had a laugh, and Lad called his men over to help weigh the gold, which they had to do in small batches because the old triple-beam scale on the premises was calibrated with only a five-pound counterweight. By the time they finished, Lad Dvorak was perspiring and salivating both. Here was a new account worth all the cotton in Lavaca County, and a fair share of the land, at that.

The men took the saddlebags to the safe, and before he wrote out the voucher Lad shook Villaseñor's hand and asked if he needed some of his balance in bills. The man raised his brows, pulled a fat fold of American currency from his coat, and removed the clip. "It doesn't seem so," he said, removing three five-dollar bills and letting them fall to the varnished bureau top.

Lad had his tellers sign as witnesses to the transaction and handed Mr. Villaseñor his voucher. "It's a pleasure," he said, "having your business. Did you need some smaller change for these?"

"The pleasure is mine," the man said. "And those bills are for you. And for your men."

"Beg pardon?"

Villaseñor lifted the lid of the box and removed two cans of shoeblack, a brush, and a felt strop. "My wager," he said, running his thumb through the stiff bristles of the brush. "The way I see it, I can leave my money here in your bank, or I can withdraw it tomorrow and do my business over in Shiner or Yoakum. I'm betting you'd rather I didn't, and I'm betting, because this is true, that when I get back in an hour from having a word with Monsignor Carew about my daughters' Nuptial Mass, you and your boys will be just about finished putting a shine to these undersized men's boots. Five dollars apiece is more than fair — don't you think? — all things considered."

Now Lad's fingers were back in his beard and his ears were flushed with blood. "I'm certain," he said, "that you would be happier with the twenty-cent shine they'll get around the corner at Wasek's barbershop, but let me be the first to congratulate you on your daughter's wedding. Who's the lucky man?"

"I don't believe I said." Villaseñor fished a cigar from his suit coat. "Not to you, I didn't. And I'd be happier, sir, if you didn't presume to tell me what would make me happy. That money there, it's yours. And so is my business, assuming these little farmwives here, who've put more men in the ground for me than yours have swindled for you, have, by hour's end, boots in which I can see myself well enough to shave."

Then he bit the tip from his cigar, ground the tobacco with his back teeth for more than a wordless minute, and sent from his lips onto the bureau top a long string of thick black spit. He lighted his cigar and the whole room went suddenly and sweetly ripe with its smoke. "There," he said, "another token of my generosity, Mr. Dvorak. If your spit's too good for my men's boots, then you can use mine."

FOR TWO DAYS thereafter, the talk about town was constant as the lowing of cattle in the pastures. While the townswomen sat together quilting or stood clustered in kitchens, polishing copper pots or latticing dough over pies filled with fruit canned the previous summer, their lips moved faster than their hands. Faster, their husbands said, than their minds.

Gathered in the icehouse, the men took long pulls on their pilsners and shook their heads, feigning indifference, but at home, even after sweating behind plows or beneath the weight of hay bales, they found themselves these days with more patience for their women's words. They'd sit at their tables long after they'd eaten, elbows on each side of their coffee cups, and they'd listen to the stories the women brought home.

The Mexican had rented the whole second floor of the Township Inn for a month. Paid in advance, he did. Then there was Sy Janek's wife, Edna, who claimed that, on her way home from delivering the Knedlik twins, she'd seen the girls, all three of them, riding black horses after dark, running the animals hard out behind Patrick Dalton's granary and into the pecan grove by the north fork of Mustang Creek. In dresses they were, with a foot in each stirrup and God only knows what, if anything, between their tender parts and the saddle leather. There was Father Carew, who'd canceled both Masses for this coming Saturday and would say, when pressed, only that this Villaseñor fellow had wedding plans, and for more than one wedding, and that to secure the church he'd brought with him a Papal Indulgence, the first Carew had ever seen, and three Sundays' worth of collections in cash. And then there was Patrick Dalton, who'd been seen taking lunch with Villaseñor and his men at the inn, and who had called Lad Dvorak to tell him that he'd run suddenly short of room at his stable, that the banker would have to come fetch the drays Dalton had boarded for him all these years in exchange for prime interest rates at the bank. These wives, the broad-hipped women who bore bad news and children both with a sad but softened look around the eyes, claimed Dalton had been seen smiling at the feedstore while he ordered two hundred pounds of molasses oats, smiling even while he shouldered them out to his wagon, two forty-pound sacks at a time.

And this is where the men of Lavaca County stopped listening.

This is where they breathed in abruptly through their noses and pushed their chairs back from the table and took their coffee out into the swirling night air, which was growing cold of a sudden and sharp with pecan and mesquite and oak from the chunkwood fires smoldering in their smokehouses. They stood out on their porches or out back of their barns, and while the low moon slid behind thin bands of clouds and they pulled tobacco from the bib pockets of their overalls and rolled cigarettes with callused thumbs, they grew more certain than ever of their wives' willful foolishness, of their forthright and feminine need to believe the world a far more mysterious and alluring place than it was. Patrick Dalton, the men knew, hadn't smiled in coming up on four damned years, not since the night when he'd for the first time lost an acreage-staked race to Vaclav Skala.

They'd been there, after all, and in their memories they'd borne witness to the race the same way their wives had borne their children — with the assurance that they'd each played a vital and thankworthy role, and with the misguided confidence that, for having done so, they would remain forever attuned to both the memory of the bearing and the born alike.

And so it was that on this March night, smoking out behind their barns, the men of Dalton, Texas, and its hinterland drew from the oft-unswept corners of their memories dozens of mismatched and contradictory notions of a night four years back, a night that, by all accounts, had seen them standing in the shuddering light of two rock-ringed finish-line fires, their undershirts starched yellow with the dried sweat of an August day's work, their backs to the creek where they'd floated their jars of corn whiskey and beer bottles to keep them cool. They'd stood drinking and smoking, comparing crop yields and woman troubles, making half-dollar bets with their neighbors while the riders readied themselves.

Some forty yards to the west, just beyond the swinging cattlegate, Vaclav Skala's youngest, Karel, sat his pop's biggest roan stallion. The boy's neck, like his brothers', was kinked from so much time harnessed to a plow, warped such that his head cocked sharply to the left and made him look a little off-kilter in the saddle. Still, there was an ease in the way he handled the animal, a casual confidence that kept his boots slid back in the stirrups so that it appeared he rode only on his toes, the reins held so delicately between fingers and thumbs, held the way a lady might hold her most precious heirloom linens after washing.

He turned the horse a few times back beyond the gate and edged him up alongside the Dalton boy on the county's newest horse, a nervous, twitching red filly his daddy had shipped in from Kentucky or Tennessee or some-damned-where. The boys kept the animals reined in just the other side of the gate while their fathers shook hands.

These were the communal truths, the recollections the landowners and townsmen shared the way they kept in common a constant worry over rainfall and boll weevils and cotton futures. What they didn't know, though they might have suspected as much, was that Vaclav had taken in those days to praying shamelessly of a Sunday that pestilence might visit the Dalton herd, and that Dalton had once that summer crept in the moonlight among the outermost rows of Skala's melon crop, injecting the ripe fruit with horse laxative. These two, given a normal night, would have sooner sat bare assed on a cottonmouth nest than exchange pleasantries with each other, but here they were, something about the night and the onlookers and the improvident stakes pushing to each man's lips at least the pretense of sporting civility — *Good luck, then, neighbor* — before they went to inspect their animals.

Dalton pulled on the saddle straps and slapped his son on the leg, leaning in to offer some last bit of advice. As for Vaclav Skala, he didn't say a word to his boy. He'd said what he needed to half an hour before when he handed young Karel his crop. His mouth moved only to work the tobacco. He spat juice into the weeds and scratched at the arc of blond curls he had left behind his sun-speckled crown, pulled a nine-inch blade from the sheath on his belt and held it up to his horse's nose, letting it glint there awhile in the flickering hint of firelight while the animal got a good, strong smell of its steel.

The men of Lavaca County looked questions at one another and shook their heads, laughing together by the fire nearest the creek. *That Vaclav's a few deuces shy of a deck,* someone said.

But he's shored up straight compared to Laddie, ain't it? Where is it you're going after this, Dvorak? Bury a bishop?

And sure enough, Lad Dvorak had been there, all turned out in one of the suits he wore to work, his eyes wide enough with unease to give the lie to the rigid set of his jaw. He was holding a little .22 revolver stiffly at his side, and he looked, when he moved, like he considered his steps before taking them, each an act of pained determination, the walk of a man whose bowels had seized up on him, or who was heading to the confessional with something venial to cut loose from his conscience.

Suspect of anything that couldn't be learned from acreage or animals, the locals wondered if that's what education did to a man. Sure, he'd drawn up the papers for Dalton, making the whole wager legal as the sale of heifers or hay, but you couldn't trust a man who walked flat pastureland like he'd gone all day plugged up by his own turds. He might have held liens on half the acreage in Dalton and Shiner, but he sure looked a silly son of a bitch holding a gun.

Still, it had been left to him to fire the shot that would send the horses and their riders churning dirt through a half mile of dust and darkness, up around the thick and twisted stand of water oaks just shy of the parcel's far hedgerow, and back to the fire-lit finish line where now all the men stood waiting, pointing and laughing at Dvorak, who held his pistol so tentatively in front of him that the barrel drooped downward like the willow tip of a divining rod.

Got-damn, Lad, that ain't your dead daddy's pecker you're hold-ing. Put a squeeze on it the way you do them purse strings of yours.

Lad squinted into the darkness and shrugged it off. There wasn't a man here who hadn't yet come to him for a loan, and if his posi-tion of power wasn't apparent in the way he held a gun, he more than made up for it with his willingness to foreclose on a loan, with the reticence of his Sunday smile, the simple withholding of which could set a man's wife to fretting in the pews, praying her husband hadn't missed a payment.

To be certain, as Patrick Dalton swung the gate out and the horses threw their heads around and lifted their tails to drop great clods to the turf, Lad would have his hand in this, too. He came out from the fenceline, watching, on account of his new shoes, where he stepped, and when he positioned himself a few yards out of the way near the pine saplings clustered alongside the creek, he waited for a nod from Dalton, one from Skala, and then he raised his arm and pointed the gun at a sky strung brightly with stars.

Since the first wagonloads of Czech settlers rolled onto the flat and fertile land of south Texas from the port of Galveston, folks had joked that if a sober man rode over these Texas plains from the coast, and if he thought, before nearing Lavaca County, that he saw in the distance even the slightest rise, even the gentlest hint of a valley, then what he was noting was nothing more or less than the very curvature of the planet. Here in Dalton, between the two forks of the creek, the land offered its first embellishment, a gentle swell that came to a two-hundred-acre plateau and then fell away to sloughs near the water's edge. And so it was on that night, despite the indecisive summer winds, that the highland discharge of such a small caliber gun brought farmwives even a half mile away to their kitchen windows and caused their sleeping children to twitch in their beds.

The horses reared and surged, and the smoke from Lad's gun flew up in a windswept whirl and circled itself like a confused spirit into the creekside trees. The boys got up fast in their stirrups, and by the time they urged their animals up to speed, hoof sod flying behind them as they tore past the cheering line of men and between the two fires and into the darkness, eleven-year-old Karel was laying it on thick with his whip.

This boy had been outriding his older brothers since he was nine, and when his old man bragged on one of his sons — which was rare and only brought on by drink and never within earshot of the boys themselves — the words he found himself slurring were always the same: *That youngest of mine, men, he could whip some fast into a common ass.*

The truth, Karel knew, though he could not have yet put it into words, was that the horse wanted the whip, wanted it the same way Karel wanted his pop's strap, the stinging and unambiguous urgency of its attention, and, for Karel, the closest he got to his father's touch.

Now he kept his crouch tight and marveled as always at the way the ride smoothed out the faster the horse ran. He would come, in later years, to find the same comfort in hard loving, in the convergence and confusion of violence and tenderness, but tonight he knew only the nervous thrill of it, the hot smelter of fear and joy found only in this kind of abandon, in riding for a stake in another man's land, in riding for the father who had refused to hold him on the day of his birth, or any day thereafter, in riding into a darkness that his adjusting vision was only now beginning to brighten, and

20

while he alternated pops of his crop on the animal's hindquarters, he kept Billy Dalton in the corner of his eye, making sure to hold him close and on his outside flank as they approached the quarter-acre stand of oaks they were to circle before heading back to the fires and their fathers at the finish line.

The horse, Whiskey, the youngest and fastest of his father's prized pair, wanted to turn it all loose, wanted to shred acres of sod with his hooves and fill the night with the hot breath of his nostrils. Karel could feel it as he squeezed his thighs to bring the horse into the left-hand turn, the rippling ribbons of muscle beneath the animal's hide, the quivering resistance to the slightest tension on the reins. And then, just before the moss-veiled cluster of trees with their low-hanging, skeletal branches, the Dalton boy stood in the stirrups and cut back behind Karel to take the turn clockwise instead.

Whiskey threw his head to the left and broke stride, and Karel snapped the crop across the right flank and crouched into the turn, keeping the horse tight against the treeline and, because of the cant of his neck, squinting his eyes against the branches that reached out, slapping at his shoulder and face, snagging and snatching clumps of hair along the way.

The Dalton boy was out of sight, orbiting the same sizable stand of oaks in the opposite direction, and for Karel, now, there was only the sound of wind and hoof strikes, the hot pumping of breath from the horse, the memory of his old man's words when he'd handed him the crop half an hour before, the stuttering seconds before two horses would meet headlong at all but full speed.

Sooner than he expected, Karel looked up to find the Dalton horse coming on hard, Billy tucked forward and low behind the filly's windswept mane, his look one of tight-eyed determination. It was a matter of who would hold his ground and who would veer to the outside, and it was, Karel knew, one horse or the other, rather than the rider, that would likely make the decision if left to the last second.

It was Karel, too, who knew that wasn't going to happen.

When the horses were ten yards shy of colliding, Karel dug a knee into Whiskey's left flank and the horse swung out to the right, away from the trees, and then, as the Dalton boy's lips turned up at the corners and he leaned in harder, thinking he'd gained an irremediable advantage, Karel pulled his crop back sharply and, just as the horses passed, he did what his father had told him to do.

What the men of Lavaca County remember correctly is that Karel Skala broke first into the firelight, and that he blew past them at full stride before standing in the stirrups, his head cocked, as always, so far off-kilter, and slowing the horse into a wide circle out beyond the cattlegate before cantering back to where his father and brothers awaited him. Patrick Dalton went red-faced with disbelief as he stood taking it in, watching his landholdings dwindle, sucking snot up through his nose and spitting it, one last time, into the soil he'd just lost. And then waiting, waiting while Karel dismounted and handed the reins to his father, waiting while the older Skala boys gathered around their brother, slapping him hard on the shoulders and laughing. Waiting a full minute or more until the other boy, his own son, came ambling atop his filly out of the night, his right arm twisted into his lap, the shoulder hanging loose of its socket, the left side of his face puffed up and split open from cheekbone to chin.

The men standing creekside, they either pulled forth or pocketed coins, crept back to the creek for their jugs, circled around the horses, and watched while Lad Dvorak handed over both fifty-acre deeds to Skala. The Dalton boy, he was protesting, his eyes awash in tears, his face gone to a sickly blue around the wound. "The son of a bitch," he said. "I was winning."

Skala took the deeds, folded them into the back pocket of his trousers. One of the men handed him a bottle of whiskey and he bubbled it good before offering it to Dalton. "Looks like your boy caught a tree branch," he said. "They hang low around that turn, ain't it?"

Dalton refused the bottle, took his son's arm and pulled down on it and then raised it straight-elbowed until it popped back into the joint while the boy howled, crying in earnest now. "It's more than enough of that," Dalton told him, and he grabbed Billy by the hair and dragged him out into the saplings by the creek. There was some breathless whispering out there, more of the boy's complaints, and then Dalton, loud enough that everyone could hear: "It's worth fifty goddamn acres, then, is it? That's what you'll have me believe, boy? A stripe on the face?"

Dalton stomped back out into the firelight, his shoulders forward. On his face, fitful furrows. He was heading straight for Karel, who took a step or two back before standing his ground beside his father.

"Skala," Dalton said, sucking more snot. "Can I make loan of your boy's crop for a spell? My boy can't seem to keep a bead on his."

Karel looked up at his father, who was working a big wad of tobacco with his molars, nodding. Karel handed over the crop and Dalton snatched it, heading back toward the trees, snapping it against his thigh until he was once again out of sight but not nearly out of earshot: "Now, you chickenshit. You little pigtailed sister. You tell me when it feels like fifty acres' worth of hurt, and we'll see when I agree."

It's KAREL WHO first sees the carriage, who stands straight against the weight of his brothers' progress and brings the plow point to its sudden and subterranean stop. "Shit, boy," his father says. "Is it someone told you to quit?"

The boy jerks his head up toward the road where the wheels and horses are stirring dust in their slow approach. The carriage is a two-seat covered surrey paneled in dark hardwood, varnished and gleaming and coming forward in the midmorning light. Harnessed abreast, the two sizable horses step with such a regulated cadence that their hooves hit the ground in tandem.

"Couple fine horses," Karel says.

"Talking when you should be listening," Skala says, "ain't it?" But he, too, is taking note of these animals, both of them shining oil black with broad blazes white as bleached cotton. The four boys stand transfixed, their necks cocked such that from the carriage they appear to the girls each to be puzzling some monumental and impenetrable question.

Guillermo Villaseñor brings the surrey to a stop and gives Skala a nod before setting the brake and climbing down. He smoothes the sleeves of his dark suitcoat and produces a handkerchief with which he cleans his spectacles. The three girls stay in the shaded back seat while the horses blow and tramp idly in the dirt. Karel's eyes move from horse to girl, girl to horse, awed in equal parts by each of these striking animals, the stallions with their brushed black manes and

24

long forelocks, the girls in their flowered dresses that scoop down at the neck just enough to afford a boy a view of their delicately ridged clavicles and the tanned topmost slopes of their breasts.

My *word,* Karel thinks, and his father lets loose the plow handles, hangs his whip there, and bends forward to swipe the spent tobacco from his mouth with a finger before pulling his plug from his bib pocket and biting off a new portion. He sets to chewing, then he heads out to where Villaseñor is waiting by the road in a tailored suit, his hands held out from the waist with the palms open to the fields as if to say that he's brought nothing of harm or help, either one.

The boys free themselves from the harnesses and Stanislav runs his fingers through his hair and tucks his shirt into his trousers. And then they stand there, toeing the soil with their boots, crossing and uncrossing their arms while their father walks to meet the Mexican at the edge of the cropfield.

All of the morning there's come a cool breeze just strong enough to rustle the mesquite trees up the road and ripple the boys' shirts, and now the sun works its way in and out of the clouds. Out east toward the creek, a red-tailed hawk has been circling and gliding, circling and gliding, and when it tucks its wings and drops to the earth in its swooping dive, a covey of quail bursts from the scrub grass and all of them make their escape but one. The boys, they have their backs to it, but the girls see it, and the youngest one, the one sitting closest to the field, the one with lovely full lips and wide animal eyes, opens her mouth slightly at the sight, and Karel stands straight and locks his knees against these new stirrings in his stomach, and those below. He has seen the wet tip of her tongue.

On the road, Villaseñor puts his hand out and Skala looks at it and spits into the dirt. "You needing directions?" he says.

Villaseñor smiles and pulls his hand back and narrows his eyes as if he's studying a man across from him at cards. "Not in the least," he says. "I'm precisely where I mean to be."

"Well, I mean to be plowing my fields, not standing around like an old woman on the church steps, so why don't you let me to it."

"I will, sir. I will. Thing is, I've got an enterprise in mind that could leave you with twice the fields you have presently. I've heard it in town you've more land than anyone in Dalton, perhaps more than anyone in the county, and I'm thinking you wouldn't mind having a good deal more." He pulls a cigar from the breast pocket of his coat, turns his back to the breeze, strikes a match with his thumbnail and puffs the thing lit.

"They're saying at the feedstore it's a Mexican in town passing time with Patrick Dalton, and I'm thinking if you're that Mexican then you can take your fancy buggy and your *enterprise* and your little split-tails there and turn them all *presently* around and go on back to town."

The man neither flinches nor frowns. He works at the cigar and lets the smoke roll in his open mouth and drift into the breeze. "Dalton's stabling my horses. Nothing more. And I'm Spanish, Mr. Skala. My ranch, sir, was down in Guanajuato, some three thousand hectares, beef cattle and horses, but that's finished now. Still, my family, I can assure you, is not of mixed blood, though that too will be finished, soon enough. Sometimes a man has choices in such matters and sometimes he has not."

"That's a fact," Skala says. "I'm expecting you've got a choice for me, then, am I right?"

"My girls," the old man says, "they're of age. They need husbands."

"Hell," Skala says, "it's a mess of needs go unmet around here."

"I'm willing to pay to see that this one doesn't. Two hundred acres per daughter, cash or land, if there's land enough around to be had."

Now Skala laughs and spits and turns to have a look at his boys, who are standing just this side of the furrows now and moving their eyes from the carriage to Villaseñor without moving their heads.

"Shit," he says. "What use is more land if I'm out the bodies to farm it?"

Villaseñor considers telling the man that he might buy some good workhorses instead of tethering his own flesh and blood to a plow, but instead he takes the cigar from his teeth, puts two fingers in his mouth and whistles sharply, waving his cigar at the carriage.

The girls climb down from the surrey and walk out front of the horses and stand there in a line like they're at auction and somehow prideful of it. They offer the boys closed-lipped smiles that appear soft and kindly but a far cry from shy, and they stand without moving their feet or swinging their arms and in this way they seem as at ease here in the bare daylight on another man's land as they might in their own bedrooms. The wind plays against their dresses, which flare out gently over their slight hips, and the hems fall a few inches below the knee and ripple there against their taut brown calves.

They do not avert their eyes, and neither do the boys.

Across the road, a threesome of Skala's shaggy heifers comes to pull at the brittle grass around the fenceposts, and then, taking note of the men, they push their square heads over the top wire of the fence and cross their eyes and commence to lowing.

Villaseñor raises a hand to his daughters and another out to the boys in the field. "They seem interested enough in one another," he says. "Why should we break their hearts?"

"*We* ain't doing a damn thing, not together we ain't. And I'll break a heap more than their hearts if they go taking Mexicans for wives, you mark it." Now he turns to make his way into the field, saying, "Boys, get back in front of that plow. I'm all talked out."

Villaseñor waves his cigar again at his daughters and then presses the kindled end dead against the heel of his boot while the girls climb back into the surrey. Stan runs a hand through his hair, takes another long look at the girls as they mount the carriage, and Villaseñor laughs when he catches sight of it. "Mr. Skala," he says. "I hear from Dalton you've got a pair of good-running horses."

Skala reaches the plow and takes his whip in hand and twirls it like a down-flung lasso in the furrows beside him. Without looking back toward the road, he says, "Well, he'd be one to know."

"Claims he does."

"I reckon he learns then, even if he learns slow."

"Perhaps, then, you'd rather wager than cut a deal. Win some land and keep your hands all the same—assuming you win, of course. Would you consider that?"

Skala coils the whip and hangs it on the plow handle. He clears his throat, turns to Karel, and looks a question at him. The clouds race overhead, and the hard wind blowing up cold from the west snaps the leather riggings against one another. Karel smiles, ducks into his harness, and tightens the straps.

Vaclav fingers the whip coiled up on the handle while the clouds throw their fast shadows onto his land, then he turns back toward the road and gives the Mexican a nod. "I just now did," he says.

In their room after dark, while the three older boys lie back on their beds, bare chested in just their long drawers, hands clasped behind their heads, Karel sits on the floor working cottonseed oil into the horses' bridles. The moonlight slants its way into the room to play there against the lamp smoke hanging in the air.

"It don't matter to me which one I get," Stan says. "So long as I get one of them."

Thomàs rolls onto his side to face his brothers while he smiles and cups a hand over his crotch. "Generous of you, big brother. Then I'll have me the little one with the kissing lips. You boys see the brisket on her? Oh, Lord. I do believe she makes my sticker peck out."

Eduard sits up, his lumpy feather pillow in hand, and hurls it at Karel, who ducks out of the way and shoots his brother a look. "Poor little boy," Eddie says. "He's going to be stuck here with nothing but his own hand greased with cottonseed oil."

"Worse," Stan says. "Stuck here alone with Pop."

"It's your dream," Karel says, going back to his work, "so have it whichever a way suits you. There ain't no way I'm losing that race."

"I aim to have it a mess of ways what suit me," says Thomàs. "I aim to have it sunup, sundown, and Sundays."

• • •

That night comes the first dream Karel will ever remember carrying with him past dawn, one that will visit him often enough over the years that he will come to wonder, when he wakes, why it so troubles him still. He's standing over his father in the barn while the man hunches forward to hold Whiskey's pastern bent back between two knees and pull from the hoof a shoe that is cracking in hairlines at the nail holes. It goes unstated, but it's clear that Karel has undershod the horse and that the hind heels are now underrun and that Vaclav Skala believes his son to be about the piss-poorest farrier on the planet.

Still, the job is routine. Karel has cross-tied the animal and now there's nothing left for him but to lean against the horse and breathe in the smells of animals and hay and sweat while he watches his father's deft hands at work. Whiskey stands patient as ever in this endeavor, but when the shoe is pried loose and Vaclav drops the hoof to the dirt unshod, the horse lifts it as if he's gone half lame and throws his head about, snorting and blowing. Karel keeps his hand on the animal's neck and talks to him softly, but when Vaclav reaches down again to have a look at the hoof, the horse sidesteps and kicks, and there's a sound like what you get if you stomp a boot heel down hard on a green pecan, only louder, much louder, when the hoof strikes Vaclav Skala's forehead and drives him back into the dirt and hay.

But this is not what jerks Karel awake in bed. Instead, he keeps dreaming as he always will, watching himself run over to his father, who lies groaning and facedown with his arms thrown out to each side, the horseshoe still in one hand, the hay dust borne up by his impact hovering over him, a thousand airborne particles glinting in a kind of murky and suspect halo over the man whose fall has given rise to them.

Karel bends over the old man, whose visible eye is open but rolling too loose in its socket, and when he stands straight again, the blood rushes to the boy's head and the whole world goes red of a sudden. He stumbles, lurching to one side to catch his balance, and there's that sick sensation you get when you're out along the creek-bed and your boot comes down on a bullfrog, all that fleshy give before the abrupt and splintering and skeletal resistance.

And then his father is screaming, sitting up and cursing red-eyed and furious, holding before him an outstretched arm and a quivering hand, the horseshoe still flat, defying gravity, against the man's downturned palm despite his fingers, which are straightened and thick knuckled and now running with blood in thin streams from the back of the man's hand, a hand tufted with blond hair and run through such that the points of two shoeing nails have come up sickly between the bones and through the skin and show themselves nesting in the swollen and bloody punctures.

Upright in bed with sweat-drenched sheets adhered to his skin, Karel blinks the dream back and sits listening to his brothers' throaty breathing while his eyes try to find purchase in the darkness. The window is so black it appears to Karel the world outside has been reduced to two unlit dimensions, and because he knows himself awake now, he has no choice but to puzzle some sense out of it. He puts the night at some late hour after the moon has passed through its arc and gone on to brighten other dark horizons. After midnight, then, long after, and the horses, always still at this hour, are complaining such that he can hear them through the dense pear grove that stands between the back porch and the stable. What the devil, he thinks, and he throws back the sheets.

After pulling on his socks and trousers, Karel slips into an undershirt and slides the suspender straps over his shoulders before feeling his way down the hall with a hand on each wall and stepping into his boots by the back door. They've lost two calves in the last six months to coyotes, so Karel grabs the J. C. Higgins .22 they keep leaning and loaded against the backdoor molding. He checks his trouser pockets to make sure he's got matches, and then he steps out into the windless night that's loudly alive with tree frogs and crickets and with the panicked animals in the stables.

He pulls the lantern down off the nail that's driven into the door frame, and when he gets the wicking lit, he heads down the steps with the rifle in his right hand and the light in the other. The horses sound like they're all but gone mad, stamping and knocking themselves against the stall planks and speaking loudly out against whatever has come to torment them.

Karel moves through the grove rather than around it, hoping to conceal himself long enough to get a good bead on whatever it is he's about to shoot, but once he clears enough of the trees to get a view of the stable doors, Karel's guts flash hot with adrenaline. The slide-to door of the stable stands gapped open a foot or more, which would be normal enough, Karel knows, were there not a flickering and yellow light at work inside and a dark horse standing in the shadows between the stable and the water tank, its head sweeping back and forth as if listening at once to the other horses and to whatever it senses moving in the grove.

Karel leans his gun against a tree and blows out the lantern. He takes a knee behind the tree, one he's climbed dozens of times as a kid on account of its low berth of branches and its sweet summer fruit, and now he hunkers there with his rifle leveled at the open door and waits while his guts work against themselves in such a way that Karel wonders if a man can set himself afire with only the friction of his own fears.

He doesn't wait long there before the stabled horses grow muted and still and the entrance falls void of its glow so abruptly you'd swear there was a darkness inside capable of consuming even firelight.

Karel's eyes go useless and he thinks about how, in winter hay season, a day baling in the freezing wind can make it so even a tepid bath is too hot to sit down in all at once. Got-damn, he thinks, and he concentrates, tries to see with his ears, to find beneath the commotion of tree frogs and insects some more human and telling sound. At first he believes he's imagining it, dreaming it as acutely and convincingly as he's dreamed nails through his father's flesh, but when the slightest of a breeze pushes through the grove and the critters stop their calling from the trees to take note, there they are—footfalls, out beyond the cattletank in the yard.

Karel tries to follow them with a gun barrel he can't quite see the length of, but then his eyes begin finally to find some depth in the darkness, to see into the black rather than only the black itself, and he leaves the lantern there among the surfaced roots of the tree and makes out across the dirt with his rifle raised.

When he comes upon them, the animal sidesteps and nickers and its ears come forward. The rider startles, lets loose the reins, and sits the horse staring at him.

She's beautiful, and he damn near shoots her.

"Get on down from there," Karel says, taking his finger from the trigger.

She widens her big black eyes at him and parts her lips and sits there running her fingers between the horse's ears and down its white blaze. "And if I'd rather not?" she says, her voice smooth and cool as river-bottom stones.

She's in the same dress she'd worn in the carriage, only now its hem is riding up on account of the saddle. He drops his eyes to her legs, bare to the thigh above her riding boots, and he feels like it's nothing inside him but hot liquid swirling around his bones. He motions at her with the gun barrel and tries to drop his voice low, tries to mean it when he says it: "Then I reckon you'll be the handsomest dead woman I ever see."

Her hair falls straight and dark in front of her shoulders, a few wisps pasted to the corner of her mouth. She looks down at the gun and works visibly to keep a smile reined in while she pulls her hair back behind her ears. Then she takes hold of the pommel and swings down from the saddle. She's slight enough that she scarcely ducks her head when she stands beneath the horse's throat to rub its neck. "Do I look so dangerous?" she asks.

Karel considers the question for a moment before he realizes the gun's still leveled at her. "Either that or you're lost," he says, and he drops the barrel and holds the rifle at his side. "The hell you think you're up to in there?" he says, nodding at the stable.

She steps from under the horse and it nudges at her with its great head and sniffs and nibbles at her hair, and Karel goes cool with something akin to envy, a kind of longing he feels often in the presence of animals. There's only the trace of a northern breeze, and he takes a sideways step, hoping he might get downwind enough of her to find her scent there in the air amidst the traces of woodsmoke and turned earth and cattle.

Gathering the reins in her hands, she holds them out to Karel. "I only wanted to see them," she says. "So here. Have your fill. Fair is fair."

There's not yet so much as a hint of light on the horizon. Karel rests the butt of the gun on the ground and leans against the barrel while the horse jerks its head up against the reins and works its jaw from side to side against the bit. "I don't have to handle a horse to outrun it," Karel says, but then he notes her hand there, extended with the reins, and curses himself. If he'd reached for them, he might have touched her.

Now she raises a brow and slides the toe of her boot around in the dirt as if she's intent on drawing something of importance, something he might understand. "No," she says, "I don't suppose you do. That's an impressive pair of horses in there."

Karel glances at the stables, then back toward the house, then down at what she's drawn in the dirt. He's gone his whole life asking himself unspoken questions about his mother, and now something about the cool, unlit morning and this girl in her dress and riding boots has him wondering if his mother ever sat horseback, ever rode while he was inside her for those months when, unlike every month since, he could touch her, even if he didn't know he was doing it, when they were together in that way and both alive and maybe riding together amidst the morning light and the fields of alfalfa and the smells of coming rain and late-cut hay.

The girl walks her horse to the cattletank and waters him. She acts, for all the world, as if she's paying a friendly, daylight visit to an old acquaintance.

"You better git," Karel says. "Pop catches you here it'll be hell to pay."

The girl reaches down between her knees and gathers her dress hems together in one hand, then she slides a boot into the stirrup and swings herself into the saddle. Her skin shines even in the darkness, and her lips look swollen and tender and wet when she smiles. "And what about you?" she says. "What if it's you who catches me?"

Karel lifts his rifle and flexes his fingers around its forearm and smoothes over with his boot the work she's done there in the dirt. "Just see that it isn't," he says.

The girl taps a heel to the horse's ribs and its oily eyes roll in its head as she swings him around, and then she tosses her hair to one side and looks back at Karel over her shoulder. "I will," she says. "Tomorrow night. When we race."

Karel tries to laugh, but what comes out of him is a sound more like that of the critters in the trees than that of a man who's filled up with certainties. "Is that a fact?" he says. "Your father lets his girls do his racing for him?"

"He likes to win."

"Well," says Karel, "seems only fair that you tell me your name, don't it? Before you leave me in the dust, I mean."

She turns the horse back at him and walks it up slowly so that she's looking directly down on him, her eyes so deep and full of their dark allure that Karel imagines she could pull him out of his boots and into the saddle with nothing more than a look. She curls a few strands of the horse's mane around her finger and wets her lips with her tongue, and, before she gives her horse a heel and gallops him into the early morning fields, she leans down over Karel such that her hair brushes against his face and he breathes her in and she smells of lavender and of beeswax and of sweet feed, and then her voice is in his ear and she's whispering: "Ask me Saturday, and I'll tell you it's Skala."

A Breeding of Nettles

DECEMBER 1924

THE YEAR'S COTTON was long in, all three hundred and fifty bales of it dried and ginned and shipped overland to Port Lavaca back in September. The money was in the bank, the Mexican pickers paid and sent on their way. Both cuts of late hay had been baled and stacked three deep in the loft—all in time for calving season—and now Karel Skala was waiting for but two withering Hereford heifers and one wide-hipped wife to drop their young into the world.

Early of the morning, with the sun striking a bright line on the horizon and the wind worrying the twisted branches of the mesquite trees behind the barn, Karel stood sipping coffee and watching his mixed herd of cattle graze beneath a low line of heavy clouds sliding in from the west. December, and still warm enough to break a sweat working in shirtsleeves. He had a habit, Karel did, on account of his crooked neck, of leaning to the right at the waist so as to set the world level in his sights. Upstairs, buried with his father's old watch beneath bank papers in his bureau, there was a photograph some fourteen years old of him and his brothers on the day of their father's funeral. They'd been standing out in the grove among the pear trees he now owned, smoking cigarettes and meaning to say something kind about their pop but saying nothing instead, looking squint-eyed into the evening sun, all four of them young and blond-haired and blue-eyed and kinked badly at the neck, compensating as best they could—he and Stan leaning to the right, Thom and

Eddie to the left. Well over a decade had gone by since they'd been together that way, standing leisurely if uncomfortably in one another's company, pretending they could ever level off a world that had put their mother in the ground and left their father standing for so many years with tobacco-stained lips, red-faced and ever ready with his whip.

But Karel didn't have time to think of such things, of his brothers and what had become of them, of their rich and lovely Spanish wives, of all the land that had fallen into their laps. There simply weren't hours enough for such thoughts, not even with the year's hottest and hardest days behind him. His Sophie had it in her mind to drive to evening Mass in Praha for the Feast, for the Jolly Club dance afterward, and there'd never been, in the five years they'd been married, any talking that woman out of a chance to spend time on her knees beneath the painted ceiling of St. Mary's, no matter how pregnant she was.

"What you aiming to do?" he'd asked her over breakfast, nodding at her belly. "Squeeze her right out in the pews?"

Sophie had whipped her apron at him and smiled. "If it's the Lord's intention, Karel, I expect I will. Besides, how is it you're so sure-fire certain it's a girl?"

"Same as always. Dreamt it was a boy."

She shook her head and went back to shaping dough for the kolaches she meant to take to the dance. "Well, Karel," she said, and now her smile drew itself tight at the corners of her mouth, "seems likely—doesn't it?—that eventually you've got to be right in your dreams about *something.*"

Maybe so, Karel thought now, but not about this. Sophie was carrying all her weight up high, and he'd seen it before, twice in three years, and he knew what it meant. He took a last sidelong look at the coming clouds, spat some loose strings of tobacco from his tongue, swallowed the grainy dregs of his coffee, and then he went to work.

In the cattle pens, he ran his hands up under the knotted tails of each red heifer, checking for inflammation or bloody show, and, finding none, cursed them both for being slow. They lowed and switched their tails, their dark eyes unblinking up high on their white faces. They bent and took in more hay, and Karel was thankful at least for this. The youngest of these girls had proven herself vengeful, an unusual characteristic for a Hereford, and he still wore a bruise on the side of his belly from her antics the week before, a dark stain of blue ringed in black scabby stitching where the teeth had drawn blood.

"You're whores, the both of you," Karel said, slapping hard on her flank the young little bitch who'd put the bite to him. "Slower than Christmas, too."

He shoveled the shit from the pens and wheeled it out back to the compost heap, which stank of rotting eggshells and chicken heads. He slung feed to the pullets who'd been thus far spared Sophie's strong hands and sharp blade. He hung pails of sweet feed in the stables for the horses, then he walked out east of the barn to the smokehouse, added some pecan chunkwood to the embers, and pulled a strip of glistening fat off one of the hams he'd strung up two mornings before. He popped the fat into his mouth and held it there in the hollow of his cheek without chewing, sucking the salt while he made his way back to the barn.

As an afterthought, he grabbed his toolbox and went out to grease the windmill bearings, which were scored badly on their races and would soon need replacing. He loosened the shaft collars and worked the bearing puller onto the housings. Once he'd pulled them free, he popped the bearings from the housings and lubed them well with a finger dipped in grease.

This was the kind of morning work Karel liked, simple little tasks he could complete without calculating figures or opening his wallet or asking his wife for help. If the world were made of only such chores, he thought, he wouldn't fret so about being without a son.

He wouldn't have to keep Sophie on her back every night in March so that, come next December, after the bulk of the year's work was done, she might finally get it right and deliver a boy. If all his work were this easy, he could spend his time thinking instead about the Novotny girl, the way her skin shined dark as a polished penny, the way her arms and shoulders rippled with ribbons of muscle from years of working at her father's feedstore, the way she hadn't grown heavy in the hips or sharp of the tongue. The way she never said no.

The wind was picking up out of the west as if bent on keeping the sun on the morning horizon, and when Karel got the bearings remounted and the drive shaft engaged, the mill began pumping furiously.

Out in the pasture, the jackass lolled its heavy head around while lumbering along, chasing the new calves in circles. The dumbest animal on earth, Karel thought. Dumber even than a cow, but just as useful. Too dumb to fear coyotes, and stubborn enough to keep them clear of the calves. Karel swallowed the pork fat, put his fingers in his mouth, and whistled loudly. The jackass stopped in place, its ears standing forward. The air was ripe with the smells of cattle and smoke and winter pine. Stray wisps of cotton swirled in the wind, and Karel couldn't help but see the waste in it, couldn't help but imagine the three or four bales his hired Mexicans had left in the fields. The ass was still motionless amidst the herd, waiting, and as Karel walked back to the barn to check on the kegs of beer that had arrived overnight, his guts stung with the recognition that he couldn't command much in the way of obedience from anything but a half-wit animal.

The week before, when the heifer had bitten him, he'd kicked her hard down in front of her udder. She'd shuddered and stepped backward, just keeping her feet, and her great white face turned away from him in a way that reminded Karel of the hiding game his youngest daughter, Evie, had taken to playing in recent months, covering her eyes with a blanket, certain that if she couldn't see, she couldn't be seen. Karel had looked down at the scuffed toes of his boots, inflamed with anger at himself, worrying over the money he'd lose if the heifer took to bleeding inside and couldn't calve. Then he spat into the soiled hay and waited for the cow to turn her face to him. When she did, he kicked her again, this time harder and higher, just back of the brisket, where it would be sure to sting her like fire without costing him so much as a cool penny.

Up in Shiner at the Spoetzl Brewery, the young brewmaster Kosmos made most of his living these days by ruining the strong pilsner he'd become known for in half a dozen counties. The Texas Senate still allowed for near beer, an all-but-tasteless concoction that could get a man drunk only if a man's definition of drunk involved a dull pain above the ears and a near-constant need to piss. By state law, Kosmos was to brew his Bohemian recipe and then boil off the bulk of the alcohol, but he could be forgetful sometimes, especially when Karel Skala paid him to forget. To be a Czech farmer in south Texas was to be always thirsty, and it was a well-known joke among the women of Lavaca County that if their men were made to choose between their pints of pilsner and their peckers, there'd be a premium on good sharp knives and coagulant salts at the general store in Dalton.

In the loft, amidst the stagnant smell of still-damp hay, Karel pulled back the square bales near the northern ladder and stepped into a long corridor of secreted beer, a single oaken row of kegs stacked two high that ran the length of the loft. From the ground level of the barn, all anyone could see of the loft was a wall of hay bales, but for four years now Karel had kept a hollow between the back row of bales and the wall. In the winter months, the kegs would stay cool for several weeks, long enough to find buyers for them but not too long to keep them hidden before the hay needed to be put out for the cattle.

The Praha Jolly Club would be good for at least three, Karel figured, and if he had to make the long trip out there today, and sit in church besides, he was damn sure going to turn a profit doing it.

He lowered the kegs one by one from the loft with a rope hoist, rolled them out to the Dodge truck he'd bought last year, for five bits on the dollar, from old Lad Dvorak's bank in town after it foreclosed on the Slovacek place over in Weid, and by the time he got the kegs loaded up and the truck's wheel bearings greased, the fast fat clouds were blowing past overhead without turning loose even a misty bit of their burden.

Inside, after a long hour spent tallying earnings and costs in his ledger, Karel shaved and changed into his suit, then he sat sipping coffee at the kitchen table, rolling sixteen cigarettes and lining them up in the silver case Sophie's father had given him for a wedding gift. The house was warm and fragrant, the milky-sweet yeast dough of kolaches browning in the oven, and when his cigarette case was full, Karel spent a few minutes chasing the girls around the house, growling like a bear while they squealed and laughed and Evie hid behind her blanket. In the living room, Karel plucked his youngest off the floor and nibbled behind her ears until she giggled and buried her face in the collar of his shirt. The oldest girl, Diane, ever hungrier for attention these days, stood below, tugging on the leg of his trousers. Karel put Evie back on the floor, squinted up his eyes and made his fingers into claws before crouching down beside his oldest. "Deenie," he said, "when I catch you I'm going to pull off your toes and eat them with mustard."

The girl, at three, was as fast as she was loud in her escape, and Karel couldn't help but laugh. "Let's to it, all you good-looking women," he said. "If we're going, we're going now."

This was a trip that gave Karel fits, that slicked his guts with a hot mix of envy and resentment and lust, and he tried, mile after slow mile, to keep his eyes only on the road, on the out-flung fencelines blurred by the dirty haze of the truck's front glass. Had it been a stranger at the wheel, someone from northern Fayette County or down near the Gulf Coast, that man would likely have taken note of the name on the passing cattlegates and assumed that he was rolling by one man's expansive spread of property. But the men of Lavaca County knew different. The land between the south and north forks of Mustang Creek, with its wire-fenced stretches of pastureland and black-soiled cotton fields, was the original Skala parcel, some of it bought and some of it won—all of it amassed by old man Vaclav before his sudden death and then deeded to Karel. Everything north, for six miles beyond the Shiner town limits, was the property of the older three Skala boys and their families. The northernmost plot, nearly four hundred acres that lined both winding sides of the Shiner-Moulton road, was the one that most made Karel wish he could drive blind.

Even with sweet little Diane in his lap and Sophie up against him, hip to hip, holding their two babies, one on her knees and one yet curled up and floating tethered in the soft and murky insides of her —even with all this family pressed so close to him—Karel couldn't keep his eyes from the stand of blackjack oaks about a mile up the road, from the farm road that ended at the gate amidst those trees. Nor could he keep his imagination from winding up that road to the house that sat, just out of view, a quarter mile from the gate, nestled among a grove of peach and pecan trees, its back porch steps leading up to the door that opened into Graciela's kitchen. Just last week, he'd seen her out front of the mercantile in Shiner, walking with her children, the little girls dressed in gingham and hair ribbons and clean white stockings, and for once he hadn't crossed to the other side of the road to avoid trading pleasantries with her. The truth was, talk or no talk, it took less than the sight of her to take him back all those years, to the wonder of her dark hair and the taut swell of her calves below the hem of her dress, to the sweet, earthy smell of her he'd taken in some fourteen years back, and to the desire that he'd begun to imagine he'd never again satisfy or suppress, either one.

It was a long trip, just shy of thirty miles to the church in Praha, and the unkempt road made the driving slow. The truck bounced and lurched, slipping into and out of the hard ruts, throwing packed clods of dirt and rock against the undercarriage. Karel steered with one hand and put his eyes back on the northernmost horizon and pulled his cigarette case from his shirt pocket. He flipped the top open with his thumb and pulled a cigarette out with his teeth.

"Time we get home," he said, "it'll be twice as much driving as praying."

Sophie turned the baby, who'd already taken to sleep, so that the little girl's cheek was against her chest. "It's always a ledger with you, Karel. You could pray now, I suspect, if you want so bad that things end up equal on both sides."

"I been doing just that," he said. "Ever since we left."

An hour later, up past the Columbus Road and into the slight swells of forested hills that rose up near the county line, Karel had yet to free himself from the thoughts of his brother's wife. He had yet to strike a match, and his cigarette still hung there, unlit, from his lips.

JUST OVER THE Fayette County line in Praha, there was medicine more than Mass at St. Mary's to be found, and by the time they arrived, both Karel and Sophie Skala were in need of one sort or another. A cool, parched wind had crept in behind the morning's clouds, evening was coming on, and Karel steered the truck behind the church and set the brake beneath an old live oak whose bare branches spanned the twenty-yard gap between the church itself and the adjacent hall, a new, two-story construction of stone and red brick where the dance would be held after Mass.

The long ride had been a rough one, rough enough that now, climbing from the cab, Sophie could tell the moment her feet touched the earth that her third child would be born in Praha, and on the day of the Feast, no less. In the shadows, the air carried a new chill, and Sophie was thankful for the warmth of her body, for the warmth of the body curled up within her. Resting Evie's sleeping weight on her hip, she pulled her shawl up to cover the back of her neck and then cupped her free hand beneath her belly, exhaling sharply.

When Karel made it around the truck with Diane, his mind still miles back on the road in his sister-in-law's kitchen, Sophie took her oldest girl's hand and, before leading her around to the front church steps, said, "I'm needing to sit, Karel. We'll keep a place for you inside."

Karel rubbed his arms against the cold and, as an afterthought, went back to the cab for his suitcoat. Stove smoke came swirling up from the houses hidden amidst the trees to the east. He wanted to clear his head, so before he rolled the kegs of beer into the hall and discussed price with old man Novotny, he walked out back of the church to the parish stables and smoked a cigarette there among the four horses and the smell of tack oil and oats. In the nearest stall, a roan gelding looked up from its bucket of feed and blew, blinking its eyes slowly, and Karel wished there was some immediate need that might keep him here—a hard foaling or a hay fire, either one—anything to keep him out of that church where he would have to sit in the gleaming pews and try to find a place for his eyes to fall without causing him pause or regret or something less forgivable.

Now he held his cigarette in his mouth and scratched the horse behind its twitching ears before turning to watch as more families arrived, most in automobiles, a few yet in wagons, all wearing their finest clothes and tempered smiles.

St. Mary's was one of the three "painted churches" in the surrounding countryside, the ceiling brushed brightly with vivid images, the most unsettling of which was a gold triangle that framed a single unblinking eye, an eye that stared down on a full congregation or on empty pews with the same unflagging and illegible gaze. Even so, Karel thought St. Mary's handsome—from the outside, at least. Erected the year of his birth, the church stood unassumingly enough between the clusters of white pine and moss-veiled oak. Trimmed in marbled stone and planked with simple whitewashed pine siding, the structure's only exterior embellishment was its tall steeple, on top of which was a burnished bronze cross that the townsfolk had paid a young bohunk a keg of beer to mount in its lead pedestal.

Karel had heard the story as a boy, had marveled at the man's bravery. By all accounts, the week before Easter, he'd climbed out the topmost steeple window and shimmied up so that, perched with the toes of his boots on the windowsill, he could steady himself such that he might raise the cross high enough to slide the bronze tenon into the pedestal's mortise. The parishioners stood below, calling up to him with encouragement and advice. Overhead, the sun flickered between passing clouds. When the young man raised the cross, one of its arms snagged on his shirt collar and, just as he worked it free, a gust of wind sent the leaves skittering across the rooftop from the nearby trees.

More than one hundred feet above the ground, the man braced himself against the wind, leaning into the steeple the way a child will lean into his mother for the shelter of her body, but there was nothing of help to be had. With one hand on the cross, the other trying to take hold of the steeple, he pressed himself against the structure, swaying there until he looked down and his boots slipped from the sill.

He fell to the rooftop, sliding on his belly down the steep pitch with the cross gripped in one hand while the fingernails of his other raked over the cedar shingles as he slid. He flailed and kicked, his boots scraping, in search of purchase, as he descended toward the eaves.

This, the onlookers would say, was a malediction, evidence more than ample of evil's due influence in a world of fallen men, and when the young man flipped himself onto his back, planting his heels and stopping himself just short of falling, and lay there pumping hot breath from his lungs before crawling slowly back toward the steeple to complete the job, the cross leaning against his shoulder, the parishioners cheered before they fell silent in solemn recognition of the Lord's intervention. They whispered, as they still did, of this act of grace, of the vision that had brought before their eyes and renewed in their hearts the savior's struggle beneath the weight of his own glorious burden. An Easter miracle, a new testament of their faith, and all for a few gallons of beer.

Now, as Karel ground the wet tip of his cigarette into the earth with the toe of his boot and walked back to his truck, the cross stood glistening against the darkening sky, and dulled only slightly by weather and time. Beneath it, inside the church, Karel's wife was forcing smiles at the other wives from her pew while the painted eye gazed down on her, bearing muted, candle-lit witness to her own struggle against the onset of a hot and cramping wave of contractions. On Sophie's shoulder, little Evie still slept, a thin ribbon of saliva strung from the corner of her mouth to her mother's shawl. Beside her, Diane sat gazing up at the ceiling and the stained-glass windows, listening to the whispered prayers and conversations of the growing congregation. The youngest child, suspended head down in the red liquid glow of its mother's womb, tucked its knees up against its chest and rolled the back of its head against the hard rope of its mother's spine.

The altar boys appeared quietly from the nave, genuflected and lit the altar candles while, in the sacristy, Father Petardus slipped into his fine white vestment. Outside, Karel rolled three kegs of beer from his truck into the hall and stood laughing with the men of the Jolly Club, taking Novotny's flask of corn whiskey when it was offered, folding bills into his pocket. Novotny's daughter, Elizka, wearing her Sunday dress and white stockings, managed a discreet fingertip wave from behind the bar where she was readying the glassware. Karel gave her a nod, his insides alive with a potent mash of whiskey and desire. He took another pull off the flask, swallowing with a grimace, while in the pews Sophie breathed hard through clenched teeth and thought, with a kind of willed determination that never fully blotted out the fear, of what lay in wait for her. She'd had hard labors with the first two, but this would be another thing entirely. The child would come from her, and she would survive it, but it would be hours yet, and the back of its skull would grind against her spine as it came.

It had begun, she knew that, but she couldn't know that it would progress in the way that it would, that the baby would be rendered from her in a fashion as protracted and inexorable as the way stones are tumbled, turned smooth by years of rushing water, and men are eroded of kindness by the slow, interminable friction of their unrealized desires.

51

HER WATER BROKE at the kneeling rail.

The church was quietly alive with the flickering of candlelight and the swirling haze of incense smoke, and Karel was on his knees beside her, amazed as ever by the serenity that overcame his wife's face when Father Petardus placed the Eucharist on her tongue. Holding Evie, who stirred now on her shoulder, Sophie kept her eyes shut, bowed her head, and when the altar boy moved the communion plate beneath Karel's chin and the priest held the sacrament before him, saying, "The Body of Christ," Sophie inhaled with a plaintive gasp and whispered, "Oh, Karel," as if begging her husband to accept what he'd been offered.

He did not.

His hearing, after these five years of marriage, was attuned to her voice in the way common only to husbands who adore their wives and those who lie to them with regularity. To Karel's mind, he practiced the latter because of the former, because Sophie was a good woman, kind and hearty and generous, so much so, in fact, that he suspected she knew when he was less than honest, less than wholly hers, and that she endured the indiscretions the way a good horse will endure shoeing and hard harness work, blinded to everything but the promise of brushstrokes and oats, of kindness and comfort. With eyes affixed only to a future worth forsaking the present for.

Now, because Sophie was speaking at the communion rail, speaking to him in an attitude she would normally reserve for her queries of God, Karel turned from Father Petardus's offering. He leaned toward his wife, his hand reaching down to support himself, and, in doing so, touching the wet hem of her skirt.

When, for years afterward, he told this story to his child, he would say that the birth had begun at the precise moment that the body of Christ had touched his tongue, that it was as if the sacrifice of one son had allowed for the arrival of another.

This was to become Karel's way, the stretching of truth in an effort to instill in the workaday the wonderful, and this was especially true in the stories he would come to tell his children. His own upbringing had been one of quiet exclusion, his father moving through the rooms of the house and the rows of the cropfields in what seemed a determined if not wholly unnatural silence. Year after year, the rain would batter the cedar shingles overhead, the sun would bake the black earth to a hard ceramic sheen around the rigid cotton stalks, the quail in the pastureland would covey and nest and hatch and fledge, each season born naturally of the one before, but on the rare day that Vaclav Skala would gather his boys behind the barn or on the tree-lined banks of Mustang Creek with fishing rods and tin pails of grubs, the very earth would cease, in the boys' minds, its slow, secretive turning, and they'd stand eager and mute, dumbstruck by the anticipation of their father's words.

Usually the stories were brief, meant to impart some lesson, and while Karel might laugh or grow solemn at the stories his father told — of his stormy voyage over high seas from the old country to Galveston, of the wolves he'd hunted alongside his brothers in the hills of Bohemia, lessons about hard work and fields sowed with stubbornness and sacrifice — he never found in these moments any new revelations that could dispute what he'd been told, since he was old enough to comprehend, by his brothers: That he'd killed their mother; that their father despised him for it and had refused, on the day of Karel's birth and thereafter, to hold him.

Now Karel realized that Father Petardus was still extending the Eucharist toward his lips, and Sophie was holding Evie in one arm while she clung to the kneeling rail with the other, her cheeks flushed and running with perspiration from her hairline. Karel brought his wife to her feet and turned away. The priest took a step back with the host yet in his hand and looked down at the couple rising from the rail. The altar boy stood blinking, a frightened grin focused on his own shaking hand and the polished plate held under the host, wondering, no doubt, just what under heaven to do now.

Karel, with whiskey and smoke still on his breath, led his wife down the center aisle of the church toward the doors, a hand in hers and another around her waist. In the pews, Diane met her father's eyes with her own. He nodded toward the door, and she rose to join her parents in the aisle.

Sitting back from the kneelers, making way for the girl, the congregants were pulled from the downcast gazes of their prayers by this unexpected procession. When he'd brought Sophie to her feet at the kneeling rail, Karel had inadvertently stepped on her hem such that now, as they made their belabored way out of the church, the back of Sophie's skirt dragged the floor and streaked the hardwood with her water.

Outside, in the gloaming, the trees lurched and swayed, animated by the shifting winds, the air chilled and sharp with dry pine and chimney smoke. Karel breathed in deep through his nose the way he did when he butchered an animal or kindled a fire, and he laughed as he held his wife around the waist. "It's turning out about how you wanted it," he said. "Ain't it?"

Sophie forced a smile between grimaces. "Not if you're meaning to let me labor in the back of that truck all the way home to Dalton."

"Why, hell no, I'm not." His pale eyes gleamed with mischief, and Sophie recognized the look as the one, more than any other, she'd found irresistible when he'd courted her with dancing and dandelion wine, with kisses and wandering hands among the hay bales up in his loft, she the eighteen-year-old daughter of a father soured by his own determined and ill-humored devotion, Karel the wild-eyed and tough-skinned owner of a vast and growing, if begrudged, fortune in Lavaca County. He was irresistible then as he was now—prone to recklessness, yes, but thoughtful enough to touch her with only the backs of his fingers so as not to rough her skin with his leathery calluses. And he was wounded, too, as anyone could see, and his afflictions opened something wide in her that only caring for him could fill.

When he looked into her eyes, he put the flat back of his hand smoothly against her cheek and pushed her face to the side so her head would match the permanent cant of his own, and in this way he seemed both to acknowledge and soften what his father had done to him with plow and harness and neglect. His smile was forever bent with a hint of impertinence, and he made it his way to say, always, any damn thing he felt like saying, as he did now when he pulled open the church door and called in to the congregation, "Is it a midwife on her knees in there somewhere, and someone to look after my girls? It's a long way back to Dalton, and my wife's taken a mind to farrow out here on these steps if she's not lent a bed instead."

Inside there was the turning of heads and the scuffing of shoe soles on the hardwoods as the parishioners looked away from the sacrament before them and toward the voice at the back of the church.

"Karel," Sophie whispered, pleading with her eyes.

Little Diane was tugging his trouser leg, and he smiled down at her and widened his eyes in such a way that set her to giggling. He looked into the church, caressing Sophie's swollen belly with the backs of his fingers while he called, "Make you a deal, gentlemen. You tend to my wife, and I'll dance with your daughters."

COME NINE O'CLOCK, in the front bedroom of her squat, lamp-lit house, the old widow Vrana had set her mind to it that they would not lose this child. She moved birdlike, shuffling about the room on arthritic bare feet, wringing cotton rags in a basin of cool well water and folding them onto Sophie's forehead as the poor woman labored beneath a single sheet.

The children had been lulled to sleep in the widow's bedroom where, sixteen years before, her husband had coughed blood so violently that it had misted the walls, and where he had died when he'd coughed his last. She had checked on them, these two darling little girls asleep in the bed of her long and fruitless marriage, and the traces of moonlight through the windows reminded the old woman of the nights of her own childhood, nights nearly seventy years gone when, wintering for the first time in this strange new country, in the one-room shelter her father had thrown together when it got too cold to sleep in the wagon, she'd awoken long before morning to the sounds of indecisive winds and coyotes and her two sisters' breathing to find their faces graced by ribbons of light that found their way in through the joints of the hastily hewn roof timbers.

But that had been so very long ago, and they were all buried, father and mother and sisters alike, in the St. Mary's cemetery, not a quarter mile from this house with nothing but densely clustered trees and a narrow footpath of fallen leaves and the indeterminate remainder of her own mortal life between them, and she could make that short walk through the little thicket with a pail of sudsy water and wash their headstones with these same cotton rags, and she could do so any time at all that she liked, excepting now, when both she and the rags had a more pressing purpose.

This baby wasn't turning, and Sophie Skala was one of Praha's own. As a girl, before her father moved the family south into Lavaca County, Sophie had run ponytailed and sun flushed through the thickets and creekbeds of Praha, and a much younger Mrs. Vrana had often taken note of the girl at Mass, sitting so prim and fair, that ponytail tucked up into her Sunday bonnet like a sweet, if poorly kept, secret. Widow Vrana, who now sat on the edge of the bed whispering Hail Marys with the woman that girl had become, helping her pray her way through these violent contractions — strong but unproductive these last two hours — this old woman, she'd pined in those long-gone days for a little girl like the one Sophie had been, one so sweet and well mannered, one so at home all the same in her best dress or in the little smocks she wore while traipsing barefoot around the countryside. It had not come to pass, and it had tested Mrs. Vrana's faith more than even she believed it was meant to be tested that, over the years, in a land of farmers and tradesmen whose wives had little money for physicians and even less faith in their science, she had attended to perhaps four hundred births, and still, no amount of her garden's herbs or store-bought tonic or time spent splay-legged and praying beneath her husband's weight had yielded so much as a short pregnancy, much less a child of her own.

And so, by her will, if not by God's, this child would live. The water had come hours ago, and she'd seen both babies and mothers lost to less dangerous labors. Already she'd applied onions to Sophie's feet and a poultice to her lower back to calm the spasms. She'd purged her with a tea of mugwort and sorrel, and now, to her mind, time was a creeping and persistent rival. The widow knew well, as did all the midwives in three surrounding counties, of the death, nearly thirty years back, that had taken Klara Skala, and needlessly so, she thought. Edna Janek was an able practitioner, and it would not have happened, she believed, had Klara been attended to sooner.

Now, after a final prayer together, she sopped Sophie's face with a new cool rag and pulled back the sheet. She checked between the suffering woman's legs, and then she struggled onto the mattress and positioned herself with her hands cupped on either side of Sophie's belly.

"I've waited as long as I'm willing to wait," she said. "Catch your breath, dear. I'm afraid this is likely to pain you something terrible."

AT THE PARISH hall, during the two further hours of the old widow Vrana's ministrations, and an hour longer of Sophie's grunting and pushing to expel this thing that had so beset her, Karel Skala would unhinge himself with drink.

It had gone full dark by the time he'd gotten Sophie and the girls over to the Vrana house and settled the little ones into bed. He'd kissed Sophie on the forehead, and the old woman had ushered him out the door as if he were no more welcome there than would have been a common cur. On the path through the thicket, without a lantern, he'd been grateful for the emerging moon, swept clean of the day's clouds by the push of cold weather from the west. It was too cool out for tree frogs, and Karel felt their absence. He'd grown up with the throaty urgency of their chirping, and a walk through woods with only the sounds of nested birds and insects was a fresh reminder of all the little disappointments that conspired to set a man to thinking about greater ones. He stepped quickly, wishing to rid himself of this thicket, and his boots crunched in the brittle leaves and pine needles underfoot until he emerged into the unhindered moonlight.

He was grateful, too, for the sight of the cemetery at the end of the path, for the muted animal sounds within the parish stables, then for the gleam from the hall's lighted windows and the muffled, brassy half step of the music that could be heard as he approached, all of which brought him closer to the promise of soft skin and hard drink.

Just outside the hall doors, Bohumil Novotny stood laughing and passing a half-gallon jug with a pair of boys who, but for the work a blade had done to one of their cheeks, could have each passed for the other. Karel stopped behind the trunk of the giant live oak so he could study them awhile. Judging from their caked work boots and oilcloth coats, they hadn't come for church, and Karel would have bet a dollar against a dime that they weren't yet sixteen. Still, here they stood, running their hands through their dark, closely cropped curls and taking seasoned, deliberate pulls on the jug. They made a habit, these two, of hooking their thumbs in their trouser pockets when they laughed. Karel noticed that they held themselves in the same way, upright and rigid as if they'd been skewered with cedar posts, but when they moved they did so leisurely, with loose-jointed gestures.

As for their company, he was about as complicated as cornbread. Between his feedstore and rail interests, Novotny had amassed as much of a fortune as one could in a town so small as Praha, and he was as well dressed as he was red-faced and overfed. Beneath his tailored and unbuttoned black suitcoat, his shirtfront had been freed from his trousers by the protrusion of his belly, and when he took note of Karel approaching from the shadows, he fell silent and scratched the underside of his down-slung stomach while the young fellows beside him toed the dirt and nodded their greetings.

"Damnation," Karel said. "You men so scared of touching a woman that you'd hide outside in the cold rather than take a turn around the floor?"

Novotny raised his brows at the others and took his handkerchief from his vest pocket to clear his nose. Then he took a pull from the jug and held it up as if raising a toast to something no less impressive than the moonlit sky itself. "I'd let you a drink of this corn here, Karel, if I thought it might quiet you down. Thing is, given your communion-time proclamations, I don't believe the last few drops I give you had that effect."

Inside, the band held the last long note of a schottische, and then came the vigorous applause from the dancers. "A few drops just ain't enough to do the trick is all," Karel said, "but I see you found a bigger portion now that the sun's not out to lay light on it." He nodded at the hall door. "Orchestra sounds lively tonight."

"Whole town's lively on account of that near beer you brung." Novotny winked at the boys and handed the jug to Karel. "You know these boys here, I believe, or did once. Villaseñor bought their pop's land down your way."

Karel bubbled the whiskey and took a cigarette from his case. When he lit the thing, the first pull of smoke fell slowly, as if of its own weight alone, from his nostrils, and then he gave these boys a look, one they didn't manage to return, as they appeared intent on studying the scuffed toes of their boots. Good-looking fellows they were, broad across the shoulders and bright in the eyes the way boys tended to be when they got the first scant sniff of their own manhood. If they had a whisker between them, Karel couldn't locate it. "Son of a bitch bought a passel of folks' land," he said, passing the whiskey back to Novotny and putting a hand out as the band took up a new number inside. "Only twins I recollect was the Knedlik boys, and they were still on the tit last time I saw them."

Now the boys turned their attention upward in unison, and the one with the scar stepped forward, smiling, and shook Karel's hand while indicating his brother with a tilt of the head. "Joe here ain't got off it yet," he said, a statement that earned him a hard elbow to the shoulder and smiles all around. "Name's Raymond."

Karel took note of the mark the boy wore, a thin and winding line of poorly mended flesh that ran from the swollen underside of his left eye to the corner of his mouth. "Someone mistake your face for a beefsteak, did they, Raymond?"

The boy put his hands in his pockets and gave his brother a glance through the corner of his unblemished eye. Novotny said the Knedlik troubles had made the paper more than once, and wondered how it was that Karel always knew the market prices of hay and cotton if he never unfolded the *Gazette*.

61

Karel shrugged and kept his eyes on the boy to let him know he was still awaiting an answer. Before they went inside, with the moon flickering between a few remaining wisps of clouds, Raymond Knedlik worked his tongue around in his mouth awhile and spat between his front teeth. He took a step sideways to square his feet with his shoulders. "It was a family matter," he said.

Karel nodded and turned for the door, but the boy took hold of his shoulder and stopped him short.

"Seeing that we're talking appearances, Mr. Skala, I'm wondering who it was what nailed your ear to your shoulder and left it there until your neck growed that way. A family matter, was it?"

Karel held his cigarette between his teeth and shot Novotny a look that had both amusement and wonder in it. *Who in hell is this little green-ass?* he wanted to say. *And why is it that I want to kick him in the ribs and slap him on the back all at the same time?* Instead, he took a long pull from his smoke and did something he rarely did, something that had always proved as useless as sowing seed in September — he tried to straighten his neck so he could look this boy level in the eye without leaning.

He couldn't any better than he ever could, so he spat his unfinished cigarette from his lips and ground it asunder with his boot heel instead. "I ain't got a family no more," Karel said, "excepting my wife and girls."

"*Excepting?*" Raymond said. "Hell, you can feed me shit on a biscuit if you ain't got me beat. All I got left is Joe here."

"That a fact? Last I heard, your pop had bought a parcel up county from Flatonia."

"Yessir. And me and Joe here just sold it. Which, so long as we're on the subject of commerce, you reckon it's some of that beer left for sale inside? We wouldn't mind drinking one to your family, Mr. Skala. We hear it's getting bigger presently."

"It damn well better be," Karel said, opening the door. "On both counts."

THERE WAS BEER left aplenty, and Elizka Novotny there to pocket Karel's coin and hand him the glass, making sure, each time, to brush his fingers with hers when she did.

The only child of the wealthiest man in town, Elizka had made use of her advantages. During the war, when enrollment fell and the University at Austin had opened its doors more readily to women, Elizka had left Praha for three years of book learning. When her mother fell to a crippling stiffening in her hands and feet, she came home before graduating to assist in the woman's care and ended up managing her father's business interests instead. She had a knack for numbers and negotiation, and once, when Karel had asked when she planned to settle down, Elizka Novotny had pulled a wisp of curls from the corner of her wet mouth and said, "I am settled. I didn't grow Daddy's business just to marry some dirt farmer who expects me to hand over the reins so he can make a wreck of it."

Now Karel gave her a wink, handed beers to the Knedlik boys, and turned toward the music. On a stage of pine planks laid over railroad ties, the five-piece band had come out of their suitcoats, and there was sweat showing beneath the arms of the bandleader's shirtsleeves and wicking into his vest as he kept time to the music with his foot. He handled his accordion with an oddly orchestrated violence, and when he stomped his boot heel sharply through a three count, the horns and drums met him on the third beat, striking up another polka.

Bohumil Novotny buttoned his suitcoat and made his rounds, shaking hands with his fellow townsmen before begging their pardon to carry a plate of food home to his ailing wife. When Father Petardus rose from a table in the back and raised his empty glass, wishing the parishioners a pleasant night, the band kicked into a droll march as the pastor walked for the doors to make his exit. The onlookers hooted and slapped at their thighs, the older among them throwing themselves forward until the laughing turned to wheezing and hacking.

Karel, for all his talk, spent most of the night on the perimeter of the dance hall, moving with the Knedlik boys in tow between the long tables, introducing them to the folks he knew while young suitors reached for the hands of their sweethearts and husbands danced with their wives, stirring the baby powder that had been sprinkled on the hardwood flooring to make shoe leather cooperate with the slide steps of the occasional waltz.

The hall had gone ripe with the smells of spilled beer and sweat and the lingering, fatty spices of the sausage and onions that had been served before the band had tuned up. Throughout the hall, between songs, rose frequent outbursts of laughter and the ivory clicking of dominoes being shaken between hands, but it was the music Karel wanted, and the band kept it coming while he drank and smoked and took a seat across from the Knedlik brothers near the door.

The boys took long drinks from their pilsners, but only Raymond studied Karel from over the rim of his glass. Joe kept his eyes on the table, his mouth pinched up between drinks like he'd been trying the whole of his short life to wash one bitter taste from his mouth with another.

Karel tapped his toe in time with the music and sat back in his chair with a groan. He hadn't found time to eat, what with all the commotion, and now his stomach was a sour swirl of beer and corn whiskey. "So, you boys in need of work?" he said.

Raymond smiled and licked a trace of beer suds from his upper lip. "It could be. You in need of help?"

There was a commotion on the dance floor, and Karel looked out to find a young girl sprawled out on her back beneath her red-faced dance partner, who was struggling to bring himself back upright after their tumble. *Hell, boy,* someone called out. *It's a dance, not a circus!*

Karel turned back to the twins, who were chuckling into the foam of their beers. "I might could use a hand or two," he said. "Your folks is gone then? I didn't hear."

"Ashes to ashes," Raymond said, and then his smile turned in on itself at the corners of his mouth. "Mother was a good woman. Deserved better than what God gave her. Died of the typhus last winter. The old man, he burnt up in his bed when the house caught fire. Just after the last cut of hay."

"God bless," Karel said, feeling, at the word of the mother's death, some old, buried connection to her clawing at him like a blind, burrowing animal awakened to find its den collapsed around it. His words, he suspected, had betrayed nothing, and when Joe looked up at him, his bright eyes glassy and red with whiskey and fatigue, did Karel think how halfhearted it must have sounded, the invocation of God coming, as it had, from a man who'd not two hours ago interrupted a sacrament. "What I mean to say is, that's a sorry lot, boys. It was good fortune you managed to make it out."

Now Raymond traced his scar with his thumbnail. He finished his beer and kept his lips closed while he held his stomach and muffled a belch. "We wasn't ever in anything what needed getting out of, Mr. Skala. We don't believe in fortune. Nor accidents neither."

Karel frowned and lit a cigarette. He started to say that a man ought to watch how much he said, and when, but he thought the better of it, saying instead, "How about work? You believe in that?"

"We ain't interested in farming, if that's what you mean. Joe here's good with animals. Sits a horse good as any. I can butcher damn near anything born with blood in it. But we don't tend to crops. We got enough money to get by a good while. Got a new truck. Got no use anymore for planting fields and mending fences. If we had, we'd have kept the land up county."

"I expect you would have," Karel said. "Anything else you won't do, assuming there's good money to be made in it, of course?"

"Just that. Crop farming. I reckon that's the whole list right there."

Karel polished off his beer and grabbed the boys' empty glasses from off the table. And then, before heading toward Elizka at the bar, he clinked the glasses together and squatted down such that his haunches rested on his heels. Now that Sophie was laboring, they'd have cause to stay put in Praha for another day or two at the least, and he'd need someone to look after his heifers and smokehouse, and there were at least four kegs of beer that needed delivering to Hacek's Ice and Coal in Moulton, but first he wanted to see how much doing it might take to spook these boys.

The orchestra held one last, long note of a polka, and when the dancers had spun to a stop and turned toward the stage to applaud, Karel put his cigarette to his lips and held it there burning orange at the ember while he leaned in close to Raymond Knedlik. "Set a house afire, would you, Raymond?"

The boy glanced at his brother and then looked hard and without blinking through the rising smoke into Karel's eyes. His bad eye twitched, its bottom lid pulsing with the measured beating of his heart. Then he pushed his chair back and stood up, his brother following suit. They hooked their thumbs into their pockets and laughed while Karel came to his feet with the beer glasses still in his hands and his cigarette hanging from his mouth.

"If what folks says is true," the boy said, "it's more than me and Joe here that's helped his old man into the hole he deserves."

It had been a long time since anyone, friend or otherwise, had dared to mention Karel's father within earshot of him, and Karel noticed that his fingers were gripped around the beer glasses so forcefully that his veins bulged beneath the tanned skin on the backs of his hands. What I ought to do, he thought, is take you little shit-asses outside and stomp some sense into you, but the brothers held their ground, moving together in such a way that their shoulders nearly touched, and Karel found himself thinking of the days he'd been harnessed with his brothers to the plow. It had been hard work, but they'd suffered it together, shoulder to shoulder, and now there was something cool bubbling up inside him, working its way through him fresh and clean the way the waters of the cold springs out west bubbled up through stone to feed the winding rivers in the hills.

Karel let his cigarette drop from his lips and ground it into the floor with his boot before moving close enough to the boys to smell their sour breath. Onstage, the bandleader pulled a red kerchief from the back pocket of his trousers, mopping his forehead and the bridge of his nose before he announced an intermission. Karel found himself whispering: "If what folks says is true, then we'd all three of us be waiting for a turn in that new electric chair they got in Huntsville, sure enough. So either it ain't true or we ain't been so goddamned mindless enough yet to go flapping our gums about it at a church dance of a Sunday night. Besides which, there's a difference between killing a man and letting one die, so why don't you just take your seats there and let me buy you another beer and listen to what I'm wanting to ask you."

HALF AN HOUR later, after the Knedlik boys had agreed to look after the Skala place for a day or two, and to stay on after that if they could agree on the terms, Karel saw them out to their truck and shook their hands, their breath steaming in the growing cold as they said their good-byes.

And then he took to drinking in earnest.

The beer did its work in much the same way he knew river water did, running through him and carrying away, grain by grain, the sediment of ill will that had embedded itself within him over the past year of hard work and worry. What was left now, he thought, as the night deepened and the hall thinned out, leaving only the most vigilant of dancers and drinkers, was nothing less than the very bedrock of him, deep and compacted such that neither plow nor music nor drink could unearth it.

Karel's earliest taste of the bottle had come eighteen years back on the night of his first race against the Dalton boy. That night, beaming with victory and the whiskey his brothers had smuggled into their room from their father's stash, he had stirred in his bed, flushed so fully of his usual thoughts that it seemed to him there was nothing left of him but skeleton and skin and the tingling thereabouts that came from having done something his pop might praise him for and from having drunk something that might send the old man reaching for his strap.

At first he'd kicked the sheets away and marveled at the novelty of it, of a night freed from the knot of longing he'd had cinched in his gut as long as he could remember, but then the room had begun its slow, almost reluctant turning, the way a windmill did sometimes when a trace of breeze crept up so softly overhead that it didn't even register on his sweat-glazed skin. He'd sat up in bed, alone in a room alive only with the sounds his brothers brought forth from their dreams, and though he couldn't have put it into words, what he knew somehow was that he'd been scooped clean inside of more than he might be able to do without, reduced to something so thin walled and brittle and hollow that it felt, any moment, like it was sure to cave in on itself if he didn't find some way, or someone, to fill it.

He'd discovered on that night, and many like it afterward, that he could manage to stay upright on horseback even when he'd drunk himself incapable of walking a straight line between the back porch and the outhouse. Fumbling with the straps, he'd grabbed the saddle by the pommel and set it aside in the hay. Then he mounted the horse and rode with only a bridle. He cantered out past the cattlegate and slowed to a walk while crossing the south fork of the creek, and when he came up the far bank he gave the horse a heel and marveled at the solid resistance of the animal, that and the surging response that leveled off into a ride so fast and smooth that he could hardly tell himself from the animal or the animal from him. There was the controlled violence of the muscles rolling beneath him, the vibrations working through him so fully that the roots of his teeth tingled in the hard bone of his jaw. In the distance, mesquite and pecan trees cast their erratic black shapes against the bruised sky that hovered over the solid line of the horizon. It was a wonder, and Karel relished the mystery of it—all these acres, so familiar beneath the bald sun, now rendered foreign as provinces in the Bible. All he needed, it seemed, was night air made fast in his hair by an animal run hard in the night, and he could find the loud landscape of his father lulled quiet by something so simple as the absence of light.

In the end, such a ride had only once failed to right him, to restore in his echoing hollows the weight of all the worry he couldn't seem to feel whole for long without.

Now, near midnight in the parish stables, a soft diffusion of moonlight found Karel leaning against a stack of square hay bales and listening to the idle tramping of the horses as they shuffled and sighed in their sleep. Outside, the thicket was loudly alive with the work of insects and wind. When Elizka Novotny came to meet him there, as she'd done twice before in the course of the last year, Karel tried to stand upright and, in the attempt, lurched forward in a fashion so sudden and awkward that at first he imagined one of the horses had worked its way free and come up to nudge him between the shoulder blades. He swung his arms back to compensate, sliding around in the loose hay underfoot before falling back against the rough bedding of the bales.

Elizka pulled the long curls of her hair back over her shoulders and moved toward him past the stalls. "If you were wanting to dance," she said, "you should have asked me an hour ago when the orchestra was playing."

He shrugged and sat up. She held his head in her hands, pulling him toward her, and he could smell her there in the dark, the bitter tang of perspiration and sour malt sweetened by the earthy, animal scent of her. Karel leaned forward and breathed in sharply through his nose. "You smell something of a horse," he said.

She went to work on the buttons of his shirt and shushed him, pushing him onto his back atop the hay. Above them, hung from nails in the joist timbers, was the old weather-checked tack that the parish had forever mended rather than replace. Elizka pulled a rusted martingale ring out so Karel could catch sight of it. "You imagine it has anything to do with this fancy inn you keep inviting me to?"

Karel held his tongue and kicked off his boots. After she'd gotten him out of his trousers, she worked her underclothes down over her hips and pulled her dress up around her waist to reveal the chill bumps rising there on the tops of her thighs. When she straddled him, he looked down as the soft cleft of her yielded to him in the shadows, and then he smiled at her with his eyes closed while she worked the slick and fragrant heat of herself against him. "No," he whispered. "I'm near certain it's you."

Elizka moved atop him for a long while, her hips shifting up and back in the smooth, rhythmic cycle of a seasoned horsewoman posting in the saddle. Karel lay there with his eyes clamped shut, remembering another astride him, the lather of her tracing cool trails down his thighs, until he could scarcely tell what among all this forgiving flesh was hers and what was his. The horses twitched and switched their tails in their sleep. Outside, the wind threaded its way through the thicket and swept leaves from the roof timbers while Elizka's breathing gathered into its own urgent cadence.

And then it was upon him, the same irrepressible breed of desire that he'd felt the night he left his father to expire in the mud after falling beneath the weight of his horse. A longing to turn loose of every damned handhold the earth afforded a man, a longing he'd managed, until then, to defy long enough to unlearn.

When it was time, he pushed himself into her and he held her hips as steadfastly as he was now held by this intoxicating urge, one stronger than the alcohol, one which compelled him to surrender to what beckoned him simply because it beckoned and he heard it. A summons as vital and insensible, Karel felt, as the one the very pull of the earth had on the unborn, that unanswerable force that landed foals and calves and infants alike in the world with the intention to let them fend, in the end, entirely for themselves.

When his body shuddered, Elizka stopped all at once and leapt off to find him smiling at her, his eyes wide with the kind of self-satisfied mischief his wife so often found endearing. *"Damn it, Karel,"* she said. *"You didn't."*

He tried to follow her, but he had his trousers and boots to contend with, and by the time he made it to the stable door, she had cleared the churchyard and was pacing up the road, her arms stiff at her sides, toward the room she kept above the store beside her father's house. Karel stopped, and as he turned away there came a

71

voice from out in the cemetery. He scanned the fenceline in the darkness to find the old widow Vrana swinging open the gate. She moved toward him with her shawl pulled over her head like a nun come out of the dark night to chasten him. Her face was creased by what Karel imagined were equal parts weather and contempt, and as she approached she kept her eyes fixed on the feedstore up the road.

When she was upon him, he shivered against the chill of her eyes or the winter air or both, and he looked down to find himself still shirtless, hay dust catching moonlight in his chest hair.

And what was there to say by way of explanation? No sense even in troubling with an attempt. Instead he said, "Evening, Mrs. Vrana," and he gave her a nod and a playful bow.

"Long past it," she said, glancing once more up the road, where now lamplight flickered in the second-story window of Elizka's room. "Your wife is wanting to introduce you to your son, Mr. Skala, if you can spare the time just now."

The wind gusted and then swirled so that it came, for a moment, out of the south. The enormous oak between the church and hall turned loose of a wind-snapped twig so slender and insignificant that it rustled down through the network of bare branches and landed soundlessly on the cool sod of the churchyard. Behind him, one of the horses shifted in its nervous, animal sleep, and Karel moved his toes around in his boots. "My *son*, did you say?"

"I did. Delivered so near on to midnight that I can't be certain which day. But he's a boy, Mr. Skala. I'm confident I've kept the difference straight in my mind."

Karel reached for the woman's hand. She allowed him to take it, and then she took a step back toward the cemetery.

"I'll be goddamned," Karel said.

The old woman let go of his hand, began shuffling along toward the gate, and without so much as turning her head she said, "I can't speak to that, Mr. Skala, but I suspect you can. Either way, your wife's waiting on you, and she's likely expecting you to have your shirt on when you get there."

72

A Sacrament of Animals

MARCH 1910

ALL OF THE COOL afternoon, a steady wind has swept across the brittle pastureland and bristled through the needles of the spindly creekside pines, and now, with the two finish-line fires whipped alive and spitting embers, a sliver of moon flashes behind the low scrim of clouds with all the coy promise of a woman's pale skin showing itself beneath the sheer guise of worn stockings. Near the creekbed, in the shadows beyond the firelight, Villaseñor's men stand watching as the onlookers arrive, the hint of moonlight glinting off the blued receivers of their rifles, which they cradle in the crooks of their arms with a collective if tentative tenderness, the way they might hold their sons, had they any to hold.

In two days, news of the wager has outrun the county mail service, finding its way north to Shiner and Moulton as if conveyed by wire, and when Vaclav Skala leads his sons and his fine snorting stallion out of the darkness of his acreage and through the gate at the pasture's westernmost fenceline, he takes slow notice of the congregation of animals tethered to fenceposts. He reckons there's fifty of them at least, two to each cedar post—workhorses, most of them, with some finer breeding and a few common asses among them. Surveying the ones nearest him, he notes a few in gleaming oiled tack embellished with polished brass rivets and hardware, others haltered in fraying rope and unsaddled, all of them steaming from the nostrils and tossing their heads against the sharp and shifting scents of nightfall. Vaclav stops of a sudden just inside the gate and

75

runs his hand down the twitching flanks of his horse, smoothing the roan hide's confusion of colors as the animal works a hoof halfheartedly in the winter sod and browses the occasional tufts of dried turf. The boys ask wordless questions of one another with their eyes and stand at the ready while their father bites a new portion of tobacco from his plug and works it back into his molars with a finger before spitting a loose string of the stuff from his tongue. Then he turns to them and tilts his head toward the long line of horses tied up and nervous in the night as if staged for some inhumane procession. "If that sight there wouldn't stiffen a horse thief's pecker, boys, I don't reckon any pretty little thing's teats would do the trick neither."

The boys laugh and give the horses a look, but Karel is scanning the shadows for another animal altogether. Two nights in a row now it has worked him awake, the sight of the Villaseñor girl with her knees bare above her fine, polished boots in the stirrups, her hair sweet smelling and black and falling toward him. Stan grips his shoulder and gives him a playful shake, but Karel knows that even his brothers are wishing failure upon him, bearing in their chests, as they surely do, the hot burden of hope.

And they are not alone.

Men are milling about everywhere. Farmers and townsfolk, tradesmen and ranchers, and Karel can't remember a time when he's ever seen so many men he recognizes standing unwarily amidst so many he doesn't, all of them telling jokes and swapping stories and smoking cigarettes, toeing the black earth and warming themselves near the fires. There are better than four dozen, Karel guesses, and there are others he can't see. Out from beyond the stand of pines rise the muffled conversations of those who are newly arrived and as yet planting sixpenny nails in the hard, dark clay of the creekbank with boot heels and securing their jugs of corn whiskey with double-knotted twine and floating them in the cold running water as if fishing for the county drunks.

Just this side of the trees, two squat Mexicans with thin mustaches and expensive rifles stand eyeing Karel and smiling, stubs of cigars planted and smoking in the wet corners of their mouths. One of them winks at him and elbows his partner, who laughs and scratches his low-slung belly and then pulls the cigar from his mouth so he can purse his lips into a mocking kiss that sours Karel's guts and slicks his palms with sweat. And then there's Lad Dvorak, laughing with Patrick Dalton and his boy, the three of them huddled close to the fire farthest from the trees, and when the banker catches sight of the Skalas, he turns and moves toward them with his lips crinkled into a smile and his trousers stiff and creased hard with starch. He makes a point of fingering the silver chain slung from his vest as he walks, and when he stands before them, he pulls the watch from his fob and looks Vaclav in the eye before springing the thing open.

"I've never known you to be early, Skala. That or late, either one."

"Never known you to give a great goddamn one way or the other," Vaclav says, "unless you're carrying a note and expecting payment, which I'll remind you ain't the case." He takes a look around, squinting into the darkness beyond the reach of the firelight and testing the scant weight of the horse crop in his hand. "What's keeping the Mexican?"

Off to the east and well out of sight, roosted mourning doves project the last of their day's lamentations from the dense and tangled stand of moss-draped oaks. Dvorak clears his throat and puts his watch away. "I don't suspect anything is, Skala. Seems to me he's unaccustomed to being kept by anyone other than himself."

Karel takes Whiskey's lead when his father hands it back to him, and then he stands, his feet squared with his shoulders and his stomach fermented by nerves, as his father forces a smile to his lips and scratches the bald and sun-spotted skin of his scalp and then smoothes the fringe of unkempt curls on his head. "Well, hell then," says Vaclav, "I reckon it might just as well be me what accustoms him to it."

"Might as well be you who tries," Lad says, then he locks eyes with Karel and opens his coat to reveal its green silk lining and a folded bundle of parchment secreted there in the monogrammed pocket. "The papers are all in order, boy, excepting your father's signature. You ready to ride?"

Karel spools the leather lead tight around his wrist and reaches out instinctively for the long neck of his father's horse, working his fingers there such that the bristles of the animal's coat prick the tender flesh beneath his fingernails in a way that is both painful and reassuring, and he's about to tell Dvorak that he's sure enough ready when his father raises the riding crop and snaps it sharply against his trousers before handing it over. "He calls you *boy* again, son, you got my permission to sign the family name for me. In welts on his hindquarters."

In the distance, coyotes have found their voices in the damp promise of weather, calling out as if in answer to the inconsiderate onset of cold. Visibly agitated along the fenceline, the horses blow and complain, their hides shuddering violently with the worried work of their muscles. To the west, when Villaseñor's surrey rolls dark and polished as a hearse to the gate, the sky hangs swollen and sickly above the distant horizon as if the whole mass of the heavens has been wounded and gauzed with clouds and backlit feebly by the diminishing moon. The coach rocks on its springs, and when it comes to a stop, the twin carriage lanterns swing in illuminated arcs from their chains. Guillermo Villaseñor ties off the reins and sets the brake. He climbs down from the seat as the onlookers stand casting long shadows in the firelight. Still others emerge unsteady and quiet as spotted fawns from their drinking amidst the trees by the creek. They watch silently as the man buttons his fine otter-skin coat against the growing cold and tilts his unlit cigar up and down playfully in his mouth. The two girls in the covered rear seat of the carriage are visible only as indistinct but animated shadows, and in the moments it takes for Villaseñor to strike a match and puff his cigar lit and take down one of the lanterns and amble to the gate, his men are there waiting, their rifles at their sides, until they exchange some words in Spanish and the two guards cast quick looks over their shoulders at the assembling crowd. They nod, and Villaseñor puffs his cigar and lets the smoke roll from his mouth and swirl out into the night before pulling the thing from his lips. He hands the lantern to one of his men, slides two fingertips into his mouth and whistles sharply.

Out west, a coyote answers and a wet gust of wind scours the pasture and swirls the fires, which throw glowing ash yawing out into the clusters of men. And then the girl rides out of the darkness with her feet high in the stirrups, her black hair roped into a single swaying braid and her face rapt in a solemn beauty that reminds Karel of a memory he can't possibly have, one he's kindled to life since the other night out by the stables. He's seeing his mother, blond and lovely and sitting a horse in the night, and he can't help now but imagine himself curled up and floating inside her, his blood an extension of hers, his bobbing movement a function of her horse's gait, his heart beating only so long as hers refuses to stop. He hears the sharp inhalation of his oldest brother beside him, and then Stan and Thomàs are whispering.

"I believe I've changed my mind, brother."

"Change it all you want. You ain't changing mine."

"I may be of a mind to change it for you, then."

Karel catches himself thinking that he'd just as soon bury them both as suffer the sight of either of them with this girl, and then something heartless and scalding blazes in his chest, and he has to lean into Whiskey's solid weight to keep himself upright. He has imagined yet another unforgivable way to prevent it, one his father might expect of him if there comes the need and the opportunity for it, and he fingers his crop silently and squints against the stinging wind and a blossoming of tears that he wipes away with the oilcloth sleeve of his coat.

The girl reins the horse to a stop beside her father just outside the gate. Their faces flicker in the outermost reaches of firelight, and Karel notices her attire—a velvet riding coat and fine leather gloves, snug trousers tucked into her boots, little shining stubs of spurs rising from her heels — and he doesn't know whether to thank God or curse Him that this girl has come ready to ride to such an extent, that she's left her dress hanging in her wardrobe at the inn back in town. Her father places one hand on her leg and the other on the black neck of his horse, and Karel forces himself to look away, to check Whiskey's cinch strap and stirrup buckles, to ready himself and his animal in such a way that he'll forget, if he can, that he's dreading, for the first time in his life, an occasion to swing himself into the saddle and ride.

IN TOWN, in the candlelit narthex of St. Jude's, Father Carew genuflects and crosses himself and then stands fraught with his own weaknesses. He's spent the whole of the day making preparations for a Nuptial Mass that may never happen, and since the first purple hint of dusk, he's fought the temptation to saddle his bay mare and ride her out past the feedstore and Wasek's barbershop, past the Township Inn and the cluster of houses that stand emptied this evening of their masters. He'd prefer to ride out past Patrick Dalton's diminished acreage in the countryside just north of town, to the Skala place between the forks of Mustang Creek, where tonight, despite the priest's prayers, sin is set either to prevent or occasion a sacrament. To be seen there, of course, would be tacitly to condone that which calls for condemnation, but his curiosity pulls at him like a kind of depraved gravity. He's a man, after all, just as surely as he's a man of God. And there are the boyhood memories, too — his father come home to stand slapping his hands together at the hearth, swaying to the tuneless music of his payday pints, his long evenings spent drinking at the pub, his pockets either loud with coins or empty even of a shilling from his time spent wagering on shuffleboard. Carew's mother would have stood wringing her hands either way. It was better, to her mind, to live on potatoes and turned lard than to buy meat for the pot by sending other men home penniless. Better to live off the alms than to occasion that humility for others.

Carew remembers it all with a shudder. It had all been so many years ago, and now, though his joints creak with arthritis and his skin has grown onionskin thin and crinkled with age, he still longs to be among the men of his parish. It seems to him so often that he's spent the whole of his protracted life trying to care for his mother, long dead, by tending to the women of his parish, by administering blessings and comfort and penances alike to the farmwives whose lives have played out so poorly at the mercy of their hard-willed husbands. And so he prays, and he's thankful for the memory that answers his prayer. He'd almost forgotten. The Knedlik woman has delivered twins, and they've yet to be baptized. He fills a phial with holy water from the font and strings a leather lace through its cork, hangs it from around his neck. Then he snuffs the candles and makes his way out to the stables.

The weather has come to call, and the stable's roof timbers groan as if bearing some immense and unforgiving load beneath the descending cold. His horse, Sarah, an old girl now like her namesake, relents to the tack and blows her hot, rheumy mist as the priest works the halter over her head, and then they're out in the night, ambling down the quiet streets, past the inn and feedstore, past Wasek's place and around the corner where the heavy doors of the bank stand closed behind a gatework of wrought-iron bars. On the edge of town, he rides quietly past the lamp-lit houses, imagining the children sinking into featherbeds and the dreams that await them there, and soon enough he leaves the last house behind and reaches the outlying pastures. A half mile up the road, he rides around the loamy slough tucked in and fringed by water oak and yaupon, and he stops briefly near a young sweet gum just this side of the southernmost fork of the creek. Fifteen minutes in the saddle, and already Carew finds himself shifting the sharp points of his hips in the leather and wishing for the simple, meaningful discomforts of his younger years. Even the years of purposeful self-deprivation at seminary had been better. He'd been able, at least, to keep some weight on his frame and move his bowels daily, to spend time amidst other men without the nagging worry of his influence on the trajectories of their souls.

He gives the old girl a heel, and the horse's hooves clop across the solid and seasoned timbers of the narrow bridge. Carew is grateful for the horse and her infallible memory, for her steady gait on the hard-packed road. Even in the failing moonlight, she knows her way, and the priest laughs and feels the bite of the cold in the worn crowns of his teeth and hunches his shoulders beneath the coarse wool of his overcoat. There's something beautiful in it, he thinks. An animal grown old and indifferent to the darkness. How many men might be able to say the same? Too few or too many?

Up on the farm-to-market road that snakes hoof pocked and wheel rutted beside the trickling of the creek's southern fork, he feels suddenly less alone. Here is the sickly sweet smell of the other horses' droppings growing cold on the road, the well-tended fence-line of the Skala property, the distant complaints of animals come alive in the night. Here, where the road parts ways with the water and turns north as it runs between the outstretched fencewires, he lets the reins fall slack and sits upright while Sarah walks at her own ancient pace and tilts her ears forward when an owl cries out. The wind comes steady from the west, and through the clouds the moon leaks only as much light as might a few long-wicked candles. To the west stands the original Skala plot, land sectioned off into cropfields that have already been turned over into black furrows in anticipation of the planting season; to the east, clusters of cattle stand sleeping and silent in the pastureland claimed from the Daltons over the last several years. A slow half mile up the road, Father Carew finds the distant stand of trees flashing in firelight, and he brings the horse to a stop beneath a low berth of mesquite branches that hangs over the fence to shade the road even of diffused moonlight. From here, he has only to cut through a cattlegate and keep himself unseen as he rides northwest past the Skala house to the Knedlik place a mere mile away.

Instead, he dismounts and surveys the dark encroachment of

clouds to the west. He walks the horse up the road until he sees, a quarter mile away, the impressive line of horses tied to the fenceposts, the dark carriage sitting empty in the distance, a single lantern hanging from its chain and flickering beside the covered coach. In his younger years, his vocation had been such that he would awaken some early mornings with night sweats and a swollen heart and a prayer already formed and half recited, his devotion strong enough to compose itself and pull him from sleep with its silent annunciation.

Now, as he ties Sarah to a post and slips himself between the two highest fencewires, he feels the cool glass of the phial bounce against his slack and hairless chest, and thinks of the Knedlik twins, stained still with the sin of Adam. He walks carefully through the pasturage of cut hay and scrub grass, moving covertly between the sleeping cattle and farther into the darkness, imagining himself no more than another man gone deaf and disobedient within earshot of a divine calling. When he's close enough to get a good view of the assembled men bantering and coughing up phlegm and lurching forward in laughter, close enough to see the two fires ablaze and, between them, Skala and Villaseñor looking down at the papers that Lad Dvorak is unfolding for their perusal, the priest lowers himself onto a half-consumed bale of hay, his hip joints creaking and popping as he settles into his place a safe distance beyond the reach of the firelight.

The men of Lavaca County are less than timid tonight with the use of their shoulders and elbows. They've seen moonlight races before, but none like this, and they jockey for position as they form long lines on either side of the two fires. Dvorak produces a fountain pen from his coat pocket, and the two men steady the papers against their horses while they make their marks. The riders shift themselves in their saddles and look at each other with only quick, sidelong glances, and Father Carew plucks a straw of hay from the bale and works it around in the corner of his mouth, his vocation now but a whisper drowned out by the insistent, anticipatory whirring of blood behind the drums of his ears.

84

A MILE AWAY, the Knedlik woman peers down into the pine drawer of her dresser where her two babies lie twisted together atop their makeshift bedding of raw cotton sewn simply into a folded blanket. They have slept most of the day, and now their eyes gaze unfocused and unfeeling into the oil lamplight of the room. Beneath her housecoat, her nipples burn, already cracked and raw and leaking with need. She leans to tuck the edges of the top blanket beneath the infants and winces when she comes upright again. She had torn during the birth, and still her husband had come in late from town last night and stabbed himself into her from behind. She'd been sleeping on her side, and when she awoke to the searing pain of him working inside her, she'd bitten her lip until she could hear her teeth grinding together through her own flesh. Now, the rags between her legs are cool and wet with her blood, and he's gone again, out in the night drinking corn mash and cheering for his neighbor's demise.

She'd been but a girl of fifteen when Klara Skala died in childbirth, but she remembers the young family well, remembers Vaclav Skala as a young man, reserved but kind, the gentle way he had with his wife. And now, long without her, the man works his boys like animals, *instead* of animals, and she's beginning to understand how you can come to see in your children only what they've left you without. She recalls the warmth of the youngest Skala boy held against her, taking from her what the child she'd lost never would, and now her own boys, her twins, blink and throw their limbs around beneath the blanket as if impatient already, restless as their father with nights spent at home. She can't help such thoughts. They have his cold, inexpressive eyes, and they look at her with only their own desires in mind. On more than one occasion already, she's found need to nurse them at the same time, one to each breast, and the sharp pull of them working at her and the weighted relief of her milk coming down has been at once reassuring and appalling. It's as if they would take all of her that there is to take, as if they'd willingly leave her drained entirely of herself and offer, in exchange, only cold looks of shriveled brows and quiet, fleeting satisfaction.

"Hail Mary," she prays, "full of grace, the Lord is with thee," and her babies twist and writhe and eye her there in the oily light.

PERCHED ON HIS hay bale and hidden in the night, Father Carew bears unwitting witness as two motherless children get up in their stirrups to do their fathers' bidding. Old Man Skala takes hold of the reins and flashes a blade beneath the nose of his horse, his lips moving in a way that reminds the priest of his most penitent daily communicants, the way their prayers are at once fully formed on their lips and yet unuttered, swallowed with the transubstantiated food and drink. Of course, Carew can't hear the words, can't think what they might be, can't imagine just how calculating and threatening a man can be when he whispers to an animal in the cool, cloud-veiled moonlight of a half-lit winter night.

But Karel can.

His father's words rise to his ears as unmistakably and lucidly as do the imagined memories of his mother's voice. His pop nicks the stallion's nose with the knife tip, and the whinnying horse throws its great head up and around in a furious nod until Karel gathers him back in with reins and clamped knees. The moon flickers above the moving clouds, and Karel steals a glance at the girl sitting horseback beside him. Her head is canted to receive her father's advice while she faces Karel with her dark brows raised into an unspoken inquiry. And then his father leans in, his face just inches from the knife, the blade all but resting on Whiskey's wet snout. "Get a nose full of that," he says. "You remember that, ain't it?"

Three years back, in the stable, Karel had stood beside the cross-

87

tied horse while his father gelded the colt's sire. It was August, past noon and blazing, and hay dust hung glinting and suspended in the slant of light from the loft window. Outside, mockingbirds called out in all their ambitious imitations, and the cattle protested the heat and ambled slowly, lowing as they went, about the nearby pastures. Inside the horse barn, the two animals stood switching their tails against the nuisance of flies. Just outside the door, Vaclav Skala worked his knife blade into a smoking pail of hot hardwood coals he'd had Karel fetch from the smokehouse, and when he wrapped the handle with wet rags and pulled it from the embers, the blade was steaming and blackened with soot.

The two horses had been tethered nose to nose, the sire cross-tied and hobbled, and Karel watched as his father held the smoking blade to Whiskey's nose. The horse twitched and whinnied, jerked its head in abbreviated motions that seemed, even to Karel, even then, a kind of uncertain consent. "Why not keep him fit to stud?" he'd asked.

His father turned the knife in his hand and smiled as he dropped to a knee just safely in front of the old stallion's rear legs. "Because I've got Whiskey to breed now, and I can sell the old man here for a handsome price, is why."

Karel stood, unflinching, as his father pulled down on the horse's thickly leathered scrotum and spat tobacco juice into the dry hay that had been forked over the dirt floor.

"But we could get more for a stud, ain't it?"

Vaclav worked his tobacco slowly with his back teeth and considered his son without looking at him. "Who's this *we* you're so fond of talking about, boy? This here's my horse, and now that I've bred him I'll be damned if anyone else will. I've gotten one hell of a colt out of him, and I'll breed Whiskey next, and when I'm finished with him, I'll cut his nuts off, too, if it's to my liking. Now hold his head. I want him to see this. And enough of your got-damned questions."

Karel was amazed as ever by the deftness of his father's hands with tools. The man could shoe a horse in twenty minutes, could

88

mend a breached fence in ten. Now it was a matter of a hot, sharp knife and less than a second. The horse screamed and reared against the ropes, stamping the hard earth and clouding the air with blond dust, and then Vaclav stood with the testicles in his hand while the horse streamed blood into the hay. "It's some folks will eat horse balls," he said, "but we ain't them folks," and he threw the whole bloody mess on the ground beneath Whiskey's head. "Get you a good look at that, by God, and don't think your time ain't coming."

Then he turned so that his eyes met Karel's, and they exchanged a strange and conspiratorial smile. "Of course, I reckon we could've had some fun with your brothers. Could've fed them a nice fried-nut supper and not told them what they were chewing till they cleaned their plates."

Karel laughed there in the hot barn with his father, and then it was time to get back to work. "Come here, boy. It's time you learn how to stitch up a gelding."

Even now, somehow, despite the shifting muscles of the horse beneath him and the creaking of the saddle and the brisk air rich with the winter smells of pine and parched sod, Karel is still in that hot stable with his father. It's not unlike the drunkenness to which he's begun, in recent months, to accustom himself. There's a comfort in the distance it affords him from the unrelenting dullness of the present day beneath the weight of hay bale or feed sack or harness or loneliness, and he can feel now, as he does some nights with a belly warmed with mash, the past start to shoulder its way into the present such that he knows, unsettling as it is in its possibilities, that there are moments and days that he'll never outrun, that he'll never bury with hoof-thrown divots of sod nor the forgetting afforded by days and months and years piled up atop the ones that came before them. Now Karel works the leather of the reins in his habitual, delicate way. He'd taken pains today, with boar-bristle brush and knife-tip alike, to get his fingernails clean, and while he'd scrubbed and scraped he'd been thinking of how much approval he'd find in his mother's eyes when he presented his hands for her careful inspection, dreaming her alive and smiling and stricken with a desire to clasp his long, slender fingers in her own.

He shakes his head now, scolds himself for thinking more fondly of a past that never happened than of a future he might occasion with hard work and horsemanship and concentration. There are times, goddamn them, that won't turn loose of you any more than they'll permit you to take hold of them.

Besides which, there's this girl sitting horseback beside him. Her father is standing next to her, leaning forward, his hair slicked back and gleaming such that it might just as well be appointed with butter as with hair tonic. He's whispering to his daughter, giving her instructions in Spanish, likely telling her to stay low in the saddle around the trees, to follow close on Karel's flank until after the turn. To make her move on the final straight half mile back to the fires.

And then he pats her thigh and whistles to his men, who tuck their rifle stocks under their arms and begin walking with the single lantern past the long lines of townsmen and into the shadows toward the stand of moss-strung trees in the invisible distance. The air is sharp with the woodsmoke from the finish-line fires, alive with the nighttime work of animals and the whispers of men, and then Vaclav Skala protests, his knife still in hand, gesturing to Lad Dvorak and Villaseñor.

"Where in steaming hell is them sawed-off Mexicans going?"

The fireside men fall silent of a sudden. Villaseñor's guards look at each other with feigned surprise and smile and keep walking. One of them holds his rifle out without slowing his pace and makes a show of levering a cartridge into the receiver. The air shifts, coming cold from the north, and the fires surge and smoke whips out in gray ribbons and casts the horses and their riders in a dreamlike haze. Karel curses his neck, leans in the saddle to set the world upright so that he can catch sight of Patrick Dalton, who smiles and elbows his son. The red-headed boy stands with his hands tucked into his trouser pockets and nods knowingly, his freckles so thick on his nose that he appears to be afflicted with a single birthmark that bridges his cheeks, on one of which a slight scar is still visible. And then Lad Dvorak and Villaseñor are stepping forward, the latter with a cigar half-smoked and still kindled in his mouth, the banker unfolding the papers and holding them forward for Skala's perusal.

"It calls for witnesses on the course," Dvorak says. "You signed it."

Vaclav waves it away and swipes spent tobacco from his mouth. "Does it now? It say they have to be Mexicans with loaded guns, too, or is that part just something you gone and dreamed up in that corn-popper mind of yours?"

Whiskey sidesteps and Karel wedges the toes of his boots into the stirrups and reins him back in line. When he glances to his left, the girl has tucked her crop handle into her boot and is running her gloved fingers through her horse's black mane, looking at Karel with eyes half-open, as if she's only now awoken to find herself sitting in a gleaming saddle with a boy's eyes on her. She wets her lips and smiles, widens her black eyes at him, and then she pulls her crop from her boot and levels it across her horse's shoulders.

Villaseñor steps in front of Lad with his hands open and his palms out in an unthreatening and diminutive way that reminds Karel of the other day, of the first time he'd seen the man and his daughters. It's off-putting, this gesture, and Karel reckons there's not another man in the county who would configure himself so in the presence of other men. There's something almost womanly about it, too, too forgiving and soft, too vulnerable, and still Karel finds himself beset by a soft pull in his chest, a sympathy that threatens to well into something not unlike kinship.

His father is having none of it, and he turns now to his older boys. "Stan," he says. "Get on up there by them trees. And take one of your brothers with you."

Stan straightens himself up into the best shape of a man he can make, a man with oilcloth trousers and hair wet combed and parted neatly on one side despite the turbulent weather, a young man with a neck bent to match his brothers' and the will to walk farther away from his father than he's been instructed to walk. He nods at Thomàs and, as the two move past Karel, Stan runs his wind-chapped hand along Whiskey's side and, ever the eldest brother, slaps Karel's boot from the stirrup.

The onlookers fall back to drinking and placing whispered wagers as the two boys trail Villaseñor's men off into the darkness, and Karel works the toe of his boot back into the stirrup and readies himself to ride.

And then his father is beside him, and Karel catches a sour whiff of the man's chewing tobacco. Vaclav grabs him by the coat pocket and pulls him down so he can whisper in the boy's ear. "I expect you think you can cozy up to little Mexican heifers out back of the grove nights and keep it a secret, is that it?"

Karel looks his father in the eye like he's been taught, but he's so stung by surprise that he can hardly breathe or swallow, much less speak.

"As per usual, I expect you're wrong. But I'll make you a deal. Win this race and you can run off with her and sire a whole house-ful of little half-breeds if she'll have you. You ain't good for nothing but riding any-damn-way, but I'll tell you this, boy—you lose and you'll never ride that horse for pleasure again."

From where father Carew sits, the whole affair might just as well be conducted in silence up until the moment when, with the papers made legal and the witnesses dispatched into the shadows and the riders prompted, Lad Dvorak steps beyond the horses and off to the side a few paces and raises his little pistol overhead. Carew sees the testament of smoke from the barrel before he hears the sharp crack of its report move over him as if ushered by the breeze, and he considers, as the horses plunge forward and the riders go to work with their whips, that this may well be the fashion in which the souls of men rise from their bodies — discreetly, soundlessly, yet all at once, as if cast forward into their everlasting fates without any outward indication to the temporal world.

Carew fingers the phial of holy water through the rough wool of his buttoned coat as the sound falls over him in such a way that he finds his senses, long stunted, have been triggered as violently and unexpectedly as by the onset of seizure or epiphany. The night now overtakes him — the wild, leering cheers of the townsmen; the chill of the breeze so damp and strong with the odor of smoke and manure that he imagines it adhering itself to his exposed skin; the gritty, broomstraw taste of the hay between his lips — all so wonderfully alive with the compulsory if tainted enticements of a fallen world.

The moon, just as surely, is overtaken again by the clouds. The horses are throwing turf, bearing their riders out of the firelight and toward whatever awaits them in a darkness so dense that, if Father Carew weren't compelled by it all so viscerally, he might liken it to the irremediable and uncomprehending darkness of which St. John wrote, to the wholly unintelligible nature of light to a world gone black.

Instead, the priest springs to his feet with a youthfulness he hasn't known in more than two decades, a sound rising from some rarely plumbed depth within him, something akin to the chants of a High Mass. But there comes, just overhead and not a yard off his shoulder, a silent and startling black flash of something winging by, fast and fleeting as the peripheral arrival of the conscience in sinners. A horned owl, banking now with a wing dipped vertically, arcing across the pasture and leveling off again, gliding out toward the running horses in search of field mice or nesting coveys of quail or a young opossum lagging too far behind its mother. Carew tracks it until it vanishes into the trees assembled just this side of the creek, and then he looks around at the congregation of nightfall and desiccated pasture grass and sleeping cattle. He had almost called out, had almost cheered the riders, and now, as the relief of the undiscovered culprit courses cool within him, he turns his attention back to the race, watching in silence as the horses carry their burdens into the indiscernible distance.

KAREL HAD EXPECTED that she would hang back before the turn, that she would test his flank and work carefully alongside him in anticipation of a final sprint back to the finish. Instead, he is trailing her from the start, her long braid whipping back at him as the ride smoothes out and he finds his balance, crouching forward and low over the horse's rhythmic exertions. Out of the firelight's reach and swallowed by the darkness, he squints against thrown dirt and the sharp gusting of the wind, and when his eyes adjust to the scant moonlight, when the slow, familiar muscular burn flares and creeps beneath his skin like a hot wicking of oil up his calves and into his taut hamstrings, he considers his options. He could do as the Dalton boy had done those four years earlier, biding time until the last moment, waiting to see which direction the girl takes around the trees and then veering the other way. Or he could follow her and hope for an inside opening as they break into the straightaway. A hundred yards from the oaks, Karel crosses the crop in front of him, applying it to alternating sides of the animal's hide until he gains some ground and is riding hard just off the girl's right flank. He has learned in these years of riding that properly sizing up the opposing rider trumps any impressions he might have about the horse. But this is something else entirely. She's fast, unyielding with her crop, but her true advantage, and one he finds himself helpless against, is that, even now, he can't keep his eyes off her. Something about the smooth and easy flexing of her knees, her backside cocked back and shuddering with the vibrations of the ride, her riding pants tight enough to reveal the swell of her hips and the sweet crease between them, the whole thing bobbing like a firm, just-ripe peach hanging from some wind-worried branch.

God bless, Karel thinks, and he whips the horse soundly.

It's been three weeks since his fifteenth birthday, and as he urges Whiskey on, hoping to gain enough ground to afford him a look at this girl's dark eyes and swollen lips, he finds himself wishing that he had a father like this girl has, one who would risk his own wealth and pride for a chance at earning, for his children, the pleasure of a lifetime of nights spent in the company of someone they might come to love. As it was, this year Vaclav had given Karel a birthday free of chores and two extra eggs at breakfast, that and a dollar that Karel spent the better part of buying bottles of beer for himself and his brothers at the icehouse. Hell, next year might warrant two dollars, but not if he didn't quit himself of all these got-damned thoughts and teach this girl and her bouncing round hams a thing or two about horse racing.

Just before the stand of oaks, where he takes note of the surprisingly loud and mechanical sound of the insects at work there in the tangled berths of the branches, Karel shifts his weight farther forward over the horse's shoulders and blisters its hide with a flurry of right-handed encouragements. Circling the trees to the left, the girl stands a bit in the stirrups, bringing Karel fully square with her on the outside while she turns her face his way against the spiderwebs and willow-thin branches that reach out from the treeline's perimeter. Karel eases up on the whip and, though he means to look blankly at her, finds himself smiling the way he has some nights when he failed to disguise the joy of holding a strong hand when he and his brothers played cards around the kitchen table for pennies.

The girl crouches and rides and averts her eyes, and halfway around the turn her forehead crinkles into delicate little ridges. Karel follows the direction of her glance to find, off to the right and some thirty yards out from the horses' determined path, the flickering glow of lanternlight and his two brothers standing side by side with one of the Mexicans, lit cigars smoking and orange tipped in the upturned corners of their mouths. To Karel's mind, though he might have expected it, though he wants as surely as do his brothers his own land and an easy life spent freed from the hard grasp of their father's hand, there's still no way to make this right, his brothers standing there in the flickering diffusion of light, smoking cigars as if they've been smoking them all their lives, filling their mouths with a foreign, sweet smoke that Karel knows they've never before had the pleasure of tasting, cigars that have all but surely come from the Mexican who stands smirking here in the shadows, his boots dusted with the topsoil of his father's land and his heart darkened with the desire to take it from him.

Casually, as if occasioned by afterthought, the man raises his rifle, swinging it level toward the oncoming horses for a moment just long enough to give Karel pause and cause sour questions to rise like bile in the back of his throat. Where in the devil, he wonders, is the other one?

Instead of steadying his aim, the man moves the gun in a continuous, sweeping motion, as if practicing for a shot at a low-quartering quail, and there's a pinched grin on his lips when he drops the barrel and holds the gun again crossways and harmless against his waist. He nods, and Karel strains against the stiffness in his neck, shifts his eyes to catch sight of this girl as her lovely face is graced by the hint of a smile, by a slight and silent and nodded reply. And then Karel is leading, if only by half a head, his crop gone cold in his sweat-slicked hand. He thinks of his father, the stink of tobacco on his breath and the bloodshot eyes, his promise and his threat, and Karel wonders if he could bring himself to strike this girl. He has her within reach, his whip in hand, and the idea works itself free in his mind the way a deep cedar splinter from a hard week of fencework will sometimes slide, as if tweezed by a ghost, from beneath the calloused skin of his hands: If he can just get her off that horse so he's sure to win, then he might do as his father has said he might and keep her for himself. Beside him, running hard and just trailing, her horse is lathered at the mouth and steaming from the nostrils, and the girl's faint smile hangs on her lips like a forgotten flirtation. Karel squeezes his crop, imagines the astonishment registering on her face, those lovely, swollen lips fallen open into a pink wet ring of wounded disbelief. And then later, after he'd won — and won her in doing so — he'd sugarcoat it so she couldn't help but understand, and she'd forgive him, and she'd close her pretty lips and put them to good use against his.

He adjusts his weight backward over his stirrups, his stomach alive with the work of rendering conviction from uncertainty, and just as he's convinced himself to swing at her comes the moment Karel will study in his memory for better than a decade, searching in hindsight for the details that might help him discern the difference between an occurrence occasioned by accident and one born of calculation. When a blast of damp air incites the trees to a violent bewilderment of leaning and lurching, the girl's boots come out of the stirrups, and she's pitched off balance and lashed forward and up and free of the saddle such that she's clinging to the neck of her animal, her crop still clenched with the tangled hair of the horse's mane in her gloved little hand, both legs flying wildly and slapping against the outside flank of the horse. Karel locks his knees and stands in the stirrups, feeling the hot wash of fear in his chest, his guts strung slick and tight as greased cordage beneath his first rung of ribs. Whiskey reacts with a tossing head and the jerking steps of a horse pulled up short and against its will into a trot, and Karel digs a heel into the animal's side to swing him well out and away from the girl so that she can come off the horse, as he is sure she will, without being trampled by another.

It's curious, though, or it will seem so later when he plays it all out in his mind, that *her* horse never breaks its stride, and with Karel lagging behind, allowing her a wide berth, the reins cool and damp in the palms of his hands, she hugs the horse's neck and relaxes her legs so that they hang insensibly toward the ground. And then, as she passes Karel's onlooking brothers and the Mexican they seem all too eager to stand beside, the girl arches her back, limber as a bottomland cattail, and kicks her feet back. For Karel, long accustomed to the gangly and lumbering company of men, her graceful and long-practiced ascent to the saddle seems occasioned all at once by a singularly feminine and fluid motion, but when he remembers it later, when he tries to duplicate it on his own horse out in the coverts of a new-moon pasture, he'll think on it hard enough to see then what he's seeing now without knowing he's seeing it — the tandem backward swing of her legs, the perfect curved line of her spine as her knees float back over the horse's thundering haunches, the slightest cant of her hips and the scissoring of her legs that returns her smoothly to the shining leather of her saddle; her feet coming forward, the toes sliding into the stirrups just as she leans forward into her crouch and, with her backside hovering above the saddle and her knees bent and absorbing the plunging force of the ride, her head turning back so that, just as she brings the whip down hard on horsehide, she's smiling back at Karel from three full lengths ahead.

And then she's running hard and away, hugging the perimeter of the trees as she widens her lead and whips her horse, her braided hair flung back and black and dancing playfully in the air behind her shoulders.

Alive in Karel's mind is only a whisper of suspicion, one muted by the astonishing beauty of what he's seen, and he smiles at the fortune of having borne witness to something so graceful and yet so capable and strong, to a girl turned woman before his eyes, to that woman flashing her white teeth at him, smiling because, for her, as for Karel, there is nothing quite so thrilling as a race run on horseback, nothing filled more with wonder, nothing so able to convince you that you are flesh and blood and alive in the world that offers so few joys other than this running.

Instinctively, he whips his horse and gives chase, angling the animal back into a tight, sweeping circle around the trees, but then it's as if a leafless branch reaches out for him from the stand of twisted oaks. He catches it out of the corner of his eye the way he sometimes notes the flash of a diving hawk in a distant pasture while harnessed to his father's plow. He leans instinctively away, but his neck is locked in its perpetual cant and the thing rakes him hard across the scalp and face. There's a flaming pain where the hair snags and rips from its roots, and he knows, from the taste of warm iron and the hornet's sting of it, that the tender skin at the corner of his mouth has been torn. He's knocked off balance but manages to keep his mount, holding the reins a little too tightly for good riding and grinding the serrated enamel of his teeth until the horse takes note of the boot heel digging into its side and resumes its running. A gust blows cold, biting at Karel's wounded lip, and he's as certain that he can still ride as he is that even the most violent of winds don't stretch tree branches outward from their trunks into the paths of riders. He looks back over his shoulder to find the branch retracting into the mossy veil of the trees, and he's still cursing when he breaks into the open pasture and spots the distant fires burning as if in self-consuming anticipation of his arrival. The missing Mexican, he knows, was up to nothing so innocent as relieving himself in the shadows, and Karel runs through a few quickly imagined scenarios of how he will take his revenge, none of which, he realizes, is going to help him gain enough ground to win this race.

The girl is running hard out front, and he swings his crop and nudges Whiskey to the left to avoid the stinging draft of dirt and dust thrown back at him by the horse he's trailing. Still, he can't quite let loose the image of the girl, of her body willing itself back onto her horse. And what to make of his brothers? Of their easy way of standing, hips cocked and arms crossed, those cigars aglow like smoking punctuation marks to all the sentences they've thought but kept themselves from saying. He knows it shouldn't, but still it surprises him — they want him to lose just as surely as he wants to win, but wasn't there supposed to be something more binding in brotherhood than that? Wasn't there something written by common blood or by God or by what Karel imagines as the fine, looping script of their mother's unwritten will that should have kept them from standing idly by, grinning and sucking on cigars afforded them by the very men who had tried to take his head off at the roots with an uprooted timber?

Karel is running five full lengths behind but holding when the moon slips out brightly from the clouds just long enough to oversee the goings-on below, and when it ducks back under cover there comes, from out north in the pastures beyond the creek, a sound like slow-tearing parchment that grows steadily louder in its approach. This is a rainfall that will defy the almanac and swell the creeks beyond their banks, a four-day flood that, before it relents, will level the furrows and float topsoil from the cropfields and drive the county's cattle to huddle loudly together beneath the shelter of mature oak and pecan trees. It will prove a nuisance to nuptials and make it all but impossible to dig a respectable grave. It will reduce the finish-line fires to soft and steaming black stacks of drenched timbers, but for now, to Karel's way of thinking, it is a welcomed relief. It's been a long, dry winter, and soft soil makes for easier labor. The cold water wicks into his clothes and numbs his scalp and face. Besides which, Karel has spent the larger portion of his life waiting for simple changes, for the sun to come out or the rain to fall, for the school bell to ring and release him to the outdoors, for the cows to show in the swollen gashes beneath their tails the bloody discharge and the hard edges of hooves that signal the onset of calving.

For now, he's simply thankful for the sudden turning of the weather, for the chance that the rain might fluster a girl who's likely been kept under roof when the weather sours, who's grown up riding only on ideal days at ideal times. Once the sweeping sheet of downpour reaches them, he feels the cool renewal of confidence at work in his blood, in the quieting of his heart and the stillness of his hands. The horse is all speed and momentum, a rolling and muscular extension of Karel himself, and the steam from the animal's breath breaks over him like windswept fog. His hair is soaked and streaming from the teeming weather. He imagines Stan and Thom, wringing wet and walking all this way back, the comfort and easy confidence washed from their faces. He pictures each brother with his shoulders hunched against the rain, walking and frowning, looking at his sad and sopping cigar with all the puzzled dejection of a man come home from his fields to find his wife run off and the breakfast dishes still stacked in the sink, hard-caked with the reminder of all she was to him besides cold hands and warm legs in bed.

He's gaining now, but not nearly enough, and they're close enough to see the lines of men hunched forward beneath the downpour, cheering with their hands on their knees as the fires fail in the pouring rain and shoot steam outward as if from the undersides of braking locomotives. He makes one last push, one of both desperation and obligation, swinging his crop and urging the horse on with sharp, vocalized exhalations—"*Haa, boy! Haa, got-dammit.*" Water seems to erupt from the hoof-struck ground, and the animal's ears twitch and fold backward. Karel pulls within two lengths, but the girl is riding with ease, streaming water from her hair and rocking forward and back in smooth, effortless revolutions, and when she senses him making ground on her, she flips the crop around in her hand and waves the knot just in view over her horse's eyes.

And that's all it takes.

The animal lengthens its stride and drives forward with such immediate comprehension that even Karel can't help but think it beautiful. Well, hell, he thinks. Would you look at that. She didn't even *touch* him.

Now he might as well sit back in the saddle, and he knows it, knows it's too late, knows that his mind, this last half mile, has been too damned often clouded with matters other than the race. Still, he puts the whip once more to the horse and holds his crouch, feeling his eyes flood with saltier stuff than rainwater as he reaches the first of the onlookers.

The Dalton boy is smirking, standing straight despite the rain, shouldering the affectionate weight of the arm his father drapes over him, the scar on his cheek faded into the slightest line and visible only because it stands pale on the boy's wind-flushed and freckled skin. Dvorak has turned from the race and is walking back toward the cattlegate, against which Villaseñor leans with his hand cupped over his eyes and his dark brows raised in appreciation as his daughter crosses between the smoldering fires and comes upright in the stirrups, swinging her animal out into the pasture past all the horses roped to their fenceposts and bowing their heads against the rain.

When Karel finishes, he avoids his father's eyes as he passes him and reins his horse in the other direction, circling out toward the creek and the canopy of the treeline. His father looks his way with narrowed eyes, pinching his lips together and shaking his head as the townsfolk gather around the Villaseñor girl and her horse, slapping her father on the shoulder and shaking his hand. Beneath the shelter of trees, Karel sits the horse and marvels at how quick these men are to shift their allegiances, at how little it has to do with their admiration of these strangers. He's known all his life that his father was the envy of his neighbors, that he was seen around the county as cold and self-interested, and now it comes so naturally, this celebration of his comeuppance. Hell, Karel thinks, if coyotes took every last one of our calves, these bastards would gather at the fenceline cheering the slaughter.

Shifting his weight in the saddle, Karel turns his face up to the cold drops of rain that find their way through the pine boughs above. His mouth burns with its wound, and he runs his fingers through his wet hair, fingering the swollen knot on his scalp. The wind shifts, and out in the distance the falling rain sways and tosses all at once like sheer drapery hung from an open window on some moonless, gusty evening. The townsmen drift about, pushing their hats down over their ears and hugging themselves against the cold, moving in small groups toward the road and their horses, back toward the creek to fetch their whiskey. Karel watches Mr. Knedlik, wiry and weaving with liquor already, labor himself into the saddle with a groan. He's a mean old son of a bitch, one whose wife has been seen about town for years with yellow bruises on her arms and eyes shot red with his handiwork. And now the poor woman has delivered twins, and it strikes Karel as telling that the man turns his horse for town, with the hope of finding the icehouse open late, rather than out through the western pastures toward home.

From out of the crowd, Eduard comes beaten looking and sloshing through the mud, hunching his shoulders as if gravel rather than rain has been turned loose by the sky. When he stops beneath the trees, he wipes the water from his face with his coat sleeve and takes hold of the horse's reins. He offers a conciliatory grin and says, "You reckon it'll rain, brother?"

The horse blows and sidesteps, and Karel leans back in the saddle, supporting himself with flattened hands reached back against the animal's haunches. He's quite certain he could go a week without saying a word and not miss the sound of his voice in the least, but somehow he manages. "Supposed to mean good luck for weddings."

Eduard studies the sod at his feet for a moment and makes a show of wincing, as if he's grown cold to the idea he'd been so ready to banter about two short nights before in their room. "Just so you know," he says, "it's nobody here who thought you would lose," but there's something sidelong and searching in his eyes that doesn't cotton to his words.

Swinging down from the saddle, Karel takes the reins from his brother and looks out to the east where the distant stand of trees is masked by the darkness out of which his other brothers will shortly emerge. "It's sure as shit some who did," he says. "It's some who were celebrating with cigars before the thing was half run."

From the overhang of pine boughs, rain spatters down onto the horse's hot hide and steams there as the animal signals its impatience with sidesteps and quick tosses of its head. Eduard stud-

104

ies his brother. "I wouldn't know about all that," he says, then he points at the corner of his own mouth by way of indication. "You're bleeding."

"Deserve to be," Karel says, nodding his head out toward the oaks in the black distance. "It's a Mexican up there with a tree growing out of his arm, and he ain't bashful with it."

Eduard offers a confused look. The gray rain comes down as if flung from feed pails, and the pastureland looks to be sheeted in roiling water as the puddles are splashed by the new torment of drops. Some of the townsmen have short words for Karel, but most either touch the horse lightly and nod at him or pass without any acknowledgment whatsoever.

Karel inhales hard through his nose and works the bitter result around in his mouth awhile before spitting it into the muddied earth. He matches eyes with his brother and plays down the whole thing with raised brows and crimped lips. Then he stands beneath the pines and looks around at the dispersing crowd of shadows as a few begin to unknot their horse leads and amble out into the darkness. Whiskey stamps and whinnies, and Karel settles him by slackening his hold on the reins and rubbing a flattened hand up and down the broad slope of the animal's neck.

Out toward the road, just this side of the cattlegate, Villaseñor is still huddled in congratulations with his daughter, the other two girls as yet sheltered from the rain in the backseat of the surrey as their sister sits wringing wet and smiling in the night while her father shakes her playfully by the shoulders and squeezes the top of her thigh and cups her cheek in his hand. And then, instead of heading through the gate out to the road, she turns the horse into the night-masked pasture and glances back at Karel as she goes. She gives the horse a nudge and walks it into the darkness of the rain and cut hay to the south. Her father lifts up on the gate, unlatching it, and steps out toward his carriage, nodding to Karel's father as he goes. Vaclav moves his head in acknowledgment without meeting the man's eyes. They're barely visible now except for the single

105

carriage lantern throwing a pale halo behind them, and Skala stands there in the tumult of weather, leaning casually against a fencepost as if the sun and good fortune both were shining down on him. His face flushed by the weather and anger, he draws his knife from the sheath on his belt and busies himself cleaning his fingernails while Dvorak and the Daltons stand talking in the rain.

The fires, burning hot and blue just minutes before, are smoking and black, and Karel catches a glimpse of his other brothers and both Mexicans walking with the lantern out of the distance. Karel studies Eduard for a long moment, watching him watch the girl as she canters into the shadows. "Where you reckon she's off to?"

Eduard shrugs. "It ain't no telling."

Karel watches as the girl moves slowly into the dark downpour, and when Stan and Thom come sloshing up with the Mexicans, he makes a point of looking them each hard in the eyes. Stan doesn't seem willing or able to hold his gaze for long, so intent is he on studying his muddied boots. But Thom, ever the most brazen, smiles brightly and slicks his wet blond hair back on his scalp with a flourish. "What say you make me a loan of that horse," he says. "It's time I go introduce myself to my bride."

Despite the weather and the wound, Karel finds his mouth inexplicably dry, so he parts his lips and gathers blood and rainwater on his tongue so he'll have something to spit at Thom's feet. But when he notes the men standing silent and armed behind his brothers in the dancing light of the lantern, he swallows the water and, with it, the impulse to ask why any man with a perfectly good rifle would have to secrete himself behind oak moss taking potshots with tree branches. Instead he shields the rain from his eyes with one hand and takes an exaggerated look out to the south where the girl has ridden into the night. Then he glances west to the cattlegate. Just this side of it, their father has put his knife away and now comes slopping through standing water with his fringe of curls hanging wilted about his ears. Karel turns toward Thom and mocks his vanity with a slow swipe of his own rain-slicked hair. "Ain't my horse to lend," he says, "but go on ahead and ask Pop if you want. He's likely in a giving temper."

When Skala joins them there beneath the pine trees, the man lets fall from his lips a thick glob of tobacco juice. Fishing his handkerchief from his pocket, he studies the boys with a stern silence that dares them to speak, and when he looks toward Karel, his eyes narrow and he makes a low, deliberate sound in the back of his throat while he wipes his face dry. He takes the boy's chin roughly in his hand and tilts his head back. "The hell happened to your mouth, boy?" he asks, but he turns his attention to the others without waiting for an answer. He scans their faces, stuffing his hands into his coat pockets and baiting them with his gaze, and when he takes sudden notice of the men keeping close company behind them, armed with their lit lantern and rifles, Skala snarls, his face deep-creased with disgust. "Oh, *Jesus*. Ain't this rich," he says. "I knew you boys had taken to Mexicans, but I didn't expect you'd favor the ones wearing mustaches! Hell, what next? You all pull your peckers at night thinking about those darkies they hired on at the wire works in Shiner?"

Stan fidgets and can't will his eyes upward, and when the sting of his torn lip throws a shiver through him, Karel realizes he's smiling. His oldest brother has never fit his role, though he's never stopped trying. Ever the peacemaker, ever the one who would relent to kitchen chores and hard labor alike rather than listen to the rest of them squabble about whose turn it was to shuck the corn or scrub the floors, Stan is a born mother hen. At nearly twenty years of age, he's been marrying age for better than two years, but he's never so much as mentioned leaving home, leaving his brothers, and he's never once outwardly crossed his father.

"Ain't no one leaving until one of you little sugar tits tells me why this boy looks like he's been chewing barbwire."

Stan swallows, shifting his weight on his feet while the Mexicans eye each other with wry looks. Eduard shrugs awkwardly, his neck as bent as his brothers', and in his gesture is a hint of relief and resentment. He'd been left behind to stand in wait with his father by the finish-line fires, and if something happened out on the course behind those trees, he damn sure hadn't had the privilege of seeing it. As for Thom, he rolls his eyes and casually plucks a string of tobacco from his tongue before speaking up over the rain. "I reckon losing gives him an appetite."

Something twitches in the ropes of Karel's guts, and Stan jerks his head toward his brother in disbelief, his head cocked sharply on his cambered neck, his brows up and his jaw locked like he's taken the tetanus. If Thom has astonished himself, he doesn't show it. He squares his feet with his shoulders and stands there pleased with himself, his arms crossed smugly across his chest. Vaclav feigns amusement, holding the buckle of his belt like he's just pushed back from a Sunday meal, nodding in mock appreciation of the boy's wit.

When he stops smiling, he hurls his arm backhanded across his body and drops the boy with a single blow that crashes into the side of Thom's face with the sharp sound of dry kindling popping in the woodstove. There is a frozen moment of adrenaline and traded gazes while Thom slops around in the mud on all fours, and then he's up on his knees, pulling a hand from his face. The chapped skin is split open along the cheekbone, blood running thin with rainwater and streaming from his chin. He studies the flat of his hand with the confused look of a lost traveler, studying the map-work of blood in the lines of his palm. Karel recognizes the look on his brother's face, knows that the shock will be short-lived, that the disbelief will sink fast beneath a blank and impenetrable gaze, his expression hardening over like the frozen surface of a pond until there's a whole undercurrent of dark and teeming things at work beneath a frigid skin that deceives as surely as it obscures. Beneath Thom's feet, a gnarled and twisting tree root juts from the wet sod like a fossilized cottonmouth. Soon enough, the boy begins to right himself, planting the toe of his boot against the thing for leverage.

"You rotten son of a bitch," he says, and he lunges, throwing himself forward, driving his head into his father's ribs and hooking a hard, stray fist into Skala's nose. A mist of blood sprays down across the man's lips, over his chin and into his son's hair, and then they're both going down, falling until the boy lands atop his father. When they hit, a rasp of hot air kicks from their lungs, and they gasp and flounder there like angry conjoined fish until Thom finds his breath and steadies himself with one hand on the ground, cocking his elbow to throw another punch. It never lands. Before it can, the man rears back and throws himself forward at the waist, his forehead slamming into his son's mouth.

Now a roar goes up from the townsmen as they rush from their idle banter, pulled by some irresistible gravity to circle around the action and cheer this perverse spectacle of a family's hell-bent dissolution. As if cued by these new, loud encouragements, Thom rolls away from his father and sits up to reveal a grimace of torn gums running dark with blood, his top front teeth folded back toward the roof of his mouth.

What happens next comes so naturally that, later, Karel won't be able to recall dropping the horse's reins, won't know if his actions were driven by some innate if misguided compulsion to protect his father or by some long-stabled animal urge toward violence, won't remember even if he lashed out first or was spurred into the fight by a blow from one of his brothers. What he will summon in his mind is the way his brother puts a hand to his own mouth and, feeling the damage his father has done there, rolls onto his side, screaming and kicking back at the man like a branded mule.

Faces aglow with amusement, the Mexicans step backward to dodge the flailing limbs, and the moving lantern throws an erratic tide of yellow light over the fight while Eddie and Stan rush in to put an end to it. They reach down to haul their father up, but Skala is having none of it. He comes up in a blind, swinging rage and catches Stan in the neck with an elbow that drives the boy staggering backward and wheezing, clutching his throat.

Beyond the cattlegate, Villaseñor finally takes notice. He rises from his seat up front in the surrey and pulls his coat tight across his chest. The wind stirs the carriage lantern, and he shields his eyes with the awning of a flattened hand held above his spectacles, then he peers out at a night of gaming turned fierce. Out in the pasture, even the girl takes note of the sudden cheering, turning her horse to give this new, disquieting diversion her audience.

A little better than two hundred yards beyond her, the priest stands on his toes atop his hay bale, and for a moment he struggles to grasp the meaning of this boisterous new encirclement of men. His coat is soaked and the wind is needling his face with raindrops, and still he remains, leaning this way and that to find a better vantage point. He can't see a thing, and then, in the irregular yellow lanternlight and haze of woodsmoke, the ring of men swells and constricts like some jaundiced heart pulsing in a miasma. Stumbling backward, one of the onlookers opens a gap in the circle such that Father Carew catches sight of what's at work inside, and he would swear — if he swore — that his lungs have forgotten how to take air just as surely as he's forgotten, this last half hour, how to pray. He has seen father and son both spilling blood, the exuberance of the crowd around them — he is bearing witness now to something far more regrettable than a race for land and bridegrooms' hands. This is the bloodlust of brothers, the vengeful rage of the father, all of it born out and somehow flawless in its wickedness, like some depraved reenactment of Genesis staged solely for the amusement of reprobates. How far? he wonders. How far may we follow one ill-chosen and descending path?

In the meantime, Skala has gotten Eduard by the hair, and before he drives the boy's head into a raised knee, he catches Karel's eye. The old man wears the twin puncture wounds of Thom's teeth deep in the sun-spotted skin above one eyebrow, and he nods at Karel with a satisfied look on his face that suggests he's been waiting for this since the first of his sons slid wide-eyed and helpless out of their mother and into the world.

Thom is struggling to stand, his boot soles slipping on the muddy sod, and Karel watches him with the same cool patience he feels when he's hidden behind a tree some mornings, leveling his rifle as dew glimmers in the tall grass all around him and a buck walks proudly out into the clearing, all but begging to be shot. And then it all churns sour in Karel's mind—the lost race and his father's bloodied, contented face; the cold rain coming down, numbing everything but the hot swell of desire that he carries for the girl; the vision of his brothers and their goddamned cigars; the smell of smoldering fires and wet cow shit; the hot hollow in his guts he doesn't figure he'll ever fill up; the metallic paste of his own blood on his tongue—all of it rendered clear by the electric spill of adrenaline into his veins. He recalls the quiet thrill of a morning spent hunting on his father's land, the trigger of memory cold against his finger, imagines squeezing it back, and while his father and Eduard exchange blows, Karel drives a boot heel beneath Thom's ear before he can find enough purchase to stand upright. Karel feels the shock of the impact in his hipbone, an abrasive jolt that makes him imagine his bones as sandy stones crushed together underfoot. Thom drops to the ground for a third time, facedown in the muck and standing water.

And then Karel shoulders up to his father, and they're all at it with fists and feet. Eduard rears back, landing a shot to Karel's temple that blazes in blinding light across his field of vision such that he mistakes it at first for a flash of lightning, and he's throwing blind punches as he awaits a rumble of thunder that never comes. When Stan leans over and drags Thom to his feet, the two of them come wildly and unwarily forward. Dazed and unyielding as a drunk, Thom still wears a look of serene release on his wrecked and swollen face. He draws back, twisting at the waist, and when he uncoils, swinging with a scream, he doubles his father over with a blow to the kidney.

Karel gasps as if he's taken the punch himself, and then Eduard and Stan are on him, crumpling him beneath their weight. They yank him up by the arms, twisting his wrists behind his back until he thinks his shoulders will come clean from their sockets. He flails and kicks back at his brothers' shins, sliding in the mud and held upright by the same muscles that restrain him as he watches his father holding his stomach, grunting under his own weight and attempting to stand. Hovering over him, Thom flexes his hands at his side, waiting for more. When Karel calls out, cursing his brothers as he stamps at their feet, his arms held fast behind his back, Thom turns and avails himself of the easy opportunity. "I'm fixing to give you your druthers, little brother," he says, showing Karel a fist. "You rather eat tomorrow or see?"

Karel hurls his body forward, trying to shrug free of his brothers' grasp, but they torque his arms harder behind his back and it burns in his shoulders enough to bring tears to his eyes and flood his mouth with saliva. He tries to spit, but the stuff catches on his swollen lower lip and rolls down his chin like drool from a toothless dog. "You ought to see yourself, Thom. Face like yours would scare a whore off a five-dollar dick."

Thom spits blood and opens his mouth wide, making a prideful show of his injuries. "I got no use anymore for whores," he says, smiling. "I'm the marrying kind." When he swings, the night flashes hot white before Karel's eyes. As the light wanes, it is replaced by a blackness overlaid with crimson. A tide of nausea crests in the hot swirl of his stomach and all the starch drains out of his knees. His brothers yank him back to his feet, his pulse throbbing hot in his blind eye, the welt over his cheekbone swelling until he can feel it buoying the tender skin of his lower eyelid.

The wind shifts again and plays hell with the trees such that out by the creek comes a clattering racket of snapped branches and fallen pinecones. Over the commotion of weather, Vaclav is shouting, "*Turn him loose*," and when Thom spins around with his fists up he finds his old man on his feet with his knife drawn, waving it there in front of him, the honed blade wet and shimmering in the flickering light.

When the gun goes off, even Vaclav startles. The blast is sharp and short-lived, the sound of an errant hammer striking milled white pine.

Karel freezes, half expecting to hear a body splash against the waterlogged earth. Startled, one of the Mexicans swings his gun up and leans his cheek into the smooth walnut of its stock, stepping back and readying himself to return fire while his partner waves the light above his head, searching the darkness to locate the shooter.

"Put that damned knife away!" Lad Dvorak shouts, stepping forward with his pistol raised and smoking above his head.

Karel shrugs off his brothers, and they turn him loose and step warily toward the safety of the armed guards as their father turns one way and then another, slashing the air in front of him with his blade, squinting into the shadows until he locates Dvorak. "Best mind your own business, Laddie," he says.

"I mean to," Lad says. "I'm going to make it my business to ride clean into Hallettsville and collect Sheriff Munson if you don't put that thing back in your belt where it belongs."

Skala grunts and shakes his head, wipes his face with the sleeve of his coat. "Put that sorry excuse for a gun away, you son of a bitch. This whole thing stinks to high hell. I ain't putting this knife anywhere but in your gut unless someone can explain to me how a boy runs a horse for a mile and comes back bloody."

Without shouldering forward from his place in the ring of onlookers, Patrick Dalton lets out a disgusted laugh. "Lord-a-*mighty*," he says. "Listen to yourself, Skala. Just look at my boy's face and listen to yourself."

"Hell, Dalton. All these years and your cunny's still sore? Why don't you limp back home and have your boy rub some salve on it if it's all that bad."

There comes a chuckle from the crowd, and then there's whispering and jostling as the circle widens and breaks open to admit Guillermo Villaseñor to its center. The man walks with his hands in his coat pockets as if he's strolling around town of a dry Saturday evening, his wavy hair as yet oiled and orderly despite the blowing rain, and when he gets within a few feet of Skala, he motions to his men with a tilt of his head and a clicking sound he makes with his tongue. They nod slowly, in unison, and only once, and then their boss brings his hands from his pockets and holds them out as if he's come down from his surrey with no business other than that of collecting rainwater by the handful. The wet lenses of his spectacles throw slanting reflections of lanternlight from their surfaces, and before he speaks he makes a sound of paternal disappointment and impatience, half clearing his throat, half sighing. "I must confess," he says, raising his voice above the din of rainfall, "that I had hoped I might afford my daughters the luxury of unblemished bridegrooms, Mr. Skala. As I had hoped you'd be a man whose word proved worthy of his wealth." He tilts his head and arcs his thick brows in a look that indicates regret and resignation both. Returning one hand to its place in his pocket, he flips the other palm down, working his fingers in a dismissive gesture one might use to give an idle servant leave from the room. "Please, let's be reasonable. Put the knife away."

Skala lowers the blade, but keeps it in hand at his side. His forehead is deeply bruised and swollen above the twin toothmarks, his speech dulled by a split lip, his shoulders thrown back as if he were bragging of an evening at the icehouse about cotton yields or bale weights. "It's been some shenanigans during the race, I'm betting. And that's got to be answered for," he says. "It's raining to strangle toads, sure enough, but not hard enough to break skin." He points to Karel with his knife. "I want to know how the boy's mouth got bloodied of a horse ride."

Karel hears his father speak the word, and he's suddenly aware that he's lost track of Whiskey. He gazes one eyed toward the creek, scans the line of trees back toward the cattlegate. When he reaches up to feel the swelling beneath his eye, there flares a searing pain beneath the skin that Karel would swear begins burning before he even touches the wound. He wonders if the worst of pain lies in the anticipation of its arrival. Wincing, he turns back toward his father, squared off and awaiting an answer from Villaseñor. The horse is nowhere to be seen.

The man nods slowly, shifts his attention from Skala to Karel, from his future sons-in-law, who now stand battered and serious and shouldered in front of his guards, back to Skala. "Well, sir. While I can't say that I appreciate the tenor of your curiosity, I certainly do recognize your right to its satisfaction. Thankfully, despite all your pleasantries here, your boys still appear to be conscious. Shall we ask them if the race was run fairly?"

"I told you at least once before, stranger, that *we* ain't doing anything. Besides, I already asked them twice — once with words and once with an ass whipping."

Out west, the moon slides into view, washing pale over the landscape for a slow moment before ducking back behind another jagged-bottomed line of clouds. The rain slackens to a drizzle, and Karel feels the hot throb of his pulse in his swollen eye. Grown suddenly impatient with all the chatter, the townsmen take to groaning and whispering, shuffling around in the mud and waiting.

"It don't look to me like you got that much the better of it, Skala," Patrick Dalton says. "Besides which, if you choose to lay licks to your witnesses, then it ain't nobody's fault but your own if they won't vouch for you."

"Dalton," Skala says, an angry blue vein snaking up his throat from beneath his shirt collar. "I believe I already invited you to leave. Ain't a man here who doesn't know you sit down to piss, and not a one who'd take two steps out of his way for your fool opinion."

Villaseñor holds a hand up to the crowd. "This is my business, gentlemen, and as much as I might appreciate your interest, I'll kindly ask you to hold your tongues until I can effect a solution." He motions to Stan, and his guards push the boy gently forward into the circle. "You are the oldest, is that correct?"

Stan's nose is bent opposite the cant of his neck, a black plug of dried blood protruding from one nostril. What surprises Karel is that his brother wears his welts with a prideful posture. He stands straight and nods immediately, then he clears his throat and says, "I am."

"Very well. Then would you tell me, as your father's witness, if there's any reason to doubt the result of the race."

Stan glances at his father, who turns the knife in his hand at his side while he returns the boy's gaze. "The girl was out front the whole way, best I could tell. She damn near lost her mount out back of the trees, but even then she was leading."

"What about your brother's face?"

"Can't say for sure. Wind came up mighty strong before the rain blew in. Gusted through them oaks pretty good, and they were riding right up tight against the treeline. I expect he took a branch to the face, but if he did it didn't look to hinder him much."

Villaseñor turns to Karel, swiping beads of water from the smooth skin of his coat sleeves. "That sound accurate enough to you?"

Karel glances one eyed at his brothers standing three abreast, their backs straight, knees locked in anticipation. In the corner of his vision, Skala weaves on his feet like he does some nights when he stays late at the icehouse. Turning the knife at his side, the man coughs phlegm and spits, and it occurs to Karel that, in all these years, he's never thought to imagine that this wiry and unforgiving man was once the very one his mother had loved. When he imagines her, dreaming her alive daily in his mind, manufacturing memories, forging connections with her that he'd never known, what he sees is a woman sitting horseback with a swollen belly, a woman pale and lovely and comforting her youngest son, stroking his curly hair and pressing him to the warm, faintly perfumed comfort of her bosom. Only now, with the wind's murmuring in the pines akin to

116

the hushed sounds of graveside consolation, does he shiver with the notion of all she's lost, all she'll never know of the family she's left alive and discontented in the world from which she must always have meant to protect them.

"Well, boy?" Vaclav says.

"She was too far gone from the start," he says. "Tree or no tree, there wasn't any catching her."

AFTER THE TOWNSMEN break away from their tight-huddled circle, murmuring at the disappointment of a fight brought so abruptly to an end, recounting the most staggering blows and arguing light-heartedly about who got the best or worst of it, Karel dodges his father's attention and goes in search of Whiskey. The horse has wandered from the dry shelter of the trees and is nibbling at the short remains of wet hay on the fringe of the southern pastureland. Beyond him, the girl has turned her horse out into the dark field and is walking the animal slowly, looking back over her shoulder as she goes.

Trudging out to collect his father's animal, Karel hears his father getting in the last words, warning his brothers, telling them that they have one hour to collect a change of clothes and get the hell out of his house. They can sleep at the inn, by damn, and on Villaseñor's nickel, too. That or they can sleep out in the rain or go cuddle up in some hayloft with the mustachioed Mexicans they've taken a fancy to. And then the man is swinging open the cattlegate, stopping to bite a new portion of tobacco off his plug, spitting and shaking his head, a hand clamped to his side as he heads out across the dark stretch of acreage in which, at least outwardly, he's always taken greater pride than in his boys.

As for Karel, he comes up slowly on Whiskey, works a flattened hand down the horse's smoothly muscled shoulder, stroking cold rainwater from the horsehair and reassuring the animal for a few moments with his voice. "There you go, boy. That's it. It wasn't your fault, now was it?" Taking hold of the pommel, Karel slips a boot into the stirrup and swings himself into the saddle, nudges the horse around with a heel and a clicking of the tongue.

What Karel knows, as he rides into the darkness to the south, is that he has nothing more to say about this night, no desire to go home and meet the silence of his father or the whispering exodus of his brothers. He'll ride the horse fully cool out here in the weather, let his stinging lip and his swollen eye and the reassurances of nightfall and drizzling rain convince him that it wasn't only his distracted riding that cost him the race. When he makes it home and gets the tack put away and the new hay forked into the stables, maybe he'll bed down out in the loft until morning. But for now he'll ride south until he finds the lower fork of the creek, and then he'll follow it around to the house. Out there somewhere in the darkness, he knows, is a girl astride her black horse, the both of them streaming rainwater, and it is toward her that Karel rides out into the night, a failure on his father's horse.

ON THE BANKS of the creek, where the remaining men stand winding frayed wet twine around their wrists, reeling in their jugs of corn mash and laughing and passing the wet coins of their wagers between them, the horned owl perches amber-eyed and ruffling rainwater from her feathers, watching from the sheltered lower branch of a sweet gum tree. Across the creek along the far bank, near the tangle of water oak and pine roots and the deep impressions of boot soles in the wet silt, she discerns the slightest distinction in the clustered dancing of bluestem spires, knowing by some sharp and instinctive insistence in the grainy fibers of her muscles that rain and wind bend the uppermost inches of grass blades while the scuttling of prey and the dragging of a tail will set the reeds to shivering upward from the tillers.

And then she's aloft and diving, her wings thrown back and rippling as she descends across the water and meets the ground with outflung wings and extended legs. The men turn their heads in the darkness, sensing amidst the drizzling rain and uncertain wind her silent and feathery slice through the air and across the creek.

Then the little opossum shrieks and writhes as the hard points of talons break the skin and dig deeply in.

A moment more and they're airborne again, the prey fighting its useless clash of twisting tail and snapping teeth, knowing in its thoughtless and animal intuition that to effect escape by the instinctive feigning of its own death is as unlikely as is this flight itself of a wingless creature over treetops.

There's the confusion of the dreamed and the dreamlike. The dying animal, only two weeks weaned and shunned from the pouch in the colder months, is shot through with a searing internal heat, the distinction blotted out between its normal downturned sleep and this new, impossible reality of hanging high above the earth without its tail coiled and clinging to tree bark.

The owl dips a wing and veers west. She clears the trees and glides over the pastureland toward the far southern fork of the creek, toward her hollowed oak and the three fledglings waiting there with eyes just newly keen enough to know the approach of trouble but helpless in all other faculties to defend themselves against it.

Riding the familiar line of fencewires beneath her, she streaks low and level as she works her wings against the downward push of the rain and follows the mile-long fenceline toward home, squeezing her claws into the hot meat rhythmically with the upward pull of her wings. Beneath her, just to the east, there's the dark movement of a horse and, with another hundred yards of wind and rain run through her feathers, another black and cantering shape, an animal too large for her consideration and too earthbound to trigger the panicked reflexes that urge escape.

The wind gusts and propels the rain horizontally out of the west. The owl angles her coverts to the wind and gains loft, vectoring out and up toward the hardwood tops before her in the distance while below, weighted by the wet wool of his coat, Father Carew flails ineffectually, ensnared between the two barbed and topmost wires of the fence. His old bay shudders and sneezes, turning her head against the windblown rain in such a way that it appears, to the priest, as if she's avoiding sight of him, of a man who is her master and yet so powerless against feebleness and gravity and fence-wires and the simple predicaments they occasion. Struggling to free himself, the priest folds himself over at the waist, reaching out to the gritty mud of the road before him as he works his legs and his boots slide in the rain-glazed weeds and cut hay underfoot. He feels the points of the wire prick through his clothes into the aged and thin and tender skin of his belly, and as the owl alights a half mile away, unnoticed to all but her waiting young, the priest digs the toes of his boots into the soft, yielding earth and finds purchase enough to propel himself through the fencewires, tearing his coat and shirt as he goes.

And then he's facedown on the rutted muck of the road, and by the time he gets his boots free of the fence and works himself slowly to his feet, there's a pointed pain in the loose skin over his ribs. He leans against Sarah, gathering his breath with his back to the weather as it hurls itself against him. He unbuttons his overcoat and shirt and finds there against his chest the hanging shattered glass of the phial and the burning laceration from which issues a cool and uncongealed stream of holy water and blood that slicks down his sternum and runs thin until it gathers at the cinched waistline of his trousers and pools in the shallow whorl of his navel.

KAREL LETS HIS horse find the way, this landscape he knows so well grown foreign, his whole field of vision reduced to the opacity of black sackcloth. The rain comes on lightly but steadily, running beneath his clothes and down the ridge of his spine and into his britches. The horse moves slowly, following the scent of the animal it has spent the night trailing. Out west, a flash of lightning wicks into the low ceiling of the clouds and washes the plains in a muted glow that lasts just long enough for Karel to see the girl and the haunches of her horse out some seventy-five yards and closing on the creek. But this he expects. What startles him, illuminated in the short second of eerily white light, is the appearance of a man on the flooded road beyond the fence, a man with his arms thrown around the neck of his horse and a face weathered by time and weighted by a cross between sorrow and surprise. His eyes are pale and wide, the skin beneath them slung low and discolored. Here's a man who, as if by intuition, turns toward Karel to reveal a muddied and open overcoat, a shirt unbuttoned and stained, something glinting and jagged hung round his neck. Unlikely and inevitable as the rising of the dead in one's dreams, here stands the old priest, bleeding and clinging to his horse in the rain, and when Father Carew parts his lips to speak, the world is cast again in black.

Whiskey takes no notice, moves forward, his hooves splashing in the standing water of the pasture, and Karel shudders against the cold, against the unexpected rise of penitential guilt. He has seen, he knows, something he was not meant to see, and on a night when all but the nocturnal are deprived of sight, and on the skin of his arms he wears the prickle of conscience-laden exhilaration, the same as he'd felt when, as a boy skipping rocks on a summer Sunday, he'd stumbled across three bathing schoolgirls in the swollen creek, their sun-flushed skin appointed with beads of water and a smooth newness from which Karel couldn't pull his eyes—the arc of their spines when they bent to splash water onto one another, the dark mystery of their nipples, so different from his own, wind kissed and erect and upturned on their budding breasts.

Karel smiles and shakes his head. How is it that seeing the priest who baptized him could occasion memories of naked girls? How is it that anything ever gives rise to what it does instead of what it should?

After half a mile spent all but blind on this horse, when the rain lets up further without stopping altogether, Karel's eyes find some discernible depth in the darkness. Whiskey blows, his hide rippling beneath the saddle, and Karel breathes through his nose, inhaling the sweet, musky smell of wet horsehair. His eye is puffed up near to closed, aching still, but only as a muted throbbing deep beneath the skin. There's something to be taken from this, he thinks. Something about the body, something about the eyes, about the flesh and the bones and the heart. About how they want to adjust, to heal, to see and feel. And they do, he thinks, if never entirely.

At the southern fork of the creek, he makes out the girl and her horse silhouetted against the trees rising out of the slough. When he pulls the horse up a few yards from her at the water's edge, he hears the swollen rush of the current over stones and the rain draining like endless handfuls of sand let fall between clenched fingers into the water. Just off his right flank there comes the creaking of the girl's wet leather tack as she shifts her weight in the saddle. Karel points his toes downward in the stirrups and breathes only through his nose while he strokes his horse's long neck. She's near, and then she's speaking, and at first Karel feels a pinch of guilt, thinking he's come unbeknownst upon a girl telling private thoughts to her horse beneath a pall of unrelenting clouds and nightfall.

"My father knows where I am," she says, her voice nearly inaudible beneath the rainfall.

"I suspect he does," he says, but he wonders how this is intended — as a warning? As a simple, startled declaration?

"He does."

"Doesn't seem the sort who abides not knowing things he just as well might."

"Yes," she says. "That's right."

"He know the priest who's set to say Mass at your nuptials is out on the road getting fresh with his horse?"

She turns her head sharply toward him. "Please don't speak that way."

Her voice comes at him so softly, but Karel can't see her eyes clearly, can't figure if it's some tenderness in her or the faint sound of the rainfall that makes it so. Another strobe of light brightens the horizon and outruns its thunder. They wait it out and sit there awhile, watching the electricity do its work out west, and when Karel looks over at her again, the girl is sitting the horse with the reins in her lap and her hands reaching back over her shoulders, unplaiting her wet hair. Karel can see rising from her collar the delicate slope of her neck. She's squinting against the rain, looking away from him toward the creek while she works, and in another instant it's full dark again and the thunder shakes the earth beneath them. The horses stamp the ground and voice their concerted complaints. Karel moves Whiskey forward toward the sound of running water and then stops when he feels the warmth radiating from her horse.

"He may know you're out here, but he'll wish you hadn't been all the same when you catch cold and can't make your own wedding."

She turns her head and laughs, and Karel bites the inside of his cheek against the disappointment of not seeing clearly the wideness of her eyes when she does. "We've seen greater danger than rain," she says.

There's a certain superior curtness to her speech that Karel can't reconcile with the smooth sweep of her voice, and all at once he supposes that she's talking down to him, the winner of the race making light of the rider she's outrun. He recalls her fall, feigned or not, the ease of her ascension back into the saddle, and it is this memory that worms itself around in his mind with enough torsion and convolution that he's somehow firmly and unexpectedly sure of his suspicions. "I don't doubt it, but then again I don't reckon much of anything seems dangerous to you, Miss. You make falling off a horse look like a game at a play party."

The rain surges with a hard gust of wind and then falls to a sprinkle again. Karel combs his fingers through his tangle of wet curls. A nervous muscle pulses in the crook of his afflicted neck, and he shifts his wet weight in the saddle to have a fruitless, squinting look overhead. The rain needles his good eye, and the sky is dark enough to suggest that the moon has orphaned the heavens. She shivers beneath her wet riding coat, and now Karel feels the cold so suddenly that he thinks for a moment that, but for distracted riding and misfortune, it could be this way with her, that he could spend the rest of his life noticing his surroundings only as they pertain to her. He waits for her to speak, for whatever's coming next of her cleverness to find words for itself, and when she sits silent for a long minute, before he can stop himself, he hears himself ask, "What's become of your mother?"

Lightning streaks silently across the distant sky and, before he can recognize it for what it is, Karel flinches at what he sees coming toward him – her hand, pulled from its glove and dripping with cold rainwater, cups the back of his neck, and there's a shuddering of electricity in him that has nothing to do with the weather.

"You're asking if she's alive?"

As if in answer to her question, he leans his neck further into her palm, which is already growing warm against his skin. In part, his vision comes back to him, and he can see her there in the shadows, the taut line of her arm strung between them, bridging their bodies above the indifferent loitering of their horses.

"My father says that if we look for ourselves in others, we're likely to find someone we don't recognize."

Karel stirs slightly in the saddle, uncomfortable but unwilling to pull away from the softness of her touch. He considers what she's said, the meaning of which flits in and out of the limits of his comprehension the same way a flushed bobwhite will weave itself into a stand of trees to elude his shot. "I'm thinking there's easier riddles than that one in the Bible," he says, and her face, leaning toward him, is visible but illegible — bottomless black eyes weighted with sadness, lips curled into a smile — the whole of it more confusing than consoling.

"It's Graciela," she says.

"Do what?"

"My name. It's Graciela. And my mother is alive to everyone but my father. Now follow me," she says, pulling her hand away and nudging the horse out into the creekwater.

"Follow you? Hell, I *have* been."

Without turning in the saddle, she clicks her tongue loudly at the horse and calls back, "You ought to be accustomed to it then. Come. We'll get the horses out of the weather."

ON THE EDGE of town, three poor horses stand tied out front of the icehouse, shuddering in their sleep. The building is the size of a modest barn, cobbled together of rough-hewn, unpainted pine. From the rooftop stovepipe coughs gray smoke, and the fogged windows glow with lamplight. Karel and the girl ride the horses by at a walk, keeping to the other side of the road beyond the meager reach of the light. Fifty yards into town, just beyond the druggist and the tack-and-saddle shop, they stop and secrete themselves beneath the eaves of the feedstore that stands next door to the Township Inn. The girl's horse takes the opportunity to lift its tail, shining and black as blued gunmetal, and leave a steaming heap on the hard-packed road such that the night smells, to Karel, of home, of the outdoor comfort of woodsmoke and horse dung.

With a hand held back to keep Karel still and quiet, Graciela peers around the corner and down the alley toward the inn's stables. Toward Dalton's town center, something moves slowly across the road, and Karel squints his working eye until he can make out the shape of the old priest, who glances back over his shoulder as he walks his horse around the corner of the church toward the parish stable.

Turning back, a hand on the cantle of her saddle, the girl says, "Father and my sisters are indoors, but the inn's stable boy is still tending to the carriage horses. It won't be long."

While they wait, Karel runs his tongue along the jagged wound at the corner of his mouth, feels the cool seep of fluid down his cheek from his engorged eye. He watches the girl leaning forward over her horse's neck, her hair falling crimped in wet ripples down her back. Even on a stationary horse, her weight is centered over her bent knees, her spine held straight. There's a seasoned confidence to her, he thinks, and she carries it in her body, in her upright and unflagging posture, a solidness in her legs and shoulders that is almost masculine. But then there is the breathtaking taper of her back, its sudden slope into a waist so slight that Karel feels certain it's smaller around than a man's hatband. There's the wide, smooth flare of her hips. If she were reclined such that you could run a finger along the side of her body from ribs to thighs, it might put you in mind of a single, perfect valley found in a landscape of irregular, rolling foothills, of a horizon you'd gladly ride all day to reach. Sure enough, she's her father's child. She has his olive skin, his dark hair and eyes, his easy assuredness, but one look at her would make any man wonder how lovely was her mother. As Vaclav Skala would say, she may have her father's features, but she sure ain't got his fixtures.

They wait there a solid fifteen minutes, and when the girl swings down from her saddle, she holds a finger over her lips and tilts her head toward the small stable set back from the road behind the inn. They walk the animals down the alleyway, the hollow sound of the horseshoes on wet stone bouncing between the brick walls of the inn and the solid planking of the feedstore. Slowly, Karel slides the stable door open and inhales the smell of animals and dry hay. The girl hands him her reins and slides beneath his arm as she slips inside to light the lantern.

When they get the horses inside and dried and curried, she scoops oats into the feed buckets and they hasp the horses into the two empty stalls. Only then does Karel get a good look at the other twin black animals, warm now and switching their tails in the opposite stalls. If anything, they are more impressive than the one the girl has just stabled, taller and hard-ridged with muscle, painted with the same distinctive and shockingly white blazes, and Karel wonders how any man could bear to harness such a horse to a carriage. He turns to the girl, who sits beneath the lantern on a farrier's stool, blond hay bales stacked two high behind her. She's removed her riding jacket, hanging it from a crossbeam to dry among odds and ends of tack. Her white blouse is buttoned to the throat, pleated and blooming across the rise of her breasts, and thin enough that Karel can see, beneath it, the lacy filigree of her camisole. Her hair falls over her shoulders, and it calls to Karel's mind shallow black water running over a gentle outcropping of stone. She's smiling up at him, her skin dark and damp still with rainwater and gleaming in the dancing yellow lanternlight. There's a pinch at the scabby hinge of Karel's lips, and he realizes his mouth is open. "Graciela, huh?" he says, and she laughs a little and nods. "You ever ride those monsters yonder?"

She shakes her head.

"Your father, then?"

"Not anyone. They're carriage horses."

"The hell they are," he says. "Just look at them."

Outside, the rain is still coming down sparingly, but the wind throws itself in dithering gusts against the cedar shingles and whistles loudly beneath the eaves. She stands, stray wisps of hair strung in wet threads about her cheeks, her eyes deep and studious, moving up and down the length of him, settling back on his eyes as she approaches him. "I've seen them, Karel," she says, and his name on her lips sets loose something warm and liquid beneath his skin, a rush of comfort that seeps into him and swirls around his bones. "I saw them born. All of them, and the best of the stable are boarded over at the Dalton place. But tell me, if horses are only ever used to pull a carriage, how are they anything but harness horses?"

Karel gives that some thought, and it reminds him of his least favorite arithmetic lessons at school, the long and pointless story problems Miss Kubek always asks last, knowing that even the brightest among her pupils will puzzle over them. But these are horses, he tells himself, not numbers, not something dreamed up to exist only on slate or paper. "Because you can look at them and tell," he says. "It's that damned simple. You can tell within an hour after they're foaled. The second they can stand without a wobble. There ain't but three kinds of horses, Miss. Those made for the harness, those made to run, and those made so poorly that you know how lucky you are if you own one of the first two kinds."

She's standing so near to him that he can smell her breath, not sweet like he might have expected, like her hair, but earthy and clean, slightly metallic, the scent of wet, mineral-rich soil at the edge of running water. As he breathes her in, she touches him again, this time with both hands cupped about his neck while she brushes her lips against the swollen mass of his wounded eye in a kiss so light that Karel thinks it either accidental or imagined.

It is neither, and when she leans back to show him her smile again, he feels as he had as a young boy when, on some rare occasion, a woman had shown him affection. What he wants now, as he wanted then, is to take hold of her, to hide his eyes in the curve of her neck and feel her fingers in his hair, her arms around him, and in this way lay claim to the moment so that it cannot be taken from him. What he wants is to accept and possess the tenderness all at once. Instead, he stands with his arms at his side and wills it to continue. Overhead, the rain spatters on the shingles while here, inside, the lamplight flickers against the rough woodwork of the stalls and crossbeams while the horses switch their tails and empty their buckets of feed.

"You may be right," she says, blinking slowly, one time, as if for emphasis. She pulls one of her hands away, traces a finger down the unnatural curvature of his neck with the other. "But how will you ever prove it to me?"

It is part beckoning, part challenge, and then his lips are on her, the warm, loamy taste of her surprised exhalation rushing across his tongue as he holds her by the hips against him. There's a pinched pain at the torn corner of his mouth, a little lick of fire come alive from stirred embers, and when she pushes him away, he drops his hands into his trouser pockets to obscure the extent of his excitement.

"Wait," she says, pulling her hair back over her shoulders as she crosses the stable toward the lantern hung from the raw timber framework of the nearest stall. When she retracts the lamp's wicking, a horse blows, and Karel knows without question that it's Whiskey, fed and dry now, and warm, but awake and restless nonetheless, disquieted by the sudden onset of shadows. Working his hands from his pockets, Karel watches the girl, steadying himself against the hot work of his own musculature, against the rolling spasms in his lower back and abdomen, the arousing arc of energy that surges from his tailbone up into the blades of his shoulders.

Her silhouette is cast against the pale remnant of light behind her, and when she approaches him, walking in slowly measured steps, Karel's breath catches, and then it comes all at once. Her hands, he sees, are at work on the uppermost buttons of her blouse.

Meander Scars

MAY 1898

NOT YET NINE in the morning, and Vaclav Skala had broken a hard sweat out in the western cropfield. He was thankful for it, for the cool slicks beneath his arms and down his back, for the ring of relief afforded by the wet band of his wide-brimmed hat. If you took the time to read the *Farmers' Almanac,* which Vaclav did, though he had recently begun to wonder why, you'd expect these May skies to be crowded with clouds, but when he whoaed his shabby draft horse and removed his hat, wiping the sweat from his face with his shirtsleeve, he looked overhead and studied the unbroken blue of it while he fished his new plug of tobacco from his pocket and unwrapped it and bit off a portion. Whatever fool it is writes that rag, he thought, probably ain't ever once set foot in Lavaca County. He was going to need plenty of dry heat in time, but if he spun all this cottonseed into the soil only to have the sun bake the earth hard before it could take, then he'd have to suffer the first poor yield since Klara had died. Just the thought of it went to vinegar in his blood. He'd have to wait another year until he could afford the lumber and shingles he needed to finish his stable, and then what would he do? Old Man Kaspar had a fine roan mare coming in season, and when Vaclav had unfolded last week's *Shiner Gazette,* he'd seen an advertisement for a monster of a horse named Arasmus, a giant stallion shipped over from Italy, of all goddamned places. He'd never seen a stud fee so high, nor a horse so imposing. After all these years, he was fed up full with all the red-faced bragging his neighbor Patrick

Dalton did about his stable of racehorses, and Vaclav had folded the paper and tucked it under his arm before pushing back his chair. He left his coffee steaming on the table, told the older boys to mind Karel and their chores, and he'd ridden straight away to see Lad Dvorak at the bank.

Two days later, for thirty dollars up front in boarding, feed, and stud fees, the whole thing was arranged. Another thirty would be due after the foal survived a fortnight, and he'd keep Kaspar's horses in hay for a year thereafter to pay off the mare's share. The mere thought of it set Vaclav to tingling with anticipation, and now, as the tobacco did its work on his nerves, he studied the straight furrows of his fields, marveling at the sound results of his own able work. He looked back toward the house, over his shoulder and into the glare of the sun. He'd kept the older boys home from school, and he'd have to tan them if they hadn't fed the hogs and chickens and gathered the eggs by lunchtime. Or if they'd let the youngest boy soil his britches again instead of coaxing him into the outhouse.

Now he snapped the reins and clicked his tongue at the ragged old horse, one that deserved nothing more than hard work and a bucket of dry oats and another day above ground, and he engaged the planter. If a man put his mind to it, he could single-handedly seed half an acre in an hour. By noon, when Skala will find his boys by the creek and slap the oldest one hard across the cheek, he will have exceeded that pace by nearly a quarter acre, and then he will come furiously back into the fields without eating, and he will work the horse into a half-lame lather, and he'll let himself cry for one last time in his life.

Fifteen years before Vaclav Skala bought his land, a storm had uprooted a hollowed-out red oak and blown it across the northern fork of Mustang Creek so that its crown splashed down in the slough on the opposite bank. It was the worst weather the residents of Lavaca County would see until the winter flood of 1910, four straight days of wind-driven rain that left the furrows brimming with water and the farmers sitting in their kitchens, watching from the windows, weathering, at once, the storm and the apron-wringing worries of their wives. As the fruitless windfall of twigs and foliage swept downstream, lodging against the downed oak, the water dammed up behind it and rolled, roiling and thick with sediment, into the slough, carving from the soft loam a deep new trench that would circumvent the fallen tree, that would last beyond the storm and the return of the sun, that would bend northward and loop back around to rejoin the stream, leaving the old creekbed dry and richly fertile and, by the time the Skala boys found it, lushly overgrown with a bed of little bluestem that made for comfortable sitting with fishing poles and lunch buckets and the collective desire to pretend, beneath the ribbons of light that slanted through the treetops, that they were not bereft of the feminine tenderness that, to young boys, is nothing shy of sustenance.

And so just before noon, with their morning chores complete, they played, today like so many days, beside the trickling of creek-water. Their feet were tanned and bare, their faces soiled with the congress of dust and sweat. Stan stood on the bank, throwing twigs and clods of dirt into the moving water while Eddie and Thom took up makeshift arms, dueling with the swords of fallen branches. The youngest, Karel, sat where the creek had once been, pulling shoots of grass from the soil and, with full fists raised above his head, letting the blades flutter down on himself, laughing with delight, shaking his head and sputtering loudly when the falling grass stuck to his wet lips. He stood, fetched a stick, and, when shooed away from his brothers' play, slapped it against the trunks of trees and then squatted on the bank of the creek to swirl it in the water, as entranced by the cloudy rise of silt it occasioned as he would be one day by the reaction a swung crop could affect in a horse. And then it struck him, the sudden constriction down low in his bowels, the gurgling urgency against which he tightened his muscles, locking his knees together and shuffling his feet with his back straightened, a cold panic shivering through him as he imagined the close, foul shadows of the outhouse.

Stan bent to find another clump of dirt to hurl into the water, and he took note of Karel there, doing his rigid little dance. "Don't you mess your pants again, Karel," he said.

Karel looked up at his oldest brother, his arms swung back and his hands cupped over the seat of his dungarees. "I won't."

Stan sighed and shook his head. "You will, too, if you don't go now," he said. "Come on. I'll go with you."

Off to the east of the house, just beyond the smokehouse and the new, half-framed stable their father was building, Stan stood with Karel, the door to the outhouse swung open on its rusty hinges, the smell of it rank and intensified by the heat and washing out over them. Little Karel stood there balking with his face bunched up like he'd licked a lemon, shaking his head. "Just get in there and do your business," Stan said. "Pop will be coming in for lunch soon, and we'll run out of time to play."

Still the boy wouldn't go. "I want Mama," he said.

"You get in there and go," Stan said, "and I'll go fetch her. Okay?"

"You promise?"

"I swear. You can leave the door open if you want. Just go, and don't forget to wipe good this time."

Inside, Karel sat holding his nose and trying to convince himself to unclench his muscles, his little, dusty feet dangling in the angle of light that widened and narrowed as the breeze swung the creaking door back and forth. His brother Thom had told him that there were snakes down in the hole, slithering around in all that filth, biding time and waiting to bite a boy's backside. Karel didn't believe it. He'd asked his father, who'd wanted to know why a snake would choose to spend its time wallowing in shit if it could just as easily do its swimming down in the creek. This made sense to Karel. His father usually did, but he still couldn't shake the vision of water moccasins coiling in wait down there, their forked tongues flicking fast in and out of their mouths. Besides which, he himself had seen the thick, leathery tails of rats sliding beneath the rough planks of lumber where the walls of the outhouse met the ground. Rats were hardly better than snakes, and just sitting perched over the hole stiffened Karel's muscles with panic. It was worse than mere darkness, worse than his fear of falling from the top fence timbers of the cattle pens where his father sometimes perched him in the sunlight to keep him out of trouble while the young bulls were castrated or dehorned. Now Karel felt the onset of movement within him, and, as much as he wanted to finish and escape the sour, confined heat, the boy found it difficult to reckon how he could let so much of himself fall from his body and still emerge squinting, just minutes later, into bright sunlight to find that there was nothing of him missing, that he was still the same boy he'd been when he'd gone in. Now he closed his eyes tight, let his muscles go, and listened for the sick splash down below. Then he tore two pages from last year's almanac and wiped himself clean.

When he emerged into the fresh air, into a light so intense he had to clamp his eyes shut and stand blind for a few seconds against the white glare of it, he found his brother standing there, the old handmade picture frame in his hands. Stan stood looking out to the west, keeping watch for his father, and then he wiped the glass with his shirtfront and gave the photograph a look before handing it over to Karel.

"Be mindful with it," he said. "We'll have to get it back into Pop's room after lunch so he don't find it missing."

Back by the creek, the other boys pulled biscuits and bacon from their pails and sat with their feet in the cool push of water while they ate. Karel crouched in the shade beneath a pine tree, gazing at the mother he'd known only this way, as the two-dimensional woman standing in white, her fair hair smooth and long, falling back behind her shoulders, her wedding dress white and high necked, fringed with lace and beaded smartly about the bodice. Her

139

shoulders square and strong, her legs long, her hips full and round and tapered up into her narrow waist. But it was her face that Karel sought, and though he had no words for it, he could imagine those bright eyes on him, softened by kindness. He could picture her hair falling over him as she knelt facing him, his face pressed into her while he said his prayers before bed, her lips brushing his forehead after she'd tucked him in. Looking at the photograph, it was all too easy to forget that she was one of two people in the image, that his father, too, stood in the frame, his dark suit crumpled and his starched collar buttoned to his Adam's apple. His face young and clean shaven, the sly hint of a smile on his lips. They stood together, her arm in his, and there was a stand of trees behind them, hazy and out of focus, that Karel didn't recognize. What Karel saw was only the woman, only his mother, and though he'd done so before, only to lapse into sadness and tears, he couldn't help himself: He tried to touch her. He put his fingers to her face, her ankles, her fancy dress, and what he felt was only the frame's glass, only the flat cool of her absence.

Then came the onset of an emptiness that, at three years old, he could already feel but not explain, and when he stood with the frame held loosely in his unsteady little hands, he walked without taking his eyes from the ground to where his brothers sat eating lunch at the edge of the water.

When their father found them, the damage had already been done. The boys had tried to remove the picture from the frame, but the water had crept between the photograph and the glass, adhering the two, and when they went to pull one from the other, the clarity of the image was lost to a broad gray smear that obscured both bridegroom and bride, rendering them both as sullied and indistinct as the trees behind them.

Now Vaclav stood over them with his hat in his hands, his face sun flushed and running with sweat. The three older boys were huddled around the ruined photograph, whispering accusations, and Karel was collapsed at the bank of the creek, his head buried in his out-flung arms, quivering with his crying, his tanned little hands clinging to the grass that grew in proud clumps right up to the water's edge.

"This don't look like chores or lunch, either one," Vaclav said. "Don't recall giving you boys permission to do anything else."

The boys rose, their eyes on the ground. Not one of them had been brave enough to stand with the evidence of their failure in his hands, and now their father stood chewing his tobacco and wiping perspiration from his forehead, shaking his head and gazing down at the boys' feet where the photograph and its dismantled frame lay in the grass.

"One of you little shitasses better start talking," he said.

Eddie and Thom moved together behind their older brother, and Stan avoided his father's eyes and glanced down at the picture frame, twisting his hands in the hem of his shirt, bouncing nervously on the balls of his feet. "Karel wanted to see it," he said.

"Well so did I, goddammit. Wanted to see it about a hundred times this morning, but I didn't leave my work to go get it, did I?"

"No, sir."

The man took a step forward and lifted the wet print from the ground, his eyes squinted and impassive and shot with blood the way they were sometimes when he came home from the icehouse of a Saturday evening and sat at the kitchen table drinking from a canning jar while the older boys played sheep and wolf or spoon before bed. "You going to stand there jittering like you're set to piss your britches, or do you reckon you can tell me why the thing's wet as a dish rag?"

Twisting his shirt tighter in his fists, Stan stopped his bouncing and willed himself to meet his father's gaze. "It went in the creek. Karel tripped over Thom's lunch bucket."

"And so it's his fault, is it?"

"No, sir. It ain't nobody's fault. Not really."

"The hell it ain't. There's nothing ever happens that ain't *some-*

141

body's fault. Even if it's God what made a mess of things, it's always someone to blame. And this time it ain't a three-year-old nor God nor a goddamn lunch bucket, boy. It's whoever took the thing out of my room without any business doing so. Now, who would that be?"

The boy turned his shirt hem loose all at once, and his mouth pinched at the corners as he took a step forward and a tear ran fast down his cheek and fell to the earth. The slightest of breezes played in the pine boughs overhead, and the boy's bottom lip quivered. "Don't strap me, Pop," he said. "Can't we fix it?"

His father put his hat back on his head and looked down at the wrecked image of his wedding day, and when he dropped the thing to the ground, watching as it floated and swayed on its way to the earth like a broad, fallen leaf, he ground his tobacco with his back teeth and then spat. And then he struck the boy square across the wet cheek with the flat of his hand.

Stan's hat flew from his head, and the boy crumpled beneath the blow, dropping to his knees and cupping his face in his hands. He was only down for a few seconds before willing himself to stand, biting his lip to keep from sobbing and looking his father in the eye the way he'd been taught.

"You're too old to strap," Vaclav said. "It ain't going to be that easy for you anymore."

Karel had righted himself on the bank of the creek. Leaf-thrown shadows played across his face, which was caked with dirt and tears and seized with a seriousness that, even for his father, seemed shamefully sad for such a young boy. Vaclav thought for a moment that he might go pull the boy from the creekside and take him into the cowbarn, let him sit there in the cool shade while they took their lunch, but his stomach was soured with anger and he thought about what he'd just told the oldest boy, about how there wasn't anything without blame or anyone blameless, either. He thought of Klara, of how light her body had been and how, even so, carrying her out of the house had been a burden he'd never be able fully to straighten

142

his back beneath. And then his mouth was flooded with saliva, and for a moment he thought he might be sick. His eyes began to water, and when he realized he was about to cry in front of his boys, he pushed the tobacco from between his teeth with his tongue, holding it in the hollow of his mouth while he bit the inside of his cheek hard enough to stop the tears. Then he sucked snot hard through his nose and spit a wad of tobacco-stained phlegm into the now-grassy silt where, twenty-some years before, creekwater had gurgled and surged downstream.

Before turning from the boys and walking back to the cropfields out west, where he would spend the rest of the day away from them, working without relief from sun or hunger or heartbreak, either one, he gave the older three each a sharp look in turn and said, "It ain't no fixing this, boys. She's ruined permanent. Now get back to your chores."

Vaclav took a deep breath through his cleared nose and called out to his youngest. "Karel," he said, "get on your feet, boy. Eat your lunch. And don't you dare shit your britches today, you hear me?"

The Blind Janus

DECEMBER 1924

OVERNIGHT, THE COLD had deepened, the mass of dry air descending as if to make amends all at once for the previous summer's heat, and before the sun was up, when it was yet a glowing, cloud-streaked promise of pale pink beyond the trees to the east, Karel Skala stood beside his truck in the yard of St. Mary's parish, smoking a cigarette and nursing a pain behind his eyes as surely as his wife, over beyond the cemetery in the old widow Vrana's house, was now nursing his child. He'd woken with his boots still on, aching about the shoulders and slumped forward in the overstuffed chair that sat in the corner of the widow's front room. Sophie had been sleeping still, propped up with pillows, the baby silent and swaddled on her chest, and the old woman stood over them, gazing down and sucking audibly at her own teeth, tucking the blankets around mother and child with her skeletal hands.

Karel rose to his feet with a groan, and Mrs. Vrana turned toward him slowly, less startled than expectant, her wispy brows raised to beg questions of him that he felt certain he wouldn't have been able to answer even had he known their content. When Sophie stirred, he told her that he had need to go check on the cattle. He didn't mention the Knedlik boys. Didn't mention the dream he'd had in which he'd arrived back at the farm to find everything in order, even improved, the fencewires strung taut and the Monitor windmill spinning productively and the cattle healthy and fat, ready for profitable slaughter, the entire operation running so smoothly that he'd recognized himself, at once, as wholly dispensable. No, he simply kissed his wife on the forehead and fetched his crumpled hat from the floor beside the chair where he'd slept. He gave the widow two dollars so she could purchase what she might need to provide for his wife and children, telling her that he'd be gone no more than two days, that he'd pay her well for her attentions when he returned, that he'd bring half a nice ham from his smokehouse, too.

Afterward, out in the churchyard, despite the cold, Karel's shirt was soured with perspiration, with the slow leaching of the previous night's beer and corn mash from his body. Across the way, the windows of Elizka's room above the store were dark, and he imagined her in there, lying awake in her bed, cursing him even more soundly than she had the night before. His stomach swirled, and he wished like hell there were somewhere nearby to take an early breakfast. As it was, he'd have to wait until he got back to Moulton, at least. He finished his cigarette, walked back behind the parish stable to relieve himself before the long drive home. When he unbuttoned his trousers to make water, dousing the thickly barked base of an old pecan tree, the smell all but knocked him over—not the diluted ammoniac odor of urine, but a biting, rank fermentation of his and Elizka's congress, the turned scent of her embittered by the hard musk of his own sweat. He finished, buttoned up, and when he made his way back to the truck and got the engine running, he gave his fingers a smell and recoiled, shaking his head and wiping his hand on his pant leg.

Well, hell, he thought, putting the truck into gear. I reckon that's about how fast a woman will turn sour on you.

Out on the road, without Sophie so big in the belly and wincing beside him, without the little one on his lap, he made better time than he had the day before, keeping the wheels in the ruts so that he hardly had to steer. After half an hour, the ride's vibrations and the crunch of gritty, hard-packed earth beneath the tires and the chilled rush of air through the window had all worked well to clear his senses so that now, with the horizon turning loose of the sun, he could sit easily in the brightening light of dawn and smoke a cigarette to mask the acrid, pasty taste of his own mouth. Ahead, the road ran straight out of the little swells of hills, and the miles of well-kept fencelines stretched out, glinting sunlight and shimmering with dew on either side. It was good country, broken black soil, cemented with just enough sand and clay to keep it all from washing away come a hard rain, and Karel thought what a fine fortune a man could make if the seasons wouldn't put an end each year to his industry, if he could take two or three harvests of cotton the same way he could get several cuts of hay.

At least there were other ways, if your spine didn't go soft at the thought of hard work or a risk worth taking, to turn a profit, and Karel smiled there in the cab of his truck, imagining the money he'd make at the cattle auction this spring, doing the arithmetic in his head, tallying his take on the feeder steers and young heifers alike. And then there was the beer, and the chance to outdo his brothers in the growing business of quenching the county's thirst. Karel had an unspoken arrangement with them, one born out of necessity, since he wouldn't exchange so much as a word with them if he could help doing so. He would run Spoetzl beer anywhere in Lavaca County, and he had customers as far north as the Fayette County line, as far-flung as Hallettsville and Yoakum and Moulton. Villaseñor and Karel's brothers did their business over in Gonzalez County, where their facility with Spanish made it easier for them to deal with the growing population of Mexicans off to the west.

Whenever he thought about it, he couldn't help but laugh, thinking that his brothers, born bohunks like all the best men of the surrounding counties, had actually learned to speak that nonsense. Over the years, because their work was so cheap, Karel had hired the same four families of Mexicans to pick his cotton, and they made for strong backs that never wilted in the September sun the way the darkies might. But they sure as fire didn't expect him to speak their language, and they got the hell off his property as soon as the work was done and the pay in their pockets. That was one thing, but speaking Mexican yourself, sometimes even in your own house, and letting your kids speak it, no matter how pretty and brown their mother's skin — well, that was another thing altogether, akin somehow to sullying good polka music with something as silly as a goddamn banjo.

Twenty minutes shy of Shiner, Karel caught sight of a father and his boy in the near pastures just west of the road, walking hedgerows with their shotguns at the ready. His head was clearing, the crisp morning air working cool in his sinuses and numbing the pain behind his eyes, and he pulled the truck over and parked it in the roadside weeds and got out to stretch his legs while he watched the hunt. They were a good hundred yards out, working without a dog, kicking along the brown outcroppings of brush and chokeweed and immature trees as they walked toward the fenceline, the boy out front of his father, turning over his shoulder every now and again to take some whispered instruction from the man. A slight breeze leaned the field of short hay eastward, and Karel thought he'd have better sense than to teach a boy to hunt from upwind, even if it was just a matter of bobwhites. Sound traveled as surely as scent, and if a windward covey couldn't smell you coming, it could sure as hell hear you.

Still, these were days of a generous, ever-yielding landscape, days of bright red wagonloads of tomatoes come summertime, of railcars piled with maize and dimpled, rust-colored sweet potatoes, of dense bales of cotton and hay, of cattle herds that had been spared the foot-and-mouth outbreaks that had so plagued the panhandle way up north, of steers so plentiful that the slaughterhouse pens down county stayed full and the stench of the Yoakum tannery could water one's eyes from a half mile away. And so as much as Karel frowned upon the man's methods, he wasn't in the least bit surprised when a brace flushed low and with the wind, breaking and quartering to the south before the boy shouldered his gun. Karel felt the skin over his forearms prickle into gooseflesh, and when the birds were twenty-five yards beyond the barrel of the boy's gun, Karel found himself whispering, "*Now.* Take them *now.*"

By the time the boy got off his errant first shot, the birds were quartering above the hedgerow some thirty-five yards off, the white feathers about their heads and beneath their wings shining like an invitation in the morning light. And then the boy fired again, dropping the trailing hen, its smooth flight stopped so abruptly, the little bird seeming leaden in its plummet toward the pasture, that Karel marveled at both the shot and its result. It was something so simple, something he'd seen hundreds of times in his life, but it was beautiful and hard to believe in a way that he likened to the onset of hard rain, to how astonishing it was that clouds could hold all that water inside and then, as if they'd been waiting for just the right occasion, turn it loose so suddenly, at once, and let it fall to the earth.

The leading bird flittered safely into the distance some forty yards from where the other had fallen, and, just as quickly as it had come up from its hunkering covert amid the hedgerow, it alighted and disappeared into the vast field of brittle hay. At dusk, if it could keep itself hidden from the predators circling overhead, it would find its way back to the covey. As if conducted by the wan light, the cocks would commence with their melodic beckoning, and all the day's dispersed survivors would reconvene. If the boy came out hunting tomorrow morning, he might have occasion to take another shot at this very same bird.

The father held a hand on the boy's shoulder now, shaking him playfully and then pointing out to where the bird had fallen, letting the boy sight down the length of his arm until they'd agreed upon where the bird had gone down. Karel lit a cigarette and thought, That ain't a half-bad shot, kid. Then he waved at the hunters, and, when he had their attention, he tipped his hat. Even from this far off, it was plain that the boy was beaming, and when Karel got back behind the wheel of his truck and steered it loudly back into the ruts in the center of the road, it struck him more fully than it had even last night, once he'd gotten his shirt on and found his way back through the thicket to the Vrana house, where he'd found the baby wrapped in a yellow cotton blanket and sucking softly at his mother, that he, too, had a son.

In the indistinct haze of his drunkenness and the meager lamplight, the child had seemed unreal to him, even deformed, his little head hairless and tapered into such an unsettlingly sharp point that Karel's first instinct was to take a step backward. But Sophie's face was reassuring, even serene, flushed and beaded with the exertions of her labor, her eyes half-closed with exhaustion but still warm and attentive. She pulled the blanket back so that Karel could have a better look, stroked the baby's hollowed cheek with her thumb.

"It liked to kill me," she whispered. "But just *look*, Karel."

He'd come toward them then, conscious of the sourness of his breath and the unevenness of his steps, and when he sat on the side of the bed, Sophie moved her hand from the baby's face and gently took hold of Karel's wrist.

"He's all right, then?" he asked. "His head looks like its been whittled down near to nothing."

"He's perfect," she said, closing her eyes. "Just wait. He's perfect. You'll see."

Karel sat for a while, wanting to light a cigarette but knowing he oughtn't, watching until the child turned loose of the wet nipple and slept against it such that it dimpled his cheek. Without opening her eyes, Sophie pulled the blankets up close around her child, who twitched and sucked intermittently at air, dreaming already of the breast. Karel waited until Sophie's breathing grew heavy and slow, and then he rose as quietly as he could manage, his hand held on the side of the bed for balance. He moved to the chair in the corner, to the discomfort of hunched, seated sleep and unsettling dreams.

Now, on the road, Karel found that possibilities broke over him as coolly and continuously as did the wind working its way in through the truck's windows. He had his own boy now, one he'd be able, in time, to take out early of the morning, their guns in hand, their breath steaming in the cold air, their stomachs warm and full of coffee and Sophie's biscuits, their voices kept low and their steps careful and quiet as they worked through the tall grass that fringed the creekside trees of his property. He'd teach the boy to work from downwind, to swing his gun smoothly to his cheek with the first fluttering sounds of a covey's flush. And when their work together gave rise to a pair of low-quartering birds, Karel would hold his own gun across his waist and watch his boy do as he'd been taught. Afterward, when they resumed their hunt after retrieving the harvest, Karel would walk behind the boy and muss the kid's hair and smile at the sight of the four little twiglike legs sticking from the boy's coat pocket. And, by damn, wouldn't that be something?

Even before he had a clear sense of what he was doing, Karel was applying the brakes and pulling the truck over once more into the thick hem of weeds on the side of the road, remembering Sophie as she had been the first time he'd seen her, all that sunlit hair spilling from beneath her new straw hat with its wide brim and bright yellow band. It had been a week shy of her eighteenth birthday, and her father had brought her down with him to the cattle auction in Yoakum, hoping to surprise her afterward by buying her a new dress in Shiner before heading home. When Karel saw her there, so at ease among the livestock, so full of light but so obviously not to be taken lightly — scrutinizing, as she was, a promising lot of sturdy black heifers that bellowed and stirred up dust in the corral before her — he lit a cigarette and started the bidding a little higher than he otherwise might have. Here was a girl stout enough to shoulder more than simple housework and easy enough on the eyes to make a man stop to watch her while she did. She'd whispered to her father, glancing at Karel just before she had, and the man nodded at the auctioneer. After sweetening his offer twice more, only to be outbid each time, Karel flashed her father a smile and shook his head, then tipped his hat at the girl. Go on and take the damned cows, then, he thought. I got my sights set elsewhere.

Now, in the truck cab, he lit another cigarette, the last he had with him, and smiled as he blew smoke from his nose and nodded in approval of his own fine idea. He spun the wheel hard to the left, eased the truck out across the road in a wide U, and gave her more gas than he had to as he made his way back to Praha the way he'd come.

By the time he made it back, the small town was alive with the workaday business of its citizenry. He parked in the same spot beside the parish stables that he had left just over an hour before, and after he'd set the brake and worked his hand around inside his hat to tidy its shape, he fixed the thing on his head and made out across the lot and up the road to the Novotny store. Inside, Elizka sat behind the counter working figures in her ledger, a cup of coffee curling wisps of steam into the dark ringlets of her hair. She looked up with only her eyes, keeping her chin tucked down against the ruffled collar of her blouse. "I thought you'd gone," she said.

"I did. Just didn't stay gone long."

And now she raised her head and squared her jaw. "Might have been better for my disposition if you had, Karel."

Karel recalled the smell against which he'd recoiled before dawn. Even this early, with her hair strung in greasy curls from the perspiration of the night before, she was lovely. Her cheeks smooth and tan, a few freckles faint and alluring across the bridge of her slender nose. But this was a trip to Praha that he hadn't made for her, and he was restless now with the desire to see his offspring. "It's just some smoking tobacco I'm wanting," he said.

"Is that so?" she said, rising to her feet behind the counter and smoothing her skirts against the backs of her thighs. "It always is something you're after, now isn't it?" She squatted beneath the counter, and when she stood, she slid a pouch of Bull Durham toward Karel. "Twenty-five cents," she said.

Karel laughed without showing his teeth, weighing the pouch in his hand as he ran his thumb over the black label. "Two bits for tobacco?" he asked. "Is it something rare about it?"

She smiled now, twisted a curl of hair around her finger and looked down at the tobacco on the counter. "There's nothing common in this store, Mr. Skala. You come to Praha from now on, you better come prepared to pay dearly for your needs."

IN THE FRONT ROOM of the old widow Vrana's house, the reception was also one of astonishment, but in this case the surprise was unbridled by contempt and instead strung wide with smiles. Sophie was introducing the girls to their brother, pulling back the blanket so that Diane and Evie could sit on the edge of the bed and run their fingers down the wrinkled red skin of the infant's legs. The girls were wide-eyed in their excitement but they caressed the child gently, and Karel recognized in their comportment a greater comfort in the company of the newborn than he had ever felt when they had themselves been just hours or days in the world. Even little Evie seemed to understand that a well-enough intentioned touch of a loved one could be cause for pain, and with only a single, feathery finger, she traced her brother's leg from the dimpled knee down to the tiny curling toes. Karel stood in amazement of them, his hat still on his head, his eyes shifting from face to face, and when Mrs. Vrana came stiffly into the front room from the kitchen out back, she offered Karel a brusque nod and then shooed the girls from the room. "It's breakfast on the table, girls. Go eat while it's hot, and let me tend to mother now."

Karel helped Evie down from the bed, watching as the girls went barefoot across the worn floors toward the back of the house, and when he turned back toward his wife, Sophie blinked slowly and smiled at him. "We hadn't thought to see you today. Is it you forgot something?"

This was Sophie's way, to greet the uncommon kindness with a teasing question, and Karel had come to expect it with the same brand of anticipated relief as he felt when, after a long day of work and the night's last cup of coffee, he slid himself into bed to find waiting beneath the sheets the cool and calloused bottoms of her feet at work against the tired muscles of his calves. And the feeling that now surfaced in him was a cool one, too, but one that went to work at the hard center of him and swept the heat from his body, a late winter breeze that began in his bones and rustled out through tissue and sinew and muscle and blood to give rise, finally, to a welcomed chill and the gooseflesh it occasioned.

The widow took the baby from Sophie's arms, and his mother threw her hands out instinctively after him as he was lifted from her, this the startled reflex of a mother who's not yet grown accustomed to her child being without rather than within, of all those who have had to surrender from their bodies what they've suffered to bear and nourish, of those who must relinquish from the safe and hot and contracting centers of themselves those whom they long to hold so fearfully in their uncertain arms.

Karel took his hat from his head and tossed it onto the chair where he'd spent the night sleeping upright, then he held his hands out to old woman Vrana, who raised her wiry brows at him and set the child hesitantly in his father's arms. The child squirmed, throwing his arms around in the gesture of falling, kicking his little legs beneath the swaddling blanket, and Karel felt the warmth seep back into him, back into the muscle and marrow of him. "Forgot all manner of things," he said, and when he looked up from the child, Sophie was smiling at him as Mrs. Vrana went to work changing the rags between her legs. "But then I remembered," Karel said, and he pulled the child in close to his chest, marveling at how the whole of the boy was lighter in his arms than a suckling pig, at how the boy's head was already beginning to take its rounded shape, how the eyes were pale blue and unfocused and still intent on seeing what they couldn't just yet render clearly. Karel didn't marvel at the fact that he was doing for his boy, in this, the first full day of his life, what his father had never once done for him. It would occur to him only later, when the boy was older and asked questions about his grandfather, and when Karel realized how few of the answers he could resurrect from the graveyard of memories put so long before to rest.

The widow was still at work between Sophie's legs, and Karel kept his eyes averted while his wife winced.

"Well, Papa," Sophie said. "We going to just call him *'boy,'* or is it you've some other name in mind?"

Karel smiled, bounced gently on the balls of his feet as he watched the child in his arms. He shook his head and looked up at his wife. "I was only thinking girl names. Thought we'd have us a little Klara this time, after Mama."

Sophie's eyes softened and she looked at her hands, clasped as if in prayer atop the sheets. Then, as if she'd cheered herself abruptly with the memory of some childhood mischief, she threw her head back on the pillows and laughed until her body stiffened and she grimaced, sucking in air. When she'd collected herself, she widened her eyes at him and then she raised her brows lightheartedly. "I'm glad you came back, Karel. And so are the girls. It pleases everyone that you did. But if you name that boy Klara," she said, "his first word is liable to be an angry one."

COME THE FOLLOWING morning, on the outlying road just south of Shiner where the farm-to-market snaked away on its unpaved and meandering way toward Dalton, Karel pulled the truck into the drive of the new filling station that had been built by Old Man Kaspar for his nephew after the boy had proven himself unsuited to running figures or machines or much of anything else at the family's wire works. The cool air had persisted all of the previous day, and Mrs. Vrana, though she mostly avoided his eyes, had taken pains to ensure that Karel made himself properly clean for handling the infant. Within an hour of his arrival, she'd drawn him a hot bath out on the screened porch behind the kitchen and set to washing his shirt and underclothes, all of which had worked to refresh his body and obscure in his mind his latest indiscretions. After a half day of thought, he'd named his boy Frank, because it was a simple, solid name, and because it rang sound and plain and honest in his ears all at the same time without sounding weak. He liked the way the Ks stacked up between the two names, like two hard ridges in an otherwise smooth downhill ride, and as he pulled beside the petrol pump, he found himself silently mouthing the name: *Frank Skala . . . Frank Skala.*

Now Karel set the brake, retrieved his hat from the passenger seat, and stepped down from the truck. The clouds had cleared to the east to render the overhanging heavens a burnished blue, and Henry Kaspar stood waiting for him in a stiff straw hat trimmed in Yoakum leather and new overalls, the fabric of which was unblemished by grease stains or scuff marks or any other testaments to actual labor. As he had ever since he'd come of age enough to grow it, Henry wore an ambitiously waxed mustache that seemed to curl around the sides of his mouth like some invertebrate creature that had slithered through cold, congealed oil only to find itself mired on a simple man's face. At this, Karel didn't bother hiding his amusement. A man takes to wearing something that big hanging from his lip, he thought, he surely hangs short inside his britches.

Wiry and pale and almost comically bowlegged, Henry had knees that aimed out toward the peripheries of his sightlines even when he stood still, which he did whenever he had excuse to do so. After a nod, he set himself to pumping fuel into Karel's truck, working his tongue up under his top lip as if curious to see if the roots of his mustache had sprouted through the other side so that he might actually taste how much of a man he was. The biting, clean smell of petrol swirled in the air. He gave Karel a suspicious look, and then he smiled. "Heard you added another little one to the stable, Skala, and I congratulate you on that, I surely do. But just so you know, it's a limit on the free tickets to the picture show."

Karel stretched his legs and worked his boot around in the gravel, pretending to mull that over awhile. "Henry," he said, "it must get terrible lonesome out here on the outskirts of town with only a few folks passing through for a tankful each day. Am I right?"

The man wrinkled his brow, checked the pump gauge, then cocked his head. "We do a steady enough business, Skala, if that's what you mean."

"I ain't doubting that. What I mean is . . . Henry, do you ever find that you're talking to yourself?"

"Pardon?"

Karel laughed, and a gust of wind flipped his collar upright about the whiskers on his throat and sweetened the petrol-laden air with the scent of pecan and mesquite smoke from the smokehouses of farms out west of town. Henry Kaspar topped off the tank and levered the pump off and hung the nozzle back in its place.

"I would have thought by now," Karel said, "that if you spoke to yourself every now and again, you might have come to realize that you make about as much sense to a sensible man as a sermon does to soapstone. A man drives in for gasoline, and here you start up talking about the picture show? You understand my confusion."

Henry lowered his eyes and ran a thumb along the stiff brim of his hat. "I'd think you could find a way to make your point without being so sharp. It must be me who's confused. Given all the gas you bought of late, I just reckoned you were trying to milk us on the promotion. It was in the *Gazette*. For the grand opening? We're giving away a ticket to the picture show with every dollar in purchases."

"All the gas I bought of late? Hell, Henry, you ain't yet been open for business two weeks, and this is the first time I've stopped in."

Henry's shoulders buckled forward a bit with the muscular diminution of a man who's discovered he's been had, of a man who's folded the best hand to a sly bluff or bought some new mail-order tonic that tastes only and unmistakably of watered whiskey and doesn't help to move his bowels or ease his wife's monthly pains, either one. "Check the oil and water?" he asked, smoothing his mustache with his thumb and finger.

"They're fine," Karel said. "Checked the both of them before I headed out this morning."

"It's those hired hands of yours is what I mean, Skala. Couple twins a few years younger than me? Said they used to live around these parts back before Villaseñor bought up all that land. They've filled their truck two times and some fuel cans besides. Said they were tending your business and to put the gas on credit for you. They had your new trailer hitched to their truck, full load of hay strapped down tight with come-alongs, so I took them at their word."

"Hay?"

"Yessir. I reckoned you'd sold some bales and they meant to deliver them for you."

"And you didn't think to send someone to the house, asking was it okay?"

"Knew you wasn't home, Mr. Skala. Heard you'd asked the whole parish up in Praha to dance with their daughters while your wife was in her pains. Only thing I questioned was how these boys had a full load both coming and going."

Karel took his hat from his head, worked his hand around inside to reshape it. "That a fact?"

"It is. Like they'd gone out to sell bales that didn't pass muster and had to turn right around and bring it all back. The quiet one of the two looked to have found some trouble along the way, too. Back of his shirt was dried black with blood yesterday evening, and then they show up again bright and early today, and he looks none the worse for the wear. Just sits in the truck smoking without a grimace and reading the paper while his brother gets out to check the trailer hitch, and I pump some air into the tires and fill some fuel cans he had in the back of the truck. And then they head out on their way."

"Son of a bitch," Karel said. "Which way?"

And now even a man shortchanged in common sense like Henry Kaspar could tell he'd made some bad assumptions. "Looked to turn west just shy of town. Out Gonzales way, could be."

Shouldering past Henry, Karel climbed into the cab of his truck, his face flushed in wide red streams that ran hard down the ridge of his jawline to a confluence of flushed rage about the stubbled skin above his Adam's apple. "Rotten little shitasses," he whispered, and he levered the truck's throttle.

Henry took a startled step backward when the gears engaged and the truck shuddered on its chassis. "You want this on credit then, too?" he asked, his eyes looking off to the side of the truck as if something out on the horizon had been called to his attention by the insistent pointing of his outturned knee.

"That'll be fine," Karel said. "But keep two accounts. I aim to have them boys pay theirs separate."

In the days before Vaclav Skala's death, the drive from the farm-to-market road to the house had been a deeply rutted cause for concern. It ran, as it did now, between the forks of the creek, climbed a slight swell, dividing cotton fields from pastures, and put a good quarter mile between all that belonged to the Skalas and all that did not, between the outlying county road upon which Villaseñor's carriage had all those years ago appeared and the shelter of the house and the pear grove in which Karel had hunkered in his boyhood, watching as Graciela slipped from the stables and swung in the darkness onto her horse until she'd been stopped by surprise and gun barrels both; between where she'd been that night, with her hair falling over him smelling of honeycomb and oats, and where she was now, tending Thom and her children in a solid house afforded by the man who'd been just capable and sharp-witted enough to win the allegiance of another man's sons.

Nowadays, this was a fine road that ran narrow and sure and absolute in its demarcations, but before Karel's improvements it had been bare, hard-packed earth that often went to slurry, deeply pocked and corduroyed with fruitless furrows during the wet spring months such that it proved a torment to wheel spokes and boys' backsides alike. And so it was now that the level, graded earth overlaid with sand and gravel dredged from the Navidad River proved a daily source of pride for Karel. Of a normal day, his satisfaction bloomed within him as surely as the twin forks of Mustang Creek

163

swelled during a deluge, providing a steady reminder of how natural and simple it was to render oneself, with only labor and diligence, straight backed and confident in a world overrun with men beaten down by their own ineptitude and softness—men like Henry Kaspar, the thought of whom leached from Karel the pleasure of riding this road, *his* road, and hearing the solid crunch of gravel grinding beneath the truck's tires.

Atop the swell, once he came round the outcropping of scrub and mesquite that made for a thorny hedgerow between meadows, the whole of the homestead came into view beneath the hard blue sky and a sun so white that it reminded Karel that the blazing thing was a star, just one of some all-but-infinite number. He eased on the brakes, pulled his pouch of tobacco from the breast pocket of his coat, and tugged the pouch's cinch-string tight with his teeth while his hands worked, as if through some half-surfaced memory made animate, to roll a cigarette while he looked at the bright star throwing pure light from the heavens onto his house and stable and smokehouse and barn. He startled with the realization: It was almost Christmas. It was almost Christmas, and he had the kids to think about, his new boy among them, and he'd need to get something nice for Sophie this year, maybe that new Delco-Light laundry machine he'd seen last month at Pavelka's Hardware in Yoakum. He sparked a match and lit his cigarette, exhaling slowly through his nose and squinting against the familiar sting of smoke as he released the brake and drove toward his barn, beside which was a lone rectangular patch of bare earth ringed by a weedy fringe that announced the absence of Karel's new trailer. Henry Kaspar might have been a fool, but he wasn't a liar.

Karel parked the truck out front of the swinging barn doors and again set the brake. Then he sat pulling on his cigarette, watching the smoke as it whirled in thick blue ribbons from his lips and nostrils through the open window and out into the expanse of light and wafting air, as if drawn by some whispered and enthralling promise of its own dissolution.

There was something to be taken from this, Karel thought. Something more than the work of the wind and the fleeting, ghostlike floating of smoke. Something more than the way a dime's share of tobacco that you'd had to spend two bits for turned, in two days' time, to something no more noteworthy than air. No, there was something else to it, Karel thought. There were things other than smoke, he reckoned, that ushered toward their own ends as if they willed it. People, too, some of them, and there was no telling but that these Knedlik boys might be just that sort. If they proved to be filching from him, Karel reckoned he'd have to give them what they must somehow have craved and render them as impermanent in the world as if he had taken them briefly into his lungs only to exhale them through his nose and mouth and watch as they whirled away and flew apart in the breeze until they were of no more consequence than a dry throat and the remaining trace of a pleasantly bitter taste on his tongue.

There was a reckoning of trouble to be found inside the barn, and the first of it was the brim-chipped bowl of blood left coagulating on the old workbench in the barn. The sight of it sank into him like some grainy weight that made him feel in his bowels as if he'd swallowed enough sand to flatten the rope of his guts down into compressed coils beneath his stomach. It wasn't the blood that unsettled him. He'd seen enough of that in his years, his own and others'; it was the sight of his mother's dishware atop the hand-hewn bench his father had made. When Karel was just a boy, his father would serve grits or oats for breakfast, and, while the boys ate, he'd stand watching, a cup of coffee steaming in his sun-chapped hands, and he'd never once failed to remind them to take care with their mother's dishes. After the only photograph of her was lost, the old man had become half-crazed with his protectiveness of the things that had been hers around the house. The dishes. The knitted blanket folded across the back of the wide oak rocker in the living room. The tiny cut-crystal bud vase on the kitchen windowsill into which Vaclav each year had placed the first bluebonnet he found sprung up in the pastures behind the stable. Now Karel seized himself against the downward pressure in his bowels and rubbed the dry skin along the curvature of his neck. He lifted the bowl carefully, hearing his father's admonishments as he did. Inside, a half-dozen beads of lead shot glinted gunmetal gray and smooth in the black tar of blood. Beside the bowl was a torn white shirt, soaked through with blood at the back of the shoulder and yellowed with dried sweat beneath the arms, its hem torn away in a wide strip from beneath the lowermost button around to the opposite buttonhole. On the workbench sat the tweezers and iodine bottle from the upstairs shaving cabinet. Karel picked the bowl up by the brim and tilted it in his hand, watched as the dark liquid oozed grudgingly to the lowered side while the shot stuck in the glue of dried blood at the bottom of the bowl. Not two days by themselves, Karel thought, and already someone's managed to get shot.

And then he looked up into the broad swath of overhead light falling on the hayloft, where the bales he kept so neatly stacked were now set haphazardly to the side in stacks of two or three, revealing the empty hollow where the kegs of Spoetzel pilsner had been. Karel returned the bowl gently to the bench and crossed the barn, climbing the ladder too quickly. When his boot sole slipped from a rung about halfway up, he caught himself with both hands, and his shin hit the rung below with the unforgiving sound of seasoned timber on bone. His mouth flooded with saliva and the pain flared into his hip bone. He cursed between his clenched teeth, got his foot up and found his purchase, then spat down into the hay forked over the floor. He went up the rest of the way in a staggered, half-lame fashion, moving one foot up and then shadowing it with the other so that, with every other step, his boots would come to rest side by side on a single rung. By the time he stood in the loft, the pain was only a stinging nuisance where the skin had been abraded along the flat ridge of his shinbone. Then he stood to prove to himself there above the earth what he had suspected with his feet on the ground:

They were all gone. All twenty-one kegs, and better than a dozen bales of hay with them. Karel sat on a bale and rolled up the leg of his trousers, trying to pry loose from the haze of his memory the drunken conversation he'd had with Raymond Knedlik two nights before. He knew they'd talked about the delivery to Hacek's icehouse in Moulton, and he knew from the past year's business that Hacek would never be good for more than six kegs at a time. That left fifteen reasons why Karel sat rubbing spit absentmindedly into the abrasion on his shin when there was a half-full bottle of iodine downstairs beside a bowl of another man's blood on the workbench, fifteen reasons why he pressed his thumb into the bruised blue flesh around the wound a good bit harder than he had to, hard enough to cause himself to wince and grind the worn crowns of his back teeth together while he thought about how best to find these boys. Wish the little son of a bitch would've been gut-shot instead of winged, he thought. They're young and their truck is new. It'd be easier to follow a wide trail of blood or the stink of a corpse, either one.

By the time he got his pant leg rolled down and descended the ladder, he'd made up his mind. He would check the livestock and the windmill. He'd make sure the cattletank was full, check to see there was hay and salt put out in the near pasture. He'd fetch his rifle from the house and head up to Moulton to have a talk with Hacek, and then, if he had to, he'd cross the county line into Gonzales and see if he could find these boys before someone else found them first and put holes in them that couldn't be mended with tweezers and iodine and bandages torn from a dirty shirt.

He went out the side door and headed between the barn and stable toward the pastures out back of the grove. To the southwest, in the flat field between the stable and the creekside hedgerow, Karel saw that one of the remaining heifers could no longer rightly be called such. And thankfully so. She stood with her head craned back to her unsteady offspring, licking the mottles of her calf's rust-colored hide with her wide pink tongue while the little one turned its head in sidelong suckling. Nearby, the ass rolled its head and gamboled in clumsy circles around the cow and calf, keeping watch like a daft nursemaid, its ears standing forward and its dusty hide quivering. Rolling his sleeves one by one, Karel walked to the fenceline, took note of the windmill overhead, spinning lazily, as if in halfhearted submission to a stuttering breeze it deemed less than worthy of its full attention. Just the other side of the fence, the cattletank was full, the water clean and clear and shimmering beneath the bright skies, his discontented and unshaven face floating on the surface. Everything he saw seemed roughly in order, and still Karel felt the sour torsion of his guts, for it was what he didn't see that gave him pause. He lowered his hat and tilted its brim forward above his eyes as he scanned the outlying pasture, focusing on the hedgerows and mesquite outcroppings in search of movement. And then came a prickling twinge in his consciousness, the work of the inexplicable, all-but-insensate perception that had, on occasion, alerted him to the concerted focus of someone's eyes on his turned back from across a stretch of landscape or a loud and crowded barroom. He turned slowly, expecting someone to be standing behind him. Instead he saw, out east of the stable and barn, four turkey vultures perched on the topmost fence braces of the cattlepen, their faces red and squeezed deep with creases and hideous in their attention to the monstrous, two-headed mass that lay expired beneath them on its side in the sun-bleached hay.

Holy hell, Karel thought. If it ain't one thing, it's two. And then he went toward the mess of mother and child, toward the conjoined remains of cow and calf. Behind the stable, he pried the upturned horseshoe from the rusty nails driven into the framework of the rear door. He planted both feet and took aim at the vultures on the fence. He recalled the day his father had finished the siding of the stable, the way the man had swiped spent tobacco from his mouth and frowned at the suggestion of the boys that they hang the horseshoe there the way they'd seen on other stables, end-points up so the good luck couldn't spill out. He had scoffed at the boys' superstitions, but in the end he had relented. Now Karel, who had, until now, expurgated even this reminder of his father's occasional kindnesses, leaned back and threw the thing hard, watching as it turned end over end and bounced with a reverberating clang, just off its mark, against a fencepost near the hunchbacked birds. They lifted, all four of them, heavy and clumsy and in unison toward the sky, and by the time Karel made it to the pen and swung himself over the fence, the loathsome things were circling overhead with their white-fringed wings casting swirling shadows onto the ground as if their famished, anticipatory flight were some winding mechanism vital to the very turning of the earth.

Inside the pen, Karel removed his hat before he got wind of the animals' decay and placed it over his nose and mouth, breathing in the soured salt of his own musky sweat. The calf was facing south, its visible eye open and filmed with the wilted, chalky remnant of its mother's sac, its body lodged inside her up to the shoulders, its neck collared by the cracked and blistered leather that had once been the swollen and bloody flesh designed to yield what it had failed to yield, to rid itself of this young, animal burden. The heifer was on her side, one eye frozen wide and buzzing with gnats and flies. Karel pulled his hat from his face, gave the air a whiff, and, finding it yet spared a stench, settled the hat back atop his head. He spat at the ground and lit a cigarette, and then he walked around the perimeter of the pen while he smoked, his path moving counter to the revolutions of the vultures overhead, his eyes flitting now and again in perverse curiosity to the heifer he'd kicked out of anger and the unsettling, unnatural thing it had become in his absence.

Unbidden out of his aimless circling arose a thought of his mother.

He shook his head, trying to clear the image, trying to tell himself that he couldn't say why the thought had nested in his mind to begin with. But when he closed his eyes he saw it so clearly — his mother's body cold and blue, her legs splayed, the blond, tangled nest of pubic hair from which emerged, as if hatched from within, his own head and neck, his own pained face slicked with the film of birth. And this was not the face of Karel as an infant, not one that wore the fatty, innocent consternation of the just born; instead, it was the face Karel had seen reflected in the cattletank, one with a day's growth shadowing its cheeks and chin and a jaw set with seasoned resentment. Inside this dead woman, Karel knew, the rest of his body was tucked and tethered and goosefleshed on account of the cold: his forearms softened by thick blond hair; his legs taut with the ribbons of his hamstrings; his solid, round knees held up obliquely against his chest; his slender feet with their yellowed, untrimmed toenails threatening to scrape away at the insides of the body that harbored him. Unmistakable as hunger or thirst, he felt the collapsed void of his lungs, the tightening around his throat, unrelenting and inflamed in its fleshy wet cordage below his Adam's apple, the angry, feminine constriction of a woman who might, even in death, strangle that which she was meant to expel.

Karel threw his eyes open, inhaling hard through his nose, and turned to face the sun while he leaned breathless against the nearest fencepost. He pushed the brim of his hat back above his hairline and forced himself to look unblinkingly into the white flare of the sun, holding it burning in his vision until tears hung glistening in fat beads from his lower lashes and fell onto the sharp ridges of his cheekbones, until he saw, when he closed his eyes, only the circular, phantom dancing of red lights cast against the flat black backdrop of his temporary blindness. Overhead, the vultures tilted their broad wings against the subtle wind. They would fly countless, lazy revolutions. They would not dizzy. They would not tire. They would outlast those who relied upon the living. They would wait.

TWENTY MILES to the northwest, the Knedlik twins reached the outskirts of Gonzales and the icehouse where things had gone so wrong the day before. Raymond drove, smoking a cigarette, and Joe rode silently as ever, reading the local newspaper and favoring the shoulder where, only a dozen hours before, lead had nested an inch beneath the pocked blue skin. It was full daylight, not the best time for what they had in mind, but it had taken the better part of the night and a good bit of whiskey and lanternlight to tweeze the shot from behind Joe's shoulder and get the rest of the beer loaded again into the truck and stacked over with bales of hay secured with cotton duck straps and come-alongs. As it was, they'd meant to hitch the dead heifer to the tractor and drag it out beyond the pasture to the creek, to save Karel Skala the sight and stink of it, but the sun had come up too fast, and they knew better than to dawdle. They might exact most of their revenge tonight beneath the guise of moonlit skies in Lavaca County, but there was a matter here in Gonzales that couldn't wait.

Raymond steered the truck past the slanted shotgun houses that fronted the road and fringed the fields just east of the railroad tracks. There was smoke coming up thinly from the stovepipes and the plain cedar siding was unpainted and warped such that the joints between planks looked each to be some irregular line on a map marking the parched bed of a stream that widened and narrowed along its horizontal path. Beyond the houses, a few Mexican sharecroppers were already out in the early sunlight doing God knows what this time of year, tending to their mules and tilling manure into the sad little garden plots set back of their houses. They looked beaten down and sunbaked even from a distance, and the way they hunched their shoulders against the bald sunlight on a cool morning was all the evidence Raymond Knedlik needed to shore up his lasting aversion to cropwork.

"Poor dumb bastards," he said, nodding out at the field. "Rather be gunshot than a Mexican or a farmer, either one. How's the shoulder?"

Lowering the paper, Joe turned to Raymond and offered a weak smile.

"Don't pain you enough to keep you from lighting a match, does it?"

Joe rolled his shoulder slowly around in the joint, the grin leveling on his lips to a squinting, concentrated expression that was neither smile nor frown. Then he lifted the newspaper to finish the latest serialization of "Judith of Blue Lake Ranch," which had been running the last two weeks in the *Gazette*. His brother ribbed him about his reading, but Joe had always rather read than speak, and besides, this story was a lively one about a horsefarm in northern California, hundreds of head of mustangs and saddlebreds both, and Joe figured he'd prefer to see in his mind the rolling hills of a ranch way out west than this same scrubgrass landscape he'd been living amidst all fourteen damned years of his life. Judith, too, he wouldn't mind seeing, and he wondered if there were women yet walking in the world with keen horse sense and big, pillowy bosoms both. In last week's installment, Judith had up and fired her ranch foreman, Bayne, who'd been robbing her blind, selling saddle-broke horses to Judith's well-to-do neighbor on the sly, and now Joe wanted to see how she'd fare without his help.

Joe liked the idea, as unlikely as it seemed, that a woman could make it on her own out in the scalded, dusty world of men who took their spurs off only to sleep or shit, and he thought how his mother would have turned out if she hadn't married Pa. He suspected she could have done better, and it didn't seem much of a sacrifice to him that he and Raymond wouldn't have been born if she had. She was a bright woman with a strong back and a comely enough figure. If she was hindered, it was only by her unwillingness to part from the literal word of the Good Book and from the conjugal expectations of her father. If she'd found enough room for doubt, enough hard will with which to entomb her selflessness in a cave sealed by a rock too heavy to be rolled away by the meddling or the miraculous, either one, she might have made off on her own, caught a train and gone west. She might have cooked her chicken and dumplings and pot roast and biscuits and tomato gravy at some outfit like the Blue Lake Ranch. She could have saved her pay and opened her own restaurant or saloon, taken men upstairs with her on her own terms at the end of the night. She could have gotten something out of the world instead of bringing a couple of boys into it too late to get them grown in time to save her.

"Put the goddamn paper down and keep a lookout," Raymond said, the scar on his face bending blanched across his cheek and down into the cracked hinge of his lips. "Remember, no shooting unless it can't be helped. And don't forget the rope."

Raymond turned the truck down a dirt road before town and followed it out beneath an overhang of mature oaks lining each side of the road until they reached the Drycreek Saloon where they'd met up with Karel's brother Thom the day before. So far as Joe could tell, there wasn't a creek anywhere nearby, but if there had been, he reckoned it had damn well gone dry.

It had been Raymond's idea to try to unload the remaining stockpile of Karel's beer here in Gonzales. He told Joe they might prove their salt this way, stake a claim to the part of the profits they'd been promised, make themselves indispensable with their initiative. They'd turn two weeks' take in a matter of days. The morning before, they'd done Karel's bidding first, delivering four kegs to Hacek's place in Moulton, moving four others to the icehouses and

173

saloons up and down the rail lines in Weid and Sweet Home, but come lunchtime they still had thirteen barrels in the trailer, and even Raymond knew a trip to Hallettsville was out of the question. Sheriff Munson had taken a fall from the saddle the previous week, the slow encroachments of age and gout making him about as steady on horseback as a bullfrog on a barbed fencewire. He'd be staying put there in the county seat, and Raymond had it in his mind to do their business well beyond the law's reach.

After their conversation in Praha, where with breath that stank of sour pilsner and corn mash Karel had whispered his intentions, the twins knew what was expected of them. Karel had told Raymond that he had all the beer business in Yoakum and Shiner wrapped up tight with Kosmos's consent, that he'd made all those local deliveries the week before, that he'd get to them again just before the holidays when they were likely to need their stores replenished. For now, Karel needed only to keep the beer cool for a week or two and find buyers in the small towns. He'd double his profits if he could sell it all, he said, and he winked and lit a cigarette, offering one each to the boys as he steamed smoke from his nose into the cool night air. And if he did, he'd be more than happy to cut the boys in for a share.

The trouble had begun just a hundred yards down the dirt road the Knedlik boys now traveled, where Villaseñor and his sons by law had outfitted an old barn's loft with floor-to-ceiling hay-bale insulation and enough ice to keep the bootlegged Spoetzel beer cold even in the summertime. On the bottom floor, where once there'd been tack and farm tools and feed bins, they'd opened a saloon. Villaseñor, who grew ever more wary the farther west, and nearer to his old adopted home of Mexico, he got, had put the surliest of the Skala boys in charge of the Gonzales concern, and this was how it came to pass that, on the previous day, Raymond and Joe had come calling, trying to peddle beer to Thomàs Skala, who had fifty kegs of his own on ice upstairs, a loaded twelve-gauge behind the bar,

174

and a merciless, motherless determination to keep fast all that he'd been granted.

To the Knedliks' right, out east, there was nothing but the blond stubble of cut hayfields, the earth gone glossy and dark after the week's rainfall. The saloon was housed in an old horsebarn, one that still had corral posts and a few fence braces rotting along its southern wall, the whole thing leaning on warped beams where the sandy soil had been swept from beneath the masonry piers by years of rainfall and erosion. Out back, a stable had been converted to house stockpiles of coal shipped in by rail. The saloon's siding curled with peeling paint the color of raw cotton, and Raymond steered the truck near the rear of the building, pulling forward and backing such that the trailer would sit broadside behind the sliding doors that had once led to the corrals. When he got the rig situated to his liking, he flicked his cigarette out the open window and set the brake. Climbing down from the cab, Raymond buttoned his vest and rolled his shirtsleeves up to the middle of his forearms as he took a look around. He knew the saloon didn't open until noon just as surely as he knew there was a tack and harness shop out front across the road. From this vantage point behind the saloon, there was nothing in sight and nobody around to take note of them. Nothing but the adjoining hayfields and the barn and granary of the neighboring farm. Raymond pulled his new Smith and Wesson .32 from the seat of the truck and tucked it into the waistband of his trousers so that he could feel the cool of its walnut grips against the knuckles of his spine. He reached around with both hands to see that his vest fell flat in back to conceal the butt. Joe pulled his lever-action Winchester from behind the seat and swung the cab door closed with his foot. Then he lifted the coil of rope from beside the full gas cans in the truck bed and put his arm through the center of it so he could balance the weight on his good shoulder and still keep both hands on the rifle.

The air was still and cool, smelling faintly of coal dust, and the sun hastened its light unobstructed down through the cloudless sky. If it were summer, Raymond knew, he'd have already sweated through his underclothes and shirt, and he was thankful for the cool, as was Joe, who had, as it was, more than enough heat burning beneath the bandages wrapping his wounds. "All set then, brother?" Raymond said. "Let's see is it anybody here what needs tying up."

Joe nodded, but before he took a step toward the saloon's back door, he glanced at the newspaper folded on the dash of the truck. He hadn't finished the serial, and Judith was all dressed up in white boots and a yellow dress, fixing to visit her nearest neighbor who'd been recently widowed. Together, they had over eight hundred acres and just as many broken horses as wild ones. Joe reckoned most readers would want Judith to fall sweetly in love and get married and live a comfortable life as the wife of the neighboring rancher. Most folks wouldn't mind that he'd been buying stolen horses from the wily foreman she'd had to cut loose, but Joe couldn't bring himself to cotton to the possibility of such a wrong given a spit shine and thereafter accepted as right. You could rub a dry turd with a whole can of linseed oil, after all, and all you'd end up with was a mess of shiny shit. As for Joe, he wanted Judith to do the man some fashion of harm, to break his fool heart or swindle him for part of his landholdings and even the score. To bat her eyes at him over coffee while she kept her shawl wrapped tight across her shoulders so he couldn't see the flash of pale skin that glistened there in the hollow of her throat, anything that would cause him even a hot twinge of unsatisfied longing.

Either way, this was no time for reading. He'd have to wait and see. Joe coughed up phlegm and felt pain sear in the stricken meat behind his shoulder. Then he levered a cartridge into the rifle's receiver and followed his brother, who was already trying the back door of the saloon.

KAREL DECIDED to leave the heifer there to rot. He'd have the boys deal with it when he found them, and it warmed his cheeks to imagine what it would look like, the boys hitching the thing behind its front legs with cinched rope, the jerk of the tractor when they released the clutch, the irregular wake the thing would make in the short pasture grass as they dragged it out toward the creek where they could set it afire with kerosene or leave it there to decay beneath the work of sun and wind and vultures and time. He thought it might make for fine amusement to sit on the fence near the cattletank, smoking a cigarette and sipping coffee while the boys worked beneath his gaze, while they broke a sweat even in the cool December air. He envisioned the calf coming loose halfway across the pasture, sliding sick and foul from the dead heifer's cavity and giving the twins twice the job to do.

He'd teach these boys more than one thing, and he'd do it soon, and with the tight smile of his imaginings pinching the bridge of his nose, he went to fetch his gun from the house. Inside, there was still the faint trace of sweetness in the air, a hint that the last food to be pulled from the oven had been Sophie's kolaches two days before. In the sink, a single cup. On the table, another sat half full of cold black coffee atop a stack of currency and a page torn from the newspaper with a note scrawled in a childish hand in the margins. *For the trailer,* it read, *and the beer. Can't linger.*

Karel remembered his father's words after he'd hit Stan that day near the creek, words that he'd since coupled in his mind with his understanding of the difference between the trouble that befalls boys and that which comes to call on men. *It ain't going to be that easy for you anymore.* So help me, it ain't, Karel thought. Besides which, what about the gasoline? What about the damned cow? He crumpled the paper and the bills and stuffed them together in his pocket, then he fetched his gun and a handful of cartridges and made his way out to the truck.

As EXPECTED, the door was bolted, and Raymond jerked his head to the side, indicating the northern side of the building. The brothers moved warily around the corner of the saloon and made their way in the shadows to peer into the dusty, double-hung windows. Inside, there stretched a long bar of unfinished pine. Three tables were set with four chairs apiece for cards and dominoes and the swapping of lies, a scalloped glass ashtray in the center of each. Between tables and near the front door, spittoons stood at the ready while, overhead, plywood signs had been affixed unevenly to the rafters beneath the loft. In painted lettering that slanted and curled with enough flourish to indicate the work of a woman's hand, they advised against gambling and the use of foul language. Beside the bar, which was fronted with stools made of sectioned logs, rawhide nailed atop the cross sections, was a long vertical slateboard with prices written in chalk. Above the slate, a tin Coca-Cola sign had rusted through at one corner's nail hole and hung askance from the other. Just the sight of it made Raymond thirsty. At just shy of fifteen, hairless though he was about the chin and chest, he would never admit it, would never drink anything other than beer or whiskey in the company of men whose whiskers had already come in, but *oh,* how he preferred the fizzing thick sweetness of a cold Coca-Cola to damn near anything, clear winter well water and his mother's sweet tea not excepted.

He tried the window, leaning into it such that a long ribbon of peeled paint came loose of the window's latticework and stuck to his palm, and then he caught his brother's eye and shrugged. He pulled his gun from the back of his pants and held it by the barrel, averting his eyes when he reared back and crashed the etched walnut butt through the pane just above the window latch. The sound was one of china hurled against a wall, and for a moment Raymond saw the twisted, fire-eyed snarl of his father come home from a different saloon some twenty miles from this one and many months ago. Joe stepped away from the shadows cast by the old barn's eaves and gave a glance toward the street out front. He shook his head, and Raymond went to work clearing the shattered shards of glass with his gun barrel until there was room enough to slide a hand safely inside to free the latch and lift the window. He tucked the revolver back into his waistband, brushed a few glinting splinters of glass from the shoulders of his vest, and then he hoisted himself up and in through the window with a grunt.

After he'd had a look to make sure he was alone inside, he threw the bolt of the sliding door, gave it a heave on its squealing rollers, and Joe joined him inside and set his gun against the back wall and surveyed the loft ladder that rose against the back wall to a closed trapdoor. Dropping the rope to the floor at his feet, he turned to his brother, indicating his shoulder, and Raymond shook his head there amidst the smells of coal dust and old tobacco spit and spilled beer. Then he crossed the room and shrugged the coil of rope onto his own shoulder and made the ascent in smoothly measured steps. When he pushed the trapdoor open, the cold air fell from above like the settling of an invisible fog that made it feel as if everything his skin contained had leached to jockey for position just beneath the skin, leaving the rest just a hollow strutted and braced by his bones. Inside, there were kegs stacked three high around a column of ice. The floor was sawdust that had mixed with just enough water to make it adhere to his boots. Against every wall, square bales of hay reached to the ceiling. In the corners, more two-foot blocks of ice stacked three high. Overhead, there were three slave-driven fans spinning lazily from the rafters, the metal fasteners of their leather drive belts clicking over their sheaves in regular, reassuring intervals. The room was so cold that Raymond's back teeth ached. These is some crafty sonsabitches, he thought, rolling one of the outermost kegs toward the trapdoor and working a cinch knot into the rope. He looped the rope one turn around the topmost loft ladder rung to act as a makeshift pulley and safety all in one, and then he got the first barrel lassoed and looked down through the trapdoor to find his brother below, waiting with his rifle in his hands and his eyes fixed on the back door. Raymond whistled softly and his brother looked up to find the first keg of beer descending from the hole in the ceiling, the rope humming its braided hymn to friction against the topmost rung of the ladder.

Thirty minutes later, they had ten kegs set sidelong atop the whole stretch of the bar, another centered on each table, and eight others hidden beneath hay and strapped down in the trailer. The exertion had reopened Joe's wounds, and just above his collarbone his shirt stuck fast with blood to the bandages beneath it. Raymond took notice and asked after him with his eyes. Joe shrugged, if only with one shoulder, and then they went to work in earnest, uncorking the barrels until all along the bar and from each of the tables there gurgled amber spills of pilsner. When they'd finished, Joe stood at the back door with his rifle while Raymond removed his hat and knelt down at the nearest end of the bar so he could take a long draught from one of the opened kegs. It fell in a pulsing stream, like a blood spurt or milk sprayed from an udder that was pulled and released by a palsied hand, and when he stood, Raymond's dark curls were drenched and he was blinking the stuff from his eyes. He smiled so that his teeth, yellow but straight, were visible to the gum lines, and Joe had seen this smile only once in the last year, when they'd stood out in the pasture lit by a full moon and the roaring blaze of

181

the house fire they'd kindled with kerosene-soaked curtains in the front room of their father's house.

Raymond leaned forward at the waist and shook his head playfully, a dog come up wet after a deep drink from a rushing creek. "They brew a damned good beer in Shiner, brother," he said, stomping a boot down for emphasis. "I hope these here floorboards is thirsty."

By quarter of eleven, Karel had made the trip to Hacek's in Moulton and found, parked between the train tracks and the storefront, the unmistakable new black Packard of Guillermo Villaseñor, the paint throwing sunlight from its polished surface like the oiled, blued receiver of a fine rifle. Karel's skin went tight around his muscles, and he pulled his pouch of tobacco from his breast pocket and rolled a cigarette to calm his nerves. He sat smoking in the cab of the truck for a long minute before swinging the door open and climbing out, hitching his trousers up and pulling his hat down low over his hairline. The town, less than half the size of Shiner, had been erected in one long row of raised storefronts along the rail line as if its founders, with transient hearts and foresight, expected one day, when a train was made that could bear the load, to roll the whole town broadside onto flat railcars and haul it to some other, more fitting, location.

Between Hacek's place and the nearby dry-goods store stood padlocked rows of slope-roofed bins in which the old man kept the coal shipped in from upstate by rail. From the telephone lines strung parallel to the storefronts, crows gave voice to their grating complaints. There were townsfolk out, walking between stores on the piered pine decking and airing themselves out front of the barbershop and the green grocer's.

Karel tipped his hat to a woman making her way from the barbershop past the icehouse with a young boy in tow, his hair cropped short and parted with a wet comb in a fine straight line over one ear. The woman nodded, pulling the boy along none too gently by his outstretched arm, and Karel remembered the cold fear of being a boy set atop a board laid over the arms of a barber's chair, of the sick smell of hair tonic mixed with the minty scent of hot shaving soap, of the swishing sound of the push broom's bristles on the hard-planked floor. He wondered how old his boy would have to be before he'd need to be taken to Wasek's shop in Dalton for his first haircut. Then he ground his cigarette beneath the toe of his boot and reached for the doorknob of Hacek's icehouse. He told himself to quit worrying over the had-beens and the would-bes and set his mind instead to the business at hand.

Inside, dust hung in the wide slants of light from the front windows, and Villaseñor stood flanked by his two men, who went hatless as children but wore their graying hair slicked back in the fashion of their master. Deep wrinkles stretched from the corners of their eyes. They hadn't missed any meals, and their smooth leather vests bulged out above their rifles, which were held, as ever, across their bodies waist high. Villaseñor leaned against the bar, his hat in his hands, his spectacles low on his prominent nose, and when the bell over the door signaled Karel's arrival, he turned from his conversation and, with a bemused, curious arc of his brows, buttoned his suitcoat and turned back toward Weldon Hacek, who'd found a rag and now busied himself with the nervous work of buffing from the gleaming bar top some blemishes of his own imagination.

Karel stopped just inside the door, made to remove his hat but then, thinking twice of it, left it on and made a show of rolling another cigarette and putting a match to it. He exhaled through his nose and crossed the room with the cigarette smoking between his lips, leaned over against the cant of his neck until his hat brim touched the bar and Hacek had no choice but to meet his eyes. "How about you draw me a beer," Karel said. "You ain't run out of pilsner, now have you?"

Hacek stopped mopping the bar, fetched a glass from the shelf on the back wall and tilted it beneath a tap. The man had a reputation for tasting his inventory at regular intervals, and his nose was a pocked and swollen bulb that hung with such a profusion of brown hairs that they appeared to be the tangled source of the thick mustache that hid the better half of his upper lip. "Was near out after last weekend," he said, sliding the glass toward Karel, "but this here is from a fresh drum I just took delivery of yesterday morning."

"Come by way of a couple boys towing my trailer, did it?"

"Matter of fact," Hacek said.

Villaseñor cleared his throat, set his hat on the bar and removed his spectacles, the lenses of which he studied with a frown before cleaning them with a pressed white handkerchief pulled from his breast pocket. "Well now," he said, keeping his eyes on his work, "if it's a new barrel, then let's all have a taste, shall we? Draw one for yourself, too, Weldon." He pulled a thick bundle of banknotes from his trouser pocket, pulled two dollars from the fold, placed them on the bar with the flat of his hand.

Karel noticed that, after all these years, the man still wore a silver wedding band. "On a first-name basis, are we now, Hacek?"

The shop owner retrieved four more glasses and commenced filling them while Karel tasted his and felt the cool tingle of the froth on his lips. He pulled on his cigarette and flicked the ashes onto the floor while he watched Hacek pour and set the glasses in front of Villaseñor and his men. The latter leaned their guns against the front of the bar and put their hands around the glasses, but they did not drink. Instead, they waited for their boss's prompting, and by the time Hacek filled his own glass, Karel had let the informality of the Mexican's address do its work on him. When Hacek turned all at once to face his vendors and customers, Karel held a finger up before the man could drink while he drained his own glass in one draught. "I do believe I'll have another," he said. "Long as my brothers' keeper here is paying."

"It would be my pleasure," said Villaseñor, holding his spectacles up to the light from the windows before putting them back on. "I was just telling Weldon here that I'd like very much to give you far more than a beer. You're the uncle of my grandchildren, after all, though they barely know you by sight. It's a shame, but it's true." He waited until Hacek put a new glass in front of Karel, nodded to his men, and they all drank together, excepting Karel, who let his glass sit untouched on the bar. "Anyway, as I was saying, Skala, it might be better for everyone if I paid you off your share of the Spoetzel concern. Especially if you insist on hiring boys without manners to tend to your business in your absence. My son-in-law tells me he had to put some birdshot into one of them yesterday. Said they came into our store out in Gonzales trying to unload some kegs and didn't like the reception they got."

"Shit," said Karel. "If you still got Thom running that place, ain't anybody likely to take a shine to the welcome he rolls out. Or have Graciela's better graces softened his temperament same as they stiffen his pecker? How many little half-breed nieces and nephews do I have, anyway? I can't keep track."

If Villaseñor took offense, he didn't show it. He squared his shoulders over his polished black shoes, let out a sigh that seemed occasioned more by relaxation than impatience, and took another sip of his beer. When he set the glass back on the bar, he spun it slowly in the condensation of its own making. Then he smiled at his men and winked at Weldon Hacek. "I was afraid you'd fail to see the sense in a buyout. But no matter. The offer was only courtesy, really. I've spoken with Kosmos. Called on him last night at his home. What a fine wife he has, too. Have you had occasion to dine with them? A woman with a proper sensibility and impeccable taste. We sat in the parlor after our meal and shared some brandy, enjoyed a couple of top-rate cigars I brought with me, and by the time I'd taken my leave, we had come to an agreement that is . . . well, that is somewhat exclusive." He lifted his glass, studied the ring of water it left there on the polished bar, and then he set it back in the same spot and began spinning it in the opposite direction. He looked up only with the corner of his eye, and Karel forced a bemused grin. "Then, just now before you arrived, I shook hands with Weldon here and agreed to take his business at fifty cents per barrel less than you've been charging him, and to deliver it upon demand rather than merely twice per month. I have several trucks, of course. It's all the same to me. And, as a matter of course, I sent Stan and Eduard down to Yoakum this morning, and I trust they are making the same offer to some of your other overcharged customers." The man smiled now, but his eyes didn't shine. They remained dull and black and entirely unamused. "You see, Karel, you can't really expect me to respect our arrangement and keep my business out west so long as you're sending children who carry firearms and make threats into my very own store, now can you?"

Karel took a slow drink and dropped his cigarette to the floor, letting it burn there at his feet without stepping on it. A dry, leathery tightness had begun to creep into the tendons of his neck, one that he recognized as having nothing to do with the cool weather, and he would have sworn it was contracting such that his ear was nearer his shoulder than normal. "If them boys have been out Gonzales way," he said, "they done it on their own. I told them only to make my deliveries here in Moulton, and to call on some others between here and Shiner. Nothing more."

Villaseñor finished his beer, took his hat from the bar, and nodded to his men. They followed suit, setting their empty glasses aside and retrieving their guns before crossing the room to flank the door. "Well, they did a fair bit more than that, it would seem. Spat on the floor of my saloon, one of them did, and used foul language. If you can't trust the men you hire, Skala, then you either hired the wrong men or you didn't make it well enough worth their while to do as you said. Either way, you carry the blame." He nodded, and one of his men opened the door, tinkling the bell overhead. "Do yourself a favor," he said. "Cut those boys loose so you don't end up having to send word to their mother that they've found an early way into the ground doing your bidding."

"They ain't got a mother," Karel said. "And I didn't come here wanting advice."

"You'd do well to take it all the same. Mind your business while you still have some left to mind," Villaseñor said, and then he settled his hat in its place and took his leave.

MEANWHILE, WHEN THE Knedlik twins slid open the back door of the Drycreek Saloon, they found Thomàs Skala perched in the trailer atop one of the square bales, his hat set beside him and his shotgun in his lap, his blond curls catching sunlight and blowing about his ears in a burgeoning wind. They hadn't heard the engine of his truck, which was nowhere in sight. Raymond cursed himself for parking right out in the open, visible from a good distance up the road, where he supposed now that Thom had pulled over and come the rest of the way quietly on foot.

"Good morning, ladies," he called out. "If I'd meant for folks to come up and help themselves to my wares while I'm away, I'd of left a trough full of beer out here in the yard with a canning jar set next to it for customers to drop their nickels in."

Joe ran his thumb over the safety of his gun, making sure it wasn't engaged, keeping his eyes on Thom all the while. Raymond combed a hand through his wet hair and hooked the thumb of the other into the front pocket of his trousers and laughed. "Might should have done that," he said, turning the side of his face to the sun. "Would've saved us the trouble of breaking your window. Broken glass is dangerous, you know. Got me a scar what proves it." Toeing the damp earth sprung through with weeds, Raymond noted the reassuring cool of his pistol against his spine. "It's going to be a rough ride on the back of that trailer. But we'll gladly give you a lift if you're needing one."

189

Thom nodded as if in appreciation of the boy's wit, and Joe looked the man over slowly. As it had been the day before, his face was cleanly shaven, his back straight and his shoulders squared over his hips, his neck cocked sickly to one side in a way that Joe found to be even more disconcerting than it had been when he'd first met Karel. With the latter, there was a telling, uncompromising plainness to both his appearance and his movements, as if he'd been cast unembellished at birth and couldn't be bothered with betterment. Karel's eyes had gazed, even in the dark of night, with a spare intensity that revealed little if anything of his intentions, and he looked deliberately unkempt, his toughness and humor evident in the way he carried himself and wore his clothes, something askew from hatband to boot heels, and in this way, for him, his warped neck seemed all of a piece. But here was a man with a starched collar and an unwrinkled vest, a polished man with polished boots, a man who wore the makings of a grin on a face that looked like it had been hot toweled and lathered and rid of its whiskers no more than an hour before. Just looking at him, Joe swore he could smell soap. Here was a man who fashioned himself so as to obscure his unsightly twin imperfections, the two top teeth folded back like someone had taken a hammer to them, and then there was that neck, bowed over like a fern blade weighted with dew.

Raymond noticed this, too, had noticed it the day before, when the thought that there was more than one man in the world wearing this affliction opened a damper in his chest and put a red glow to the coals of his kindled anger. Now he freed his thumb from his pocket and traced the jagged scar tissue that fell away into the corner of his mouth as if he'd been made to eat the tail end of the wound he'd sustained. As if the wound itself, then, had for a while sustained him. And then he took note of his brother, the round stains of dried blood showing dull and dark as well-handled pennies through the cotton fabric of his shirt.

"Tell you what, girls," Thom said. "You go ahead and drive off and I'll sit right here, and we'll see if this trailer comes with you or not. I been having a long talk with it out here while you were lost inside my establishment, trying to find your way out, and it told me it didn't like the recent company it's been keeping. It's a Christian trailer, it turns out, and can't cotton to all the sinning it's been drawn into of late. I reckon it might like to stay right here among more honorable, God-fearing folk."

"That so?" said Raymond, his hand still at the corner of his mouth.

"I believe it is. Also, I unhitched it from your truck and let the air out of the tires on the other side. So there's that to consider."

Raymond scanned the trailer, saw that it was so, that it leaned gently back and away from where he stood, that the hitch bolt had been removed and lay, missing its nut, on the shaded bare earth beneath the truck. He swallowed his bitterness along with the souring taste of beer that remained on his tongue. "We been considering a few things ourselves. Spent the better part of the night considering how birdshot finds its way out of your gun when someone turns their back on you."

"And so you came right on back for more, did you? It's even mice that learn, when they lose a tail, not to go sniffing too close to easy cheese. I'm a better shot than to have missed what I aimed at. If I'd of wanted your little sister there dead, he'd of been heaped over with dirt before sundown. A man's got to make his expectations clear. I can't have every sharecropper in town thinking he can come into my place and spit on the floor like what you done. There's spittoons enough in there for whatever tastes too bad to swallow."

"And that's that? You shoot a man because his brother spit on your floor, but now you're just going to teach us this lesson here by stealing our trailer. What's to keep your gun in your lap while we drive away?"

"I had a peek under the hay," Thom said. "And through the side window, too, while you were having your fun. It's you who's been doing the stealing, and I'd call the law if I thought he'd be amused by a mess of real beer being sold around his county. What I get for the trailer will make up for what you've drained onto my floor in there. We'll call it a fair swap, and as long as me or my brothers don't see you anywhere near our property again, then I can go back to selling beer instead of mopping it off the floor and wasting bird-shot."

"How many brothers you got?"

Thom squinted against the sun, and he put his hat back on his head while a gust of wind blew a few loose straws of hay from the bales around him. "It's three of us," he said, "that we claim."

"What if I told you that trailer don't belong to us? That it's on loan to us from the one you don't claim?"

Thom caught a laugh halfway up his throat and squeezed it off. He nodded once. "I'd say you're right about it not belonging to you. It belongs to me. And I'd say a man can count his brothers however he damn well pleases, and that you might should get that truck running and git while your brother still has one left to count himself."

Raymond turned to Joe, pointing at himself and jerking his head toward the truck, and his brother stood with his rifle at the ready. Raymond strode over and got the engine cranked while the wind came up again in a hard gust that seemed both dishonest and point-less without any clouds in the sky to be blown about. When the en-gine fired, Raymond worked the choke and throttle, and exhaust came coughing up from beneath the bed and floated back over the trailer. Thom Skala rose from his seat on the trailer, lifting the stock of his gun up to his shoulder but keeping the barrel down and away from Joe.

Raymond swung the truck wide out to the side of the old barn and circled back around, reaching over while he drove to open the passenger door for his brother before pulling alongside him. Joe slid his rifle behind the seats and climbed in, reaching for the news-paper on the dash before slamming the door shut behind him. And then the truck jerked with the release of the brake, and Raymond Knedlik pulled forward for one last word with the man who made him burn, two days straight, with the knowledge that he'd been out-witted and outtalked, both. "It's going to be a hot one tonight, I'm guessing," he said. "You try to keep cool, now."

Thom fingered the trigger of his gun, the idle caress of a man who's managed to make his point without having to make it loudly. It felt to him better now than it had to have taken aim and executed his shot so well the day before, measuring the distance and the breadth of his shot pattern so he could pop the boy with a few beads while he walked out to his truck, so he could do just enough harm to send a clear and stinging message. And still, it hadn't worked, or it hadn't for long. Maybe this wouldn't either. Who knew? He wondered what had possessed Karel that he'd hire them to do his bidding. These boys were clearly half a head shy on horse sense. After all, the wind had come up again, and out of the northwest, carrying a chill that was as trustworthy a sign as a green, hailstone sky in September. "You need to check the date on your almanac, son. It'll be cold enough to light the woodstove tonight."

"We'll see," Raymond said, winking and clicking his tongue. "Never can tell about the weather, though, and I'm guessing it'll be too hot for good sleeping."

The other boy turned his attention away from the conversation, opened the newspaper and commenced reading. The engine stuttered and then caught with a gray cough of exhaust. While they drove away, Thom stood watching for a while until the truck was clear of his own and out of sight. He had work to do, and a lot of it, the little sons of bitches. The wind came up again and played violently in the upper branches of the old oaks across the road. They were in for some weather, sure enough.

AFTER A LONG DAY in the truck spent chasing those whom he hadn't been able to catch, Karel made it home just before dusk. He propped his gun in the corner of the kitchen, filled the coffee pot with water and grounds and settled it on the stove to brew. In the course of the morning and afternoon, he'd driven to Moulton and Weid, out west to Gonzales, and back home to Dalton by way of Shiner. No one he'd spoken to had seen the Knedlik boys since the day before, when, according to a boy working at the feedstore in Gonzales, the quiet one had been winged with shot as he walked unarmed to his truck out back of the saloon, but it was the sight of the man to whom he hadn't spoken — his brother Thomàs, decked out in his fine vest and shined shoes — that worked cold and sickening in his blood like a kind of distemper. He halved a sweet roll that Sophie had baked two days before from the leftover scraps of kolache dough and folded each half around a fatty hunk of the cured ham he'd brought in from the smokehouse. He ate standing up, wiped his hands on his trousers, scraped a chair back from the kitchen table and took a seat. After rolling cigarettes mindlessly until his case was full, he cinched the pouch of tobacco closed and sat smoking, listening to the growing wind wheeze through the window screens until the smell of coffee brought him again to his feet. He took a cup from the drain board, poured it half-full, then topped it off with whiskey from the jug of mash he kept in the cabinet over the sink and went to sit on the back steps facing the grove while he drank.

It was uncommon, such a wind without even a trace of clouds to diffuse the pink glow of the sunset. Back when he was a boy, there'd been a comfort to the approach of weather come evening time, to the way you could know that something was on the way without quite knowing what. It might blow, it might rain, it might well do both. Depending on the season, there might fall a clatter of hail until it sounded from inside the barn or stable as if there were men doing roof work overhead.

Most often, whether anything dropped from the sky or not, Karel had busied himself in those sunset hours with work about the stables. He'd fill the lanterns with oil so he could leave them lit overnight. He'd muck the stables and shoulder a new bale over in front of the stall doors and break it open there so he could fork it quickly into the stalls. There were extra oats for Whiskey, who could get skittish when the wind blew and he was cooped up inside. Ride him out in a thunderstorm, as Karel had so many times when dark skies slid in fast from the west and caught him too far from home to outride the clouds, and the horse would switch his tail and whinny happily and never break stride. He was spooked only when stabled, and Karel had grown to feel much the same way. He took pride in his home, in the new white paint on the house and the green window trim that Sophie had so wanted, in the graded road and the expanded smokehouse and the new cattlepens he'd fenced in behind the barn, but preferred to see it all from out of doors, where he could lay his eyes on the work his hands had done.

And so it was, though it had been years since there were fine horses in his stables instead of draft animals and spools of baling wire and cans of oil and kerosene and tins of grease, that Karel preferred to be out of the house when the sunlight was failing and some change of weather looming. He liked it better when there were chores to do and the promise of darkness or rain or both became a clock against which he could measure his work, and tonight, when he finished his coffee, he rose to his feet and stretched his sore back with his hands twisted together high above his head, and then he fetched a length of rope and some chain from the stable and carried them out east of the smokehouse to light a small fire beneath the crankcase of his new Fordson tractor so he could get it started in the cool weather.

A half hour later, when he made it around to the cattlepen, he was thankful for the long gray shadows of dusk, for he was sure, by now, that the vultures had made more than one good meal from his losses. He left the tractor idling loudly outside the pen and unlatched the gate and let the wind swing it wide. While he tied the rope like a noose around the half-born calf's neck, he held his breath against the stench and thought of the knowing look on Villaseñor's face, letting himself fantasize for a moment that he was hitching a rope round that son of a bitch's throat. Karel worked bent over at the waist, winding the rope from the calf and then around the front of the heifer's hind legs, looping it in two tight circles from behind the heifer's udder up over her haunches and knotting it along the spine so that the calf couldn't come free from its mother's body when he dragged the whole mess of it across the pasture. When he rose, his hips popped such that he could hear it over the wind, and his back began to throb in deep spasms that felt like steaming water was being wrung upward from the small of his back to the stiffly warped knuckles of his neck. He would bet, goddamn it, that his brothers didn't ache this way, never mind that they'd all once worn the same harness and pulled the same plow. If Thom's youthful good looks were any indication, they were aging handsomely, like their wives' father, who, if possible, was more infuriating now in his polished appearance and disposition than he had been when he'd first come calling in his carriage. His speech was, as ever, salted only by his choice of words, never with the tenor or volume of his voice, and he wore suitcoats and hats that made him stand everywhere in Lavaca County a head above even the wealthier Czechs and Germans. And now he'd rubbed off on his daughters' husbands. Karel tied another two loops just behind the heifer's front legs and pulled the remaining rope tight before looping a cinch knot into the end of it and doubling the chain through that.

When he had the whole affair rigged to the tractor, he climbed into the seat and worked the hand clutch while looking back, easing the slack out of the chain until the cow swung around smoothly in the hay with the calf's head trailing behind. Then Karel throttled it up and steered out through the pasture, straightening his back to brace himself against the jostling ride of the steel drive wheels as he angled between the wide swaths mowed through the old hedgerows. While he drove toward the southern fork of the creek, he pictured his brother Thom as he had seen him from his idling truck earlier in the day just after the wind began to pick up, a man engaged in the deliberate, slow work of the well-to-do, his hair grown longer than it had been the last time Karel had seen him, his face with some sun in it but smooth and otherwise unweathered, his lips held together to hide the wreck of his front teeth, his curved neck carried in such a way that the man assumed a quiet and thoughtful show of satisfaction as he carried buckets full of mop water out to the wide front porch of his saloon and dumped them carefully over the porch railing so he wouldn't splash his shoes or trousers. Sitting in his truck, Karel couldn't help but wonder if his brother still held suspicions about what his wife had done before their wedding day, if she had gone to him seeking to clear her conscience. Karel supposed it wasn't so, saw in his brother an innocence born either of ignorance or denial. And then it occurred to Karel that it wouldn't do him or anyone else any harm to swing his door open and join his brother there on the porch, to lend him a hand. It had been so long since he'd had the company of another man in his work, so long that he now felt almost a longing for those hours and days spent hitched to the plow with his brothers, their boots sliding and sinking in the fine black soil, the sun blistering the backs of their necks where their straw hat brims proved too narrow. It had been enraging and unnecessarily hard work, but at least, linked together by leather, they had felt the common hard resentment, a kind of ill will whose tongue was held in check by fear, for the same man at the same time. If anything, this was what Karel missed about the company of his brothers — their hardness and loathing had shored up his own, given him title to his own hatred. But there was something else: The older boys had also admired their father — his stubbornness and sharp tongue, the way he refused to beckon the help of other men — and so had Karel, and it was this admiration that he couldn't cotton to, the reverence for a man you surely hated, the hard plaque of respect that all the bad blood couldn't scour from your heart. This, too, he and his brothers had shared, and the bile of a common indigestion that rose from the two brands of unsuited feelings had been easier to swallow when there were others around who were burning inside with the same struggle to choke it down.

Karel wondered now, as he neared the line of water oaks fringing the creekbed and the sky darkened to a deeply bruised blue, if it was this aspect of brotherhood that had made it near on to impossible for boys like Billy Dalton to come home from the war, if the mud they had tasted and the gases they'd dodged in those trenches had hardened them together in the same way that countless grains of sand, compacted and fired so long underground, were baked together, in time, into stone. Dalton had lasted only a year back in town before clearing out to take a factory job in Kansas City where a pair of brothers from his regiment overseas had gone to work after their homecoming. Karel had seen him at the icehouse in town some four years back, standing at the bar, drinking alone, young still but no longer a boy. His red hair looked dulled as if by a wash with diluted lye, and the scar Karel had occasioned on his face had faded so that it appeared, in the lamplight, to be little more than a birthmark. Karel had bid him good evening, and the young man had nodded at him, and they'd had a drink together without saying another word, the deep-rooted rivalry of their history buried and smothered by all that had since been shoveled by time over the top of it. Karel hadn't seen him since. He'd left his father and mother and the town that carried his name, this for something akin to brotherhood that probably had no name at all.

Earlier in the day, sitting across the road from the Drycreek Saloon, this was the kind of thinking that had nearly spurred Karel out of his truck and onto the porch to have words with his brother. Each time, though, that he'd found his hand on the door, he'd seen his cigarette burning in his hand, and the red glow of the thing and its smoke had reminded him of Villaseñor's cigar, of all the business he'd threatened to take and of all that Karel had already lost — the girl, Graciela, whose loamy sweetness he could often smell in the air after a hard, cold rain; the exhilarating release of riding nights on a fine horse; the close, stale comfort of a bedroom filled with the loud breathing of brothers; the allegiance, bitter though it may have been, with the father who had staked his final wager with a family that he could never, whether he won or no, make whole. And this was the difference, after all, between Karel and his brothers. They had gone, and he had remained. They had found a way out, or it had found them, and Karel reckoned now that their destination had been one that allowed them to cull all the resentment from their respect just as surely as he now, reaching the creek, slid down from behind the steering wheel and unhitched the dead animals from the chain before climbing back onto the tractor and leaving them there to broadcast in the cool wind their reeking and indissoluble end.

THEY WAITED UNTIL an hour after dark, when the nearby farmers were likely done with the evening chores and gone indoors for the night, and then they kindled a small fire beneath an overhang of sweet gum trees a mere twenty yards from the dirt road where they'd parked the truck. After leaving Gonzales, they'd driven north until they reached the Fayette County line and then turned back east to make their way through Flatonia and over into Praha. There they'd stopped into the druggist's and the general store where, while Joe gathered provisions of potted meat and canned beans and dried sausage and sweet potatoes, Raymond had struck up a conversation with Elizka Novotny. She offered that Karel had left for Dalton that morning, that his wife was recovering still from her labor at the Vrana house, and she wondered what it was that had brought the twins back so soon to Praha. Hadn't she heard that they'd hired on to help out around the Skala farm?

"We run some errands for him," Raymond had said, "over in Flatonia. But my brother there lost his footing beneath a load he was carrying and fell backward into a window. Cut his shoulder to ribbons. We're going to get him dressed up and head on back to Dalton."

"And the food?" she asked, following Joe with her eyes while he made his way around the store, filling a crate. "Won't Karel share meals with you?"

"We don't take liberties, ma'am. We tend to do for ourselves."

Now, with two opened cans of beans warming on flat stones near the fire, Raymond sat on a fallen timber beside his shirtless brother, cleaning his wounds with alcohol and dressing them in clean cotton bandages. When he'd finished and Joe had gotten his shirt and coat back on, they ate upwind of the fire and watched as smoke and orange embers swept up through the branches of the nearby trees. The moon had come timidly off the horizon to find the sky wide and cloudless, a few proud stars already shining.

Raymond fed himself a mouthful of beans, then sat with his eyes on the fire, pointing his spoon at Joe while he chewed. "I been thinking on what you said. If you got it in your mind to go west, that'll suit me fine. One place is as good as another, I guess."

Joe nodded, tilting his can toward the firelight so he could see into it and scraping the bottom with his spoon. When he'd emptied it to his satisfaction, he tossed the can into the fire and tucked the spoon in the front pocket of his coat. Raymond had wrapped the dressing too tight, and Joe propped his arm on his knee to take the weight off his shoulder, which was throbbing at the joint and stinging still from the alcohol. He listened to the gusting of the wind, the rise and fall of it in the tree branches, and he imagined the ocean, wondering if that's how the waves sounded when they rolled up onto the land and slid back down. Somewhere shy of Flatonia, he'd finished the serial in the paper, and now he was glad to have used it beneath the kindling to get the fire started. Judith had let him down, growing soft when the neighboring rancher sweet-talked her, falling into his arms like some pitiful, spoiled, breathless woman in a picture show who'd taken faint upon the sight of approaching Indians or the receipt of a telegram bearing news of her doting father's death.

If he'd been there, Joe thought, he'd have made her look at his shoulder while he unwrapped his bandages and pulled off the scabs where they were stuck to the dressing, and then he'd have squeezed the flesh around the wounds until the blood came up from beneath the skin and rolled down his arm. He'd have accustomed her to the sight of pain and the sounds of danger until she toughened up, and then he'd have told her about the horses her handsome, sugar-tongued neighbor had bought from that son of a bitch, Bayne. After she came to her senses and remembered who she was, Judith of Blue Lake Ranch, not some little ninny who rode sidesaddle, they could have taken a ride together and crossed out to the westernmost meadow of her property. They could have sat horseback together, looking out over the cliffs that fell away down to where the ocean ran up onto the shore below. They could have grown the ranch and found some way to run her rotten neighbor out of business. But he was a long way yet from California, and the damned story was already written, and now it was ashes beneath the glowing kindling of the fire, where it belonged, and it was too late to change it, too late to save her or to remind her how to save herself, and this realization recalled to Joe's mind a picture of his mother, withered down near to nothing after three weeks in bed, the points of her hips and knobs of her knees sharp as sheared rock beneath the blankets, her voice the sound of two dry stones rubbed together, whispering in Joe's ear for water, more water, *just another sip of water, dear,* until, after three late-night trips out to the well, he'd fallen asleep in the chair beside her and awoken to find her dead with an empty glass beside her on the table near her bed.

Raymond stirred the ashes of the fire needlessly with a stick and said, "We'll just do this one thing tonight and then drive north a few days, into Oklahoma, maybe. Sell the truck there and catch a train."

"We could head out now," Joe said. "Drive all night to San Antonio and catch the Sunset Limited. Leave it be. You didn't have to spit on the man's floor, Ray."

Raymond looked up from the fire and then gazed at the moonlit sky, his eyes red and watery from the heat and smoke, his scar irregular and dead white on his flushed face. It was the third time Joe had spoken since sunup, and Raymond wasn't accustomed to his brother being so damned talkative. "I suppose I didn't," Raymond said, tossing the stick into the fire. "I might have spit in his face instead."

Joe hadn't counted on so many horses. In these parts, most of the small-plot farmers kept only enough mules and draft horses to plow and plant their cotton fields. Down south near Yoakum, where there were still sprawling cattle ranches, you might expect a full stable, but not one with horses the likes of these. Near on to midnight, the boys had smothered their little cook fire with handfuls of dirt and driven back south past Moulton until they reached the stand of blackjack oaks on the eastern side of the road, and Raymond swung the truck around so that it was pointing north and parked it in the weeds next to the drainage ditch between the road and the fenceline. Raymond climbed from the truck, tucked his pistol into the back waistband of his trousers, and closed the door softly. Peering up and down the empty midnight road, he walked around to Joe's side of the truck and then lifted the three cans of gasoline from the bed of the truck. The moon was up in earnest now, and Joe thought he might almost be able to read out here without a lantern, and when he looked at the worry on Raymond's face he could tell his brother was thinking too about the light, and not so kindly. Joe left his rifle in the truck and lifted one of the cans with his good arm.

When they'd made it over the cattlegate and walked the quarter mile up the winding dirt road to find the dense grove of fruit trees standing bare between the house and the stable, they stopped and listened while the wind worked the tree branches together and drove the whirring blades of the windmill set out on the near side of the barn. The house rose in fine white siding from the bottom story up to a screened sleeping porch that ran the length of the second floor. Raymond put a finger to his lips, a gesture so pointless, given his brother's penchant for silence, that Joe stifled a laugh and shook his head. Raymond ducked through the grove and slipped between the barn and the new Ford truck that sat outside the sliding doors with Karel's trailer unhitched and empty beside it. Just beyond it, the stable loomed quiet and twice the size of the barn, its new red paint visible beneath the unabashed moon.

Raymond slid the door open one slow inch at a time and marveled at how well greased and silent and true the runners were. The brothers set their cans down just inside the door and Raymond pushed it mostly closed. They stood for a while, letting their eyes adjust to the darkness and breathing the warm air rich with the sweet mix of manure and hay and damp saddle blankets and breathing animals, each scent distinct yet muted, overcast by the strong smell of fine, oiled leather.

Joe lit a match and cupped it with his hand, biting back the bone-deep throbbing in his shoulder as he walked past the loft stairs toward the stalls until he located a hanging lantern and pulled it down from its nail. He got it lit, dialed the wick down low, and then the brothers got their bearings in the new spill of light around them. Before the stalls, a wooden loft chute angled down to the floor from above and hay bales were stacked three high against the wall and beneath the steps leading up the loft. Raymond nodded and they walked down the wide alley, flanked on each side by stalls with brass door bolts and hardwood walls that gave way to polished slats rising from chest-high on either side of the opened feed doors, the horses within breathing and clopping softly in their fresh bedding. A few lumbered forward, blinking their enormous eyes and hanging their heads sleepily over the stall doors to see who had come to tend them in the night and what new comforts they had brought. Raymond pulled another lantern from the beam between two stalls and got it lit, and then they walked two abreast between the long rows, holding their lanterns up and peering into the stalls. Joe counted eight on each side, and only a few of them empty. A dozen horses at least, but really the same horse twelve times. Some mares, some stallions, a gelding or two and, in the last right-hand stall, a nervous little filly that shook her mane and paced within the confines of her enclosure, all of them black from hoof to head excepting their socks and blazes, which shone so white they made him squint even in the dim, oily light of the lanterns. He thought of Raymond's scar, the way it had looked too white to be real in the light of the cook fire, and then he turned to the back of the stable where the wide aisle opened into a wash-down and grooming area with stacks of nested pails on the floor and eyebolts secured in the load-bearing four-by-fours for crossties. On the crossbeams near the wall, an assortment of brushes and currycombs and hoof picks sat waiting for need of their services. Against the opposite wall, fine saddles, many of them strangely lacking pommels, sat atop what looked like wide, varnished hardwood sawhorses. There was tack strung from the rafters and two farrier's stools stacked in one corner beneath a wall hung with sets of new shoes and nippers and rasps.

Mindful of Joe's shoulder, Raymond put a hand flat on the small of his brother's back to get his attention. Joe turned, the yellow lanternlight softening his features so that Raymond saw himself as he'd been years ago before his father put his face through a window the night he'd refused to surrender the pay he'd earned baling hay all one Sunday at a neighboring farm. "Quite an outfit," Raymond whispered, holding his lamp toward the swinging double doors on the back wall. "Crack them doors so we get a cross breeze. I'll go soak the loft."

Joe nodded, watching his brother's wiry frame move between the stalls until Raymond reached the fuel cans, bent to lift one and then rose, enfolded in soft light, up the loft stairs. He gave the filly another look, and she turned from him and pressed her side against the back wall of her stall. He set his lantern on the dirt floor and pulled the bolt from the back door, pushing it slowly outward until a hard gust of wind caught hold of it and Joe found himself going with it, clutching the thing with the wrong hand and dragging his boots in the loose dirt, the back of his shoulder shot through with a deep screaming pain that sucked the breath from his lungs and flashed a blanket of crimson over his vision so that he found himself, when his eyes cleared and he registered the moonlight on his shoulders and the wind whipping the hem of his coat at his back, moaning with a long, throaty exhalation that rolled up into his sinuses until it came out, muted but audible, through his nose. Tears welled up hot in his eyes, and he stood there for a long minute, his forehead holding the door against the exterior wall of the stable, the paddock fenced and well tilled by horse hooves and empty behind him.

When he caught his breath, Joe dug the toe of his boot beneath the door to hold it fast, squatting down as he did to find a stone he could use as a doorstop. He worked with one hand in the sandy earth until he'd convinced himself there was nothing to be found, and, righting himself, he worked a small mound of dirt against the door with the side of his boot and stepped on it to pack it down. Then he retrieved his lantern and listened to the splashing of gas and the soft scuffing of his brother's boots on the floor of the loft overhead.

He was supposed to empty a can in the downstairs hay bales and splash fuel along the walls, but there was something about seeing this little black filly in her stall while his shoulder burned and throbbed, something tender and undeserving of harm, something in her dark, wide eyes and the twitching, tentative way she worked her ears. She was alert and wary, her flanks smooth and well groomed, her legs solid and long, and in her Joe imagined that he could see the many generations of long-considered breeding, the daily vision of her the cause of someone's prideful assurance that, with foresight and honest intentions, a man could see before him all the evidence he needed that he'd made some mark in the world that could not be erased by his own demise.

Overhead, Raymond's footsteps were faint now, approaching the far side of the loft. He'd be coming down soon, ready to put a match to the place, and Joe's feet grew cold in his boots thinking about it, a tingling running up his calves to prickle the hollows behind his knees. Raymond had been born first, by ten minutes or so, and Joe had been following his lead ever since. When their father was alive, prone to all his drinking and the quick ignition of his rage, it had paid to do so. There was something in Raymond, maybe some dilution of their father's hot blood, that readied him always for action, for whatever running or fighting might be called for. Joe had found as a boy that, given the rise of their father's voice in the hall, he would be caught frozen in thought, just lying in bed and thinking, until Raymond grabbed his shirt collar or wrist and dragged him out of his daze toward the window and the long, bare-foot run across the pasture to the safety of darkness and trees. But earlier, by the fire, there had been a distant, ponderous look to Raymond's face, an uncharacteristic refusal to look Joe dead in the eye when he agreed to go west. It had been Joe's idea, after all, and he thought now that even his brother's consent was a kind of follow-ing, and he didn't know if Raymond's pride would allow him to make good on it.

Outside, the wind threw itself in loud waves beneath the eaves, and from the stalls came the occasional, nervous sound of a horse stamping and blowing. The little filly came forward, tossing her head, and Joe hung his lantern outside the stall and unbolted the door and stepped inside. He reached out for her, smoothing the hide of her neck with the flat of his hand, and whispering, "Shh, girl. It's a way out for you now." He heard a bale come whisking down the loft chute at the far end of the stable, then another, and when he went to meet his brother, he left the filly's stall unbolted.

At the foot of the steps, Joe stood cupping his elbow in his good hand when Raymond appeared, his lantern held low in front of him so that he could see the steps as he descended. When he got down, he narrowed his eyes at his brother and held a palm up at his side. "What is it?" he whispered, stepping into the alley and peering down to see that the opposite door was open wide.

Joe just nodded at his shoulder, shook his head.

"Goddamn it," Raymond said. He'd log-jammed the loft chute with bales, and after they'd hung their lanterns on nails in the nearest stall's siding, he went to work soaking the bottom half of them with fuel while Joe turned the other can of gas over atop the stack of hay beneath the loft stairs.

When they'd finished, Raymond shot his brother a grin and said, "Hope you ain't too pained to run." He fished in his pocket for matches, and Joe stood listening as the stable timbers groaned against the wind and then stopped in a wheezing sigh that sounded to him like the final, raspy exhalation of some infirm animal.

Of a sudden, then, the wind changed directions, swirling hard out of the southeast, and when the paddock door came free from its makeshift dirt stop, it slammed shut so sharply that the horses went wild, crying out in panicked shrieks and throwing themselves against their stalls, this booming midnight sound no less frightening to them than would be a clap of thunder unleashed indoors. "Shit," Raymond said, fumbling with his matches.

When he steadied his hands and threw the struck match, there came a blue flash of flame that leapt up the chute into the loft, and Joe took a step backward as the heat washed over him and he stared up into the blaze overhead, a rush of air roaring in his ears, surging upward as if beckoned by some undeniable and infernal summons above.

And then Raymond shoved past, knocking into Joe's shoulder to get around the blazing chute, running toward the sliding door while Joe went to his knees and looked up, mesmerized by this loud flare of light, the bite of burning fuel and smoke stinging in his throat, the terrified sounds of animals rising until they became for him a disorienting extension of the roar of the fire and the loud rush of blood in his ears. Flames rose from the bales beneath the loft stairs and slanted up the chute, whipping toward the door when Raymond leaned into it hard and slid it open until the rollers banged against the outermost framework of the runners. Overhead, the flames fed a thick clot of smoke that hovered over the chute's opening, and Joe squinted against the blast of heat on his face and shielded his eyes against the thickening swirl of glowing ash. He heard his brother screaming at him from the open door, saw his face flickering and yellow and cast against the moonlight looming soft and unwavering behind him. And then there was a danger looming closer than the fire, certain but inanimate and all but silent, a thought given voice as if from the growing smoke itself, a quiet, urgent voice the sound of which reverberated only beneath the skin, in the sinew of muscles and the soft meat of marrow, in the blood that surged with adrenaline, and when he broke for the door, his brother turned from it, bolting out into the night.

Overhead, fire glowed blue through the joints of the loft decking, and then the fuel that had run through the seams caught in a raining curtain of flame before the door. Joe stopped, pulled his coat up over his head, and even with his ears covered, the stable was just deafening with the screaming panic of animals and the hot rush of spreading fire and the unmistakable approach of hoof strikes. When they were upon him, he turned, ducking and throwing his arms out, to find the filly towering above him, rearing and kicking, trapped between this raining blaze of fire and the door slammed shut behind her at the far end of the stable.

When Joe turned once more toward the door, the horse reared again and fell, its shod hoof hitting just above Joe's calf in the hollow of his knee. His leg buckled and snapped, the sound louder than the popping of dry oak in a woodstove, and he was shot through with a searing pain as he flew forward, the impact kicking the breath from his lungs when his chest hit the dirt, his head snapping forward to slam against the hard-packed earth, and then there were moments of darkness and quiet, of the haunting sound of his mother's voice, of her whispering in the night for water, of a body whole and calm and cool and unaware of fire or animals or the bone splintered and jutting wet through the wrecked skin of his shin.

When he came to, he worked his tongue over a scab of dirt stuck to the spit at the corner of his lips. The filly was still wild, pacing and wheezing beside him, unwilling to break through the smoke and fire that now obscured the front stable door, her hooves shaking the hard earth beneath him when they struck. Joe rolled over and the bolt of pain leapt up his leg hot and tremulous and sick until it twisted through his stomach and up his throat, and it all came so quickly there was no turning his head, no stopping it, and Joe's eyes flooded as he wretched into his own lap, the sour spew of beans clogging his throat in abrasive waves until, when he'd finished, he was fully conscious, the heat and smoke and glowing embers falling over him as he ground his teeth and grunted and cried out and kept an eye on the frantic pacing of the horse while he scooted himself back with the palms of his hands and his good leg, working his way to the rear of the stable until he could feel his spine braced against the solid wood of the rear door.

He bent his good knee, wiped the tears from his eyes and a thick smear of blood from his nose and the muddy bile from the corner of his mouth and, with one sharp arch of his back, pushed the door open and felt, all at once, the hard bite of pain that jolted through him in the squeezing of his guts and the shivering skin and the breath expelled with a cry that could only be squelched by biting down hard on his lower lip. The horse came out wildly behind him, and he flinched as she galloped harmlessly over his outstretched legs and circled herself out against the far perimeter of the paddock's fenceline. He found that he was holding his breath, and when he exhaled, he reached back again and clenched handfuls of the loose, sandy soil, feeling the grainy cool of it between his fingers, a sensation so commonplace and familiar that there came into him a startling cold relief. He was out of the stable. It was December. His father was dead. His brother out here somewhere in the night, looking for him or assuming him killed or racing toward the road and the truck. As Joe worked backward, dragging himself over the uneven earth that lay churned up into mounds and pocked with divots, he heard the sound of voices come alive in the night — his name called out like a desperate question in the parched, hoarse voice of his brother; the screaming of trapped animals; the barked, uncompromising orders of a man brought out of his dreams to find the night afire, his family sleeping beside him wrapped in sheets that would burn atop mattresses that would burn in a house made of timber that would burn, all in a world overseen by a god who had long since forsaken water.

Beneath the high moon, with the yellow bone quivering outside of the skin, the blood pulsing up around it and pooling warm in the leg of his trousers, Joe didn't notice the gunshot wound of his shoulder in the least. He didn't any longer curse or scream or call out for his brother. He had to keep himself conscious and moving, and he set all of his mind to the sobering intake of every sensation other than pain, to the slow progress across the paddock, to these handfuls of dirt and the whispering of his mother's voice somewhere inside of him, to the thirst that crept from her dry lips into his own throat, to the hard whipping of the wind and the tingling chill in his scalp and cheeks and shoulders as the blood siphoned down to feed the pool in the leveled leg of his pants, to the reaching and pulling and the gritty soil packing beneath his fingernails, to the sound of the horse blowing behind him and the vision of flames bursting up from beneath the stable's eaves such that the thick, wind-borne smoke thinned smooth and flat into an unrolled bolt of threadbare fabric, doing the work of clouds on a cloudless night, skimming over the near-round moon. It was as beautiful as it was terrible, and a mass of certainty hardened like enamel around the cage of Joe's ribs, and he knew that Judith had changed her mind, that she'd come to her senses and denied her suitor, that she was sitting her horse on this very night, waiting out on the rolling meadows of her Blue Lake Ranch in California, anticipating his arrival, and by the time Joe made it to the far fencing of the paddock and dragged himself groaning and upright on one leg and took the horse by its mane, leaning his chest over her warm hide and squeezing his arms around her neck so he could pull himself up and swing his good leg over her back, he was laughing and crying what all at the same time.

The blood ran out of him now as if displaced by the hydraulics of his own new certainties — he would ride, and he would mend, and he would go for her — and his hands were groping now, and now his vision blurred and narrowed and tinted by the faintest film of red. And here was the filly's neck. And here her mane. And here the splintery fencerail and the thick, draining weight of his boot coming full, and more fence timbers, and the gate, and here the warm undulations of the animal beneath him, the sweet steaming of her breath in his hair, and here the cool cast iron of the latch and the sighing whine of the gate swinging open. And then they were out in the night, only countless outstretched miles of swirling wind and the merging cadences of heartbeats and hoof strikes and the wide black pastures before them.

Testaments to Seed

MARCH 1910

THERE IS OPPORTUNITY enough—whether with hired women in the stale rooms above the Bio Saloon in Shiner or with country girls made pliant by cider in the nearby woodlands on beds of fallen foliage—for the young men of Lavaca County to occasion the satisfaction of their near-constant urges. Over the course of the last two years, it has not been uncommon for Eduard and Thom, their needs strung tighter or their wills wrought of stronger stuff than their brothers', to return after midnight with hushed laughter and drunken bragging to the boys' shared bedroom. When they wake Stan and Karel, as they invariably do, their talk of the flabby, over-used whores with whom they've purchased an hour is seasoned with descriptions of living but inhuman things, of animals and ripe fruit. Teats heavy and soft as muskmelons left too long in the field. A backside wide as a sow's. Brisket. Hams.

And so it is that when this girl, Graciela, comes to Karel in the lowered light of the stable, unbuttoning her blouse and then smoothing a saddle blanket on a bed of hay bales, he is struck, as a young man is wont to be in the first fortunate moments of his exposure to the delicately unencumbered wonder of a woman's body, by his own ineptitude, by the inaccuracy and insufficiency of all his feeble, boyish fantasies. Here, with the ticking percussion of rain at work on the rooftop and the unmoving air of the stable cool and redolent of damp horsehair and dry hay, there is simply no way to watch this girl shedding her boots, pulling her camisole over her head, and to see her in terms of anything other than the startlingly novel and in-comparable vision that she is.

She sits him on the bales and stands over him, her still-wet hair hanging in front of her shoulders, draping over the gentle hollow of her throat and falling fanned over her breasts, and stops him when he begins to remove his coat. "No," she whispers. "I'll do it. Just sit."

Karel obeys, in part because he hasn't a notion how to defy her, in part because to sit yielding to her will is, in itself, the unexpected satisfaction of a long-untended desire. And so he listens to the rain as the sight of her body gives rise to gooseflesh on the tops of his thighs. He lifts his feet, one at a time, so she can remove his boots, straightens his elbows as she pulls his coat and shirtsleeves from his arms. When she leans over him, kneeling to unbutton his trousers, a breast grazes his knee and he sucks in breath as if in anticipation of some violent submersion.

Then there comes a honing of his senses, and Karel sits naked and marveling at how all his fifteen years in the sunlit world have come to less than this, at how bearing daily witness to outstretched plains and sunset horizons blistered with clouds has taught him no more about the bright surprise of being alive than does the way this girl shifts first onto the ball of one foot, then the other, as she works the waist of her riding pants down over her hips. If he had to, he re-alizes, he would trade all those years piecemeal, a year of *then* for a minute of *now:* the sight of Whiskey's glossy and frothing and wrig-gling emergence from his mother for the acute work of his nerves, for his ability to distinguish, in the rough fabric of the saddle blan-ket beneath him, the coarse, individual threads of the wool's warp and weft; the walks among tall, white-tufted fields of August cotton for this glimpse of the thick, dark hair narrowing down to the proud pleats of glistening skin between her legs; the hours spent imagin-ing his mother's tenderness for the protracted seconds in which this lovely girl ceases to be anything less than a woman, in which she po-sitions herself astride his lap, a cool hand reaching down to take hold of him, to run the engorged tip of him back and forth along her slick folds until she nests him there just outside of her body, until she moves her hands onto the flexed muscles of his shoulders, and, with a pained push of breath rendered low in the back of her throat, takes the whole of him in one slow and shuddering descent.

Karel recognizes, in this moment, that his brothers must be either liars or fools, that there is nothing of the truth in all their lewd talk of creatures and fruit, that there is nothing so common in the sweet heat of this woman atop him, the wet flexing of her muscles taking hold of him, releasing. At the very tip of him, at the deepest point within her, there is a tightening, a hot wire of pleasure that is tethered to the base of his spine, strung from there to his navel and down to his tailbone. His face flushes hot with blood, and then there's a cool prickle on his forehead and cheeks that yields to numbness. The girl works against him, her hands clasped firmly behind his neck, her hips shifting forward and back in their own insistent rhythm, her breath pushing quick and warm in his hair, and Karel is all but helpless beneath her, his injured eye seeping fluid, his hands cupped fast to the tender, rocking tops of her hips, and all the while he watches her.

Not once does she look at him.

Instead, she keeps her eyes shut, fluttering with the intake of breath. Her hair is pasted to her shoulders and breasts, her nipples darker than Karel would have expected, widely encircled by brown bands of skin that he traces with a thumb, the ridges of her clavicle flecked with the faintest little constellation of moles.

He drops his hands from her, bracing them behind his back for leverage, but when he tries to thrust, moving forward with his hips, she drops all of her weight on him, pinning him in place while she breathes hard through her nose and continues her steady and measured undulations. Then a horse blows in the stable, and Karel closes his good eye, listening to the soft play of the weather overhead, to the horses shifting in the stalls, and all the while the wire within him is tightening as if wound by a winch. When he allows himself sight of her again, her head is thrown back past her shoulders, rolling from side to side as if in some makeshift dance for which there is no intended audience. There is the sweet leaking of her body running down onto him, the friction of her work giving rise to a rash down low in the hair beneath his navel.

My *word*, Karel thinks, and he wants now to stand with her still clinging to him, still pressed into the wet saddle of his lap, to take hold of her hips and lift and turn and lay her back onto the blanketed hay, to put his weight on her and feel the solid cinching of her smooth legs around him as he moves inside her. But when he begins to stand, she tightens her arms behind his neck and holds him in place. She centers her weight over him and shakes her head without opening her eyes, and while she increases the speed of her movement atop him, she leans into him and puts her mouth over his swollen eye, sucking at it as if it's her aim to take the whole of it into her mouth, to claim it as her own. Karel's muscles seize and his hands flex hard, his fingernails digging into the flesh of her hips, and a quivering wave shivers through the length of the wire strung hot within him. His eye burns, but her mouth is so soft and wet, her tongue moving in slow circles around the tender skin of his eyelid, and after a while he feels only the remnant of pain, only the heat held in the heart of the metal when a branding iron is dropped hot into well water.

And then it is upon him, the final winding of this unsustainable torsion, and just before the surge of release runs up the length of him, from its origin within her into his stomach, up the switchbacks of his ribs and into the hard buckling knuckles of his spine at the base of his neck, she drops a hand and pulls him from her body. But she doesn't stop, doesn't slow her tempo in his lap, and when his own spasms wane, he pulls his face from her lips and watches as she begins to shudder about the shoulders, her hand working furiously between her legs, her dark eyes sprung wide and fluttering with the perfect, startled bewilderment of something newly born.

GRACIELA LEAVES the lantern low, the stable dimly aglow. She moves quietly, attending to her clothes, her breathing slowed, her actions deliberate and composed, and Karel watches uneasily and wonders what is expected of him. He notes the splotched bloom of flushed skin above her breasts, but then she pulls the camisole over her head and slips into the sleeves of her blouse, her eyes downcast. When she reaches for her boots, Karel is almost surprised to find himself naked, still seated on the blanketed hay. Outside, the light rain announces yet its muted arrival on the rooftop, the horses still clop the hard dirt of their stalls in their animated sleep, and while, excepting the animals and the night and whatever god is attendant upon these shadows, Karel is still alone with this girl, he can't help but think, as he rises from the hay and pulls on his trousers, that this is not the same stable, not the same town, not the same world in which he'd found himself just a dozen short minutes before.

When they are both dressed, Graciela unhasps the nearest stall door and walks Whiskey out beneath the lamp and crossties him there, running her little hands flat against his rippling shoulders, smoothing the roan hide as the horse nudges sleepily at her with his great head and nibbles gently at her hair with his lips. Karel takes the hint and pulls the bridle from a crossbeam hung with tack, and while he coaxes the bit into Whiskey's mouth, Graciela fetches the blanket and places it over the horse as naturally as she had placed

Karel onto it. And then there is the saddle, the bellyband, the cinch straps, all of it worked silently into place and secured with a wordless cooperation that triggers in Karel's imagination a sunlit day in which they might work together in just this way – he out in the fields, manning the planter behind two good horses, spinning the tacky wisps of cottonseed into the earth, she out beyond the stables, hanging laundry on the line, their billowing bedsheets snapping in the wind. And later, with full bellies and the sun pressing itself into the horizon out west, he'd come up behind her and cup his hands on her hips, nuzzle her hair and breathe the smell of her into his lungs. He'd untie her apron and lift it over her head, leading her to the table where he'd sit her down and put a cup of coffee steaming into her hands so that she could rest awhile, enjoying the sounds of calling quail and mourning doves while he finished the dishes. They wouldn't have to say a word, and then, just before full dark, they could walk out into the yard behind the grove and pull the laundry from the line, and they could make the bed and snuff the candles and weave their legs together there between cool sheets that smelled of the floral spring breeze and the clean, broken earth. And then, if they needed the sound of voices more than the sweet give-and-take of bodies, they could talk.

When the horse stands ready for riding, Karel surprises himself as much with the sound of his voice as with the dream he's suddenly willing to share. "Good horses like these, we could be across the county line by sunrise."

She smiles without showing her teeth, finds his eyes with her own. Stroking the long neck of the horse, she wets her upper lip with her tongue. "Which one?" she asks. "Which county?"

"Whichever one you fancy."

"Karel," she says, and the serious, almost instructive turn of her voice muddies his fantasy the way his hand reached into shallow creekwater has so often obscured his own reflection. "I fancy this one. And so does my father. And your father."

"I'm not so attached just now to what Pop wants."

"And still you'll fight your brothers with him?"

Karel feels the cool trail of fluid seeping from his eye down his cheek, and when he wipes it with his sleeve, it sets to stinging again. Only minutes before, she would have done this for him, but she's not touching him now, not reaching for his neck or brushing his face with her lips. Instead, her hands are on the horse, and Whiskey is saddled and ready to ride, switching his tail idly, his great, oily eyes glinting in the low light. "Believe that if it suits you, but to me it felt like fighting for you just as much as fighting with him."

Now she pulls her hands from the horse and reaches forward, buttons Karel's coat for him, every gesture a nudge that seems bent on getting him out of the stable and into the night without her. "You can't fight them for me," she says. "You'd have to fight my father, and you wouldn't win. No one ever has."

"Excepting your mother," Karel says. "If she could get free of him, you could, too."

"He didn't go looking for her. Not the last time. Her going was his doing."

Then, with rain coming down on the shingles above, she tells him about a storm that had moved through the mountains of her father's ranch in Guanajuato when she was twelve, of high winds that had taken down trees, one of which had fallen onto the fencing of her father's corral of unbroken horses. "They ran off into the storm, and by morning they weren't visible even from the southern ridgeline. My sisters liked the comfort of the parlor, liked sitting with my mother and drinking tea and practicing their needlework, but I always preferred to be outside, to be on horseback, to be with my father, and so he came into the house where I was taking my breakfast and asked if I wanted to go with him. Told me to bring a bedroll of blankets and a change of clothes, told my mother we'd be no longer than a day and a half, and by noon we were riding in the mountains with four of his men and four pack horses loaded with provisions and rope. Over the first rise of mountains, my father stopped and chewed on his cigar and dismounted, toed a pile of manure and smiled. He winked at me and pointed out toward the next rise of ridges three hours' ride away. 'Can you smell it?' he asked me. 'The river? The green meadow up the far side of the canyon?' I told him I couldn't. It was twenty-five kilometers off at least. He laughed, the same laugh he always had when we were children, and he would try to balance all three of us on his lap at night before Mother sent us off to bed. 'I can't either,' he said. 'But the horses can. They'll have found it, to be certain.'

"Later that day, when we came over that rise, there they were, grazing in the thick grass along the river that cut through the canyon. Father smiled, sent his men down to round them up, and then he built a fire and I cooked us lunch there in the mountains. We watched while, until nightfall, the men did their work. The next morning, we rode back to the ranch with all but one of the lost horses tied and trailing behind us."

Karel smiles. "Well, then there was one what got away."

She shakes her head. "No. The one had been snakebit. Father shot it."

"It don't make much sense," Karel says. "Riding all day after some horses and not going after your own wife when she runs off."

Graciela strokes the horse and frowns, her eyes downcast and dancing with little filaments of lamplight. "She didn't run, Karel. She never ran. She took up with another man, another rancher. The war was coming, and he promised he'd take her back to Spain so she could be with her family. Father's men found them at an inn together. Father would have forgiven her, I know he would have, but it wasn't the first time she'd gone. There was something in her that needed to live only for herself, to do what her body told her to do. She'd disappear for a day, for a week, and Father would sit nights in his chair, smoking his cigars, and then we'd wake one morning and there'd be three horses missing from the stables, three saddles from the tack room, and when my father's men rode back over the ridgeline, she'd be riding behind them with the feathers of her hat waving at us in the breeze and a smile on her lips. She was no one man's woman, but when the skirmishes started and Father began to speak of moving east, she told my sisters and me that we should go only if we wanted, that we should go only where and when we wanted, that women were only beholden to men if they chose to be. And of course I told Father. He had always stayed with us, had never gone away only to be brought home by men sent to fetch him. I never once thought of leaving him. He never leaves, and he shouldn't be left. He never forgets, and he didn't forget any of the men my mother had been with, either. One morning the horses were gone again, and so was Mother, and so were the saddles. And then the men came back without her, blood on their boots, the receipt from the depot in one of their pockets. They'd put her on a train to Mexico City. Father fashioned a cross from saplings, a tiny thing, just twigs tied together, really, and he planted it on the ridge before we left. He said you didn't always need a body to have a funeral."

Whiskey stands fully alert now, ready to ride, sighing and tossing his head and lifting a hoof repeatedly, dropping it to the hard earthen floor as if to punctuate these hints to his rider. Karel puts a hand on the horse's neck to settle him, and then he looks this beautiful young woman over slowly, from the gentle swells of her calves and the slight rounds of her hips up to her hair, still damp and so dark. Her eyes shine wide, unabashed. Unapologetic. She has some of her mother in her, and she's proud of it, that much is clear. "If your father's so good to you, he would give you what you want."

"I haven't decided what I want," she says. "Not beyond tonight, at least. Until I do, I'd do well simply to take what he offers me." And then she does touch him, but not in the way he wants. She cups a hand firmly on his bent neck, pressing her lips together either in sympathy for his history of harness and plow or for his wounded eye and mouth or to keep some other, gentler words inside. Karel can't tell which. When she turns loose of him, she exhales, the hint of a smile pinching together at the pink corners of her lips. "I've told you about my mother," she says. "Wouldn't you like to tell me about yours?"

Karel turns from her, takes his wet coat from the hay bale behind him and shrugs it on. The cold weight of the thing sets him to shivering. He wraps the horse's reins around one hand and leads the animal to the door. Graciela doesn't follow. He opens the door and the hard, clean sound of rainfall makes it so that he has to raise his voice to be certain she hears him. "You already know all about her. She was just like you. I was inside her, and then she was gone."

ON THE FARM-TO-MARKET road, just across the old plank bridge spanning the southern fork of the creek, Karel nudges the horse into a trot while the rain streams down through his hair and cools the torn corner of his mouth and the swollen wound of his eye. Even in the darkness, it seems to him a strange limitation of sensation to have no peripheral vision on his right side, to see through a single eye into a world that had been reduced to near opacity by the cloud cover and the feebleness of the moon and by the girl's quick dismissal of all his fantastic hopes. The horse whinnies when Karel gives it another heel, moving between the outstretched barbed wire on either side, past the southernmost reaches of his father's land and the occasional squat clusters of scrub and mesquite this side of the fencelines. As the horse's hooves splash down, cantering in the puddled road, it comes clear to him of a sudden that the scant light of the night is narrowing into his good eye with the same concentrated reduction as the hot liquid of his resentment funneling down through his ribcage and into the hardening core of his heart. What kind of woman, he wonders, would give herself to a man only to send him away so that she can get her sleep and marry his brother the next day? What kind of woman brings a boy into the world only to leave him there without the warmth of her bosom or the swirling softness of her skirts or the caressing comforts of her hands and lips and gentle words given voice to rid a boy of the fears that find him wide-eyed and alone in the night?

Loud enough that it reaches him through the rain, the call of a horned owl, low and triadic and hollow sounding in its own solemnity, filters into his thoughts and makes room therein for the sorrow that has so often afflicted him. It is nameless and old, something that has preceded him, that came before his father and mother both, something tireless and bodiless and indifferent to the interminable aching it occasions, and when it sinks into him, Karel feels the stinging salt of his own tears burning within the engorged lids of his throbbing eye, and he lets himself go limp in the knees and jostle there in the saddle while the horse moves on heavily into the night and farther from the rushing creekwater behind them. The owl doesn't call again, though Karel listens in anticipation, waiting for something familiar to make itself known in the darkness. Which it does, but only in the way that wholesome and straightforward prayers are so often met with perverted answers. Out before him on the road, maybe seventy yards ahead, there is laughter and hooting, the clamor of the happily delirious or the drunken, and Karel recognizes the voices at once — his brothers coming to town, leaving the deep furrows and sharp words and burst blisters and leather harnesswork of their father's farm behind them in the wide wake of their elation.

Karel leans over Whiskey's neck, whispering behind the animal's ears, which have come forward at the unfamiliar sounds of men's voices pitched high with joy. "Whoa now," Karel whispers, bringing the horse up short, sitting still in the wet saddle so it doesn't creak, cupping a hand over his good eye and scanning the road ahead to find the pinprick of yellow light swinging toward him, the lantern's flame casting a cold, misty halo in the rain. He angles the reins and presses a knee into the horse's side, coaxing the animal off the road and against the easternmost fence. He slips his boots from the stirrups and lets his legs dangle there against the reassuring warmth of the animal's hide.

When his brothers get near enough to notice him, they quit their laughing, and Stan holds the lantern up in one hand while Thom and Eduard square their shoulders above their hips and clutch the canvas handles of their duffels in front of them with both hands. Thom is smiling despite the blood-encrusted gash on his cheekbone and the gruesome teeth slanted back in his mouth. He cocks the dripping brim of his straw hat back on his head to get a better look at Karel sitting above him on the horse. "Been nursing your wounds at the icehouse, little brother?" he says.

Stan looks down at his boots, shifting his weight from one foot to the other. In the faint light, he appears unmarked by the fight and henlike in his reluctance for any further scuffling. "It ain't too late yet," Eduard says. "Turn that animal round and come tilt one back with us."

Thom clears his sinuses and spits, unable to conceal either the pain in his mouth or the disdain for his brother's peacemaking. He lowers his hat back over his eyes and shoots a look at Eduard, who only shrugs and looks toward Stan for support. When the eldest nods, Thom sniffs the air as if gauging it for some foul remnant of the evening's ill will, and then he slings his duffel over his shoulder and hitches the thumb of his free hand in his pocket. "Hell then," he says. "Why not?"

And here is the moment Karel will recall so often without recounting it once even to the likes of his future wife, the slow seconds of his consideration and the unexpected, fleeting blossom of appreciation that unfolds soft and sweet and delicate within the parched cavity of his chest, the cool drizzling of rain on his hatless head and the expectant eyes of his two braver brothers, the twitching of horsehide beneath him and the weight of his waterlogged boots dangling down beneath the stirrups. The cold. Overhead, a thick quiltwork of clouds gathers and bunches until, pulled forth by the wind, it flattens out as if by feminine hands pressed into its airy batting to smooth it over a mattress. The horse stamps and blows, tossing his head gently against the slackened reins, and before Karel even considers the choice laid out before him, there rises within him a remembered scent of the girl's hair, a recollection of that tightening at the base of his spine that had uncoiled at once and so wonderfully beneath the wet weight of her in his lap. And then he's seeing his brother touching her, their fingers grazing as they pull the sheets from the laundry line, their legs threaded together in bed, the images stamped out as if by some loud machine fueled by envy alone. He sees the girl riding horseback, waving to Thom across their fields. He imagines his mother, round bellied and smiling, her arms full as she tries to balance all three of his brothers on her diminished lap.

Then, what has only just bloomed within him curls brittle and brown at the edges, and he believes now, in the slow seconds of understanding, ephemeral as they ever are, that what lies behind a man in the expanding landscape of his past can never be left behind entirely, that even the blazing, cotton-flecked fields of the summer can't sweat from him the hard, fallow crust of so many winters. He can almost put it into words, but it's fleet and then it's gone, and all that's left is the caustic certainty that there's no moving forward unbridled, that the weather-checked harness will never give, that the weight of all that is dragging behind will know no abatement.

"I ain't thirsty," he says, lifting his feet back into the stirrups. "I been sucking your girl's teats till I can't stomach another drop."

Stan flinches and then looks down again, resuming his studious consideration of his boots. Eduard smiles and shakes his head, his eyes glinting with disbelieving appreciation of his kid brother's gall. Thom gives them both a look, lets his duffel splash to the ground. "I never heard such a steaming pile of horseshit," he says.

Karel stands in the stirrups and locks his knees so that he looms high above his brothers when he spits in the road without taking his eyes off Thom's. "That's the thing about shit," he says. "It ain't something you can hear, but once someone's stepped in it there's no doubting the stink. Give her a sniff, big brother, and you'll know yours ain't the first toes she's squished up between."

When he lowers himself back into the saddle and puts a heel to the horse, he does it harder than he needs to, and when he hears behind him the sound of his brother's voice beneath the splashing of hooves and the drizzling of rain, what he makes out is the anger and weight of it but not the words. A swirl of nausea sloshes around sour in his gut, and when he notes the ache in his jaw, he realizes he's grinding his teeth. The horse is running hard, the cold rain needling them, the speed whipping Whiskey's mane back into Karel's face. Still, it's not fast enough, and Karel kicks the horse again.

HE SLEEPS PAST dawn and wakes to find hay pasted with dried blood to his mouth, his eye throbbing and his toes clammy and cramped from the night spent wet in his boots. Up in the loft, he sits forward atop the hay upon which he's slept so soundly and listens to the rain and the pained animal sounds below. When he'd gotten home, dismounting at the cattlegate with his stomach turned by a hunger that he had no means to feed and a rising regret of the hasty words he now couldn't unsay, he'd walked the horse the last quarter mile across the brittle stalks of cut hay and found the downstairs windows flickering with the irregular light of the oil lamp. He'd had enough by way of family talk for one night, so he'd come quietly around the outermost fringe of the pear grove to the stable, where he'd lit a single, short-wicked lantern so that he could see his work while he removed Whiskey's saddle and the heavy, rain-soaked blanket and then dried and curried the horse and bolted him into his stable beside that of his seedless sire. Then he'd climbed the ladder and pulled his arms from the wet sleeves of his coat and burrowed himself into the piles of hay straws on the floor.

Now he's come awake all at once from his short, dreamless sleep, and when he plucks the hay from the corner of his mouth, it tears the scab and he finds, even before breakfast, the jolting taste of his own blood on his tongue. His legs have gone stiff, as if his bones have been sunk into mud that's been left to dry overnight, and he works his toes around in the swampy wool of his socks while his head clears and his father's voice rises amid the echo of rainfall on the shingles above and Whiskey's distressed complaints down below.

By the time he gets to his feet and makes his way down the ladder, his father is standing with his steaming knife in one hand and the testicles of the gelded horse dripping blood from the other down into the hay. The horse is thrashing its head about, stamping with two hooves in unison against the ropes crosstied from the load-bearing beams. Just emerged from sleep, Karel has to steady his one good eye on the gore in his father's hand before it registers — the cleft between the two testicles pinching a seam into the horsehide such that it appears as if two heavy peaches have been dropped down into a soft brown cinch-purse made of leather with the hair left on it. On the workbench, just this side of the nearest stall, there's a cup of coffee and an uncorked jug of mash, and when Karel looks up to find his father's eyes on him, shot through with a fine lacework of blood and slowly blinking and glazed over from a lack of sleep or from drink or both, the man just stands there, his back molars grinding tobacco and his bottom lip stained brown from the juice.

"A man ain't no better than his goddamn word, boy. And it don't matter if he gives it to a man or an animal or only to himself. Now sew him closed and put some salve on it. He's a plow horse now, and his day's just getting started."

An hour later, after stripping down to his drawers and scouring himself with a brush dipped in a pail of soapy cold well water, Karel changes his clothes and swabs iodine onto the cut at the hinge of his lips. He sets his boots beside the stove to dry, then he soaks a rag in water, puts it atop the half-melted block in the icebox. He fries four eggs and eats them with a cold biscuit and a cup of coffee. When he finishes, he washes the plate and cup and places them on the drain board beside the sink, peels the rag from the block of ice, and sits at the kitchen table with the ice-crusted thing held against his swollen eye. By the time he gets his boots back on and fetches a hat and heads out through the kitchen door onto the back porch, the morning has darkened further and still the rain is coming down steady and gray onto the distant silhouette of his father, who has gotten the two horses braced to the plow and is trudging through the slop behind them to work useless muddy furrows into the land out west. Karel glances out toward the cattle huddling together beneath the weather in the near pasture, to the sheets of water falling over the sides of the full cattletank, to the windmill shimmying in the desultory wind, its tail whipping from side to side as the gusts shift, the blades churning out pointless revolutions. In the distance, his father slips and catches himself against the handles of the plow, working out toward the farm-to-market road where, just two days before, Karel and his brothers had been working when the carriage had appeared and Villaseñor set the brake and climbed down; when he had paraded his handsome daughters before the Skala boys while they stood sweating and wind chapped, their boots caked with the soil of their father's acreage; when Graciela had parted her lips, astonished at something unknown to Karel in the distance, and he'd seen the pink, wet tip of her tongue. And now, out along the fenceline, with the sun above incapable of mustering even enough light to throw a respectable shadow, Karel's father snaps his whip at a pair of gelded horses he will work until nightfall. Karel reckons there's no sense in helping a man plow a field that will have to be plowed again when the soil dries anyhow, ducks through the grove and walks out beyond the eastern side of the barn and into the field to the south, his boots already wet again and sucking in the mud when he lifts his feet. He's seen enough of this, more than enough of his father and the animals he works toward his own ends, more than enough rainfall and wind. Still, though Graciela has wrung him dry of pride, he can't say that he's seen enough of her. He can't say for sure that he ever will.

By the time he cracks the side door leading into the narthex of St. Jude's, Karel is wet through once more to his drawers, chilled even deeper than that, and he welcomes the relative warmth of the church and the biting cedar scent of incense hung thick in the air. The narthex is obscured by a long screen that separates this, the narrow realm of catechumens and penitents, from the nave, and Karel eases the door closed behind him and stands listening to the cracked, mismatched voices of the country parishioners who sit singing hymns in anticipation of the nuptials of the town's newest brides. At his feet, dripping rainwater pools, slicking the stone floors, and he removes his hat and runs a hand gingerly over his face to clear his good eye. Before him rise two pillars, flanking the entrance to the nave, and as Karel moves quietly behind the screen to lean against the nearest of them, he struggles to make sense of his own presence here. He's been inside this church so many times, on Sundays and holy days, for the yearly anniversary Mass of his mother's death and for his own boyhood sacraments, but it has felt, on these occasions, like nothing more than an echoing and all-too-orderly indoor auction house, filled only with the improbable hopes of those who sit and kneel within, fashioning of their own desperation a god whose intercessions they rely upon for help amidst all the hardships for which they somehow hold him faultless. Karel's earliest recollection is that of his father's words, the furious, adamant claim that there is always blame, always one upon whom it falls.

When the skin is split, there is ever a whip or a stone or a fist or a knife just as there is always someone behind the lashing or throwing or punching or slashing. Karel's eye throbs and his mouth stings, and when he presses a palm against the smooth, cool stone of the pillar and peers around at the congregation, he finds the chancel glimmering with candles, the altar wreathed in greenery but otherwise empty. Smoke curls in blue ringlets from the censor dangling by its chain against the back wall where, for as long as Karel can remember, overarched by red brick trellised in white mortar, the bloodied Christ has hung suffering.

The singing stops, and there comes the gritty whisk of shoe leather slid restlessly over old stone, the muted knocking of heavy missals returned to the hardwood book racks mounted on the backs of the pews. A few heads turn, and Karel sees that the Daltons are here, as are Lad Dvorak and the Waseks and the Kaspars, maybe two dozen others, all of them seated left of the aisle. On the right-hand side, there is only Edna Janek, her long hair dusted gray by time and the early loss of her husband, her gaze focused on the line of boys she's brought into the world as they emerge now, arranged by age with Stan in front and Thom trailing, from the transept, their best trousers and suitcoats dry and clean but wrinkled, their necks cocked, their faces graced in various parts by smiles and injury. Karel leans back behind the pillar and touches his cheekbone, feels the slightest pressure of his fingers roll through the tender flesh and center itself into a sharp, concentrated point behind the hard sphere of his eye. He grits his teeth and pulls the swollen lid up and holds his breath against the pain, and when he sees the girls and their father emerge with Father Carew from the sacristy into the far side of the narthex, it's as if he is watching them from some submerged vantage point beneath a murky surface of still creekwater.

When he turns loose of his eyelid, his vision narrows again through one eye, and when Father Carew catches sight of him there, shivering and dripping rainwater, the expression on the priest's face is one of confused sympathy, the look of a man who's had his heart wrenched by the incomprehensible sight of a woman crumpled into some mournful posture, undone by tears of joy. The girls are unveiled, their long hair pulled back into braids embellished by tiny dianthus blossoms, their dark skin offset by dresses white and delicate as sunlit dogwood, their calves half-hidden by airy hems of scalloped lace. They are smiling at something their father has whispered to them, their faces blooming with some undisclosed joy and yet still demure and composed, all but absent of the sly pride they'd worn two days before when they'd climbed from the carriage on the farm-to-market road, beckoned by his will and his whistle. But as they near Karel, gathering behind the screen beyond the opposite column, his kneecaps prickle with a chill and the cords of muscle twitch in his warped neck. Father Carew leaves them, glancing at Karel through the corner of his eye while processing down the aisle toward the bridegrooms, but then Graciela turns to whisper something into her tallest sister's ear, and Karel is pierced by the certainty of it—she's wearing a bruise, a dark, upturned crescent fringed with blue beneath her left eye. Karel recalls the sweet pain of her mouth on his eye, and he'd swear his heart has fallen a hitch in his chest, that it's dangling from some fraying wet thread in the cold and constricted insides of him. I ought to be able to return the favor, he thinks, whether she'd want me to or not. When he steps out into plain view, he returns his hat to his head and stands dripping rainwater until Villaseñor catches sight of him and shoulders hurriedly between his girls.

From the nave, the music starts up again, signaling the arrival of the brides, and when the parishioners turn expectantly in their pews, what they see instead of the three virginal girls in white they expect to come in gracefully measured steps down the aisle is Karel Skala in his rain-soaked clothes, his hat on his head in the house of God, standing his ground against the approach of the girls' well-dressed father. And then Villaseñor's men rise from their pews at

235

the front of the church, their hands hung awkwardly at their sides, the thick fingers working in the empty air, unaccustomed as they are to the lack of gunmetal.

Karel glances toward their approach, toward his brothers, who are standing frozen in their lock-kneed anticipation, and then he turns to Villaseñor, who is standing so near him that Karel can smell the clean, smoky warmth of his breath. "Who was it hit her?" Karel asks, nodding over the man's shoulder toward Graciela.

Villaseñor pushes his spectacles up high on the bridge of his nose, clearing his throat and righting his suitcoat on his shoulders by tugging at its hem while he studies this boy before him. When his men reach him, he brings them up short with a single hand held palm down at his side. Inside, the pews are alive with whispers, and Graciela has come to her father's side, her face beautiful despite the bruise, her hair so dark against the feathery white bodice of her dress, her eyes urging him silent with their conspiratorial wideness.

"Who struck you?" Karel asks.

She shakes her head, and her father silences her with a look before stepping toward Karel and issuing him, with a hand behind his shoulder, toward the door and out of the congregants' view. "Come," he says, the promise of satisfied curiosity in the calm, low tone of his voice.

Karel goes with him, his blood pulsing hot in the lid of his damaged eye, and Villaseñor's men follow, affording enough space between themselves and their master for the discreet exchange of confidences. At the door, Karel shrugs the man's hand and plants his feet, stealing glances at the girl, who remains in the aisle between the columns with her groom's eyes and his brother's equally upon her.

"Don't think you can go so easily unnoticed, boy," Villaseñor says. "By day or night, it makes no difference. You've had all of her you're going to have."

Karel's astonishment at such straight talk clots fast into something he can't swallow in the back of his throat, and the nervous resentment of a scolded boy gives rise to an angry trembling in his hands. "But you'll let him have her, sure enough? Marry her off to a man what hits her?"

Villaseñor smiles at such foolishness, pulls his spectacles from his face and produces a pressed white handkerchief from his breast pocket with which to wipe them, though they appear to Karel to be free of even the trace of a smudge or a fleck of dust. "Boy, if he'd struck her he'd be nursing worse wounds than what you and your father have laid on him. He's mostly of a mind that all your talk last night was just that, only talk. I assured him that it was."

"I wouldn't pay a pail of pig shit for what he thinks. I'm asking about her face."

"It's a hard way to go in life without brothers. You'll likely change your mind, and you might see to it that it's not too late when you do."

"It's too late already. You've seen well enough to that. You going to tell me who hit the girl, or do I have to ask her?"

"Your father didn't have to take my wager, boy. It wasn't all my doing."

Karel stuffs his hands into his pockets and runs his tongue over his teeth as if he might taste the bitterness of his words before he speaks them. "You call me boy again, and your men are going to need their guns."

Villaseñor laughs without parting his lips, a half-swallowed dismissal that balls Karel's hands into fists in his pockets. "Well, they aren't far from them if they do. But I've seen you fight, and you don't want to tangle with either one of these two men, much less the both of them. They may have some gray in their whiskers, but there's nothing but black in their hearts. Still, I see your point. You're more man than boy, *Mister* Skala, and I expect you'll act like one. I'll answer your question, and then can I expect you'll take your leave?"

"I ain't much for weddings or church, either one, so I reckon that would suit me fine, long as you don't mean to tell me that she fell in the night or ran into a doorjamb. She's been hit, plain enough."

"Yes. Plainly she has. Plainly. And it was the doing of the only man who has the right to do it. The only man who ever will. Now, if you don't mind, I have a wedding to attend to. I've got my guests to think about."

It takes a slow second to sink in, and when it does, Karel's hands come fast out of his pockets. "You're one rotten son of a bitch," he says. "It ain't no wonder your wife up and left every time some other man came sniffing around."

Villaseñor smoothes his fingers over his sideburns and shakes his head as if considering nothing more personal than the antics of some intractable, half-broke colt. Still Karel notices on the man's face the first suggestion of his vulnerability, an involuntary twitch in the fleshy lower lid of his eye, and while Karel focuses in, trying to discern in the arrhythmic pulsing some predictable pattern, Villaseñor unbuttons his suitcoat and, with an exhalation more akin to a resigned sigh than to the breath of exertion, he doubles the boy over with a solid, grunting blow to the stomach.

Felled and gasping, Karel slumps forward on his knees, his throat soured with the rise of bile, the stinging of sacramental incense ablaze in his vacant lungs. The man is standing before him leisurely, buttoning his coat, fishing the handkerchief from his pocket again and wiping his face while his men wrench Karel's arms behind his back and bring him to his feet such that it feels like his limbs might tear loose of his shoulders at the joints. And then he's swung toward the door, his face turned to protect his injured eye as the men use his body to push open the door, his forehead knocking against the seasoned oak with the same muted thud of the parishioners' missals dropped into the backs of the pews. Outside there's the cold, reviving bite of wind, the splattering of rain in the rutted and puddled road, the helpless fluttering in his chest as he's turned loose with a heave toward the slick descent of the church steps. When he lands, his breath comes back to him all at once, and he takes hold of the railing, righting himself, surveying the torn knee of his trousers and the abraded palm of his hand. There's a compacted, leaden weight in his gut, and he imagines that his heart, dense and still throbbing, has been jolted free of its frayed tether and has splashed sickly into his stomach so that it might be consumed by one of the very organs that it has failed with its frailty.

From just inside the doorway, flanked by his men, Villaseñor throws Karel's crumpled hat to the boy's feet and then stands with his arms at his sides, palms up. Overhead, the clouds roll curdled between the horizons, and Karel can make no more sense of the man's gesture than he could two days ago, though it seems now, as then, neither apology nor promise, neither benign nor threatening. He leans forward beneath the weather to pick up his hat, gestures with it at the man, and then sets the sopping thing on his head. "I'm betting it's a lot more of her mother in her than you care to think," he says. "She gets it in her mind to go, she'll be gone for good."

Villaseñor whispers to his men, tilting his head and looking toward the interior of the church, into which they disperse. Turning back toward Karel, he smooths his lapels and squares his coat again on his shoulders. On his face he wears the impatient disinterest of an undertaker at a late wake. The tick beneath his eye, too, is gone, shed with the mindless, deciduous ease of a single glinting fish scale cast toward the creekbottom by a meandering school. Before he closes the door and the bolt scrapes into its socket, he averts his eyes so that he appears to be looking over Karel's shoulder, speaking to the storm or the Township Inn across the road or some other boy, one he expects might listen. "Boy," he says, "I'd expect you'd have sworn off betting after last night. Besides which, I've heard all the stories, and you don't know any more about my daughter's mother than you do about your own."

THREE HOURS LATER, near on to two o'clock, Karel sits in his still-damp clothes near the blue crackling of the wood-burning stove at the end of the icehouse bar, tracing with his thumb a swath through the cool condensation that has fogged the side of his glass. Excepting him and the new barkeep, the place is empty. Bern Chytka has learned in short order to pull Karel a new pint before the foam of the previous draught slides to the bottom of the otherwise empty glass. And even more to Karel's liking, he's settled into silence and sits behind the bar reading the *Gazette,* keeping a distant vigil over his solitary customer. In the first ten minutes, he'd spoken often enough to keep Karel in his wet coat, to prove himself interested enough in his own reflection to keep the bar polished to a reflective sheen in which he could heed the wet-combed part in his dark hair. A young man who, due either to his pale, willowy physique or his townie temperament or both, Bern has chosen, even before taking a wife, a life spent tending the slurred needs of Dalton's thirsty over the shin-deep frustrations of his family's rice fields out east in El Campo. Karel knows this and more, cares to know none of it, but now there has grown a common comfort in the hot popping of hardwood in the stove and rustling of the newspaper and the bitter cool of pilsner fizzing in his throat. He wonders how it's become so that, at fifteen, he can feel like he's been in the world for an eternity, that he can watch this man behind the bar with the knowing amusement of an old man watching a boy spit between his teeth or stand with a thumb hitched into his trouser pocket, playing at an age the trials of which he can't possibly fathom.

He's far from drunk, but he knows it will only be a matter of time, by damn, so when the swollen door groans open behind him, he shakes his head at the wavering nature of a fate that has rendered him half-orphaned and brotherless only to refuse him a few hours of quiet. He keeps his shoulders hunched forward and his eye on the white rise of bubbles through the amber beer, posturing himself against intrusion, but when Bern says, "Afternoon, there," and the stool next to his scrapes back from the bar, Karel figures it's no use to pretend he's any longer alone. What he doesn't expect, when he turns to bid some rain-idled farmer good afternoon, is to find sitting next to him the quiet, gray-haired woman who'd pulled him into the world.

"Little early for drinking, ain't it?" she says, nodding at his glass.

"No use putting it off," Karel says. "It's late enough somewhere."

Bern has folded his paper and taken hold of his dear bar rag and come with a relieved smile over to a customer he must assume might like to converse. "We don't stock cider, ma'am," he says. "We don't get many women in here. There's some blackberry wine."

She smiles, winking at Karel before she looks up at the new barkeep and extends her hand. "I'm Edna Janek," she says.

"My pleasure. Bern Chytka."

"Well, Bern, if it ain't considered proper for women to drink beer where you come from, then you might just as well start making yourself accustomed to it now."

Bern tucks his rag into the waist of his trousers and his ears flush red beneath his overtended hair. "Where I come from," he says, "it's a woman's privilege to have whatever pleases her."

While Bern pulls her a beer, Edna settles into her seat and works her fingers through the wet tangles of her hair. Karel reckons he's seen her in town or up county a couple times every month of his life without ever, excepting the occasional pleasantries at Sunday Mass, speaking more than a few words to her. She smells, always, airy and clean, faintly of jasmine and talcum, like a woman half her age and still casting her charms in search of a husband, and now, when she takes a sip of her beer and perches her chin in her hand as if she'd been summoned to meet him here but hasn't yet learned the purpose, Karel clears his throat and widens his eyes at her in a resigned invitation.

"That's a considerable shiner you've got there," she says.

"I've considered it some," he says.

She smiles and her eyes soften, little wrinkles pleating the corners of her mouth. "My boys say those heifers your father sold them last spring paid for themselves already."

"Yes, ma'am. Herefords is good enough stock. Breed them with that Angus bull of theirs and they'll have some nice Black Baldies. Stout enough, and less of a handful than most when it comes time to put them through the chute."

"Well, they claim they like them."

Karel nods and takes a pull of his beer. "Don't know why they sold off them longhorns. It was a nice herd their father had."

Edna spins her glass on the bar, and to Karel it seems an orchestrated act, the feigned idle habit of a woman who has none. "Say it takes too long to bring them to weight. And that's true enough, I guess, but it don't take too much thinking to reckon it was hard for them, working their daddy's cows."

"It's hard working any cows," Karel says, and when he finishes his beer, Bern is already setting a new glass down in front of him. Karel nods his thanks, feels the woman's black eyes on him, and the barkeep retreats to his newspaper. "Keeps raining this way, it might could float all the livestock clear out of the county."

She tilts her head such that Karel thinks at first she's paying mind to the rainfall on the roof, but then he realizes that she's mirroring the angle of his own bent neck, that she's doing what she must to level her eyes on his. And then her hand is on him, holding his forearm, a chapped, working woman's hand with the pale-veined traces of her age strung beneath the skin like rivers on some sun-bleached map. She wears, still, her wedding band, and it squeezes a half-size too tight into the flesh of her finger. "I spoke to Father after the wedding, at the reception at the Township. He wanted me to give you his apologies if I came to see you, said it would have been his druthers to have you there, to have all four of you there. And it would have been for me, too. I tended all four of your births, and he baptized the lot of you. It was something lacking without you there."

Karel puts a thumb to the corner of his eye. Almost numb. The beer is doing its work on him, and he suspects that, after so long on this stool, the floor will tilt beneath his feet when finally he stands. He'd rather not be talking, sure enough. He'd rather sit and drink and draw mindless lines in the frost on his glass, run through his remaining money and drink until dusk and then stumble home through the rain and slop to a father who's spent himself aimlessly in the fields and gone early to snore alone in his bed. Still, there is a comfort in Edna's touch, and Karel guesses there hasn't been a time since he was weaned that he's had occasion to have a woman's hands on him two days running. He wishes his sleeves were rolled up.

"Your father at home? He's going to need a lot of help, Karel. Especially now."

"He's home. Plowing water, last I saw him."

She brushes a damp strand of hair from the corner of her mouth. "I wish you'd have seen him when your mother was still alive. Wish you'd seen them together. He wore a smile you couldn't scour from his face with hog bristles. At the parish dances, he wouldn't give her a rest, had her on her feet for every polka and waltz. Even in church, in the pews, he'd have his arm around her shoulders. She was a handsome woman, your mother. All that pretty blond hair. You've seen pictures."

"No, ma'am," Karel says, pushing back his stool. "Not in a long time, I haven't."

A Reaping of Smoke and Water

DECEMBER 1924

THE WIND HAD broken before daylight with an abrupt and violent certainty. Karel had fallen asleep to the labored groans of the weather raking over the rooftop and rattling through the bare branches of the pear trees out back in the grove, and then, an hour before dawn, he'd come upright in bed when, all at once, the world was beset by silence and stood hushed and bright, coddled by moonlight. He rose, his back and neck stiff from all the jostling of the previous day spent in the truck, and he pulled back the quilt and went gingerly over the cold hardwoods, his feet bare and his long drawers sagging at the seat, to peer out the back window toward the stable. He knew before parting the curtains that there would be no vehicle other than his own parked out there in the drive, no trailer, no twins come to make amends for their time away from the farm and the animals they'd promised to tend. He'd been had, of that he was certain, and without the plaintive wind and the high-pitched voices of children, the house had fallen too quiet even for the comfort of a man who breathed always a little easier when left to his lonesome. He'd wasted a day, and there was no telling how much business he'd lost around the county, and now his pursuit of the Knedliks would have to wait. He'd get dressed and make a pot of coffee. Fry some eggs and potatoes. He'd fill his cigarette case and tend to the livestock and wrap a nice, fatty hunk of ham in paper for the widow Vrana, and then he'd go collect his family and bring them home.

If those boys hadn't shown up by then, he'd hunt them down and make them wish to hell they had.

After breakfast, when the topmost arc of the sun neared the treeline on the easternmost fringe of the Skala property, foretelling its return with a faint flourish swept up in pink streaks from the horizon, Karel straightened his back from his work slinging feed to the chickens and turned toward the sound of an approaching motor. By the time Karel dumped the last of the feed and made it back around the barn with the empty pail swinging in his hands, Father Carew was unfolding his tenuous, ancient body from behind the wheel of his Ford. At better than eighty, the priest had a full head of hair, his brows lush, overgrown tangles that, had he found an outdoor occasion to stretch himself onto his back during the previous day's gusts, would have made for his eyes more than adequate windbreaks. In all other ways, he was an old man, one who hunched and shuffled beneath the mass of his own prolonged history, and for the last year or so it had surprised Karel each time he saw him about in town and, upon doing so, realized that the man was, yes, still very much above ground. Karel tossed the empty pail clanging into the barn and tipped his hat. Carew came slack and sliding his feet up the gravel drive, buttoning his coat with palsied hands and meeting Karel's eyes with a mournful tightening of the lips that had in it, to Karel's thinking, both sadness and suspicion.

"Morning, Father. You're about early."

Carew took a handkerchief from his trousers and hacked wetly into it. "Not early enough, it would seem," he said, studying the product of his cough in the handkerchief before folding it back into his pocket and making the sign of the cross. "There's a dead boy on your property, over where the road crosses the creek."

Karel massaged the curvature of his neck with a thumb and narrowed his eyes. "*God bless.* Who is it?"

"I don't recognize him. You ought to get yourself a telephone, Karel."

"A telephone? They making them now so you can call a dead man and ask his name?"

"He's just a boy, Skala. There's a black filly with him. Looks like one of your brother's animals. If you had a phone, Thom might have called you same as he did me. His stable burned last night. His girl is hurt, bad I think. I was on my way out there when I drove up on the horse wandering just this side of your fenceline near the road. The boy's facedown in your creek."

Karel squinted into the glare of dawn, his ribs chilled of a sudden so that it felt to him like his bones had been left to soak overnight in the cistern. He pulled his cigarettes and matches from his coat pocket, offering one to the priest, who shook him off. Striking the match, Karel looked to the north where, faint but unmistakable, dark smoke haloed with white steam hung above the horizon. He took a pull on his cigarette, saw the girl as she'd been all those years back, the dark hair pasted to her chest and the hips slid each in turn from her pants, the little moles up high above her breasts. He exhaled smoke, which rose white and pluming in the aimless winter air. "Which girl?" he asked. "Graciela? His wife?"

The priest sucked on his teeth and shook his head, his eyes creased with curiosity at the corners. "His *little* girl," he said. "The third child, I believe."

The coldness ran out of Karel, and he took another deep drag on his cigarette, his relief rising within him unburdened for a moment before buckling beneath the dense compression of guilt that found him recalling the recent occasion on which he'd seen the girls following their mother outside the mercantile in Shiner, each of the older two in her store-bought gingham and pigtails, the baby perched on the still-alluring swell of her mother's hip. Over the years, when a chance meeting in town with one of his brothers or their wives occasioned it, Karel had taken to crossing the street, keeping his distance, avoiding even the exchange of feigned pleasantries. There had been times, sure enough, when he'd turned the corner and found himself face-to-face with one of them, but last week there had

249

been nothing unavoidable about their meeting. He'd seen her a full block away, and something about the baby perched on Graciela's hip and her girls all decked out in town made it seem to Karel all the more spineless to dodge something so simple as a conversation. Still, when she smiled at him without showing her teeth, a cautious sadness on her lips, something bitter rose in his throat such that, when he removed his hat, he had to swallow when he would have preferred to spit. "Quite a little stable full of fillies you and Thom got there," he said, returning his hat to his head and reaching for his cigarettes.

Now the smile washed from her face altogether. The two older girls stood at her side, each reaching for their mother's free hand, and Graciela worked her fingers such that one could have the pinkie, the other the thumb. Even now, Karel thought, there's not enough of her to go around. "Is it all still about horses with you, Karel? I heard you sold all your best stock years ago."

"Wasn't anything but geldings left to sell," he said. "Anyway, horse farming didn't suit me. Ain't nothing ever come out of a stable but disappointment."

She nodded while he lit his cigarette, and Karel could see in the dark widening of her eyes that it was a nod of understanding, not agreement. "Well," she said, "it's easy to expect too much, I suppose, out of any animal."

"Expect much of anything with some and it's likely to be too much."

"Too much for the animal, Karel? Or for the one with all the expectations?"

Before she'd guided her children around him and walked down the street, she'd watched him furrow his brow, and she'd laughed with such kindness that he'd wanted to laugh with her. It had been so long, so damned long ago. All of it. And still he couldn't bring himself to cheapen it with a smile.

Even now, when Father Carew spoke of her family, he saw her. Not Thom. Not her father. Not the children. He saw her, felt her long hair falling over him. He couldn't help himself, and then he remembered the nameless boy he'd seen out hunting, working downwind with his nameless father in that pasture up north of Shiner. He saw his own son, just hours in the world, sleeping and sucking quietly at the memory of his mother's breast. "Jesus," he said.

The priest frowned. "Yes. May He help us. I need to go. There could be need of a sacrament. Can you tend to the horse and the body?"

"Better than they can tend to each other, I expect. Tell Thom I'll be there in an hour. I show up unannounced, it's liable to surprise him more than a stable fire. I was heading up to fetch Sophie and the kids in Praha. I'll stop in on the way."

HE FOUND THE filly nibbling at the fringe of yellow grass along the farm-to-market road just north of the creek's southern fork. Karel set the brake and left the truck idling in the drive while he fetched the rope and harness from the bed and cleared his throat, spitting into the earth that he owned outright. The sun was up in full now, its proud rays striking brightly against the gravel of the drive Karel had so improved since the farm fell entirely to him, and the horse looked up and whinnied when it took note of his arrival, her slender head bobbing in little, anticipatory nods. From her nostrils came punctuated bursts of steam. Karel held a cigarette between his lips, the smoke coming up thin and curling like that which routinely rose from the snuffed altar candles of St. Jude's after Mass. Karel buttoned his coat, left the door of the truck open. He slid his boots as he made his way to open the gate, comforted, as he always was, by the feel and sound of gravel crunching underfoot. With the passing of the previous day's wind had come a distillation of the county's cold-weather fragrances, the sweetness of burning oak from wood-stoves given edge by the mesquite of the smokehouses, all of it over-laid by the cool black newness of the awaiting soil, the sappy hints of sweet gum and pine.

After swinging open the gate, Karel surveyed the horse. She was a flawless, glossy black except for her blaze and socks, and there was no mistaking her owner. She worked her jaw cross-hinged against a mouthful of winter grass, and Karel's eyes followed a trail of bent, blood-painted weeds down to the sick sprawl of the body in the slough on the soft bank where water trickled and gurgled timeless secrets intelligible to the creekbed stones alone. He let the cigarette drop from his mouth and steadied the animal with a hand smoothed down her neck, whispering to her as he did. "Who the hell was it brought you here, girl?"

She snorted as if in answer, and Karel coaxed her into the harness and roped her up short to the corner fencepost. It was an inconsiderate job of horse-tying, a lead too stingy to allow for easy grazing, a half-assed knot, and Karel knew that, had he found her this way, he'd have thought the job done by some prideless, townie fool, by a man who meant to return either directly or never, and who, either way, couldn't be bothered to feel the same way Karel usually did about the importance of doing even the simple, workaday things right.

Down at the water's edge, squirrels were at work in the high branches of the pine and water oak, and when Karel approached the body, a pair of mourning doves launched themselves loudly up and across the creek, flashing the white fringes of their wings in the sunlight as they went. One of the dead boy's legs called to mind a thick and dangling storm-sheared bough. It was broken through such that the trousers creased unnaturally, folding over on themselves at mid-shin, the calf and muddy boot hanging at a tortured angle as if by only the fabric of the pant leg itself. The boy's face was in the creek, the shoulders of his coat darkened with water. It made Karel's stomach sour just to look at it, and he squatted down, picked up a fallen twig and, perching himself on his boot heels, drew a row of imperfect little circles in the wet silt as he considered whether to drag the body or carry it. It was one of the Knedliks, sure enough. From the looks of the broken leg, it was held together by muscle and skin alone, so Karel guessed he'd best lug the boy from under the arms or lift him like some sleeping, overgrown child from bed.

Either way, he'd have to get him out of the water and turn him over. There'd either be a scar on the boy's face or there wouldn't be, and Karel figured he'd know soon enough how at least half of their story had ended. Karel came back to his feet with the groan of a much older man, and when he bent over the boy, flipping his coat-tail up to find that, thankfully, the little son of a bitch at least had the common courtesy to be wearing a belt, he took hold of the leather. The boy wasn't much heavier than a week-old bull calf, and Karel pulled him up through the mud and into the weeds before flipping him onto his back with a grunt.

It was the quiet one, Joe, and Karel stared down at the boy, who stared blindly into the brightening sky. His lips were the chapped, peeling blue of a molting water snake, lips that Karel realized now he'd never heard utter a word, and something about this new certainty prompted Karel to turn, surveying the pastureland behind him for any sign of the boy's brother. Recalling the way the twins had stood together in the moonlight, their loose-jointed confidence and the easy allegiance of those who'd known each other even before they'd drawn breath in the world, Karel couldn't imagine one wandering too far from the other's sight. It would have taken something violent and unforeseen to wreck a leg that way, something even more so to allow for the dislocation of these brothers one from the other. Out two hundred yards to the north, just this side of the nearest hedgerow, a dozen head of Karel's herd stood grazing around two broken bales, switching their tails and paying no heed whatsoever to the mindless, maternal circling of the jackass. Far behind them, smoke churned in the sky like storm clouds. If Raymond was yet around, he was well hidden, but Karel reckoned it was unlikely. He'd heard stories about twins, about the twinge of fear or pain that might vex one if the other, no matter the distance between them, had stumbled into some trouble.

Karel looked into the hard sunlight until his eyes watered, and then he shut them tight and thought of his own brother. He was but a handful of miles away, and his stable had caught fire in the night. If Carew had the story straight, if one of the children was bad off, Thom might be grieving the loss of more than the lumber and tack of his horsebarn. Karel kept his eyes closed and thought hard on it, but he didn't feel a thing. They weren't twins. Hell, they weren't hardly anymore even brothers. Only one of them had ever known his mother; only one had suckled a stranger.

Karel turned and opened his eyes, looking the dead boy over and shaking his head. He leaned over the body, reached down and shut the boy's eyes one at a time with his thumb, the slick, clammy skin of the eyelids no more human to the touch than would be two wilted, frostbitten leaves. He wouldn't drag him to the truck. The boy may have been a thief. He may have been worse. Surely, now, he wasn't any damned thing at all, but it hadn't been even three full days since they'd sat together in Praha, listening to the same waltzes and polkas, licking beer froth from their upper lips and tapping their feet in time to the music. If Karel had found the boys yesterday, he might have broken their legs himself, but by his reckoning you couldn't give the dead any more of what they deserved than they'd already gotten.

He planted his feet and kept his back straight as he squatted beside the body, sliding his arms beneath the thighs and shoulders, and when he came upright beneath the young man's weight, the broken leg swung down with a sick grinding of bone and the boy's boot heel spurred sharply against the side of Karel's knee. "You little shit," Karel said, catching his breath. "All of a sudden you got to have the last goddamn word, do you?" His eyes had come full with tears, and while he waited for his vision to clear, he bent his knees such that the boy was very nearly lying in his lap. He looked him over, noticing now what he had missed before: The blue lips were upturned faintly at the corners. Not a smile so much as the promise of one. "Go on ahead, but you start laughing and you can walk your own dead ass to the truck, you hear me?"

He frowned at his own foolishness, at the fact that he was talking to a dead man, making play threats to the only kind of person who can no longer fathom fear. And then something cracked wide inside him like some parched fissure that opened deep into the baked earth during drought season. His eyes had cleared, the pain in his knee just a twinge of memory, but now he was seeing his father, the blood dark at the corner of his mouth, his body sucking into the mud of the land he'd tried the whole of his adult life to work toward his own ends, his tobacco-stained lips whispering to his one remaining son, the one to whom the land would fall now that he had fallen, the son he couldn't lose because he'd never quite had him to begin with.

Karel looked down at Joe's body in his arms, bore its weight over the very same land where his father had fallen, and when he got to the truck, he lowered the dead boy carefully into the bed. He drove the body to the stable and laid it out on a narrow bed of hay bales against the nearest stall, and then he came back on foot for the horse. It would have saved time to ride the filly bareback up the drive to the homestead, but when Karel untied her and stroked her white blaze, he was still all those years back, staring down at his father, at a man who was talking nonsense, asking, unless the impossible could be done, to be left for dead, and Karel couldn't set himself right for mounting an animal that had so recently carried a dying man toward this parcel of black soil where more than one had found his end on horseback.

ON THE NORTHERN HORIZON, beyond Shiner on the road toward Praha, white steam and black smoke rose together like the slow wind-borne ascension of a ghost and its shadow from behind the distant trees, and Karel kept an eye on it above the treeline as he drove toward his brother's farm with all the lingering, sluggish reticence of a man beholden to a task that promised to increase neither his pride nor his property. In the truck, with lips pressed tightly enough together to flatten the butt of his cigarette, Karel let the ashes drop into his lap and kept his grip fast on the wheel while his mind took only occasional note of the road. In the last ten years, they'd come to him only rarely, these memories of his father, but once they dug into him they were as biting and stubborn as the needle-sharp tip of a mesquite thorn embedded and broken off beneath the skin.

He and his father had fallen, in the gray days after Karel's brothers left, into a restless but silent pattern of parallel work. The rain came on in taunting waves, waning of a morning only to return before the bobwhite cocks began their melodic, eventide beckoning. During the day, rain or no, his father worked the horses to a useless, steaming fatigue before the plow while Karel tended to the other wintertime needs of the farm—mending fences and setting out bales of hay for the livestock; waking early to sling feed and gather eggs; milking the dairy cow and breaking, when it froze overnight, the skin of ice that formed over the surface of the cattletank. In the early afternoon, he'd come inside to find the cold remnants of his father's lunch on the table, and while he ate with his boots on he'd make a mental list of the chores that remained for him. The laundry, which had to be hung from makeshift lines in the hayloft to dry. The seasoned firewood he had to split and stack to dry in the smokehouse for a day or two before it could be piled into the bins beside the house's two stoves. After lunch he'd move through the day with the same halting, nearly imperceptible progress of the enfeebled sun descending through the begrudging mass of clouds toward the murk of the horizon.

When it was all done, before his father stabled the spent horses, Karel would take a dollar or two from the roll of petty cash his father kept stashed in a tobacco pouch at the bottom of the old milk can set just inside the kitchen door. With a link of smoked sausage or a hunk of bread folded around cold ham or bacon in his coat pocket, he'd make out on foot toward the icehouse in town. Since the wedding, his brothers had been kept busy scouting the surrounding county with their father-in-law for farms they could buy out and, Karel imagined, come nightfall, in the warm beds they shared with their wives at the inn, and he took a resigned, if uneasy, comfort in the knowledge that he wouldn't find them about town after dark. At the saloon, he'd sit apart from the other locals and spend his money quietly, pint by pint, hoping that he'd get home to find the stable lantern out, his father's boots outside the door, and his mash jug corked in the kitchen.

More and more, as the rain kept up and the days began to bleed one into another, this would prove a fruitless hope. His father, after working the animals through all the sunlit hours, had taken to drinking whiskey by twilight and riding Whiskey by night, whipping the gelding and running him hard out near the creek in the moonless rainfall, throwing muddy turf, racing the animal against some phantom rival across the flooded black stretch of pasture, around the leafless stand of moss-draped oaks, and back between the drenched clods of ash in the fire pits toward the fenceline where, absent the agitations of tethered horses, the taut barbed wire quivered in the breeze as if charged by some cold electricity generated by unspoken compunction alone.

Now, on the road between the shimmering, sun-struck fencing, Karel shivered in the cab of the truck. He kept the window cracked despite the cold, and cigarette smoke caught the draught and threaded its way out the window in a fine, unwavering line of white. He was going to see his brother, to see Graciela, to find there some charred remnant of stable and family both. There was a dead boy in his own horsebarn, and in the stall where Whiskey had once found relief from his harnesswork, sleeping and breathing heavily, sheltered from the weather, waking only to nuzzle his bucket of dry oats and blink his eyes slowly before returning to sleep — there, now, Graciela's black filly stood, tired and curried, keeping the company of Karel's sad, underused team of draught horses. It was all the truth of the present, but he had let his awareness of it slouch back into the recesses of his mind the way the guilt stricken, in time, fold their sins into the gray creases of their consciousness, into the musty and neglected shadows of all that is not quite forgotten.

As if supplanted by the present, then, comes a night disinterred from those same rarely robbed graves of memory, and in the short drive from his farm to Thom's, Karel considered neither the bright sky nor the red-tailed hawk riding thermals before funneling down toward some promise of prey to the west nor the face of the boy he'd met only once before carrying his corpse. Instead, there is hard, dark night. There is rain, no longer a downpour, but a sheeting of mist that overlays the landscape in a black, lacy haze, that drips from the lantern he holds in his half-numb hand. There is the cattlegate, swung open and sagging earthward on its worn hinges, the sound of some dull and distant locomotion at work beneath the hissing of the weather. Karel stands with his hat pulled down low on his brow, steadying himself with a hip on the fencepost while he unbuttons his trousers and relieves himself after a dollar's worth of drinking, his head muddled with pilsner, his mouth dry despite the rain, his injured eye yet blue beneath the bottom lid but no longer swollen or tender to the touch.

He's come home to find the stable lantern lit, the back door of the house cracked open, his father's jug uncorked beside an all-but-empty jelly jar on the stable workbench. And now his father, he knows, is out here somewhere on the horse he promised would never again race. Refastening his trousers, Karel looks up to find horse and rider emerging from a night unadorned by moonlight, the animal steaming toward him, churning water up in a wild confusion of spray to meet in midair the persistent rainfall. His father is red-faced and beaming and unsteady in the saddle, his hat brim wilted and streaming, one cheek bulging so with tobacco that he appears to have come directly from some visit to the town dentist gone wrong. When he brings the horse up short before the fence and speaks, Karel can't tell if it's his own drunkenness or his father's that thickens the words with such a gauzy slur.

The horse blows, a gluey froth slung from its mouth, before sidestepping, lurching beneath the weight of days and nights both at this crazed man's mercy. Vaclav reins the animal around and sits there in the yellow haze of rain and the halo of the lantern's flame, his labored breath smoking as he digs into his coat pocket for his watch, which he tents with a cupped hand before springing it open. "Holy hell," he shouts, turning the illegible face toward Karel. "I should've run the thing myself, boy. Even at my age, and in the goddamn slop, too, I can outrun your scrawny ass."

There comes, despite the cold, a hot, crawling wash of blood along the skin of Karel's throat, and he tilts his head the easy way, with the curvature of his neck, and opens his parched mouth to the falling rain. He swallows, his fingers clenching and relaxing around the lantern handle, prickling with cold as the feeling returns to them. "It must be some awful cocksure whiskey you're drinking. You couldn't outrace even Stan, and his nuts turn to mush just *thinking* about running a horse full out."

His father comes off the horse so fast that Karel startles, throwing his free hand up to protect his healing eye while the lantern swings from its handle, casting the staggering man's face and the standing water at his feet in oscillations of jaundiced light and shadow. Vaclav spits tobacco juice and swipes the rain from his face, on which furrowed disgust has displaced the wide flush of pride. "Hell, boy, of course I can't. And neither can you. Ain't no outracing a goddamn ghost. But you look flesh and blood enough." Balling the reins in his fist, he thumps his knuckles into Karel's chest and reaches for the lantern. "Go on ahead then and make me a liar. Show me how fast you are. You sure as shit didn't show nobody nothing the other night."

Now, in his truck and less than a half mile from his brother's spread, Karel remembered little about his own ride that night other than that he'd been prideful enough to take his father's bait. There had come an eagerness, too, to feel the animal once more beneath him, to ride him again while his father was drunk enough to have either forgotten or neglected his promise. And while Karel eased up on the truck's throttle, stretching the short drive even farther, he saw himself handing the lantern to his father, surrendering the only light to be found on the quarter section of flooded meadow. In the memory, the rain is constant, coming down in a mist so fine that the individual drops prove indistinguishable one from the others. Karel climbs, as he has so many off-kilter nights, into the saddle while his father's eyes flash in the oily flickering like twin filaments sunk deep in the sockets of some otherwise insensible skull. Vaclav checks his watch, gives his son the signal, and Karel nudges the horse, feeling the trace of extra give in the overworked gelding's joints but coaxing him forward nonetheless, crouching forward and low over the shoulders of an animal that makes clear, with a violent, steaming snort and the rearward slant of its ears, that it has lost all of the will but none of the instinct to run.

After he circles the trees in a night so absent of animal sounds amidst the sheeting rainfall, he slaps the horse with his wet hat on the homebound stretch, then he stands lock-kneed in the stirrups and watches his illuminated father as the horse circles, favoring now its left front leg, in a half-hobbled, elliptical pattern like some scorched and humbled planet coming timidly round its sun.

When they stop, Karel puts his drenched hat back on his head and strokes the long roan slope of Whiskey's neck while Vaclav lurches forward, the lantern swinging erratically and the watch held out. "The hell'd you even mount the horse for if you didn't aim to run it? You ain't even broke four minutes, and I done that twice tonight already. Done it twice each night this week."

Karel takes the watch and holds it close so he can see the second hand spinning in an orbit of its own beneath the timepiece's primary face, and here he realizes the pointlessness of his father's challenge. Swinging from the saddle, he says, "It's no way for me to tell if I did or didn't, so we might as well just say you won and stable the horse. It's something wrong with his leg, anyway."

Vaclav spits and frowns and pushes his hat down low, reaching for the reins. "Horseshit," he says, handing over the lantern. "If I say you didn't, boy, then you didn't. And I don't care if the animal's ground down to stubs, I'll be damned if I ain't going to prove to you just how slow you are. Just wait until I'm set and tell me when."

Once his old man heaves his weight up into the saddle, Karel nods the signal and shields his face against the splattering of mud slung back at him. The horse jolts forward and then falters, and when Vaclav prods him with two heels thrown back at once, Karel stands in the muck and feels the numbness creep back into his hands. It looks shameful, his father spurring the horse this way, with his knees slack and his backside heavy in the saddle, throwing his feet backward like some moving-picture cowboy gaining fast on some moving-picture Indian so that he can pretend to shoot him with his shiny pretend gun. Karel sloshes his boots around in the standing water, and after a few minutes he holds the lantern high with an extended arm, searching the impervious distance for the emergence of the man for whom he feels a cold flash of embarrassment. He checks the watch, shielding it from the rain, and when five minutes have passed, he snaps it shut, drops it back into his pocket and makes off across the pasture toward the circle of oaks from which pain so often comes unforeseen.

It takes him longer than he would have thought to find them. He had expected to come upon his father drunkenly sulking and dismounted, leading a half-lame horse through the standing black water, the bitterness of his disappointment narrowing his eyes, but when Karel makes it all the way out to the stand of trees without a sign of them, he thinks at first his father has outwitted him once again, that the old man has loped the animal out to the far fence-line and ridden around the perimeter of the pasture in the dark until he's made it back to the stable, leaving Karel out here to drip and shiver in the cold and keep time for a race that was never intended to be run in full. He imagines his father grinning while he stables the horse, chuckling while he warms his hands in front of the kitchen stove and splashes mash from a new jug into the makeshift glass of his jelly jar.

Karel trudges through the mud and the drowning brown grass, holding his lantern out so that he feels the weight of the thing in his shoulder as he circles the stand of oaks. Just audible beneath the rainfall, twigs snap and rattle down through the brittle tree branches, landing in the brushwood below. The red eyes and ghostly mask of a mother opossum peer from within a high red oak hollow at the fringe of the treeline. The rain comes down heavier, and his boots suck ankle deep with each step until, when the light finds the twitching muscled haunches of the crippled horse, Karel stops and feels himself sinking beneath his own weight as if the earth itself were consuming him, little by little. Whiskey lies, slick with mud, on his side, working his rear legs periodically in frantic attempts to render himself upright, and Karel can see the front legs twisted and splayed, one of them clearly broken through above the pastern, a swath of disturbed earth trenching out from beyond the reaches of the lantern such that it appears the horse has dragged himself out of the darkness toward the feeble comfort of radiating light. Karel moves with caution around the horse's rear legs, circling the animal until he can squat, sitting on his soaked boot heels, near its head and run a hand over its neck while he peers into the dark where he knows his father must be. The horse exhales with a shudder, its breath coming in labored bursts of steam, the hollow music of the rain striking its hide like that of a wet-skinned drum played only with the fingertips of children. Karel has never thought of his love for the horse, has never thought of what he felt for the animal as love, and even now he isn't sure that's the word he would choose. But it is certainly something akin to affection, something as fluttering and warm as the fine quivering of the horse's musculature now at work beneath its damp hide. The trouble with animals, with caring for beasts, is that, if you do it very long at all, you have to witness the end of something you've seen born. Karel curses under his breath. He thinks of the rifle leaning by the kitchen door, of the long walk through the rain and mud he'll have to take so that, when he returns, he can do so equipped for a loud and necessary and violent kindness.

The horse, absent the heavy breathing, sprawls so quietly, its pain sustained without much of any outward complaint. Karel marvels at it, at the inborn capacity for such silent suffering. He recalls the crucifix behind the altar of St. Jude's. The way Stan had come to his feet all those years back, biting his tongue and crying unvoiced tears after their father had struck him down by the creek. He considers the countless times he's imagined his mother, the length of her hair, the crinkling pleatwork of her skirts, the soft blue consolation of her eyes. He'd never seen any of it, but now he can't check himself, can't help but think that he might very well have heard her voice, that he might have known the sound of her even from within her body, that she might have sung to her unborn while she went about her chores or cried out in those final moments of her labor pains, and that, though he can't recall it or reproduce it, he's been carrying it around inside of him, the memory of it, an actual memory of her, a real memory, for the whole of his life.

Stroking the horse, Karel blinks rainwater and runs his fingers down the smooth hide between Whiskey's eyes. The horse's ears come up in an attentive gesture of recognition, the only absolution an animal is equipped to offer, and then Karel forces himself to shake off these memories and fabrications, these fruitless distractions, and turns his mind to his father, listening for the sound of his need given voice over the racket of the rainfall. With a hand on the horse's neck for balance, he pushes himself back to his feet and moves forward, the lantern held before him, to discover what he knows he must.

WHEN HE REACHED the bare stand of blackjack oaks, Karel steered the truck onto his brother's drive and rattled over the cattle-guard, bouncing in and out of the deep ruts until he got the tires tracked into them and could drive without even a hand on the wheel. A quarter mile up the drive, when he came around the grove, it looked, for all the automobiles and wagons parked in hasty clusters about the property, to be a barn raising or an auction. Past the grove, between the barn and the cattletank, Villaseñor's Packard stood absent its sheen, the black paint chalked over with dust. Behind it, his brothers' new Dodge trucks and Father Carew's Ford. Black smoke climbed skyward, fringed with steam, from the other side of the barn, and a line of Shiner locals Karel recognized from the brewery and the wire works were busy dragging coupled lengths of hose and coiling them onto the back of the new Speedwagon pumper that the town had displayed so proudly at last autumn's Harvest Day parade. Karel set the brake and climbed from the cab, his sinuses ringing with the bite of cold air, with the tang of smoldering wood and fuel and hay, all of it soured with the foul traces of charred meat and singed hide. He pulled a cigarette from his case with his teeth, struck a match, and stood leaning with a hand on the warm hood of his truck while he let the smoke do its work, scanning the townsfolk for his relations and puzzling at the slow, defeated movements of all the men ambling about while, judging from the dense smoke coming up from behind the barn, the stable still burned.

266

When he made it around the grove to the pumper, he glanced into the windows of the house, where the soft silhouettes of women moved about behind the sheer kitchen drapes, drawing them now and again to peer out at the progress of the men or the fire or both. Up on the rear deck of the fire truck, catching his breath, Henry Kaspar stood in the center of a muddy coil of hose. If it hadn't been for his bowed legs, which flared out even when he stood still like he'd spent the whole of his life astride a dairy cow instead of some suitable mare, Karel might not have recognized him. His coat was torn at the collar and black as a coalman's, his hat dusted with ash, his new blue overalls left at home in favor of worn hurricane-cloth trousers and a sweat-stained cotton shirt, his mustache untamed by wax such that it appeared the thing had grown down from his nostrils rather than up from his lip. Karel touched the brim of his hat and held his cigarette in the dry hinge of his lips when he spoke. "Didn't make you for the pumper team, Henry. Looks of that smoke yonder, you're quitting a job when it ain't yet done."

Henry's eyes were shot through with the blood of a man who has seen, of recent, too much smoke and too little of his bedsheets. He stood with his boots encircled by the orderly coils of hose and looked down on Karel from his perch atop the back of the pumper, shaking his head at the gall of a man who'd no doubt close the Bible halfway through an early chapter of Genesis and then presume to tell the first of God's subjects how to better go about their begetting. "It's nothing left to do, Skala. We pumped the property dry in two hours. The well and the cattletank both. You want to lend a hand, you're more than welcome to go piss on the embers, see if that does the trick. Maybe resurrect all them horses while you're at it."

Karel bit down on the butt of his cigarette to keep himself from smiling. By damn if Henry didn't have a little salt to him after all. Karel gave the rising smoke another cursory look and then gave the man an appreciative nod. "They didn't get out? I've heard of horses that's kicked a stall door down just dreaming of fire."

Henry shook his head, reached down to pull more hose onto the coil. "Then they ain't dreamed of a fire what burned this fast," he said. "Looks of it, this one went up quicker than most. The men found a couple fuel cans set just inside the door. It ain't a horse one had time to make it out, but it's more damage inside the house than out. Your brother ain't said a word that I've heard since we got here."

Now Karel let his smoke fall and ground it into the damp soil with the toe of his boot as if trying to extinguish the thought that this bowlegged son of a bitch had brought flickering to life with a simple pair of words: *your brother*. It occurred to Karel that this was the way the whole county must see them, as the family that everyone but they themselves recognized as such, and the thought of being the kind of fool who called for fair weather when green clouds folded up in hail-bearing corrugations on the horizon wicked at him until he felt parched and withered and longing, like a cotton plant wilting in a monthlong drought, for the unabated battering of that which might save him. Henry looped another three yards of hose onto the coil and looked up from his work, his tired eyes weighted with fatigue and softened all the same with concern.

"It's one horse made it out," Karel said. "That's for certain. And a dead man riding it. Father Carew said one of the kids was hurt. House looks like it didn't even get singed."

Groaning as he rose from his labor, Henry squared his hat on his head and then put a hand on his hip and leaned backward, stretching his spine. When he'd come straight again, he shot Karel a curious look and spat between his teeth. "Word has it Thom dropped her trying to hurry down the stairs when he saw the stable was lit. Was afraid they'd take on too much smoke on the sleeping porch, I guess. Anyhow, she ain't woke up yet, last I heard."

"Mercy. So he's inside, then?"

"Came out soon as we ran dry of water. Just stood there and watched it burn for a while with the rest of us, then walked round back to the corral. Eddie and Stan gone with him."

"That a fact? Misery loves company, I reckon."

Henry worked his tongue up behind his lip so that it looked to Karel like the man's mustache had come alive and was readying itself to inch across his face. "I don't," Henry said, returning to his work. "I don't reckon misery loves any damn thing at all."

When Karel had circled around the barn, weaving through the automobiles parked in the drive, he noted his trailer sitting unhitched and grayed by fallen ash. Just months ago, he'd been so proud of the thing, of the smooth welds and the sturdiness of the chassis, of the fine black paint of the frame and the wheel wells, of the fine, straight craftsmanship of the bed's lumber. Now it was nothing more to him than an unsettling series of questions on wheels: How had the damn thing gotten here? Whose truck had towed it onto Thom's property? He couldn't imagine that even Raymond Knedlik would have come rolling onto this spread encumbered by a trailer, and so he must have lost it somewhere along the way. He must have surrendered the thing, knowing it wasn't his to begin with, and a boy like Raymond wouldn't have shrugged that off and let it lay. He'd been outsmarted or outgunned, either one, and he'd come looking to retake what he'd lost. For Karel, the questions promised little other than indigestion and the certain prospect that, buried in the unbroken soil of the truth, some stray seed was likely yielding the determined green sprout of his own culpability.

He cleared his throat and spat, reached for his cigarettes, but then, when the wind stirred the fire and its heat washed over him, stinging his eyes, he thought better of it. There was enough burning here, enough flame and smoke, and he turned his attention to what remained of the stable. The roof had caved, buckling the loft beneath it so that the center joists had sheared, splintered in the middle, and now speared jagged and charred into the inflamed confusion of burning stall timbers at the heart of the fire. In the heap of glowing embers lay black ribbons of metal, warped door runners and tack and hardware, all of them twisted amidst the burning lumber like steely tangles of innards within the scorched remains of some mammoth beast that had fallen prey to its own infernal fate. The remaining fuel spat and sizzled, the smoke climbing and billowing, each outward rush blooming so that, from its center, another could rise. Karel leaned against the cant of his neck, trying to puzzle some whole out of all the smoking pieces, but the wreckage lacked any discernible order. The loft staircase had fallen and lay like a colossal and outstretched and steaming accordion, the former rise and run of the steps now inverted and meaningless and forever unburdened by the prospect of footfalls. Twin leg bones slanted up black from the embers like wet, axed forks of a diseased tree rooted and floundering in a steaming and tannic swampland. The stubborn, improbable loft chute still angled upward as if buttressed by some concession of gravity. Karel squinted against the smoke and squared his shoulders over his feet, the senseless remnants of the stable akin somehow to the way it seemed, when he stood in his own cropfields at dusk, that a horizon he knew to be true tilted nonetheless beneath the weight of the sun.

And then the faintest little breeze spiraled the smoke into a hazy tunnel through which he could see, out back of the stable, sitting hatless on the topmost fence brace of a corral meant to contain horses that were nothing more now than roasted bone and greasy ash, his brother. Stan and Eddie were with him, sure enough, standing with hands gripping the fence like it needed holding up, their attention turned to their brother, and when Thom caught sight of Karel, he slid off the fence and took a step forward as if he meant, with his brows furrowed and his hair swept behind his ears, to walk through the fire.

The wind whipped and then again settled, obscuring the view through the stable, the smoke filling the empty space as readily as water found the void of displaced water, as naturally as regret and fear seeped into the fissures of a man's cracked heart. Karel went again for his cigarettes, and this time he didn't stop himself. If the pumper team couldn't put this fire out, if a cistern and a cattletank full of cold water couldn't douse the flames, then there wasn't any harm, by damn, in lighting a little fire that a man could consume and, in doing so, control. He sparked a match, lit his smoke, tucked his cigarette case back into his coat pocket. Then he made his way around the stable, giving the fire a wide berth, wondering as he went how it had looked before the sun had come up, the orange embers drawn up into the sky, the smoke blooming white against the cold night sky. Karel had seen some impressive fires in his years — grass fires sparked by negligence or heat lightning come the parched months of summer, an explosive dust fire once at the cotton gin in Shiner when he was yet a boy — but this would have been different, the panic-stricken voices of animals and men alike rising above the familiar sound of the fire, that loud rush that could all but convince a man that something unstoppable had been set into motion, roaring its way nearer, bearing down on him. Karel wondered how many fires his boy would see in his life, how many he might watch idly before one burned closer to home. Fire was one of so many things that could render a man helpless, and now, as Karel reached the corral fence and circled around to the gate, his brothers' eyes unblinking and tepid and fixed on him, he reckoned that family was another. A man couldn't any more choose which one he was born into than he could will it to stay together when so many things abraded and raveled the fibers that were meant to keep it bound. Try to hold it all together with force, with a harness and a hard hand the way their father had, and it grew so thick with the cordage of resentment that you couldn't even get your hands around it.

Now, as Karel reached the unbolted gate and swung it open, he watched his brothers, the three of them huddled silently, their boots sunk so deeply into the loose soil of the corral that they appeared to be held upright by their trouser hems alone. Behind them, the fire licked and sizzled, the dark rush of smoke issuing from the ruins of timber and tack to sully the quiet blue skies. When Karel stepped into the corral, leaving the gate wide, he studied the lit tip of his cigarette as if he could find there, in the pale glow of the thing, the words to explain his ready proximity to these men after all these years of measured distance. Eddie took a step his way and put a chapped hand on his shoulder, and Karel looked up to find some of the blue gone out of his brother's eyes, which were faded as if from sunlight or submersion and flecked with gray. Unlike Thom, Eddie and Stan kept their hair cropped short, and when Eddie pulled his hat off in the exaggerated pretense of a greeting, Karel noted the weathered crown of the man's scalp showing pink through his thinning hair. Eddie returned the hat, winking at Stan when he did, and then he took his hand from Karel's shoulder, pulling a pint bottle of clear shine from his coat pocket and bubbling it with a grimace before handing it over. "Tastes a trace like kerosene what someone's made water in, but it makes for a warm enough breakfast."

Karel exhaled smoke through his nose and let his cigarette fall to the hoof-pocked earth below. Before him, the flaming loft chute collapsed at last, roaring blue as it fell and giving rise to a loud rush of sparks that launched skyward in the updraft as if of their own hot volition. He accepted the bottle and took a polite, tentative taste of the concoction, just enough to set him to thinking that, given enough fuel, even a man's insides might take to smoldering. When it came right down to it, there wasn't all that much in life that wasn't flammable.

"Don't know that it's deserving of thanks," he said, handing the bottle over, "but it's worse poison in the world, I suspect."

"Oh, it's plenty worse out there," Eddie said. "World is full up to the brim with worse and running down the sides with worser. Get Thom here to say a word one, and I'll give you another sip."

Karel tried to clear his throat again but came up empty. He turned to Thom, who had leaned back against the corral fence like he'd just finished a hard day of working horses and set his mind now to the idleness of a man who'd earned a few minutes of stillness and quiet spent reclined into the solid, reassuring support that only a good tree or fence could offer. Stan stood unkempt beside him, arching his brows and hitching up his trousers with the frustrated effort of one who believed that even the very pull of the earth was out to reveal him in some shameful way. Thom gave Stan a sidelong glance and frowned, and after he ran a hand over his face and sighed, he pushed himself from the fence and stood upright. "You think you were invisible, little brother? Sitting yesterday in your truck up the road from my saloon?"

"Here," Eddie said, pushing the bottle into Karel's chest. "Deal's a deal."

Karel took another, deeper slug of the foul stuff, keeping his eyes on Thom as he did. "Wasn't trying to hide, if that's what you mean. You looked busy. Didn't see any reason to get between you and your work."

"You ain't seen reason to do much of anything within spitting distance of us since Pop died. Now you come around two days running. Something got you feeling lonely all of a sudden?"

"Carew came by this morning. Said one of your horses was on my land, and a body in my creek. I had to make the trip north to Praha no matter what else. I figured I'd leastwise come by to tell you I had some of your property. That it ain't going anywhere and that the boy who took it from you ain't either."

"Which one was it?"

"What's that?"

"The boy. Which one?"

"The mute one, without the knifework done to his face. If it's one of them that deserves a lungful of water, it's the other one that got it."

"Ain't that the usual way? It's rarely the ones deserving that does the getting."

"I reckon that's right. It hardly ever adds up the way it should." Karel had meant to ask after the child, but there came of a sudden from behind the barn the consumptive coughing of the pumper truck, the burst of the engine's ignition and the increasingly urgent rumbling as the throttle was levered up, all of which gave rise to a loud flushing of doves from the grove. The brothers stood watching, turning their warped necks in concert and squinting as the proud-breasted birds came into view above the barn before angling—their wings tipped sharply down and flashing and stroking beneath a blue sky hazed with smoke, their bodies too heavy to be kept aloft absent this constant effort—in a sharp vector around the rising heat of the fire.

Once, so long ago now that Karel had all but surrendered it to the whitewash of forgetting, he had come first to the breakfast table while his brothers readied themselves for school. He must have been four, no more than five, and his father sat palming his cup of coffee, his face running with sweat so that, even at so young an age, Karel knew the man had been out already at his chores, doing what men do before dawn, milking the cows and moving the cattle, startling the hens from their eggs. On the table, dripping clots onto a doily knit by his mother or her mother, either one, sat a congealed pot of gray oats, an oily slick of butter glazed over the surface. Not a week before, Karel's brothers had taught him the game of spoon, and now, to be sure that the final card didn't catch him empty handed, he'd taken to carrying his supper spoon with him everywhere in the bib pocket of his overalls, proudly washing it after meals that called for its use. When he climbed into his chair, he pulled it from its appointed place and set it beside his bowl. His father, who normally rushed through meals and savored his work the way most men did the opposite, sat for a long while before he dished the breakfast into Karel's bowl. Outside, so loud that Karel mistook the windows for open, the crows had begun their shrill, seasonal bickering over the loose kernels of maize left behind after the recent harvest.

"Ain't no reason for them to be so loud, is it, Pop?"

Vaclav didn't startle. Karel never could remember the man startled, but he turned that morning with a look of some stricken, warmed-over fondness in his bloodshot eyes, with an expression too bare and full of remembrance to have been meant for sharing. He dipped into the oats and scooped a second spoonful into his youngest's bowl. "They don't need a reason," he said, scraping his chair back on the hardwoods so he could pull his pouch of tobacco from his trouser pocket. "It's things aplenty like that, you'll see. It's some women who like the sound of birds raising Cain before even the sun's had enough coffee to top the trees. It ain't no reason for that, either, but that don't make it a bad thing."

Now, after the doves had vanished into the distant treeline to the east, Stan hitched his trousers up again and stepped forward. "Was good of your wife to come, Karel," he said, "so near on the heels of her labor. She's a fine woman. It's nobody with any sense doesn't like her. Good of the Novotny woman to bring her, and to bring the medicine Doc needed from the druggist in Praha."

It was cold out, sure enough, but now Karel realized how flushed he'd become standing sandwiched, as he now felt, between his recollections of the past and the diminishing flames of the stable fire. Still, he had the feeling that he needed to pull his coat more tightly across his chest, button the topmost buttons where the air was finding its way to the hollow of his throat. Fever. That's what it resembled, the feeling of being baked and chilled what all at the same time. A shiver ran in ripples down his sides from his shoulders, and he recalled the other night in the stable, the way Elizka's skin was at once covered with chill bumps and hot against his own. He wanted a cigarette, but his mouth was parched, his tongue so dry, and still he knew his brother was awaiting some acknowledgment of his compliment. He wanted to ask how it was that Stan knew Sophie beyond passing, how it was that any of them might. He wanted to ask them if they'd ever, any of them, seen a calf stone dead and staring dumb eyed at the sky without having put a single hoof to the earth. He wanted to know if any of them could recall their mother ever speaking kindly of blackbirds, but he'd learned well enough that there were questions that revealed too much, that sometimes a question showed only that you knew less than you should. "I hadn't realized she was here. I'd aimed to go fetch her before noontime. Go fetch all of them."

"She saved you a trip, then. She's in the house. The kids, too. It's a good looking boy," Stan said. "The baby, I mean."

Searching his older brother's eyes, Karel found only forthrightness and fatigue, a look too worn down by hard work and early rising to be anything other than earnest. "I appreciate that. We're giving serious thought to keeping him."

Eddie smiled, lifted his bottle in a mock cheer, but before he could put it to his lips, as if in afterthought, he turned to Thom, whose pale eyes glinted in the wet corners where the sunlight found the slightest upwelling of tears. "I think you should," Thom said. "We might all ought to keep what's ours."

Karel nodded, and then he turned with his brothers to watch what was left of the fire consume what was left of the fallen stable. There was some burn left in it, but it would dwindle before nightfall, and then there'd be nothing left but the hard work it would take to raise another horsebarn in its place. For now, the four brothers stood there, shoulder to shoulder, as they had on that cold day so many years ago after putting their father in the waterlogged ground, as they had when the photographer Lad Dvorak had alerted to the occasion fetched his fancy equipment from his carriage and urged them to line up, oldest to youngest, to stand closer — *a little bit closer . . . that's some fine fellows . . . and straighten up now, boys . . . What's with the heads leaned so? . . . You missing your pillows already this morning or . . . Oh, heavens . . . of course . . . I beg your pardon* — until Karel could feel the pressed sleeve of his suitcoat touching Eduard's as they waited for the townie with his unscuffed boots to take the photograph, each of them bristling in his church clothes at the uneasy proximity to what he had surrendered out of pride and now refused, out of the same, to reclaim.

With his arms crossed over his chest, Karel watched the low flames lick up from the embers, shook his head at the waste of it all, at all that good, solid wood reduced to ash, at the blackened, twisted remains of animals shrunken sickly there in the coals. And then his brothers were turning, shifting their attention from the fire, and when he followed their gaze he found the slow approach of men in suitcoats skirting the burning stable, walking in Karel's boot prints as if tracking him across whorish terrain. Villaseñor and his men, the latter pair with their shining rifles held loosely across their thick, squat bodies as if they'd been fastened there at birth and had been worn, over the slow course of years that had grayed their sideburns and slowed their steps, slack as the muscles of their shoulders and wan as the skin slung beneath their eyes. As for their master, he led their procession with his spectacles pushed up high on the bridge of his nose, his face shadowed by his dark hat, his suitcoat buttoned and black and unworried as surface water on a still, moonless night. With the wet plug of a cigar planted in the corner of his mouth, he came forward with the smoothly assured gait of a man who'd seen enough trouble to have convinced himself, long ago, that walking toward it was no more taxing than was walking away.

Eddie corked his bottle, hurrying it into his coat pocket while Stan busied himself tucking his shirttail into his pants, and it was then that Karel saw what he hadn't once considered before, that while his brothers had found a way clear of their father, it had led them to this: to farms purchased for them with another man's wealth, to wives given to them only for walking away from what remained of the family into which they'd been born, to lives and livelihoods beholden to a man no more yielding or forgiving than their father had been. It must have been, Karel realized, for them, like waking, morning after morning, from colorful dreams of manhood to find that they were still, all of them, playing with sticks down in the grassy shadows on the bank of the creek.

When Villaseñor came through the gate and the brothers turned to face him, he unbuttoned his coat while his men settled in behind him, their eyes serious and slow to blink, unlit by the lively mischief Karel had come to expect. Then Villaseñor pulled the cigar from his mouth and held it at his side, his mouth working as if accustoming itself to this flavorless new absence. "How considerate of you to come calling, Karel. There must be so much you'd like to explain to my son-in-law here. That or to Sheriff Munson, one."

Karel stole a look at Thom, whose face registered none of the nervousness that his fingers, moving idly at his side, made plain. "There's a mess of things I'd like to explain that I can't," Karel said. "I told you yesterday, I hired those boys to deliver some barrels and watch after my livestock. Whatever the hell else got into them, or why it did, I can't say."

Villaseñor waved the cigar beneath his nose and nestled it back between his lips. Then he removed his hat and slicked a hand through the silver sheen of his well-oiled hair. Before he took his matches from his coat pocket, one eye narrowed in disgust and he extended his hat toward Thom. "Do you suppose you can manage to hold on to this for a time without dropping it?" he asked.

Now Karel noted Thom's fingers curling into fists but held tight at his sides, saw, as he had the night after the race, when Thom had taken his father's first blow rather than hold his tongue, all the hot life at work beneath his icy expression. "I suppose you might could just as easily put the damn thing back on your gray head, is what I suppose," Thom said, his voice steady and controlled, quiet but honed as if by a whetstone.

Villaseñor smiled and played his tongue against the cigar such that it seemed to bob there like a reprimanding finger. He handed the hat back to one of his men and turned to Karel, then made a show of striking a match and twirling the cigar above the little flame until smoke fell from his nose. "I spoke to the padre," he said. "Seems he found one of my daughter's horses on your parcel of land."

"He did. Found a dead boy on it, too, but I'm sure the horse concerns you more than that."

"Please, Skala. You've been sure of so many falsehoods since we first met that I'd think by now you'd have grown weary of sharing them so readily. Quite the contrary, really. I am interested in the boy, who almost certainly had a hand in this fire, and in the injury to my granddaughter. It's just that I'm more taken by where his brother might be. One dead is one shy of what would satisfy me. I need to know where he is. As you're aware, I don't make it my habit to involve the law in my business, but the fire patrol is not bound to such discretion. They have people to report to, and if the sheriff ever gets his boots on again, he'll want some answers out of you. You'd be well served to answer to me first, and I can assure you that I'll vouch for you when the time comes. I need to know where that other boy might be, where he might have reason to go." Villa-señor pulled his glasses from his face and set to work cleaning them with his handkerchief. When he had them settled back in place, he cocked his head toward his men. "They get restless when too much time passes between serious errands, and I intend to give them a chore to keep them occupied."

"If that's the case, then they oughtn't to be restless for a hell of a long while. Unless they're equipped special to track ghosts. Them boys weren't real talkative, and the one laid out in my stable ain't likely to speak up anytime soon. If there's one left breathing out there somewhere, he's likely putting fast miles between himself and here. Check all the filling stations and the train depots and hunt the little son of a bitch down. That would suit me just fine. He took off owing me money, and I don't cotton to setting fires, but you're likely going to need more than two men to hunt him down."

"Two has always been enough," Villaseñor said, sending his men away with a single hand held out to his side, the fingers working as if he were brushing dust from a coat sleeve. "You don't have to know where to look, Skala. You just have to know *how*."

"Stan and I could go with them," Eddie said. "Lend them a hand."

"I hardly see that you have a hand free, Eduard. Seems to me that bottle you keep glued to your palm leaves you shorthanded enough as it is. You go with Stan. He'll have to run the saloon while Thom tends to his wife and children."

"I been in there since the doctor showed up at sunrise," Thom said. "It ain't nothing for me to do but sit and wait like everyone else. I'd be better off at the saloon. The work will keep my mind off it."

"And just why in Jesus' name would you want to keep your mind off of your family? You dropped the child, Thomàs. You *dropped* her. And now you want to go off and leave Graciela alone with all the worry, is that it? You don't leave men above ground if they can harm you, especially if you've given them cause to do so, but you did. You shot one of them when you didn't have cause, and then you let them go when you should have shot them both. You aren't going anywhere except inside your house. It's bad judgment that has brought you to this, and there's no escaping one's own bad judgment. Come now, inside. The rest of you, too. Tell your wives and children good-bye before you go."

Karel stood perplexed by how quickly his brothers fell in line, at how Eddie caught his eye and gave a dirt clod an aimless kick before following his father-in-law out of the corral gate. Stan went, too, hitching his thumbs in his trouser pockets and studying the black acreage and the distant trees to the east with a kind of round-eyed fascination that plucked a string of envy in Karel's chest. How goddamned simple the whole mess of living would be if you could see a stand of oaks a thousand times without ever quite recognizing it or relying on it. Say a single leaf had curled brown and fallen over-night, carried away by the breeze and then rolled along the ground until some animal trod it into the earth. For Stan, that might change the whole tree, the whole treeline, the whole damned county. For Karel, it would have meant only that something he owned had been lessened, even if he couldn't say how, and he thought now, stand-ing beside his brother while the sharp bones of Thom's jaw worked the cud of this most recent humiliation, that the two of them were made of this same stuff, and that it had come to them through their father's blood.

"Jesus," Karel said, "but he reminds me of Pop."

Thom put a hand on the gate, swung it back and forth on its hinges like he was testing it for need of oil. "How's that?" he asked, his eyes fixed only on this invented work.

"Ain't nothing that ain't someone's fault."

Thom swallowed, let his recognition of the words show only in a short exhalation that bore the muffled, wordless sound of his voice. At their backs, the fire had quieted to a hissing bed of embers and heavy, reluctant smoke, out of which rose only the ruined black remnants of the stable's framework.

From out near the drive, Villaseñor called back to them. "*Now, Thomàs.*"

Thom flinched at the man's voice, and now he shook his head until he broke into a smile so that Karel could see his father's work in his brother's mouth. Opening his mouth wide, Thom ran his tongue over his damaged teeth. "I don't need no more reminder than looking in the mirror," he said. "Tough old son of a bitch, wasn't he? Tell you what, Karel. You'd have burned Pop's stable down, he wouldn't have sent someone else to find you. He'd have come to stomp the shit out of you himself."

"I got it coming, I expect."

Narrowing his eyes at Karel, Thom let a laugh and a sigh out in tandem through his nose. "Not from me you don't. I ain't talking about you, little brother."

"Well, all right, then, but I ain't talking about the fire. It's other things that ain't been squared between us."

"You needing to say penance, Father Carew's right up there in the house. But don't say it for me. A whole lot of years have gone by, Karel. Graciela and me been happy together. If something ain't square, I reckon all you have to do is square it with yourself. If it'll help, though, I'll let you do me a favor. You get wind where that other little bastard twin is, don't tell Guillermo. You come to me with it. It's my little girl up there hurting, not his."

"That'd suit me fine."

"All right, then. I need to go see how my little one's doing. You ain't supposed to have favorites. That's what Graciela's forever telling me. Maybe if I had a boy, things would be different, but Tina puts a burr in my heart that won't turn loose. I was only trying to get her clear of the smoke. Anyway, there's about a hundred women up there at the house. Let's see if one of them will pour you a cup of coffee."

FOR THE WOMEN of Lavaca County, the harshest of whispered judgments was reserved for the wife or daughter, not common in these parts, who might be found sitting idly with her apron off in a kitchen, her own or otherwise, and when Karel left his boots in line with a half-dozen other pairs in the mudroom and followed Thom inside, the rich smells of baking kolaches and creamed ham made his insides brew as audibly as the strong coffee on the stove top. Women were everywhere, their hair pulled back into hasty braids and pasted in little wisps to their flushed cheeks, their satisfaction in their work masked only by the seriousness of the occasion that had brought them to service in their neighbor's house. Thom made his way quickly through all the consolations toward the back of the house, where the stairs creaked beneath his steps as he climbed toward news of his little girl.

Karel heard his wife's voice in the parlor, but before he could go to it, a steaming cup of coffee was being put softly into his cold hands. He nodded his thanks and smiled at the tallest of Villa-señor's girls, who'd grown full in the hips over the years and wore her hair in a single rope that dangled past the small of her back. She turned, shaking her head when Stan came waddling in from the parlor, his lock-kneed steps encumbered by two young boys, one straddled around each leg like they were in training for the pumper team that had just rumbled off the property for its fire-house in Shiner. Cinched around his waist were the dark arms of a girl, his eldest—Could she be ten already? Eleven?—who clung to her father with such a fierce affection that Karel knew at once all he needed to know about his brother's inability to keep his trousers from riding down on him.

"You remember Violeta, surely," Stan said.

Karel took her hand, which was softly padded and dusted with flour. "Morning," he said, nodding.

"And these monkeys here is our meal ticket," said Stan, shaking his legs, one at a time, until the boys turned him loose and fell in a tangled, laughing mass to the floor. "Gonna raise them to do tricks and sell them to the next road show what comes through town."

After Stan kissed his wife's cheek and shooed the kids into the other room, he took his hat from the rack near the door and ran his hand around inside to give it shape. "I gotta git. It's nothing says you can't pay us a visit at our place some Sunday, you know. It's sometimes a barrel of beer and a block of ice that find their way from the saloon into my cattletank."

Karel nodded. "Ain't but one way to teach strays like that a lesson."

"That's a fact," said Stan, and with a wink he ducked through the door and closed it gently behind him.

In the parlor, where the dark curtains had been tied back to let the light in, Karel wished, from his first sight of his wife sitting hip to hip with Elizka Novotny on the sofa, that the room had been left awash in shadows. His newborn son slept wrapped in a blanket in Elizka's lap, her sensible blue dress creased between her knees and riding up on her calves so that Karel had to will his eyes from her white stockings. Father Carew sat opposite them in a plush chair the color of August corn tassels, a cup of coffee cradled by his liver-spotted hands in his bony lap.

Sophie came off the couch slowly, wincing as she rose, and Karel put his cup atop the glowing woodstove and opened his arms to her. He would have liked to close his eyes, to smell the comforting confusion of soap and perspiration that, for these last five years had announced to him, every evening when he came in from the fields, that there had been, in his absence, nothing lacking of cleanliness or order or honest work, either one. But now, with his wife's breath warm against his neck, Karel saw Elizka looking from the child in her arms to his father and back again as if there was some arithmetic, some simple ciphering, that might explain how sweetness could spring from such questionable seed.

"Where are the girls? What was I to think if I'd driven all the way up to Praha to find you run off with all the children?"

"They're fine. They're playing out front. Eddie's girls are looking after them." He felt Sophie smiling against his neck. "Maybe you would have thought you'd finally gotten what you deserved, Karel. But I doubt it. You'd have found me eventually, if you looked hard enough."

"I don't know. I'm not much good at finding what I'm after these days."

"How flattering," Elizka said, coming to her feet, the baby held out and away from her body as if she were carrying a bundle of soiled laundry. Sophie turned to take the child, then stood back begging questions of Karel with her eyes while Elizka bent to shake Carew's hand. "Pardon me, Father, I pray the child will heal, but I've got to get back up to the store before Dad forgets we're running a business instead of a charity. Tell Thom I'll have the druggist send him a bill."

"Of course, my dear. My thanks to your father."

Karel had never accustomed himself to the way a woman's joy and sorrow could sound so much the same when given voice. He'd grown up around boys, in the midst of men, for whom pain was weathered in silence and pleasure announced in exaggerated groans of relief. So when Graciela's voice carried down the staircase, so high-pitched and trembling, he found himself reaching for his son, taking him from his mother's arms in an attempt to protect him from the virulent spread of female grief that he felt certain about to overtake the house. In the kitchen, dropped utensils clanged against the stove and the floor as the women rushed into the parlor, their faces lit with expectation, their damp hands smoothing their flour-dusted aprons until Graciela appeared in the doorway at the foot of the stairs, her father behind her, her weight carried high on the balls of her feet with her heels off the floor. Her hands were at her mouth, her shoulders shaking with release, and then Sophie crossed her arms over her chest and embraced herself, whispering, "Oh, thank *God.*"

"She's awake," Graciela said, her dark, dark eyes brightened by a glaze of tears. "Come see. She's awake!"

Nearing noontime, once he'd pulled the truck off the farm-to-market road and onto his drive, the gravel grinding pleasantly beneath the tires, Karel steered with one hand and arched his back beneath Diane's weight in his lap so that he could work his handkerchief out of his pocket and wipe the window glass with it. "Deenie," he said, blowing into her ear to set her squirming, "it's so many of you kids in here now that you're steaming up the glass so I can't see. You're the oldest, so you're going to have to either ride in the back from now on or hold your breath, one or the other."

The girl cocked her head back to find her father's eyes sad and blinking apologies at her. "I can try," she said, taking a deep breath.

Sophie nudged him with her elbow, cradling the infant in one arm and stroking Evie's hair while the youngest girl slept with her feet up on the seat and her head in her mother's lap. "Don't listen to him, Diane."

"Well that's a fine thing to teach a little girl, Mother. It's a Commandment tells you you're supposed to listen to me, Deenie. You just remember that. Don't you let your mother lead you astray."

Karel gassed the throttle through the creekside lowlands and up the swell, where the road came round the hedgerow and mesquite trees, and against his hip he sensed his wife's body tense in a way that told him that she'd had her fill of his teasing. "You want to talk about being led astray right here and now, Karel, or do you suppose we should wait until the kids are asleep?"

Had it been her words that caused Karel to brake the truck hard, sliding it to a stop on the gravel and reaching out with one arm in an instinctive attempt to keep his family where they belonged beside him instead of letting them fly forward to crumple onto the floor-boards or crash headlong into the window glass, Sophie might have sat silently staring forward for a long moment, willing her heart to slow and then checking on her children, asking were they hurt. She would have known, by his hot-tempered reaction and by the way she could see, in the grainy flexing of the muscles roped between his shoulders and neck, that he was doing something that he only ever did when he was bewildered or when he was readying him-self to tell a lie. She would have known, even if he didn't—and he usually didn't—that his body was asking an impossibility of itself, that it was trying to right the wrongs that had been done to it long before the bones stopped growing and the boy he'd been found himself, at last, in the warped shape of the man he'd become. She would have known that her husband, clutching the wheel so hard that the tendons on the backs of his hands fanned out like the teeth of a hay rake, was working to straighten his neck, and this alone, to her mind, would have settled the issue. Had it been true, she could have begun enduring the weeks of cold nights, sleeping on her side, sliding her hip from beneath the warm weight of his hand, showing him with her body what it meant to be without it. She could have begun punishing him and, in doing so, wrapping her mind, day by day, around the inevitability of their reconciliation.

Instead, she found herself flooded with a cold surge of fear, with a prickling chill in the palms of her hands, her scalp, the bottoms of her feet. Karel was gripping the wheel, testing with some sub-conscious force the inflexibility of his neck, his sight fixed on their homestead. It had proved such a comfort, always, to Sophie—the house and barn, the smokehouse and stable, all of them rising up clean and orderly the way they did against the backdrop of the pear trees, amidst all the straight furrows of the cropfields and the golden stubble of cut, sunlit hay — but now, as Karel sat with his eyes moving over the expanse of it like he'd seen coyotes slipping between hedgerows of recent and was taking stock of his calves, Sophie knew only that he saw something she didn't.

"Son of a bitch," he said, pulling Deenie, who was holding her breath in earnest now, from his lap. Beside Sophie, little Evie had come out of her sleep and sat upright with startled eyes, a thread of saliva strung from the hinge of her lips to her mother's lap.

"Karel," Sophie said. "What on earth is it?"

As he eased off the brake, rolling the truck down a swath of yellowed grass toward the front of the house rather than following the drive down to the outbuildings, he pointed in the direction of the horsebarn. "In all our years together," he said, "how many times is it you've known me to let the stable door ajar while I'm away?"

Inside the house, with the girls planted in the deep, underused cushions of the front sitting room sofa, Karel bolted the front door and made his way to the kitchen where he found his rifle leaning barrel up where it always had against the backdoor molding. He levered a cartridge into the receiver, and something about the crisp metallic acceptance of the brass quieted the blood in his ears so that he was aware of his wife behind him, her son cradled tight against her bosom, her questions coming out in unpunctuated twos and threes. "Damn it, Sophie," he said, turning the doorknob. "You reckon it was Thom's horses set his stable afire? There ain't a question I won't answer once I've had a look out back, and not a one I got time for until then, you understand?"

Outside, while he wove himself into the grove, tuning out the desperate, wintertime scuttling of squirrels overhead, he kept his finger on the trigger. Still, he couldn't help noting the bellowing of his herd in the back pasture. They'd been neglected, and there was the new calf to check over. They'd need hay set out before long. So often, his days were spent cataloging the need for chores while doing others, and he busied himself with this ingrained list-making even while he kept his eyes on the front stable door swung out a good foot from flush. When he reached the edge of the drive, he tried to step lightly on the gravel, hearing still in the solid friction of the stones compressed beneath his weight the inventory of tomorrow's predawn undertakings. Wood for the two stoves. Milk. Eggs. Cattle to move and ash to collect from the smokehouse. By the time he considered that he'd have to find time to ride the filly back over to Thom and Graciela's, he was peering into the stable where the cold slant of hay-dusted light revealed a vacancy that made him wonder, even while he knew it senseless, if all he'd been taught those long hours in the hardwood pews of St. Jude's had been but a portion of the truth. If there was a Holy Ghost, then oughtn't there to be an Unholy one, one that could bring even the undeserving dead upright and walking and altogether alive enough to swing a stable door open with all the ease of an angel rolling a stone from a cave mouth?

Karel widened the door with his boot, the gunstock cool in his hands, and from the stalls came the indifferent breathing and stamping of the animals. Farm boys in Lavaca County were taught to use a gun the same way they were taught to use a hoe or a baler, and there was nothing more shameful, more deserving of ridicule, than some townie boy stalking imaginary game in the outcroppings of oak and sweet gum just off the road to town, the fancy new .20 gauge his father had bought for him held in his hands like he meant to strangle it. For the boys raised by fathers who fired their shotguns to put dove and quail on the wintertime table, who leveled their rifles to take a deer or keep a coyote from taking a calf, guns were tools, used only when there was no better one for the job at hand. When a boy who'd grown accustomed to the sting of weeping blisters and the weight of caked mud on his boots saw the loaded gun leaning against the back door every morning when he went out to milk the cows, he didn't give it any more thought than he gave the milk pails when he found a cottonmouth in his mother's garden.

Which isn't to say that even these boys ever got over the thrill of squeezing the trigger — *You don't never pull it, boy. Pull your little pud, you want to pull something. A trigger you squeeze. Gentle, like this, when you exhale. You want the shot coming out same time as your breath does.* He never did get over it, never altogether cooled to the importance of what he held in his hands, to what it could do when used well, to the little god it made of him while the rest of the looming world — his father's enormous, hairy hands or the hay bales he couldn't yet shoulder alone or the horizon he could never toe with his boot no matter how long he walked toward it — made him feel so very small.

No, when a boy or the man he'd become had cause to take up his gun, he expected to feel the loud kick of it against his shoulder before he put it down. Karel was no different, and neither, he imagined, would be his boy, his Frank, so when he stepped inside the stable, his eyes adjusting to the shadows and to the fact that there was no longer a boy's body laid out where he'd left it on the four bales of hay before the stalls, he became all at once aware of the nervous slicks of sweat under his arms and lowered his rifle with both relief and disappointment.

Neither of which lasted.

When he'd strode half the length of the stable's alley, he sensed the shadows shift overhead, and by the time he planted a foot and swung his gun up toward the loft, the boy had taken to talking.

"He ain't walked off on you. I got him up here with me."

Karel squinted up at the childlike figure of Raymond Knedlik, who sat swinging his legs over the loft, his pistol dangling from a hand resting on the bottommost brace of the loft railing, his dead brother laid out beside him with his head in Raymond's lap.

Karel sighted down his barrel, centering the bead on the boy's chest. "You got a fuel can up there with you, that or a book of matches, it's fixing to be two of you that's done the last of your walking."

The boy tilted his head back slowly so that a trace more of the scant sunlight shone in his pale eyes, which looked to have lost forever the wide aperture of youth, to have seen more than they could have at his age if he'd slept every night with the both of them frozen open. He shook his head slowly, the way Karel's father had when his sons had disappointed him, and the boy's scar flashed bloodless and white when it caught the light. "I ain't come here to burn you out, Skala. I come to pay you what I owe, maybe borrow a horse for half a day. Walked in here an hour ago to see if it's anything worth riding, and look who's waiting for me but my clumsy little brother here. Any of yours like that? Tell them to run and they fall down crying with a leg snapped in half instead?"

"You don't want to be disappointed in brothers, don't tell them what to do. Where's that shiny new truck of yours? Out rolling around on its own looking for my trailer?"

"It's cash in my pocket is what it is. All I could do. Sold it at sunup to some thick-rimmed son of a bitch at the bank. Wouldn't give me but seven cents on the dollar." He tugged at his pocket, snagging a bit of the dead boy's hair when he did and flinching because of it. "Which, some of it's yours. For the bill up at the filling station. And to put this boy here in the ground proper for me. I can't dally, or I'd dig the hole myself."

"You might as well give it all to me. Otherwise it's just a couple of midget Mexicans with rifles going to take it out of your pockets when they're done with you."

Raymond considered this, his eyes registering no more surprise than they might if he heard church bells ringing of a Sunday morning. "They might. But I'll lay two to one they're heading fast to Fort Worth, thinking I'm on the nine o'clock I was on before hopping off when it weren't no one looking. It was half a dozen folks saw me buy the ticket, and just as many what watched me get on the train."

Not fifteen feet from where Karel stood, the ladder rose up from the hay-strewn dirt to meet the loft where the boy sat, and Karel lowered his gun and held it across his body, his finger still on the trigger, his eyes shifting to the close-cropped curls in Raymond's lap. "The hell'd you haul him all the way up there for? He looked comfortable enough where I left him."

Raymond put a finger in his nose and worked it around as if he might find the answer in there and bring it to light. Then he wiped his finger in the hay beside him and said, "He liked it up high. Used to find him reading way up top of the oak tree out back of the house. All that climbing and sitting way up with the bird nests, and he breaks his leg with both feet square on solid ground."

"He deserved it same as you, Raymond. It's a bunch of dead horses up at my brother's place. That and a little girl who took a hard spill and only just woke up, and you come back here thinking to borrow a horse?"

"I ain't got nothing to do with any little girl."

"That you know of."

The boy cocked his head, sucking at his teeth audibly when he did. "You don't want to loan me a horse, just say so."

"I don't."

"Fair enough. See how easy that was?"

"You can't burn a man's horsebarn down and expect his brother to help you make away."

"You ain't got any brothers, Skala, unless you're talking about me and Joe here. Them others won't claim you. You and me, we drank our milk from the same good woman's teats, and whether you'd like to forget it or not, she never did. The old man never let her, called her a whore for the one she bore when she was yet a girl, said it was God's punishment what took it from her. Said she ought to get used to being treated like what she was, no matter how many rosary beads she prayed."

Karel raised his rifle again, watched the boy tighten his grip on his pistol, thought how good it would feel to shoot the little shit, like scratching finally some old itch that had worked itself down beneath the skin so you couldn't get to it without drawing blood. The Knedlik boy wasn't telling him something he didn't know, but it stung nonetheless to have it come back to the surface the same way it hurt to work an old splinter back out through the hole it made going in. "Not remembering ain't the same as forgetting," Karel said. "Besides which, I been drinking cow's milk my whole life and I ain't once called a bull calf brother. Called a lot of them veal, though."

Now Raymond's face revealed a restless resignation, an impatience in which Karel could detect not even a seed of fear. The boy dropped his eyes into his lap and ran a thumb over the cold blue face of his brother, mussed his hair, slid his own weight from beneath that of his kin, and eased the boy's head back down onto a pillow of hay. Then he rose frowning, tucked his gun against his spine in the waistband of his trousers, and stood wiry and hay dusted and taken with thought at the top of the ladder. "Your wife," he said. "She give you a boy?"

Behind Karel, the little filly whinnied and tossed her head, and it occurred to him that he hadn't yet had occasion to tell most folks about his boy, to walk into the icehouse and buy a round of beers and beam with the pride of a man who'd done what his father had done before him. But then he thought of his own father, of all that a son's birth could cost a man besides a few dollars spent celebrating with neighbors. "Why?" Karel asked. "You take a job with the census?"

"No, but that wouldn't be a terrible way to earn a dollar. Go around keeping count of people, asking men how many little ones they've managed to make." He glanced one last time at his brother in the hay, and then he turned his back to Karel and put a boot on the topmost rung of the ladder so that he was talking all the way down to the ground. "Who knows. You do that job long enough, it might all tally up even. Joe up there does the last of his breathing, but then come to find out it's some other boy born right about the same time. A man could find some sense in that."

Karel took a step forward, keeping his gun down across his waist but balanced in both hands and at the ready. "You can make sense of damn near anything, you look at it cross-eyed long enough."

"I'm just saying," Raymond said, reaching the ground. He turned toward Karel, pulling a roll of paper money from his pocket. "It's better when things even up than when they don't. Here. It's thirty dollars more than we spent up at the filling station, plus another fifty to take care of Joe up there."

"I ain't taking your money. You ain't got enough. There's a stable full of horses up the road you can't afford to square, and you want to stand here talking about making things even."

"Way I see it, that ain't your debt to collect, Skala. Thom can settle that on his own. You want to tell him I'm still in town, then go on ahead. I been in your house. It's not a telephone in there. That's all the head start I need."

"You ain't made it out of this stable yet, Raymond."

The boy smiled, balanced the roll of money on the third rung of the loft ladder, and nodded at Karel's gun. "Not yet," he said, "but to stop me you're going to have to shoot me in the back knowing my momma fed you at the breast."

When the boy turned and took his first careless, loose-jointed steps toward the open door, Karel found his gunstock cold against his cheek, risen without summons like the weeks of nighttime fantasies that would afflict him thereafter, visions in which he'd imagine himself squeezing the trigger and knowing, with the blast from the barrel and the jolt in his shoulder, that he'd set something right other than his pride. Instead, he steadied the gun's sights on Raymond's back until the boy reached the door, and then he called out, "Your mother got paid, did she not?"

The boy swung the door outward and the stable was flooded of a sudden with harsh noonday light. "Not near enough," he said. "Ain't a woman ever been paid enough for all that gets taken from her."

IT WOULD PROVE a wearisome night, all that sleepless darkness coming, as it did, on the heels of a long day that had found Karel Skala answering the questions he'd promised he would after fretting over matters left so long untended on the farm. In the end, the chores and the outdoors, all these years his sanctuary, had failed him, and he'd come inside before suppertime, his socks left on the back porch, salted with the sweat of his nervous work and stuffed inside his boots. For now, the baby was asleep, the two girls playing in the other room, their usual squealing tempered by the charged quiet of the home, by the way in which a house where a newborn sleeps becomes, through some mystery of its own and through the ready, unquestioning complicity of those inside, a series of rooms constructed as baffles against sound so that there, where the infant dreams in the warm heart of them, the silence can incubate the silent.

Karel hung his hat on the rack and lifted the chair rather than scraping it back, suppressing even the groan that usually announced the end of his labor and the beginning of his evening meal. Sophie turned, her apron tied loosely at her padded waist, and poured a cup of coffee, placed it on the table with an ashtray and a halfhearted smile. Karel laced his fingers around the cup and sat for a long minute in appreciation of its warmth against his calloused hands, of the strong smell of it hanging rich in the air, of the sureness of its arrival before him, all of which made him think that, if God had been a woman, she would have sent Adam from the garden all the same, but not without a cup of coffee.

Outside, floating sluggish over the southern fields, a stray cloud carried about its fringes a touch of color so that it appeared to Karel that the thing had made off with some of the unsuspecting sunset. "I know you'll be hard at it awhile," he said, "and you'll need what rest you can get. You strip the bed linens tomorrow, I'll get them washed and hang them on the line for you. Skies look to hold."

She was mixing batter for an easy supper of pancakes, a meal she knew certain to find no complaints from the girls, and when she let the wooden spoon drop against the side of the bowl, Karel closed his eyes and massaged the bridge of his nose. And then Sophie was lowering herself gingerly into the chair beside his, and when he opened his eyes and took his cigarette from the ashtray, she was waiting with her elbows propped on the table and her chin in her hands. "I'd appreciate that, Karel," she said. "But you're giving me butter when what I'm wanting is the biscuit."

And so he had told her, wanting to touch her pale arm while he did but settling for the comfort of the sturdy seat beneath him and the coffee in his hands. He told her about the boys and the beer, about the lost heifer and calf, about the body in the stable and the boy he'd found there swinging his legs from the loft with his dead brother's head cradled in his lap. About the talk he'd had with his brothers while they watched Thom's stable smolder. As he spoke, moving from the story of one day to the story of the next, watching his wife's eyes for the eventual softening that told him he'd said enough, Karel reckoned that she'd stop him short in time, that she'd return to what she'd come so close to saying those hours before in the truck, that she'd want to know, though he felt sure she already did, what he'd been doing out past midnight while she'd suffered their son into the world.

Instead, she sat listening, baiting him on with neither comment nor nod, asking only the occasional question, rising periodically to refill his cup, to feed the stove, to check on the baby, returning each time to lower herself slowly into her seat and set her head in her hands and her eyes upon him, and when the girls came asking after their supper, she set the table and poured the batter onto the griddle and flipped the cakes onto the plates. Then they'd sat together, watching their children eat while the last of the light bled out of the day. When Evie had finished her supper, her pink lips glazed with syrup, the girl hopped down from her chair to help her mother clear the table and stood with her plate in her hands before carrying it to the sink. "That baby is lazy," she said. "He needs to wake up."

Sophie laughed, wincing and pressing a hand down low over her apron when she did, and the sound of her, so unexpected and full of her easy demeanor, brought Karel out of his chair until he was standing behind her, the soft taper of her waist in his hands.

She leaned into him and shook her head. "You'll be hearing all you want to out of him soon enough, sweet pea. He's a Skala, and the Lord doesn't make any lazy ones."

She was up three times with the child before midnight, and when Karel awoke each time from less than an hour of sleep to find the baby crying again, he propped a pillow beneath his head so that he could watch the silhouette of her against the diffused moonlight that found its way between the bedroom's curtains, so that he could watch her bend over the bassinet to change the baby's diaper and then sit with her back against the headboard while she nursed him.

When they'd first gone to bed, Karel had undressed and slid into the cool sheets while Sophie changed into her nightgown, and when she'd fed the baby before joining him there, he'd been heartened by the cool points of contact between them, by the milk-dampened cotton of her gown against the skin of his bare back. Since then, each time the child had come awake, the sounds he made like those of some nocturnal animal who'd grown terrified of the night, Karel had wanted to go to him, to see in his angry little face the confusion of all his needs and to hold him, but he couldn't bring himself to do it, couldn't bring himself to deprive the child of the one soft and able answer for all of those needs. And so instead he'd prop his head up and watch, and at some early hour during the fourth feeding, while the boy suckled, Karel turned onto his side and put a hand on his wife, squeezing the solid round of her knee. "You want me to hold him awhile after he eats?" he whispered. "I'm not in any danger of sleeping anyway."

Sophie worked a finger gently into the corner of the baby's mouth to unlatch him, and then she turned him to the other breast, his tiny arms thrown up as if he'd found himself unmoored and falling from the night's only comfort when she did. "What I want, Karel, is for you to think about him if you have to."

"I have been," Karel said. "I am."

"That's not what I'm saying. What I mean is, I want you to try thinking about him when thinking about me isn't enough."

Two hours before the reluctant winter dawn, Karel pulled his trousers on and buttoned his shirt. Child and mother both were sleeping, and before he went to make the coffee and light the stoves, Karel stood over the bassinet where, in a sliver of moonlight, the child lay with his face pinched up and a fist at his mouth as if he were conscious, even in slumber, of his mother's distance from him. There was something familiar and unsettling in the seriousness of the boy's expression, and Karel couldn't help himself. He reached down and flattened a hand on the boy's chest, felt the faint, fluttering rise and fall of his breathing, and then, before he turned to the awaiting labor of a day not yet fully made, he traced a finger over the little furrows creased into the tender skin of the boy's fine neck.

After an hour of chores in the barn and about the house, before even the suggestion of dawn backlit the eastern treeline, Karel unlatched the stable door and found the lantern in the dark. The air was close and stagnant, the scents of urine and hay and animal exhalations soured overnight by the onset of decay up in the loft. Karel breathed deeply through his nose, growing himself used to the smell while he led the filly out of the stall and cross-tied her, stroking her long black neck and speaking softly to her about where they were going and who she'd soon see until he had gotten her saddled and coaxed the bit into her mouth.

Outside, after he walked her from the stable and down the drive and out to the cattlegate, she nibbled at the yellow tufts of hay left uncut along the fenceline while he worked the latch. Clouds had come chasing the previous day's stray overnight, and their undersides blushed as the topmost arc of the sun came beaming like some proud suitor over the distant trees. From the water oaks and pines along the northern fork of the creek, a mockingbird called out the first of the day's admonishments. With the gate latched behind them, Karel stood beside the horse and put a foot in the stirrup as he took hold of the pommel and swung himself astride the animal, who sidestepped, tossing her head in protest while he sat her and gave her the slack of the reins and waited her out.

And then they walked, the two of them, out toward the stand of oaks that rose up out of the grazing land and stood old and gray and strung heavy with moss over the soft sod once worn to bare earth beneath the hooves of racing horses. He nudged the filly with his heel and turned her loose with his knees, and while Karel cantered her out toward the trees and then around their wide perimeter, he watched her breath come in steamy jets from her nostrils and thought how long it had been since he'd been on horseback and what a damned fool he'd been for keeping himself from it. And still, he couldn't discount his own hesitation any easier than he could avoid the acreage in which it had taken root, growing as it had alongside cotton and cattle and mesquite trees and farm boys reared on absence and fear. He lived on it, was riding toward it. He had seen it in the labored, moonlit frown of his sleeping son's face, and now, when he brought the filly up short and sat her there beneath the overhang of the trees, the past comes to meet the present, the connection between the two no less certain than the tethers strung taut through time between a man's father and son.

It comes. The hard, mineral scent rising from the soft, flooded land. The raw wind and the stinging rain. The swinging lantern throwing its transient light onto the standing water. The ankle-deep mud and the heavy steps away from a suffering horse, and then there he is on his back, Karel's father, his shoulders driven into the mud, his eyes squinting against the rain, his mouth bubbling at the corner with a dark upwelling of blood and tobacco. Karel sees himself kneeling beside him and feels the cold, puddled water wick into the cloth of his trousers. He sets the lantern burning by his old man's shoulder, and when he puts a hand on his father's chest, the man groans and his eyes come wide and Karel feels the damage done there. The ribs caved inward, crushed and sunken. "Jesus, Pop. The horse come down on you?"

The lantern throws the man's shadow long against the ripples of rainfall in the pooled water, and Vaclav's lips move in a pale whisper, his arms twitching at his sides. "You boys promised me a bale of cotton before my birthday," he says, "and here it is almost daylight and you're just now out of bed." Sliding his boot heels in the mud, he gasps and bends his knees as if readying himself to stand.

The cold works into Karel as if born up as liquid from his soaked trousers and into his skin, washing up in little waves until he's shivering in earnest and shaking his head. "It's wintertime, Pop. Cotton ain't even planted yet. Hold still. I'm going to get you out of here." But before he can stand, his father's hand is on him, gripping the same arm that, just days before, the Janek woman had held. He can't remember the last time his father has touched him any more clearly than he can fathom, now, how he'll get the old man to the house. The breathing comes labored and gurgling, little spent strings of tobacco floating in the blood that films the man's teeth and bubbles along the seam of his lips. He needs his brothers. He can't get it done without them, and he knows the old man is going to die here on his back in the mud.

He coughs, spraying Karel's face, moaning and cinching down harder on his son's arm, and the boy tastes the sour metallic mist of his father's blood on his own lips. He wipes his mouth with the sleeve of his coat, and the wind shifts such that a wet nest of moss falls from the oaks onto his head and blinds him with his own soiled hat. He jerks the thing off and blinks his eyes and pries his father's hand from his arm. "I'm going to get you to the house," he says. "I'm going to rig the other horse and pull you out of here."

Vaclav glares into the lanternlight, his eyes washed yellow with rage around their hard gray centers. "The hell you are. Ain't none of you setting foot in the house until you've picked me a goddamn bale of cotton. Now get your brothers and get your scrawny asses into the fields."

In the heartwood of Karel's history, at the onset of his remembering and way back in the days when his father was first teaching him to sit a horse, when his brothers would bet him a day of their corn shucking on a game of spoon, the end of which they'd foreseen with a careful orchestration of cards, when bobwhite cocks still came out brazen and pale-bellied from their coverts to steal some seed beneath the sunlight, and when a boy's sleepless thoughts told him, as they ever do, to play at being a man without ever once telling him how — there had come a Sunday when Karel sat pressed between his brothers in the pews of St. Jude's while Father Carew's homily had found the priest leaning over the lectern, his eyes afire despite the tears welling up in them . . . *So often, when we pray for the dead, we fall prey to the belief that they must so long for their earthly lives, for those they've left behind, for us, when what is certain is that they long, in the company of the Lord, for nothing at all. So don't pray for them because they might now be suffering. Pray for them because they have been released from the temporal world, because they have been lifted from the binds of time as we have yet to be. Pray because for them there is no past or future, and, inasmuch as this is so, our prayers can ease the pains they suffered while they walked the earth as sinners among us.*

Now, astride the black filly, Karel reins her out to the creekside pines, and together they weave themselves through the trees as the sun breaks free of the horizon and squirrels come alive in the branches overhead. When they reach the bank, Karel sits watching the shadows of the trees on the water, waiting until the horse folds her ears softly to the sides of her fine head and begins working the bit gently in her mouth, and then he takes her into the water and guides her toward good footing and leans forward in the saddle as she comes up the other side onto the soft silt of the slough, where he bids her to stop so that he can look back as the evidence that they've come through the water widens behind them before it subsides and heals itself and slides downstream.

He's not sure he can bring himself to do it, even now, even with Sophie's words so clear in his memory, and so he comes down from the horse and walks her out of the slough and up into the unplowed field where he can smoke a cigarette and run his eyes along the outstretched fencewires until their shimmering melts into the distance.

Some hundred miles to the west, there's a boy slumped in his seat with a gun in his pants, his scarred cheek pressed against the window glass as the Sunset Limited gathers speed on the outskirts of San Antonio, its locomotive trailing smoke out over the length of the cars rolling behind it toward California. Behind him, a dead brother but not the thorn of his memory. That he'll hold with him as surely as, back in Dalton, at St. Jude's parish, Father Carew holds the Eucharist before the aging, penitent few who've come for early Mass.

In her room, with her daughters curled up beside her in the quilt and giggling softly, Sophie Skala holds her hungry, sleeping boy to her breast. She shakes her head at the thought of her husband, at the memory, only two hours old, of his awkward, half-dressed frame leaning over the bassinet so carefully, so quietly, to touch his son while she pretended to sleep.

Outside, beneath a sky flung wide over Lavaca County and hung sparsely with sun-blanched clouds that promise, instead of rain, only shade, the youngest of the Skala brothers smokes the last of his cigarette while the black horse turns her head toward the gen-

303

tle sound of creekwater behind her. In time, Karel will ride her three-quarters of an hour to the north, stopping to open and close his neighbors' gates along the way, and when they arrive, they'll find Graciela emerging from the chicken coop with an apron full of eggs, her husband on the back porch cleaning his gun, awaiting news, raising his head at the arrival of his brother. But for now Karel stands of a bright winter morning in an unbroken field not far from his house, seeing his boy's face, so much like his father's, as he grinds his spent cigarette into the earth. He gathers the horse's lead and puts a foot in the stirrup, wondering just how in the hell a man is supposed to go about asking the dead to forgive him for ever finding comfort at another woman's breast. Or for going on living at all when she could not. Or for doing his father's delirious bidding and leaving him to die in the mud alone. Or for leaving their children so long at odds with one another in the world.

And then he wonders if he's just done it, if it could be that simple.

The horse sidesteps, and, when Karel corrects her, she offers a coy little halfhearted buck. Her body shudders beneath his weight, sensing, before he gives her a heel, that they are about to run.

A New, Warm Offering

FEBRUARY 1895

COME EVENING, she appeared with Edna Janek on the back porch, and Vaclav Skala opened the door to find a girl who looked, despite her slumped shoulders and tired eyes, like she mightn't be old enough to do what she'd come to do. Edna made the introductions, and Skala took the girl's hand, which was rough-skinned and cold and so fragile in his own that he felt, just holding it, as if he might do it some harm. He glanced at her compact frame, looking her over, wary as a bidder at auction. The girl's slight bosom only just swelled the front of her dress, which was black and home stitched, the uneven hem a testament to the haste of its seamstress, and, estranged by grief from reason and amenities, he nodded to the hallway, toward the sound of the crying baby in the back bedroom, thinking the girl had sewn the dress out of respect for the dead.

She had, but not for *his* dead, and while he returned to his cup of coffee at the kitchen table, this girl who would one day bear twins listened to the hollow sound of her own footsteps echoing beneath the floorboards, hearing again the empty, earthen sound of her son's little box coming to rest on the hard bottom of its grave.

Edna led her past the front bedroom, where long, shapeless shadows fell over a bed frame orphaned of its mattress, and in the back room they found the boys in the bedclothes they'd stayed in all day, the younger two on their bellies in their shared bed, watching while Stan stood leaning over the bassinet, his hands gripping the rail while he whispered some consolation to the crying infant.

When the women entered the room, the boys looked up with the startled, expectant faces of those awakened from troubling dreams to the blinking, muddled hope that the known world would now be returned to them.

Stan loosed his hold on the bassinet and took a step backward. "I was just counting to him. I can count to fifty."

"You're a bright boy," Edna said. "This is Miss Hildi. She's going to feed the baby."

Stan turned toward the window where the day's last light fell against the panes. "My mama's in heaven now," he said.

"Yes," the girl said. "I know. My little boy is there, too."

Stan considered this, his hands gathering and releasing the soft cotton of his nightclothes. "Then maybe . . ." he said, turning to watch as Edna helped his brothers off the bed. When the woman led the boys from the room to give the wet nurse her privacy, Stan looked back as if awaiting the spoken answer to his unspoken question.

"Yes," the girl said, her voice soft, her smile a weary one. "Maybe so."

Alone with the child, Hildi gathered him in her arms and sat in the lone chair in the corner with her dress unbuttoned to the waist. The infant was hungry but unaccustomed to this new, warm offering, and the girl winced when he found the nipple only to turn it loose, wailing, his legs working beneath his swaddling, his little muscles seizing with the frustration of his effort. She whispered to him, adjusting his scant weight on her lap and cradling his head more firmly in her hand, brushing the nipple against his lips until he opened his mouth and she felt the sharp stab of him taking hold.

It would take time, but this would become, at last, on some evening later in the week, an undertaking softened by ease and familiarity, by skin, by the soft, wet sounds of satisfaction. For now, the girl leaned back into the chair as he floundered, as he started and stopped, took and surrendered and screamed, until at last he found a way to work from her what was meant for another.

When his rhythmic suckling began to yield in earnest, a cold eddy swelled beneath her collarbone, building in pressure until she found that she was holding her breath. Outside, the dark came on, and she closed her eyes as the child's hand came up, his tiny fingers curling and relaxing against the side of her breast. And then her milk let down, the cool weight of it falling within her and warmed all at once as if by the friction of its own motion or by the newfound proximity to the heat of her heart. It felt so loud that she imagined she heard it, imagined the hot surge of it falling through the flume of her body, and for a time, before she opened her eyes and moved the child to the other breast, she pretended that the comfort she felt was her own.

ACKNOWLEDGMENTS

I am indebted, first and always, to the teachers: Lee K. Abbott, Stephanie Grant, Jim Robison, and Melanie Rae Thon.

For their steadfast friendship and encouragement, I thank Steve Almond, Michael Bell, Johnny Goudie, Michael Lohre, Andy Mullinax, Bryan Narendorf, Daniel Rich, Chuck Rudolphy, Craig Schilling, Ron Wight, and Marvin Williams.

I'm beholden to Brenda Lincke-Fisseler and the other fine folks at the Friench Simpson Memorial Library in Hallettsville, whose holdings and help were essential to my understanding of Lavaca County history and culture.

My greatest debt is owed to my readers — Matthew Batt, Marya Labarthe, and Steve Sansom — whose insights were so often keener than my own.

I have the deepest fondness and appreciation for my intrepid agent, Irene Skolnick, and for Adrienne Brodeur, my insightful and impassioned editor.

I thank my parents and siblings, who have dealt with so much, and sometimes so little, so that I could do what I do. To Marya, for graces innumerable and nameless. And to my darling boy, Dalton Zane, after whom I've named the geography into which I've let wander these ghosts of my imagination.